the brink

PRAISE FOR *THE BRINK*

"Dark as a moorland winter, *The Brink* is a gorgeous tale of sacrifice, hunger, and inherited evil. Folk horror rewilded."

—**Hollie Starling**, folklorist and author of *The Bleeding Tree*

"Gripping and gruesome in all the best ways, *The Brink* combines classic folk horror and gothic terror. With gorgeous prose, Adamowicz thrills readers with a tale that keeps you wondering if all hope is truly lost."

—**Donna Freitas**, author of *Her One Regret* and *The Nine Lives of Rose Napolitano*

"*The Brink* is the sort of book that devours you. A meditation on violence, family and redemption, the story crackles with intrigue and ancient power. Jane and Isaac's growing tenderness against the bleak and beautiful Derbyshire landscape will stay with me for a long time."

—**Danielle Giles**, author of *Mere* and *Gentle Things*

"*The Brink* drags you into its eldritch depths and doesn't let go. This is historical folk horror at its finest."

—**Kristen J. Sollée**, author of *Witch Hunt: A Traveler's Journey into the Power and Persecution of the Witch*

"From the very first page, *The Brink* plunges you into a twisted folk horror tale of conflicting family dynamics that digs straight to the bottom of the well of human emotion. A novel that delves into the darkness hiding at the core of our loyalties and beliefs. Be careful! One wrong step and it may devour your soul."

—**J.R. Blanes**, author of *Portraits of Decay*

"Deliciously dark and strangely familiar, this assured debut gives us a glimpse into the weird and wild heart of old England, though Sophia Adamowicz's voice is modern and resonant."

—**Elizabeth Sulis Kim**, author of *The Book of Beasts: Reclaiming Animal Wisdom*

the brink

Sophia Adamowicz

RUADÁN
BOOKS

Boston, MA

The Brink

ISBN 978-1-968143-17-6 (trade paperback)
ISBN 978-1-968143-18-3 (ebook)
ISBN 978-1-968143-19-0 (audiobook)
Library of Congress Control Number: 2026937299

Edited by R. B. Wood

Cover Illustration by Kip Ayers

Design/Formatting by Leah Donell

First Edition

RUADÁN
BOOKS

RuadanBooks.com

To my parents.

'whether fear
Immoderate distracted him, or 'twere
From the swift motion as the Rope might wreath,
Or spectrums from his fear, or Hell beneath
Frightened the wretch, or his Soul's citadel
Were stormed or taken by some Imp of Hell,
For certain 'twas he raved; this his wild eyes
And paleness, trembling, all things verifies.'

— Thomas Hobbes, *De Mirabilibus Pecci: Being the Wonders of the Peak in Derbyshire* (1636; translated into English, 1676)

'And he, that standing on the Brink of Hell,
Can carry it so unconcern'd, and well,
As to betray no Fear, is, certainly,
A better Christian; or a worse than I.'

—Charles Cotton, *The Wonders of the Peake* (1681)

Table of Contents

September, 1642

Chapter One

When a death so unnatural happens in our own yard, it means we've not offered Her enough. It means She's hungry again.

This time, it's not just one death, but four: hens, the whole flock. My throat tightens as I edge towards the bodies that lie like heaps of fallen leaves. I should never have named them.

Blinking away the drizzle, I nudge one—Pertelote, I think—with the tip of my shoe. I hope to God that I'm wrong, that this is the work of a ravaging animal and nothing more. But not a single drop of blood speckles the feathers, and I'd expect gore if a fox were the culprit. With a heavy dread in my belly, I look past the fields and the copse where the rooks slash the air, to the thin clouds that blow across the hilltop. Elden Hole is hidden from sight, but I sense Her craving.

The other day, I fed Her a sheep's skull. The wind had razored off all its flesh so that it gleamed in the dirt, and inside the hollow of its nose were thin whorls of bone, as delicate and puckered as an oatcake. After I threw it down Her throat, sounds came bouncing off the steep walls. The clatter of bone against rock, the flapping of rooks, aye, but that's not all. There was another sound that set me running down Elden Hill without turning back. It came from the very bottom of that abyss. So sad, it was. So lonely. If I close my eyes, I can still hear it now—the mournful dirge of a sheep, bleating.

It was a warning: a message that animal skulls won't fill Her.

Guilt twists in my chest. I should've known what'd happen. I've been putting off giving Her what She wants, so She's punished us. Next time, our crops will turn black and blue as though pinched by the Devil. From there, it'll only get worse: our cow will drop dead, and then the rot will spread across the whole village. Unless I do my duty.

But I don't have room in my head to dwell on all that entails, not when birds lay at my feet, cunning poison pooled in their blood. I'll bury them out on the wastes, far away from where we eat, drink, and sleep.

I go in to fetch the spade. It's barely warmer inside the little house than it is out. The walls breathe damp, and the earthen floor has been churned up by the stomp of wet shoes. This side of the house is the biggest mess, with Will's lead mining tools among the butter barrels and firewood, his bed pushed up next to mine. What I'd do for one extra chamber, where I could have some room to myself. I move the hatchet and sieve to one side, reaching for the spade at the back, and almost die of shock when I find Lordsmeer lurking behind it.

"Come on, puss." I give my leg a tap, trying to convince him, or me, that all will be well and good.

But when I put my hand out, the cat leaps away to the other side of the house and curls himself on Mary's chaff bed. Doubtless he can smell the evil on me. Once I've buried the hens, I'll give myself a proper scrub, though the thought of stripping bare in this freezing house makes me shudder. I'll make up the fire soon and get some heat into my bones. That's what I need: warmth and a wash.

I breathe into my cupped hands a few times and rub them together, shushing the voice that insists death clings to my skin, and take the waxy leather covering off the spade. It's the same one we used to bury Mam's last bairn—a sister for me, Will, and Mary—who came into the world before her time and left too soon, taking what was left of Mam's spirit with her.

Heavy footsteps splash through the mud outside. Some childish part of me, nestled under my ribs, leaps up and sings, *Da's coming home! He's back!* But those are not Da's footfalls; Da's been lying in the churchyard at Chapel-en-le-Frith for the past few months. The man of the house now is my brother, and the moment he finds out about the chickens, his rage will blast these walls to dust and splinters. Before I can prepare how best to deliver the bad news, in sweeps Will with the drizzle, cheeks aglow.

I lean the spade against the wall and stand in front of it, steadying my breathing.

"You're back early," I say.

"I am. But I dropped in at the White Hart on the way. Mary has a message for us."

"What?"

His eyes glitter. "You know what."

The three words crash down on my head, blurring my sight. The room wavers, then comes back as a picture that's too sharp, too real.

Will peels off his cloak and the leather waistcoat beneath. "Mary thinks he's a merchant of some kind. He's lugging a sack of goods to Liverpool. A solitary traveller, Janey! We're in luck."

He shakes the rain off his hat—still circled by a scrappy ribbon of black crêpe—and hangs it on the back of Da's chair. With his fringe slicked down, there's nothing to soften the planes and edges of his face. If someone stepped too close to him, they'd bleed.

At last, I find my voice. "Are you certain he doesn't have company?"

If he's not certain, there's a chance I can talk him, and myself, out of what we're about to do.

Will tilts his head. "You really think Mary'd be telling me about him if he did?"

"But he's expected in Liverpool. Someone'll be waiting for him."

Nerves ferret around my insides as Will strides across the floor like he's always owned the place. He pours himself some ale from the jug on the table, and I watch his Adam's apple bob up and down with each thirsty gulp. Two, three, four, then up he comes for air. He fixes me with his gaze. It's the darkest thing in the room, darker than the gap under the cupboard where the spiders breed.

"There'll always be someone waiting, Jay Bird. The important thing is, no one's with him here, tonight."

"But is he the right sort? You said yourself, we've got to—"

"I know what I said." He wipes his mouth on the back of his sleeve. "What's the matter with you? You better not be trying to get out of this."

My throat's dry, as if I've gulped down dirt. "No."

"Then why do you look as though you're about to shit yourself?"

If I tell him, I know what'll happen next: he'll use it as a good reason, a very good reason, to go ahead with the plan. My soul will be forever marked. But how can I *not* tell him? I'd be putting the whole village in danger if I kept it to myself.

I say, "Something's happened."

He stares. "What?"

"Something terrible. It's the hens."

He heads to the door. I want to shove him, grab his sleeve, anything to stop him seeing the massacre outside, and yet I'm pinned to the spot as he braves the weather once more. He trudges round the back of the house, and then a torrent of curses erupts from his mouth, continuing in a filthy flow until he comes inside again and slams the door behind him.

"This. This is why we need to act now."

"Please, Will." A desperate plea jumps to my lips. "We can use a living animal."

"It's not enough!" He paces in half circles, one way, then another, running a hand through his hair. "You know full well it's not enough."

"You sound—"

"What?"

Like Grandam. It wouldn't be wise to say it out loud, not when he's like this. "You sound like you need some time to think."

Will leans over me. I'm a child again under his shadow.

"We've thought and thought. And we concluded that it's all of us together or not at all. Isn't that right?"

An age passes before I find the words. "That's right."

"So, are you with us?"

The air is tight, hard to suck into my lungs. How can I be against them? Grandam told us what happened before our family made a deal with the darkness: the death of crops, animals, bairns. Four dead chickens is nothing. We've got to give Elden Hole something substantial, or else She'll close Her thorny teeth around our village.

My brother cups my chin and lifts my face to his. "Me and Mary, we need to be able to trust you. This is the best thing for us. It's the *only* thing. And we need to act now, while we've got the chance. We've waited too long."

He's right, of course. It's been three months since Mam and Da died and we were left to take charge of the sacrifices. Only a handful of people have passed through Peak Forest since then, and I've said, *no, not them*, or, *no, not now*. I've thrown only bones, dead things, down Elden Hole. She's losing patience. If we give Her enough, She might leave the village be for a time, and we can live our lives without this fear hanging over us.

I say them in my head before I speak out loud—the words that'll set me on a course I'll never be able to change. "I'm with you."

Will steps away. "Good. That's what I wanted to hear."

Da's old penknife is resting on the table. The handle's worn down where his steady fingers once gripped. He used to whittle for hours by the fire, fashioning marvellous carvings of bears, wolves, and deer. We'd play games with them, Will, Mary, and me, back in the days when Mam and Da set the hearth aglow and kept a bit of the darkness and cold at bay.

I flick out the blade. It's the size of my little finger but sharp enough to make a clean cut. It won't be used for killing. Killing's not my job—Will assured me of that. All I'm doing is setting the trap, making sure whoever stumbles into it can't get out again. A simple part, I tell myself. I can do it, if it means saving our skins.

I slip the knife under my bodice, in case there's a struggle.

"Let's go, then," I say.

We find Mary the moment we arrive at the White Hart. She's on her knees, cleaning up a pool of vomit by the door. Judging by its purplish colour and herbal stink, the culprit's been treated to one of Alyson Bagshawe's speciality blood puddings.

"Fine evening, isn't it?" Will's lips twist into a grin.

Mary wrings her cloth over the bucket of grey-brown

water, slaps it back onto the floor, and flicks her glistening finger at him. Of the three of us, she's most like Mam. I take after Da, with shoulders made for carrying heavy pails, a square jaw, eyes small and brown as cobnuts. Mary is a slight, pointed thing, and her eyes protrude from her face, green as moss. It gives her an otherworldly look that's led Will to quip that Da was cuckolded by the Devil. Sometimes, I wonder if it's true.

Still grinning despite Mary's best efforts to rankle him, Will crouches in front of the vomit. "He's in the back room, then?"

There's a guffaw of laughter from one of the tables where old Harry Needham, his dolt of a son Nathaniel, and a couple of other lead miners are sat. I only catch the end of what Mary is saying: "...stable round the back."

"Much obliged, Magpie," says Will.

"Obliged enough to give me what I want?"

"I've told you—no keepsakes."

"Just a little thing? A button? A single hair?"

Da used to call her Magpie after the rhyme: *Three for a girl*. As she got older, she started to shape her interests around it. Every so often, she'll come home with a treasure she picked up on Elden Hill: a shard of bone, arrowheads, the occasional coin dropped by a traveller. From the moment Mam and Da died and their duty passed to us, she's been hankering after more personal items.

"We feed and we sell," Will says, and that's the end of the matter.

As me and Will pass her, a few customers lift their heads

from their trenchers, meat juice dripping from their chins, and murmur to each other. *It's one of them nights*, I bet they're saying. *Keep your eyes down.*

The only person who doesn't look troubled by us is Mrs Bagshawe, who's round by the casks, having her ear talked off by Walter the Weasel. Judging by the tankard in her chapped hand and the far-away look on her face, she's been indulging in her own supply of Derbyshire ale for a while. Soon, she'll be too sottish to think about what she allows us to do under her own roof.

As we walk by the Needhams' table, Harry glances up and says in that dry, wheezy voice of his, "Evening, evening. How're you all?"

"Very well," says Will as he disappears off to the back room.

Harry's toady goitre bulges under his chin. "He's keen on his own company tonight."

Nathaniel glances up at me from under a strand of auburn hair that's fallen across his eyes, grinning like a hob who's turned my milk sour. "I think we know why that is."

"Gets sick of us, no doubt, after a day up at Highpit Rake," Harry says quickly, blowing a puff of air out of his nose as if trying to clear it of miasma. The duty of the Vernon family has always been a bothersome subject for him, one he'd rather not face.

"Keeping yourself busy these days, Jane?"

"Looking after the animals and the house," I say.

Nathaniel crosses his arms. "Shouldn't Mary be helping you with that?"

"Mrs Bagshawe gives her a lot to be getting on with."

Mary, having finished cleaning up vomit, has moved on to scraping the trenchers. A brown and white dog sits looking up at her, swishing its tail across the floor. After glancing over her shoulder at Mrs Bagshawe, she slips it a scrap.

"You ought to marry soon. Twenty-two summers!" Nathaniel clicks his tongue. "Time flies, eh?"

My jaw tightens. "Are you making me an offer, Nathaniel?"

Old Harry can't help himself. He smirks.

"I'd soon as rather have you as a washer than a wife," Nathaniel continues. "There's plenty of ore that needs cleaning up." He takes a swig of ale and wipes his mouth on a sleeve sullied from his day's work of following a vein of lead. Then he says, all quiet, "Certain jobs, a husband can stand. Other ones, he can't."

That pale streak of piss! He'll benefit from my work tonight, along with the rest of them. Does he think I like this, being stared at and shunned by the only people I've ever known? Ungrateful sod. I clear my throat and say with as much sauce as I can muster, "Ta. I'll bear your words in mind."

He taps his head. "A fount of knowledge, me."

"Well, I'll leave you to share your wisdom with others who are much in need of it."

"Aye, you go, lass," wheezes Harry.

"Godspeed. Have a profitable night!" Nathaniel says, far too loud for my liking. Someone ought to give him a hard smack across that grinning face of his. Tosspot.

Once I've got away from them, I hover by the casks, waiting for Walter the Weasel to finish talking at Mrs Bagshawe. The hostess gives me a tight smile and puts down her tankard.

"…third handout she's had in as many months," Walter's saying. He either hasn't marked that I'm standing there, waiting, or doesn't care. "The warden's got a liking for her, I can tell you that. Wouldn't surprise me if he were tupping her. Eh, did I tell you what happened between her and Johnny Wilkins the other day?"

"No, but give me a moment to sort this lass out." She nods at me.

"Well, John's wife was sick in bed," Walter blithely continues. "You know how she is…"

Four sharp nails dig into my arm. I whip around to find Mary.

"What were you doing, speaking to Harry and Nathaniel Needham?" she hisses in my ear.

"Couldn't help it," I say. "They started talking to me."

"We don't want anyone sticking their nose in tonight's business. You know what Nathaniel's like, with that great big gob of his. I heard what he said to you."

"About what he wants in a wife?"

"No!" Mary snaps. "*Have a profitable night.* What if the merchant overhears?"

I sigh. "He won't. He's—"

"Sorry to keep you waiting," slurs Mrs Bagshawe, who's managed to break free from the Weasel. "What'll it be?"

"Three quarts of strong ale." I clear my throat. "It's a working night, so—"

"I know, no charge. Don't fret—I'll honour the arrangement I had with your Da." She glares over my shoulder at Mary. "Did you clean up that sick?"

Mary nods. "And I scraped the trenchers."

Thinking up the next task seems to take some effort, and the hostess loses her footing and stumbles a little to one side. "Go and check on Edward. No doubt he needs some help getting food ready."

"I checked earlier. He was handling the orders well enough on his own."

"That was earlier," she says, an edge in her voice. "This is now."

As Mother Damnable bends to the casks, I whisper to Mary, "Don't fret about Nathaniel. He's had a few japes at my expense, and now he'll leave us be."

"He'd better," Mary says. She makes for the kitchen, but not before glowering down at the bobbing head of the hostess.

The back room is a pantry. It's also the place where traders make deals, gamblers cheat the unwise, and whores overcharge, surrounded by the waft of cold roasted meat and pie crust. Mrs Bagshawe thought it'd be ideal for us, despite the chill in the air. Tonight, it's like walking into a tomb.

Will's already busy talking to a man—he must be *the* man—who sits smoking at the table. Waves of iron-grey hair fall over his shoulders. His face is tanned, wrinkled round the brow, but there's an air of mischief about him that makes him seem younger than he might be. Some might even call his strong jaw and laughing eyes handsome.

"Didn't fancy joining the other recruits, then?" he asks. "Bushell didn't persuade you to fight for your king?"

"Understand me," says Will, "I have no love for that money-grabbing Presbyterian, John Gell. But neither do I want to fight for one in a long line of monarchs who've claimed the Forest of the Peak as their own royal hunting ground but have done nothing to better it."

"I understand you very well, son. Between them, the king and the dissenters are bringing this country to the point of ruin. How long since His Majesty was here last?"

My brother scoffs. "Time out of mind. The fence running around the boundaries of the royal forest has fallen into disrepair. And did you see the old hunting lodge opposite? A ruin, now. There are no deer left either—they've all been shot. We did that." He bangs a fist on his chest with pride, disguising the truth that he was too young to fire a gun at the time of the culling. "Anyway, now the king is finally releasing his grip on the royal forest. Not that it'll make living here any easier. The surveyors came a couple of years ago to divide the wastes and commons between tenants' land and the king's. The commons! By the time they're done, there'll be hardly any land left for grazing."

"And what's your share?" asks the man.

Will waves his hand dismissively. "Yet to be decided." He

turns to me. "Ta for the drinks."

I put the tankards on the small table, the only one in the room, and take a seat near the man. The smell of tobacco is so strong that it takes me back years, to Da puffing away in front of the hearth at home and telling us stories. Tall tales, they were, about capturing a wolf cub up on Elden Hill or spotting the knocker, a shrivelled old man half the size of a child, who tried and failed to frighten him away from a rich seam of ore. Da was always the victor in his stories. Did he see the Vernon duty as something heroic? I wish he could have taught me how to feel proud. I want to walk off. But I can't leave Will and Mary with this stranger. It's all of us together or not at all.

We practise the act together most nights at home, round the table where we used to eat with Mam and Da only a few months ago. Each of us has our roles. Will always starts off, like he's doing now, with, "You know, as we've been sat here talking, I've been thinking. We've met before, haven't we?" His voice isn't usually this shaky.

More often than not, Mary plays the dupe, furrowing her eyebrows just as the man by the fire is doing. To calm the jitters in my stomach, I pretend this is only one of our rehearsals. The man's not a stranger; he's my sister, dressed up in borrowed garb. I'm almost surprised when he opens his mouth and a low voice rumbles out.

"Have we? I don't remember—"

"The market," Will interrupts.

The man cocks his head to one side. "The market? Which one?"

His accent is foreign to these parts. He could come from round Manchester way. Will's eyes drop down to the large leather sack between the stranger's feet. He bites his lip.

"Chesterfield, I think it was."

He picked a market that attracts many a hundred. The man could be anything from a lead merchant to a trader in corn, and he'd probably have sold there in the past.

But he frowns. "Did you buy anything from me?"

Will looks at the sack again. If he guesses at the man's wares and gets it wrong, tonight's antics will come to an end before they've even begun. I almost let him wander into a trap of his own making. But if that happened, we'd only have to start all over again.

"John wouldn't buy much from you," I find myself saying. "He's a miser."

My brother shoots me a surprised glance. I hope to God he's not introduced himself by a different name. We'd agreed on John and Elizabeth Jackson—common, forgettable names that we could shrug on and off.

A smile pulls at the corner of the man's mouth. "Were you at the market as well?"

There's something in his tone that suggests he doesn't quite believe the market story.

"At home, wasn't I?" I jerk my thumb at Will. "He always leaves me when he goes gallivanting off round the county."

"I work too, you know!" my brother replies in mock outrage.

"Aye, if you call standing in the market and gossiping like

a washer woman *work*." I groan inwardly as I speak. Neither of us is likely to join a troupe of players any time soon. I hold out my hand. "Elizabeth Jackson, John's sister. Pleased to meet you, Mr…?"

"Mace."

His grip is strong. He could pin you against a wall with one arm, this man. I try to squirm out of the handshake, but he holds on.

A silence curdles the air. Does he suspect me? Can he see through my bodice, all the way to the penknife and my thrashing heart?

He lets go of my clammy palm with a chuckle.

"Are you going to drink up?" he asks.

I'm trembling as I reach for my tankard. I knock it back in a few deep gulps, just like Will does. Over the brim, I see my brother giving me a 'don't you dare get soused' stare, but the man applauds.

"That's it! Think you can manage another?"

I glance at Will, seeking his permission. His waxy eyelids fall slowly.

"If you're offering," I say, "I'm not going to say no."

Mr Mace unfolds from the chair and, my God, he's not tall, but he's solid as a carthorse. On his way past, he lays a hand on my shoulder. He's close enough for me to see the two items hanging from his belt: a fat purse and, guarding it, a sheathed dagger.

"Good lass." He gives my shoulder a squeeze. I feel it deep in my bones long after he's taken his hand away.

Chapter Two

His name is Thomas. It would have been better if he'd never told us. I could have lived the rest of my life without meeting another Mr Mace, but Thomases are everywhere. Now whenever I hear that name, I'll think not of Thomas Rawcliffe the wheelwright who lives down Perryfoot way, nor doubting Thomas who probed the wounds of God made flesh, but Thomas Mace, the stranger who we're going to kill.

His tongue has been getting looser by the minute. After three quarts, he's moved on from the dire state of England and now he's telling us how much better it is in foreign lands.

"I've often thought about living in Venice—a republic in the marshes." He tips his tankard towards Will. "You'd like it. They're a law unto themselves. Word of advice: if you're ever heading that way, take care not to pick up anything close to a fever on the way. They're so wary of visitors bringing the plague that everyone has to go into quarantine, and when they saw the state I was in, they almost chucked me onto the Old Lazaretto island with the sufferers of the pestilence. Now, that would've added quite a bit of time to my stay, I'll tell you! As it happened, they realised it was none too serious, and I got out after the usual forty days."

"And you think I'd like that, eh?" Will asks.

"Not *that*, son. But the market is one of the best in the world. Fresh fish. Fresh fruit. You won't have seen anything like it before."

"Better than Chesterfield, then?"

Thomas chuckles and looks at me. "He's sharp, your brother, isn't he?"

In more ways than you know.

"He's got his fair share of wit," I reply.

As Thomas drains his tankard, Will holds up a finger. *One more*, he mouths.

I take a sip from the second quart Thomas bought me over an hour ago. I like the ale at the White Hart as much as anyone, but it's a fine line between encouraging merriment and drinking too deeply. Besides, I'm all in knots. If he's travelled across the sea and through France and Venice as he claims, he'll be able to spot a trap a mile away. He's got a great deal of strength and a dagger to boot. My only hope is that our kind attention and Mrs Bagshawe's beer have blunted his senses. Already, his speech has lost the crispness it had at the start of the night. Another quart, and he won't know whether he's coming or going.

"One last drink, then," Will says, standing. "I want to hear more about your adventures abroad when I return."

With his back to Thomas, he wrinkles his nose at me. *What*

a load of bull.

It may well be. In his time, Da met a few merchants passing through Peak Forest, and none of them had tales to tell of pest houses in Venice. You never know, though. Thomas seems more worldly than anyone I've met before. His blue eyes roam over me like trespassers.

"You like living here with your brother, do you?" he asks.

"Yes, Sir." In case he can hear the lie, I add, "It's not as if I've known much else."

"Got a husband? Children of your own?"

I'd rather he spoke about the pestilence again. "No, Sir."

"That's for the best. Love! What is it? A struggle towards a castle in the air, and when you get there… you find nothing but a pile of rubble."

He can be poetical when he wants to be, this Thomas Mace.

"So, after all your travels, there's no wife waiting for you back home, then?" I ask. Never have I spoken to a man outside my own household so boldly.

"No one I care to call a wife. Marriage is a punishment. It shackles us, denies us what's natural." He sits back, weighing my value. "What d'you think, Elizabeth?"

I agree, Sir. That's all I've got to say to keep him keen. Three words. They're simple. They should be so very simple.

"I…"

It sounds more like a creaking door than the start of an answer, and then a door *is* creaking, and it's Will, charging through with more sloshing tankards.

"Here we go!"

For the first time tonight, he's saved me from something I don't want to do.

Once Will settles, their talk moves onto the Turks who attack the English ships that sail across the Channel and take their passengers as slaves, but I'm still thinking about Thomas's intentions towards me. Will never said anything about leaving me on my own with the stranger, being used as bait. Doubtless, he thought I'd refuse. Other lasses in the village say the strangled, plucked-looking thing between men's legs gets hard and pulsing when it's excited. It's beyond me why they'd let it anywhere near them. When I used to hear my parents from across the house, it always sounded as if Mam were in pain.

I'm mighty glad when Mary comes in to clear our empty tankards and announces, "We're closing up soon. The hostess wants peace and quiet."

Thomas covers a belch with the back of his hand. "What time is it?"

"Late enough, Sir," says Mary. "Time you were abed, don't you think?"

We wait for his reply with baited breath.

"You got rooms here?" he slurs.

Da and Grandam knew what they were doing with this routine. First, the strangers get merry. Then, they get drowsy. They'll do anything for a bed once they've drunk enough. Kill them with hospitality.

"I'm very sorry, Sir," says Mary, "but the hostess said we've not got any rooms left. We've a whole party of folk from

Buxton staying here."

Will's next line is rushed. "There's a good inn nearby, if you're in need of a place to stay: the Black Feathers. A couple of miles over the hill. It's quiet there. They always have rooms."

A silence follows.

We've talked about this moment at home. *It feels like we're giving the game away,* Mary said. *Like we care too much about their answer.*

With this in mind, no doubt, she starts to clear up the empties on the table. The clunk of the wooden tankards breaks the atmosphere.

"That's the nearest one, is it?" Thomas asks.

"Yes."

"And are you sure they'll—"

One of the tankards slips out of Mary's hand. It's mine, I think, because half the beer's still in there—or rather, it's on Thomas's breeches. Anger cracks his handsome features.

"Oh, look what you've done, wench!"

"I'm sorry, Sir!" Mary curses, dabbing at the damp patch with the hem of her dress and fussing over him. Her nerves are fraying at precisely the wrong time.

"No need to buzz around me," he says, wafting her away. "Off with you!"

"Are you sure, Sir? I can get you a cloth. Oh, I'm such a dolt..."

"Let me be!"

He shoves her out of the way. Clumsy as the movement is, there's fierce power in those limbs, and Mary bumps her hip against the corner of the table with enough force to make her cry out.

"Learn how to serve properly," he says.

As she passes us, her eyes flick up at me for an instant as if to say, *Make sure he gets what he deserves.*

My resentment towards Thomas Mace burns. "The inn's not so easy to find, you know, in the dark."

"Don't worry about me, Elizabeth. I'm more than capable of looking after myself."

He loses his footing as he stands and grabs onto my shoulder to right himself. My skin shrinks away from his touch, but I hold my breath and let him keep his hand there until he's found his balance.

"No, you don't understand, Sir. They're dangerous, them hills," I say, rising so that he's finally forced to let go. "They're scarred with mining rakes and pitted all over with shafts."

It's a risk, snatching these lines from Will. But Thomas is more interested in me than my brother and Mary.

"You don't know where you're stepping. If you're not careful, you could end up…" I shake my head. "Well, it's not worth thinking about. You're best off travelling with us. We don't mind coming some of the way."

The back of my neck tingles as a leering gash opens up in his face.

"And how much will that cost me?" he asks.

Will chimes in with, "A shilling. Each, if you'd be so kind."

"*If you'd be so kind* indeed!" snorts Thomas.

"How about 10d?"

Will's going in far too high. It has to look like realistic haggling, but we can't put him off altogether. "6d. A shilling between us," I say.

There's a pause while Thomas drinks me in. He knows I want to lead him deep into those lonely hills. He knows I'll sacrifice my own comfort and rest just to keep him company. The only thing he can't guess is that She's out there, Her jaws wide open, waiting to swallow.

"All right, then," he replies at last. "If you're offering, I'm not going to say no."

We should've rehearsed under a night sky and in a gale. That way, I'd have been much better prepared. With each gust, the candle flames in our lamps bend and quail. The wind tears up the clouds and throws the tatters in the face of the moon, plunging us back into cave-cold darkness just as we've welcomed a bit of light. The only blessing is that it's dry, but even so, the earlier rainfall has turned the path to mud. Every time I put my foot down, the ground shifts, as if the earth itself is shying away from what we're doing.

Will doesn't seem to have such qualms; he strides several paces ahead, sure-footed as ever.

I've persuaded Thomas that it's safer for me to lead his mare without him in the saddle. He walks on the other side of me, occasionally veering close. The heat of his attention has started to cool. Relieved as I am not to have him staring or touching me, I've got to keep him occupied.

"Was it your work as a merchant that took you overseas?" I ask.

He clears his throat. "That, and I was curious."

"Is that why you're off to Liverpool? The port?"

Too late, I remember that he hasn't said a word about this to me. He doesn't seem to notice my mishap, though, saying, "Many an opportunity awaits there for a man who's prepared to work at anything. And what have I to lose?"

"You're not inclined to be contained at all, Mr Mace."

"No, I'm not. The difficulty is finding others who feel the same way. A lot of people will go along with a proposition, but when faced with real consequences, they get frightened and want to scurry back to the safety of what they know. Are you like that, Elizabeth?"

"Oh, no, Sir."

"You dare to do the things that frighten you?"

"Yes, Mr Mace."

His hand creeps across my lower back, and the night tightens around me like a net. I'm trapped by my own device. I can almost feel the weight of him on top of me and his hot, sour breath at my neck as he slits me open.

"How much further, then, lass?" he asks.

"Not far."

"You said the Black Feathers was the nearest inn."

I take one step away from him. "Not long now."

No more words pass between us as we squelch along the path up to the top of the hill, where the wind is at its sharpest. The lumpen shapes of sheep and cows lurch through the darkness like great clods of earth that have been charmed to life. When we skirt by the copse, I look down at the village. Will-o'-the-wisp lights in farmhouse windows try to tempt me down to where it's warm and sheltered. Alyson Bagshawe will soon be abed, her head resting in the nook of Walter's arm, the two of them steaming in each other's heat. The Needhams will be snug in their two-chamber house. If a nightmare should trouble the smallest of the bairns, they need only cry for their mam and she'll be there in the space of a breath, rocking them and whispering, *Hush, my sweet.*

I wonder if anyone is thinking of us, out here, and what we're doing for their sakes.

Why did we end up drawing such a bad lot? Why did our family need to bind us to this fate? If my grandfather hadn't met the Spirit of Elden Hole that day, perhaps I'd be living in a place like the Needhams' house, in a different village altogether—one where folk came to me and said, *Janey, duck, do you know how best to sweeten a cat's breath?* Or they'd ask how to make a sheep love a lamb she didn't birth or how to rid the bed of lice, and I'd solve each and every problem without having to get my hands dirty, and at the end of the day, I'd wrap myself up in clean sheets and dream.

"Tell me more about the Black Feathers," says Thomas. "Do they have good fodder?"

I suppose he means for him, not the horse. "The best."

"And good ale?"

"Strong and bitter. Cloudy as a misty morning."

He grunts. "Strange."

"What?"

"Never heard of it."

My heart jumps to my throat. "You're not from round here, though, are you?"

"I'm a Bolton man, but I spend a fair amount of time in inns and taverns. I've come to know the best ones."

"It's a well-kept local secret," I say.

"Right, well, I suppose I can't know everything."

No, you can't, Thomas. You can't know how close we're getting. I envy his ignorance. It's me who has to lug about this weight of dread.

"Let me check with Will how far off we are." Taking the horse with me, I catch up with my brother.

"Hurry," I say.

"I'm walking as fast as I can," he breathes. "Remember, you keep him busy and grab his arms if you have to."

"You've not felt how strong he is."

"He's had enough to drink."

"He was asking questions just now."

"About us?"

"About the Black Feathers."

Will pauses. "It's nothing to worry about."

"Are you certain?" I ask, the voice of caution nagging in my ear.

"I'm certain."

He turns towards an old sheep pen on the right—the spot where, if all goes to plan, he'll feign a fall and rise again with a rock. Then, it's a matter of running at Thomas before he knows what's happening and taking a swing at him. The rest of it is supposed to be simple: search his bag, his pockets. Take what we want. Give the Hole Her fill. It's how the Vernons have carried on since Grandam's time.

Will lifts a hand to his angular face and brushes away his fringe. "This way," he calls.

But Thomas has stopped walking. He bends, his hands resting on his knees.

"No. I don't think so."

I shoot a look of panic at Will, who gabbles, "It's better not to turn back now. The inn's just—"

"Oh, I know there's no inn." Thomas straightens his back. "*'Grab his arms?'* Do you think I'm deaf or an idiot?"

There's the penknife close to my heart. If Will can't reach the rock in time, I can stab. To harm, to distract. Not to kill. That's not my role. Whatever happens, that's not my role.

I tighten my fingers around the reins of the horse. She stamps and throws her head to the side with a whinny, now as reluctant to be here as her owner. The sound draws Thomas's attention. I lift my lamp higher to catch the expression on his face, but all I can see is a black bulk, still as a boulder.

"You've not been doing this long, have you? Luring strangers into the hills so you can…" He coughs. "So you can rob them?"

My throat clenches.

"Sir," Will says, polishing his words, "you've misunder—"

"Don't *Sir* me! I wasn't born yesterday. *You* were though, judging by the way you've been carrying on, you ass-headed fools. That sister of yours can't even remember the name you're supposed to have, *John*. She called you Will just now. So, which is it? John or William?"

Will scowls at me. If we survive this, I'm going to pay later.

"Come on, if you think you can take me!" shouts Thomas. "But listen. The grass'll be splattered with your blood by the end of it."

I don't move. We *are* ass-headed fools. Everything about Thomas screamed risk. I never should've agreed to this; Will wouldn't have gone through with it without me.

"Why did you come with us, if you think you're so clever?" snarls Will.

Thomas steps into my light. His face is creased in mockery. "Because when someone tries to take me on a merry dance, I like to trip them up." He spits on the ground by my feet. "You couldn't even keep up the simplest of acts, one that most women mastered a long time ago. You should've spent some time in a whorehouse. At least you might've learnt how to lie to a man's face."

I wait for Will to leap to my defence. He doesn't.

"I meant you no harm," I say, fear welling up in my chest. "Please—"

A wet chuckle erupts from Thomas's throat. "Whatever you meant to do, *Elizabeth*, you wouldn't have done it. Despite what you told me, you are a coward. Even so…" He reaches down towards the sheathed dagger in his belt. "Mustn't leave anything to chance, must we?"

The next few moments stretch out, long as a sleepless night.

I tug the horse's reins and give her a hard smack on the rump. She bolts straight past Thomas, distracting him, and I take a look at the soft skin of his neck before dropping the lantern and plunging us into the night. I dip my hand down my bodice, and my fingers close around the handle of Da's penknife. I leap towards him, but instead of sinking into skin and sinew, the blade swishes through thin air. One moment of panic and confusion, then my shoulder feels as though it's being wrenched out of the socket. He's twisting my fingers off, trying to pry the weapon loose, and the knife almost slips from my grasp. Its blade bites into my flesh. I don't let go. *You're not getting it, you bastard, even if you slice my fingers down to the bone.*

Pain bursts through my hand, pure and red hot. I close my eyes, grit my teeth, keep my screams battened down. I won't give him the satisfaction, I won't…

Someone smashes into Thomas. Bellowing in pain, he's ripped away from me.

For a second, I can't move. My hand feels like it's on fire. I bring it to my face and smell blood. Warm life gushes from my fingers and drips off my palm, pattering to the ground. My legs buckle. Knees smack the earth. I fall face forward, pain raging through me like I'm burning from the inside out.

Shouts in the distance. The clouds clear. Moonlight bathes Elden Hill.

So that's why Thomas let me go—Will's grappling with him. Together, like two hares locked in battle, they've gone tumbling over each other towards the Hole.

Watch yourself, Will. Don't, for God's sake, fall.

When I open my mouth to warn him, all that comes out is a whimper. He knows what he's doing, though, doesn't he? Doesn't he? Those can't be *his* moans I hear. They can't be *his* breaths that wheeze out in time to the kick, kick of a boot.

"Will!"

Where's my knife? I feel around on the ground for it, but all I touch is damp grass and rocks.

Thomas coughs up his lungs between kicks. He'll let the elements finish us off, or else he'll slit our throats. Worst of all, he might throw us down the Hole, alive. He hasn't got our scruples. We'd have made sure his heart had stopped before offering him. *A small mercy*, Will said when we discussed it. It's not small. Imagine if you were alive, down there—falling and falling past the creatures with flitting eyes and folded wings, ending up in a jumble of bones and mouldering flesh.

I mustn't let that happen to us.

Thomas is leaning over my brother, who's flat on his back. My insides turn to water. I'm too late.

And yet.

Only a few paces behind them, the ground gives way to a slope, and at the edge of that, there's the drop into nothingness. If I can take a run at him, I'll be able to send him toppling over the edge. If I can take a run up… if I can…

But I don't have to.

A figure rises from the dank soil. It's small, lithe. Its head is obscured by the hood of a cloak as it flows, smooth as black silk, towards Thomas. A chill creeps down my neck. Da's tales of the things that live down the mines don't seem so ridiculous now.

The shadow figure wraps itself around Thomas. His body stiffens. A gurgle, not quite a scream, bubbles into the sky.

The moon is veiled once more. All is darkness.

There's the sound of something heavy and blunt thwacking into flesh and bone, again and again. The gurgle bursts into a strangled cry and he's begging whatever it is to stop, "I pray you, I pray—"

Shhh, says the wind. *Shhh*.

The thwacking gives way to a soft, slushy pat, like clots of thick porridge falling from a ladle. Cries become silence.

Feet that barely feel like they're mine carry me over dips and ridges. I shout Will's name and scour the ground for a shape that could be him or Thomas or that thing that came from nowhere, from the ground, from Elden Hole.

"Over here." His voice is weak but—thank merciful God!—he's alive. His answer comes from a few feet away, but where exactly, I can't tell. The darkness has muddled my sense of direction.

"Where?"

"Here!"

The Hole could be a step or two in front of me. I lower myself onto the ground again and crawl, feeling along with the hand that hasn't been sliced into ribbons.

"Keep talking, Will. I'll…"

There's something sack-like in my path. The merchant's

bag? No, it's too large. Warmth rises from it. My whole body quaking, I feel along the bumps of a belt, up to a nest of curls, along leathery folds of skin, and then I get to where Thomas's face should be and find only a slick, warm mess in place of a nose and loose teeth in the bloody pulp of a mouth.

Freezing fingers close around mine. Before I have a chance to scream, another hand clamps my jaw.

"It's me."

It takes me a moment to work out who's talking. If it were the Devil himself squatting there, I couldn't be more surprised. My sister removes her hand.

"Mary? What…?"

"I followed you."

"So, that cloaked thing was you? How…?" I can't get my head around it all. In the end, I flee to the comfort of familiar words. "You shouldn't be here."

"And if I hadn't come after you, where would you be now?"

I'd be dead. Will would be dead. As much as I wanted to, I know I didn't have the nerve in me to take a run up at Thomas. Coward. Bloody coward. I lick the blood from my lips and realise after I've swallowed that it's his, not mine. I spit out the taste of him.

"What did you do, Mary? I mean, how…"

"Stabbed him in the neck. Then finished him off with the rock, like we'd planned."

"But how did you find my knife? Did *he* have it?"

Strange how it's the little details that concern you at

moments like this. I don't want to know how she feels just having slaughtered a man. I don't want to know if she'd been thinking of joining us for the kill all along.

"I took his own knife off him in the White Hart, when I spilt the beer on him."

"I didn't even notice," I say, wondering at her. "You must've been quick as lightning."

"Mary? Janey?"

Will is crawling towards us, panting like some animal.

"Are you all right?" I ask.

"Been better." His hard body presses against my shoulder. "You're quaking. I could hear your teeth chattering from half a mile off."

"It's cold," I say. "I've never felt so cold in my life."

All three of us sit around Thomas's corpse as if we're about to dine on it, or set it alight and tell tales around the blaze. The only part of my body that has any feeling left is my hand, and that burns with pain.

"What do we do now?" I ask, trying to keep my voice steady.

"Now," Mary replies, and I could swear it sounds like she's amused by the whole situation, "we see if this bastard's got anything of value on him. Then, we give Elden Hole what She's been hankering after."

Chapter Three

The first bird of dawn begins its mad, looping song as Mary's needle sinks into my flesh. I draw a breath through gritted teeth and close my eyes, leaning back in Da's chair. The past few hours dissolve like a dream. The pain's real enough, though. The pain, and the dreadful feeling that we've done something that can't be undone.

"That's it," Mary says, tugging on the thread. "First stitch in. It'll be over soon."

"How soon?"

"Give me a minute."

I give her a minute, and longer. Once or twice, I'm tempted to look down, but even the sight of the blood-smeared cloth that she used to clean the wounds on my fingers makes me queasy.

Will presses a drink into my other hand. "You're doing all right, Jay Bird."

Any other time, I'd be grateful for a rare show of kindness. Now, though, the bitter smell of ale hauls me back to the inn and sends my head spinning.

"How did Thomas come to his senses so quickly?" I ask. "It was an effort getting him out of the door of the White Hart without waking up half of Peak Forest. Do you think he was pretending all that time?"

Will crosses his arms. "He was duping us. You heard what he said—he had his sights set on attacking you."

Thomas's words writhe in my ear. *You should've spent some time in a whorehouse.* Why was he so eager to shame *me*, to show up *my* lack of worldliness, when Will was even more confident than I was? Was it purely that Thomas delighted in tormenting the weaker sex, or was there something else about me that set his teeth on edge—a sense that I'm rotten at the root? Whatever I did to provoke him, it almost cost my brother his life.

"I'm sorry I called you *Will* and not *John*," I say. Best not mention the Liverpool mistake.

Will grunts. "Not as sorry as I am. What a moment to have a slip of the tongue! That's what made him turn on us."

"Even if we'd never intended him any harm," says Mary, "even if you were actually leading him to a nearby inn, he'd have gone for us anyway. He was like that. A villain. A violent rogue looking to wet his fists with blood. I bet he went from one inn to another, amusing himself by beating up lads and lasses like us. You saw how he leapt on me when I spilled that beer."

He gave her a shove. To say he *leapt on* her seems fanciful. Then again, I wasn't on the receiving end of his anger that time; Mary was. It might've felt more forceful than it looked.

"We were defending ourselves," Mary says with finality. "We did nothing wrong."

Not even when we searched his body for valuables? Or when we took his sack of goods and horse, or when Will kicked him over the edge and we heard him crashing through the ivy and nettles into a darkness that gave nothing back but a whirr of startled rooks?

I keep these thoughts to myself and say, "Thank you, Mary."

Outside at the back, Thomas's mare snuffs. The hens are still lying there. I'll need to get on with burying them soon, after we've taken the horse to market. Then, there's a whole day of work ahead: animals to feed and muck out, the cow to milk, food to make, clothes to mend and wash. So much to do, and I'm so tired.

"All sewn up now," Mary says at last, snipping the thread. "Just giving it another clean."

She dabs a cloth with vinegar and presses it to my wound. The sting and the stench make my eyes water.

"There you go. Almost as good as new."

I take one look at the line of stitches across three of my fingers before my stomach turns over and I empty it all over the floor. The vomit's mostly liquid, but it keeps coming up, more than I ever drank.

"Bloody hellfire, Jane!" Will shouts, sounding exactly like Da in a temper.

Mary lays down the cloth. "Before you ask, no. I'm not cleaning it up."

"You're used to it, though," says Will.

"It's about time you started learning then, isn't it?"

"I'll clean it," I say.

Mary puts a hand on my forehead. "It's bed rest for you. We don't want you coming down with a fever."

"But I have to sell the horse."

"Will can sell it."

"No." I get to my feet. The room wobbles. "I'm all right."

Lordsmeer sniffs the reeking puddle by my feet. I nudge him out of the way, and he totters a few steps on white mittened paws, then headbutts my shin as if to repay me for a loving gesture.

"Sit down," Mary says. "I've got to finish your hand before you can go anywhere."

"You've done quite enough to my hand," I say, but I let her pull me back down into my seat and tie a piece of cloth round my fingers. "Do you have to bind it so tight?"

"Do you have to whine like a stuck pig?"

Will prods Thomas's bag on the table.

"Don't look inside until I'm ready," says Mary.

"I'm not. Hurry up, though."

"Done." She dips her hands into a basin sloshing with scarlet water and shakes them dry.

The bandage is clean and fresh, a barrier between my stitches and the filth that surrounds us. I marvel at Mary, the only girl in the whole of England who can bash a man's face in with a rock one moment and tend to her older sister's injuries the next.

We gather around what's left of Thomas's worldly possessions—the ones he took on his travels, at any rate.

Will squeezes the bag as if he's feeling for puppies inside a dog's belly. "Soft goods. It'll be cloth in there. Wool. Maybe fustian. I think there's something else in there as well. It jangled a bit as we were walking."

"That was his purse," I say. The leather pouch that we cut from his belt sits empty on the table, its innards arranged into three piles of two pound and ten shillings each, with a few pence extra going to Mary as a reward for her help on the hilltop.

"It wasn't just that."

"A hidden stash?" asks Mary.

It makes me shudder, the way they're talking. These are things that, only a few hours ago, belonged to a man who was walking about, guzzling beer and laughing. Much as the Hole makes demands of us, much as Thomas might have deserved what was coming, he was a living person.

"Anyway, let's stop playing guessing games and see what's inside," Mary prompts.

Will loosens the string and reaches into the sack to draw out its contents: undyed fustian, as he predicted. He lets out a breath and digs deeper, his tongue poking out like it always does when he's putting his mind to solving a problem.

"I did hear jangling," Mary says, her eyebrows drawing together.

I shake my head. "It might've been the horse's reins."

"No. Wait a moment." She unfolds the sheets with care. Her hands, still a tad wet, leave damp, rose-coloured patches where she touches.

"Careful!" barks Will. "You're getting blood on them."

"I am being careful." She wipes her hands on her petticoat.

The third sheet down does make a dull rattling noise as she pulls it towards her. Her eyes meet mine, then Will's.

She pulls back the cloth.

Nestled inside it is treasure: a gold wedding band; a necklace of glass, glinting like early morning dewdrops; and another pouch, this one bursting at the seams.

I can only stare at the hoard, dumbstruck.

Never did I think we'd end up with this. A bit more coin, a ring, but nothing like what's before us.

Will claps his hands. "Christ all-bloody-mighty! We've struck a rich vein here, eh? Eh?"

He pummels the table, laughing, and the jewellery bounces on the sheet. Mary breaks into a wide smile, lifts Lordsmeer into her arms and goes dancing round the room with him, singing one of the drinking songs you hear over at the White Hart.

There's many men get store of treasure
yet they live like very slaves:
In this world they have no pleasure
the more they have, the more they crave.
Hang such greedy-minded misers,
that will ne'er contented be.

Singing along, Will puts his arms round Mary and she drops Lordsmeer in favour of the better dance partner.

"How much do you reckon is in that purse?" I ask.

"Let's find out, shall we?" Will stops dancing and tips the contents of the second pouch onto the table. Gold rushes out. It's more money than I can count.

"This is the end of our troubles!" grins Will. "We can buy more animals to replace the hens. Another cow. Land, even. My God, we can buy our own piece of the commons!"

"It's a reward," says Mary. "A blessing for once. She must be satisfied."

I want to vomit again. Yes, She's satisfied. She's sated with our blood offering. Here we are, celebrating a man's death—a man's death that *we* brought about.

"Quiet," I say. "You'll wake everyone in the village."

Mary frowns. "What's the matter? This is a miracle."

"Summat's not right here." I nod at the jewellery. "Do you think it belonged to *him*?"

"I expect he bought it for his wife or daughter," says Will.

Mary nudges him. "Or sister."

"Not likely," Will replies. "I wouldn't spend this much on either of you two."

"He didn't strike me as a man faithful to his family," I say. "Could be he was buying it for a mistress."

"Quite the man of honour, wasn't he?" Mary slides the wedding band onto her finger and holds it out in front of her, swivelling her wrist in semi-circles. The rich, buttery yellow of the gold looks gaudy against the dirt and specks of blood lodged down her nails.

"You shouldn't be touching that," I say.

Mary pouts. "I'm guessing how much we'll get for it."

"Well, don't. He'll have stolen it."

"How do you know that?" Will crosses his arms, but a twitch of his lips tells me he's holding himself back from agreeing.

"Why would he be carting round jewellery like this?"

"To give to his lady love," says Mary, still toying with the ring. "Or loves. He probably had a lot of them, judging by how much he got around."

"It wouldn't be easy for him to buy this sort of jewellery in these parts."

Will sighs. "He could've brought it from anywhere. If he did go abroad, he might've bought it there."

"You've changed your tune! Back at the inn, you thought he was making it all up."

"Wherever he got these things, it's no concern of ours." He scratches the side of his face. "Don't ruin this, Janey. You've been determined to make a mess of it all night."

I laugh in disbelief. "What? I'm the one who got him to come with us!"

"And you were also the one who led him to attack us."

"He overheard *you* talking, Will."

Will waves me away. "In any case, Mary's right. No matter what we said or did, he'd have attacked us anyway. Look at the knife he was carrying! He'd have gutted us like pigs if Mary hadn't come along."

The dagger my sister took lies on the table next to the pile of treasure. Up close, I'm able to make out the initials carved into the side of it: TM.

"Anyway, stolen or not, we need to get these things sold straight away," Mary says, sliding the ring off her finger.

"Agreed," says Will after a pause. He gathers the cloth and jewellery back into the sack. "Can you do it then, Jane? Sell the horse this morning?"

I'm not at all sure I can do it. My stitches tighten as if Mary's still pulling a thread through my skin. But it's better to be out of the house, keeping my hands and my head busy. The shame of knowing I could've let Will die up on that hill—the shame of the whole damnable night—slices through me.

"I'll manage it," I say.

"Good, you can take the mare to Tideswell, and buy some new hens and a cow while you're at it. I'll sell this cloth and jewellery in Castleton. Mary, you stay here. The animals need sorting. The place needs cleaning."

She narrows her eyes. "If you want me scrubbing the floor, you've got to do me a deal."

"What?"

"Let me keep the knife."

"We should throw it down the Hole," says Will. "Get rid of anything linking us to Thomas."

"It'd be a waste, good weapon like that. It might come in useful. It *did*. Besides, we can use it next time," she says. Ignoring Will's earlier ruling against keepsakes, she places it in the crack between her bed and the wall.

Next time. A reminder that this is only the first of many.

Hours pass in a haze of cleaning myself up and traipsing over the hills. By the time I reach Tideswell, the market traders are setting up their stalls in the meagre sunshine. Leading Thomas's mare, I pass a grocer burying worm-eaten apples beneath his plump and shining offerings, and a man shouldering a sack of flour almost twice the size of his head. Salty wheels of cheese and slabs of butter are laid out on tables; normally, they'd make my mouth water, but this time I walk straight past them, my guts feeling so loose that I wonder if I'll ever want to eat again.

At one stall, a man is folding sheets of fustian. I stop dead. Iron-grey waves flow over his broad shoulders. My heart gives a heavy thump.

Thomas?

His large, vein-scored hands stop moving.

"After some cloth?" he asks, his head snapping up. I stare not at the weather-worn face of the merchant we killed last night but at a paler and younger man. His hair's not even grey, now that I look at it properly; it's a dark ashy brown.

I let out a breath. "No. I'm selling."

He gives the mare a quick glance and nods. "Good animal, that. Should be a fine day for making money. A lot of people are here from over Manchester way, staying out of trouble, I expect. Rosworm is gathering a militia as we speak to fight Lord Strange and his army of papists."

I've no room in my head for other people's fights. "Anyone here from Bolton?"

"Not that I know of."

"But there could be?"

He lifts a shoulder. "Anything's possible in times like these."

What if someone recognises Thomas's horse? She's not particularly distinct, but given the way I'm feeling now, she might as well be painted bright yellow and dotted all over.

I lead the mare over to a corner of the market where ewes blunder inside a cramped pen and chickens croon in stacked crates, feeling more and more light-headed with every step. A boy, too young to be out selling wares, stands with a horse of his own. Although it's bigger than Thomas's mare—twenty-odd hands compared to twelve—the poor creature's ribs stick through its coat. The boy turns to me.

"What're you gawping at?" He gives me a look as filthy as the bottom of his trousers.

If he wants to know, he can know. "Needs a good meal," I say.

"You what?"

"Your horse," I say slow and loud. "It needs to be fed."

The boy sneers. "Get out of my spot, wench."

"I'm just saying, you're not going to get much for selling a starving horse."

I move as far away from the little bastard as I can. It's lads like him who grow up into men who cause trouble. *Men like Thomas Mace*, Mary would claim. I picture the boy aged two-and-twenty, swaggering into the White Hart, spit and oaths swilling round his mouth. He's ushered by Mary into the back room where Will is waiting with a drink, and another drink, and another. I'm there as well, offering to guide him home.

The cries of the trapped animals and their musty sweet smells reach me wherever I stand. Today, the gates of all my senses are wide open, letting in far too much. I try taking in short, shallow breaths, and run out of air. Despite the muck on the ground, I have to sit.

In a daze, I watch the shoes of buyers hurry past me. Their voices blur into a background hum. I don't have the strength to sell to them. All I do is pick at the bandages, which are already streaked with dirt from the horse's reins. One end comes loose. I pull at it, wondering vaguely if the stitches have already popped open to reveal the glistening wound beneath.

It's with me again: the slipperiness of Thomas's smashed-in head… the scattered teeth… nubbles of bone, poking through raw flesh…

Squeezing my eyes shut, I conjure up my other life in my mind's eye, where a woman has come to ask me about the brown spots on her oat leaves and I say, *Oh, that's simple*, and give her a bag of special manure from my cream-white cow and tell her to replant in a different spot, somewhere there's no blood running down the side of the hill like a river.

"Are you hurt?" asks a silken voice.

I open my eyes. The pair of shoes in front of me better befit a manor house than a marketplace, though they're coated in mud.

"No," I reply, without looking up.

"Here."

A gloved hand appears. I grasp it, and soon I find myself on my feet and looking at a light-haired man with a heart-shaped face and dark eyes threaded with gleams of gold. He's well off, judging by his patterned yellow doublet and matching blue breeches and cape.

"You seem unwell," he says, his broad forehead creasing.

"I'm not." Even as I'm saying it, I pick at the bandage. "You don't want to buy a horse, do you?"

"I'm sorry, but no. I'm not here to purchase anything. Do you happen to know where I can find the Ebbing and Flowing Well?"

"The what?"

"It's a sort of… attraction around here," he explains. "The water rises and falls depending on the pull of the tide, or at least that's what some people say."

"Oh, the Tiding Well. It's just up that road, in a field off Water Lane." I point north, out of the village. "Follow Brook Head river. It's not much of an attraction, though."

"That doesn't matter. I'm not here for sightseeing. I…" He looks at the sky, as though he's sending up a prayer, then back down at me. "Have you seen a young lady pass this way by any chance? Her name is Sarah Pulmer. She's my cousin. We look alike, with the same complexion and cleft chin, though she's shorter than me by about six inches or so."

The cleft is hidden by a neatly trimmed beard, a shade darker than his hair. It looks impossibly soft. "Sorry. I've not been taking much note of passers-by."

"Of course, of course." Clouds of worry muster over the man's brow. "I'm sorry to bother you. It looks as though you've got enough to think about."

"It does?"

He nods at my hand. The bandage round my fingers is blotched with scarlet.

"I got it caught..." I trail off. For a long time, I can't think of what to say. "Did I already ask if you're interested in buying a horse?"

"Yes, you did."

"Oh. Oh, God, sorry, I'm being so... so..." I rub my hands over my eyes, hoping that, when I open my lids again, this humiliation will have come to an end. Instead, the man is still before me. He reaches into his pocket and takes out a handkerchief.

"Here," he says. "You have blood on your face."

The handkerchief is a fine thing, patterned round the edges. A word—I-S-A-A-C—is stitched into it. "I can't use this. It's too fine."

"Nonsense."

His smile wavers and blurs, and tears spill, hot, down my face. I dab the handkerchief on my cheeks as carefully as possible and hand it back to the man, muttering thanks.

"I'm sorry I can't help with the sale." He strokes the horse's velvet nose with the back of his long, gloved fingers and turns to leave. "I do hope you get the rest you need."

"'Scuse me, how much for this here horse?"

A hulking great man is by my side, his arms folded.

I wipe my sleeve across my face. "Seven pound and sixteen shillings, including the saddle, reins, and bridle."

He raises his eyebrows. "You've got some nerve, woman."

"She's a good mare. Very sturdy."

"Not seven-pound worth of sturdy."

I look to see what the kindly stranger makes of it, but he's gone. Did I dream him? Surely no man of that status, of that beauty, would take an interest in me in waking life.

Answers I give to the possible buyer's questions after that are brief and ratty.

"I'll have to look it over properly tomorrow," he says after much back and forth.

"I'm not here tomorrow."

"I can't buy it now. My brother'll come and check it over. Can't be worth as much as seven pound."

If I turn up at the house trailing the mare behind me, my own brother will have a few choice things to say. Better to get the money now and wash my hands of this business.

"Six, if you take her today."

"Four."

"Five."

"Done, if I can have everything else thrown in with the horse: saddle, reins, bridle… the lot."

I blink away the white dots that are floating before me. "All right. Done."

Coins fall into my palm, cold as sleet. He tugs on the horse's reins, a little too rough, and they weave between marketgoers and merchants till they've blended into the crowd.

Well, that's the sale accomplished, bad as it was. Now I've got to buy a few chucks and carry them bumping and squawking about in a crate all the way across Tideswell Moor, as well as tugging a new cow along with me. The thought of it makes me want to curl up on the ground and never rise again. Not just the journey. The village. The house. The talk between me, Will, and Mary.

I wish I could spend the rest of the day here—follow in that man's footsteps to the Tiding Well and bathe my stained hands in its waters.

A fountain sprung from the earth would do no good, though. Only God's blood can scrub my soul clean after last night. I look back at the spires of St John the Baptist, piercing the clouds over Tideswell. A yearning to be forgiven, to right my wrongs, floods my veins.

The grand church was built back in plague times, but death's ravages seem to have bettered, not ruined, the beauty of the building. It's twice as big as the church in Chapel-en-le-Frith, with a carved font, and oak pews shining as if they're covered in oil. Between the pews and the altar is a carved screen—a great barrier between myself and salvation. I get as close as I can, standing almost right under the cross on the upper gallery, and pray for mercy to drop upon my head like a heavy rain. I pray for a life free from fear, a life of giving back to the world rather than taking away. When I've finished praying, I open my eyes and wait to feel different.

Above the altar are a couple of paintings, side by side. One shows Christ crucified, the lamb slain to take away the sins of the world. The world is so big. Some people's wrongdoings could've been missed out.

Next to it, an angel in streaming white cloth hovers over Abraham, staying his hand before he can plunge the blade into his son's pale body. Abraham sets his teeth into a grimace and pulls away. Already, he's crossed over the boundary between the everyday and the stuff of cautionary tales. The shock of finding out that he's not who he thought he was ripples through him. He can't stop now. He'd rather kill what's most precious to him than turn back.

And the sheep in the bush won't solve anything. Granted, the boy's blood remains in his body, but what will father and son say to each other on the way back down the mountainside or over supper? Will they ever tell the boy's mother what nearly—*very* nearly—happened?

I suppose she'd know, in her heart of hearts, what they were doing. But she wouldn't mention it. Plenty of families are like that, pretending not to know why everything feels so wrong.

Isaac! That was what the gentleman's handkerchief said. I-S-A-A-C.

My gaze lifts to the boy in the painting, Abraham's intended sacrifice. His bare skin is as luscious as cream. He's looking away, but then again, he has to, given his head's being pushed down. Those full lips are open in a gentle gasp of surprise. His wrists are bound. It's almost like he's praying. He might well be.

"Excuse me, are you of this parish?"

A crabbed little man stands in the middle of the nave. He looks at me like I've been parading naked around the place.

The jellies of my eyes jump in time to the thrum of blood. "No. I'm here for the day. Are you the warden?"

"I am."

"Good. Well…" I take out my purse. "I want to put some money in the poor box."

"Oh?" he says, like he doesn't believe me.

I have five pound from the horse sale and seven from Thomas's purse. I should give it all away, but I daren't leave Will and Mary empty-handed.

I take out two pound. Then I put one back. As I press the single coin into the warden's wrinkled palm, it feels as though I'm adding to the burden of guilt on my soul, rather than lightening it. Guilt over what? Trying to buy my way out of sin? Giving too much, too little? Or using money that's grown from a tree with its roots soaked in blood?

"Pray for me," I say. Avoiding the warden's eyes, I leave the church with my head bowed.

Chapter Four

ISAAC

I hardly know what to expect as I turn down the lane to the Ebbing and Flowing Well. If I am to believe you, Sarah, this so-called Wonder of the Peak consists of two fissures in the middle of a field. A curious visitor may place an ear close to the narrow openings and hear stirrings deep below, in the womb of the earth. As the waters rise, boiling as if heated by flames, pressure builds in the passageways and, when the ground can contain the flood no longer, a fountain shoots, glittering, to the surface.

"A miracle of nature," you told me, a coquettish smile on your lips. A smile not meant for me.

Water is your element, Coz. It goes where it wills.

Even when you lived in Bolton, before your mother passed away, you were always seeking an escape. Do you remember when I visited seventeen summers ago, and you proposed walking to the River Tonge? Naturally, your parents knew nothing about this little escapade. 'Little' was what I thought it would be, in any case: a gentle, quiet stroll outside the town, the two of us sketching and talking and stretching out on the riverbank like a pair of idle cats.

I'd have followed you anywhere at that age, and so it did not even occur to me to look over my shoulder as we squeezed through a gap between the rose bushes, the hidden route out of your garden. A thorn snagged your sleeve. You pulled and tugged, scowling as if Nature had conspired to hold you in one place.

"Here." I unhooked you. "You wouldn't want to tear your gown, now, would you?"

I ran my thumb over the soft wool, where the thorn had left a bump in the garment.

"You should be more careful," I said.

"No time for that." You let your arm drop, pushing past the roses and trampling their fallen petals underfoot. "Hurry, let's go before my father notices we're missing."

The paths that led to the river shaded us from the honeyed heat of that summer's day. As we went down to the water's edge, it became cooler, darker. Rocks rose from the water like leviathans. You hopped along them, while I tiptoed behind you, issuing unheeded warnings. As soon as you had made it to the other side, off you went, following the river to where it widened out and calling, "Isa, Isa, come now! Look at this."

I imagined you'd point out the best tree to climb, a rock the shape of a ship or a secret hiding place. When I saw the knotted rope, dangling from a branch that reached into the middle of the river, I laughed. Would you really dare to do it?

You, ten years old and such a slight thing?

As if anticipating my challenge, you grabbed a long stick—I'm sure you must have positioned it by the tree for that purpose—and pulled the rope towards you. It took you only moments to climb up it and launch yourself from dry land. The branch creaked overhead, bending in the middle.

"Sarah! Be careful!"

Flashes of afternoon light streaked across your face as you swung from one side of the river to the other, your small feet resting on the doubled knot at the bottom of the rope, your high laughter skimming the surface of the water.

If anyone saw you behaving like this... Or worse, if you fell... There were rocks under the surface of that river. Could you even swim?

"You'd better get down from there," I shouted. "It's not safe."

"I will. Watch me!"

A blur of grey and white hurtled towards me as you came swinging back, and then you were flying, your face a mask of delighted terror.

I caught you in my arms, the force of your body knocking me to the ground. Breathless, you did not stop to apologise but leapt back to your feet and caught the swinging rope in your fist, holding it out to me.

"Now you try."

You had not given any thought to how a branch could bear the weight of someone almost twice your size. I gave it no thought either, keen as I was to impress you. Well, you know the story, Coz. I was dangling above the river when a crack came from above and down I went, into the water. The cold rushed up above my head. My clothes sagged, dragging me down, and as I thrashed and gulped muddy mouthfuls and wondered if my life would end at the tender age of twelve, my greatest sorrow was not swinging on that rope, but the thought of missing future adventures with you.

Then, through the murky waters, a stag swam towards me. I could only see its antlers, but they were great and sturdy, and I grabbed onto them. They pulled me up and out towards the bank where I was reborn, blinking and sputtering. You threw a large stick to the ground and patted me on the back. No stag, then. Only you, coming to my rescue.

"There, there, Isa. It was good, wasn't it?"

I sloshed up the bank. "Glorious."

It was a relief to strip off my top layers of clothes, heavy and burdensome as they were, and leave them to dry in a patch of sunlight. When I saw you watching, my chilled cheeks became hot.

"The water makes your hair go very curly," you said, not taking your eyes off me. "Almost as curly as mine."

You took the sketchbook from your satchel and captured my likeness as I sat looking out towards the rippling wavelets, legs apart, elbows resting on knees.

"Isa," you said as you worked, "you'll visit again soon, won't you?"

I smiled. "As long as I don't end up in the river next time."

"That's the very last time I'll let you fall."

"You swear it?"

"I swear it."

"Then to you," I said, gallant despite the pile of soggy clothes beside me and the taste of river water still in my mouth, "I make the same vow. We'll protect each other—always."

It was a simple thing to say as a child, a harder thing to do now that we are both grown and pulled in contrary directions by our wills.

Come back to me, Coz. I shall hold out my arms and catch you. I shall stay by your side no matter how much distress you have caused me.

Chapter Five

At the market, I spot a sturdy-limbed cow, tan brown with a white horned head. The farmer tells me that she's lately finished weaning and, though she can be a stubborn creature, her udders are full as ripe fruit, and she'll yield wholesome milk. For the first time in hours, my belly grumbles. I say I'll take her, and the cow is mine for five pound, ten shillings.

He wasn't wrong about her being a stubborn creature; she strains against the rope tied about her neck all the way back home and stops every few feet for a chomp on the grass. Instead of allowing herself to be driven round the back of our home for a milking, the beast—I'm beginning to think of her as Fie, short for Defiant—pulls and tugs on the rope, insisting that we go all the way down the lane towards the pond. Water's what she's after. She draws me to the bank and slurps greedily with her thick, pale tongue.

"Look, Mam!"

A little lad runs on unsteady legs to the edge of the pond, his arm stretched out in the direction of me and Fie. The cow lifts her head and stares gormlessly at the disaster that's about to unfold.

I let go of the rope and dart towards the child, grabbing him by the waist. He wobbles in my arms, staggers like a drunkard and stills. Red-raw hands snatch him away from me.

"Christopher! Don't run off like that! I've told you, haven't I?" A woman gives him a smack on the back of the hand. The lad starts to cry. "I've told you to be careful round the water. What if you fell in? What then?"

I look up at the woman's fierce face. It's Margaret Needham, Harry's wife. I feel a great urge to jump under the surface of the water myself.

"I caught him in time," I say.

She hoists Christopher up onto her hip, not thanking me. Instead, she looks from me to the cow and back again and kisses the still-wailing boy on the side of the head. A hand, dry and flaking from all the time they've spent washing and breaking up lead ore, caresses his cheek.

"No harm done this time," she replies. Though her words are forgiving, the way she says them is anything but. Without looking back, she walks off with her son, her chiding now lullaby soft.

I ache, then, for my mother's arms. For how things might have turned out if she'd been well enough to keep us away from the dangers that lurked all about this village.

She left that up to Grandam and, well, Grandam had her own way of doing things. It was her who first told me and Will about the Spirit of Elden Hole: not Mam, who went and sat by the mouth for hours at a time; not Da, who made the sacrifices when we were growing up. We curled at Grandam's feet, me about eight and Will three years older, listening to the story of how an angel had fallen from heaven into the Hole and was so full of torment that She sent a plague upon the land; how my grandfather was the only Peak Forester brave enough to go down and face it, and how he'd emerged a changed man, having made the deal that would seal all our fates.

"She vowed to let us be." Grandam leaned forwards on the stool so that her long, ashy plait brushed the tops of our heads. "As long as the Vernons continue to give Her our offerings, She won't bother our village. So now we feed Elden Hole, which Her angelic spirit inhabits like a body. It *is* Her body. The Hole and the Spirit are one being, like God the Father and God the Son."

I didn't understand all she was saying. I thought it was a story to make us shuddery, like the ones Da told. Yet if it weren't real, why was Grandam's face so sombre?

"How do we know She's an angel and not a devil?" asked Will.

"Because She shows great mercy," Grandam said. "If you were as far away from your home as She, would you not be mightily vexed? And would you not take out that vexation on everyone who had a decent life, like the people of this village?"

Will nodded, so I did too.

"She shows great humility by taking what we provide for

Her in place of heavenly manna. But woe betide us if we forget to give Her an offering. She'd smite us then. If we don't hold up our end of the bargain, She won't hold up Hers."

"Aren't angels supposed to be good?" Will asked. "She wouldn't do anything to us, would She?"

A shadow passed over Grandam's face and, for a moment, I thought she'd give Will a smack. Though she was our mother's mother and not young, she was far from decrepit. But she sat back and, after taking a shaking breath, said, "Did not the Lord send angels to destroy Sodom and Gomorrah? He's the Lord of vengeance as well as mercy. The sooner you learn that lesson, lad, the better. Now you're the son of this family, which means you've got to show your sister here"—she waved her hand at me—"how to take care of us all."

"How do I do that?"

She patted her knee. "Come here, child. I'll tell you what to do."

He sat on her thin legs while she whispered into his ear. I watched his grin crumble and his cheeks go pale. I watched him move away from that tongue that wagged near his face. Still, he listened. She ruffled his curls when she finished, his body stiff beneath her grasping fingers.

He didn't act straight away.

A new year unfurled. The sun melted the snow on the peaks. Spring came, and maids strewed the church at Chapel-en-le-Frith with wildflowers and carpeted its floor with rushes. Sheep wobbled as they ploughed along the grass, their bellies bulging with unborn lambs. Outside our house, a sparrow flitted through the air, insect wings and legs sticking out of its beak. It had built a nest right by our window, and whenever it came near the chicks, they chirped their little hearts out.

"Lift me up!" I asked Will one day. "Lift me up so I can see them."

He wouldn't have noticed the nest if I hadn't asked him. I blamed myself for it afterwards. One glimpse, he gave me, of those scrawny bodies with worm-like, craning necks, and the frightened black eye of the mother. Then he put me down.

The next day, no sound came from outside the window save the flutter of the mother's wings as she flew from bush to bush, searching for her young.

Grandam gave Will five shillings—one for each chick.

On his return from Castleton, Will chucks fat bags of money at me and Mary and asks us to count our share. I scoop up my bag cautiously, as if handling a toad bloated with poison. I'm nauseous at the thought of the coins slipping into my hand.

"Later," I say. I put it behind the butter churner.

"And how did your sale go?"

I hesitate. "I sold the horse and used that money to buy a cow."

"What's left, then?"

My stomach shrinking to the size of a fist, I shuffle to the table and tip out the remainder of Thomas's coins from my purse. Two pairs of eyes stare at me. Will's face twists into anger, and, before I can dart away, he grabs my wrist.

"How much did you get for the horse?"

"Four." I won't tell him about the offering I gave to the church.

"Four pound? Four?" He shakes me like a dog worrying at the neck of a bird. "It was worth seven at least!"

"The man wanted to take it today."

Humiliated, I watch Mary busy herself with counting out her share from Will's pile and my smattering.

"How much did he give you for the saddle and bridle?"

"They were in with the price," I say, flinching in case he hits me on the face. He only makes a circle with his hands and shakes. I've never seen the throat-wringing mime performed with such passion before.

"What did you think you were doing? You didn't even buy the bloody hens!"

"I can get the chucks," says Mary, not looking up. "Jane's hurt."

"That's beside the point."

"It's not, Will." She stops counting. "She's done well enough going there and back after all that happened last night."

"You're too soft on her. She can cope."

"Who are you now?" I snap. "Grandam?"

He glares at me. I run to the other side of the table, behind Mary, as if she can shield me from his blows. She might do an' all; he'd never lay a finger on her.

"Leave Janey be," she says to him, like she's telling Lordsmeer to stop playing with a spool of her thread.

Will curls his lip. After a moment longer of looking at her, he grabs his coat. "Right. Right then. I'm off."

"To work?"

"I'm not going to the rake today."

"Where, then?" asks Mary. It's becoming a habit of his to disappear when things get difficult.

His hand lingers on the black mourning ribbon as he puts on his hat. "Nowhere you need to worry about."

When he leaves, a peace settles over the house. I can breathe.

Mary rubs my arm. "Look, I'm going to the White Hart. Can you get by on your own?"

"Get by? Aye, I can do that. But don't ask me to be glad at heart."

"I'll nab a pie from the parlour. That'll lift your spirits. Till then, there's enough in the storeroom for oat cakes." She gives me a kiss on the cheek. "Take care of yourself, Janey. I'm sorry Will's got to be such a blockhead."

I don't bother with food, settling for a cup of Fie's fresh milk—which, as promised, is wholesome, and she didn't resist too much when I milked her. At least I've made the right choice today in buying a new cow, and I'm pleased to have given a whole pound to that warden. Though it didn't seem a lot at the time, I doubt many people like me, not even a member of the parish, would give alms so freely. That's two good deeds. Oh, and telling that gentleman where the Tiding Well was. I wonder if he found his cousin.

I get into bed early, making the most of the fact I don't have to share this side of the house with Will for a few more hours. Moonlight leaks through a gap in the old, oiled sheet draped across the window. My brother had better be careful, for the phantom of Tideswell Moor comes out when the moon is high.

Strange, how that story used to be such a comfort. There was the outside, full of wild, unknowable things, and there was the inside, a warm refuge and—on some nights, at least—a charmed one. No one could tell that tale like Da! He'd save it for evenings when a full moon sailed through the sky, blowing out every candle so that the only light came through the windows.

"It was on a night like this," he'd say, "that Robin Moody was stolen away by a spirit."

And we'd sit by his feet, me, Mary, and Mam, our eyes shining in the near darkness. A smile would creak across Grandam's face, for she'd heard the story many a time. Even Will, when he said he was too old for fairy tales, would shuffle cards on our bed, keeping his ears open.

I can hear Da recounting the tale even now.

"Once, not so long ago, there was a butcher in Tideswell named Robin Moody. Robin was a lazy sod, and a drunk. He whiled away hours at the alehouse with his good-for-nothing companions: the smith and the pardoner. It came to pass that one summer's day, his wife gave him the job of taking a cow hide to a tanner in Whaley Bridge. He set his slow mind to the job, but as he passed through Chapel-en-le-Frith, his companions tempted him into the alehouse. Oh, he said he had a charge to keep. But the smith said he could still make good time. He said he daren't turn up at the house drunk again; he'd get it in the neck from his wife! But the pardoner said God would forgive his sins—for a price, that is. In the end, the lazy butcher couldn't say no. He got off his horse and drank with them until nightfall.

"With his mind addled and the cow hide still untanned, he got back on his horse and set off for home. He passed by the king's hunting lodge and heard a noise. He stopped riding and looked up to the trees, where the sound had come from. A great white beast, wings spread like a terrible angel, swept over him.

"But it was only an owl. Then, he passed right by our house and saw a dark shape leap out in front of him. It had horns on its head, just like the Devil. Robin staggered back.

"But it was only a deer. He told himself, *You're being daft now, Robin. The ale's making a fool of you.* Off he went again and soon reached Tideswell Moor. The moon, which had been hidden behind clouds, shone forth. For miles and miles, there wasn't a soul in sight. His heart working like a miner hacking his way through rock, Robin rode on. Then, he saw a curious thing out of the corner of his eye.

"It was a shape of deepest black, crouching on the ground.

"Robin dug his boot into the horse's flank and clicked his

tongue. He lurched forward. The creature of darkness followed, silently flowing alongside the horse's rear legs. Giving into his nerves now, Robin began to ride faster. A trot became a canter; a canter became a gallop. But no matter how fast he went, he couldn't get away from it. Always, the thing kept pace. Always, it was just behind him."

I pull the flimsy bedsheet tighter about me and curl up with my knees almost touching my chest. The cold wind that squeezes through the gaps in the roof nips at the uncovered parts of my body. What a time to go telling myself stories like that. The phantom scared me then, but even more so now that I've committed greater sins than Robin Moody.

When at last I drift into sleep, I'm plagued by visions of something made of bristles and spines, crawling up Elden Hole with hooked, bat-like wings. A burst of flame lightens the endless depths below it. In the reddish glow, its skull gleams, a skull that seems to be attached to its body the wrong way round. Cries of animals keening echo off the walls. Slowly, the head begins to turn.

I jolt awake with a cry.

"Shh, it's all right," says a figure at my bedside, dabbing at my stitches with a wet cloth.

"Mam?"

Mary's moss-green eyes flash at me in the candlelight. "Not feverish, are you?"

She puts a hand against my forehead. It's warm and scented from the lavender water she's been using. "Hm. You're sweating."

"I was having a nightmare."

"What about?"

"Her. The Spirit of Elden Hole."

Mary takes her hand away, displeasure written across her features. Not concern. It looks more like envy.

She clears her throat. "I'm going to put honey on them stitches to help them heal. No picking at that bandage. Do you hear me?"

"I hear you." I smile at her. It's strange to think she's only spent nineteen summers on this earth. At times, I feel three years younger than her, rather than three years older. "You're good at this, you know. Looking after folk."

"You can say that once your skin's knitted back together, but not till then. Mustn't tempt fate." Mary drapes the cloth over her wrist and picks up the still-steaming pot of softly perfumed water.

"Have *you* been having dreams, Mary?" I ask, sitting up.

Her gaze is steady. "I dream all sorts, me."

"You know what I mean."

A flicker passes over her face, so quick that I can't make out what it means. "Listen," she says in a voice close to a whisper, "if I start dreaming things I don't want to see, I tell them to go away."

"Does that work?"

Her shoulders tilt from side to side like a balancing scale. "Most of the time."

I take her in as though I'm meeting her for the first time. She's a scrawny thing, but there's a pride in the way she holds herself, with a straight back and a chest pushed out as if she's already seen a few bairns through infancy. The ease with which she sewed me up, after covering her hands in Thomas's blood and brains, is both wonderful and frightening.

"You really aren't bothered about it, are you?" I say. "What we did."

She takes a deep breath. "Don't waste any more time feeling sorry for that rogue, Janey. You saw what he was like—he deserved it. He'd have been killed in a tavern brawl in the years to come if we hadn't cut short his pitiful life. He was just out to make trouble for himself and for any lass who happened to cross his path. Worthless filth. All right?"

Mary goes back to her side of the house, taking the bowl of water with her. Over and over, I repeat Mary's words in my head. At no point do they feel like my own.

Mary's asleep by the time Will returns. It's me who has to put up with all the clobbering about and grunting as he wrestles stiff leather boots off his feet and pushes his chaff bed up next to mine.

"Where've you been?" I ask.

"Where *haven't* I been?"

He lies back, putting his arms behind his head, nudging me as he does so. He stinks of unwashed bodies.

"With that woman in Castleton? The one with the birthmark—Bess Jenkins?"

I've never met her. According to Will, though, she's got a well-earned reputation and a talent for making you forget everything else that's going on in life. I don't like to think about him doing *that*. I've heard how men carry on with whores in the stables at the back of the White Hart: the fevered breathing, the slap of thighs, the grunts and yelps that better befit a dog than a person. They're all scrabbling about down there in the dirt together, beast and lover, a tangle of tongue and tail.

"Haven't you got better things to do with your money?" I ask.

"Only the smallest portion of my share is going on women."

"What's most of it going on, then?"

A shaft of moonlight through the window cuts his head in two.

"The Needhams think we're idle. Harry with his mine and his fifteen acres—he thinks he's so much better than us. And Nathaniel! You know what that knave is like. Irritating little bugger. Well, I thought we'd show them. I thought we'd buy a few acres off them, and then, mayhap, that portion of the royal forest they've had their eye on."

The royal bloody forest again! Does he ever stop thinking of it?

"You can't go round buying land straight away. They'll wonder where you got the money from. We're meant to be making offerings, not stealing from folk."

The village will tolerate us doing our duty if we stay out of everyone's way and don't come across all high and mighty.

Lord knows what they'll think of us if we draw attention to the wealth we've stripped off dead bodies.

"I'm going to bide my time," says Will. "I thought we could all put some money towards buying a goat first. After a bit of time has passed, we'll get a horse."

"The money'll only stretch so far."

"That's right, when you bring next to nothing back from a morning at the market."

He's still not forgiven me for that, then.

"Even with a lot, it'll run out," I say.

"Which is why we spend wisely and keep a look out for any other solitary travellers carrying around big bags. Not just any stranger from now on. *Rich* ones."

He turns onto his side, grabbing at my sheet and taking most of it with him. I lie on my back, listening to the wind pipe through the holes in the roof. We can't go to sleep angry with each other, not after what we've been through together.

"Will?"

"What?"

"I'm sorry about the money."

He grunts. "I'm sorry for losing my temper. You're not too upset at me, are you?"

Should I say yes, while he's handing me an apology like a hunk of warm, buttered bread?

"A little bit. Not much. Do you remember that story Da used to tell us? About the Tideswell Butcher?"

"The Tideswell Butcher?"

"You know… He was riding across the moor when a phantom started chasing him."

"Oh, that. What of it?"

"I was just remembering it."

It's so quiet that I can hear the saliva slipping down Will's throat.

"It wasn't a phantom," he says.

"Eh?"

"On the moor. Don't you remember?" He looks over his shoulder at me. "The butcher wasn't being chased by anything. It was his own shadow he saw."

Chapter Six

"'B*ehold, he findeth occasions against me.'"* The minister clutches the lectern with all the passion of Job himself, his eyes pleading for mercy. *"'He counteth me for his enemy.'"*

I never meant to become anyone's enemy.

For all of Thomas's hateful words against me and his rough handling of Mary, I wouldn't have done him harm if I hadn't been put in a place of desperate need. Mam always used to say it was a rare thing to find someone as gentle as me. Now, everywhere I go, I'm reminded of my role in the slaughter, even in church. Especially in a church that's named after him—St Thomas's in Chapel-en-le-Frith. Tomorrow marks a week since we broke at least two of the commandments.

A few pews in front of us, little Christopher Needham pokes his elder brother, John, and mutters to him. Both snigger. Margaret Needham spits words of rebuke at them, and Christopher hangs his head. As soon as his mother has turned away from them, he hides a laugh behind his chubby hand.

A draught smacks the back of my neck. No matter how

much they beautify this chapel with new pews and an altar table at the eastern end, it's still bone-numbingly cold. I press into Will for the measly bit of warmth his body can give. He's not listening to a word of the reading, I can tell from the way he's gnawing at his bottom lip. Back when his beard grew in wispy patches, he'd nibble the soft flesh so often that it was constantly bloated and bleeding. It was only after Katherine Frith spat some of the blood back in his face during a dalliance that he made himself give up the habit.

I elbow him, and he comes back to himself, straightening his back and re-crossing his arms. Whether Reverend Daniels has noticed that certain members of the congregation are struggling to follow his words, or whether he's rehearsed this moment beforehand, I don't know, but all at once he drops his voice.

"'In a dream, in a vision of the night, when deep sleep falleth upon men, in slumberings upon the bed; then he openeth the ears of men, and sealeth their instruction.'"

He lifts his face from the book. His eyes, bulging in their sockets, come to rest on me. I want to crawl out of my skin. *"'He keepeth back his soul from the pit.'"*

Does he know? Does this man in flapping white sleeves, who's only been in this parish for the past year, know that three members of his congregation stripped a man of his life and his possessions but six nights ago?

Keep back my soul from the pit, O God.

Mary shifts, causing the pew beneath her to crack like a whip. The noise catches the attention of Nathaniel Needham, who turns his head over his shoulder to look first at Mary and then me, adding weight to the rector's stare. There's a stark difference between the man of God and Nathaniel, the man of earth. The man of God looks at me from a high summit, with cold, distant authority. The man of earth is down in the dirt with me. A smile creeps over his lips.

He mouths something that looks like, *You, me, after*, making subtle gestures to follow him out. Whatever he wants, he can't approach us until we're out in the churchyard. It's not a communion day, and even if it were, it's harder to talk now that the altar has been moved to the east end of the church and surrounded by a rail. A decade ago, gossip would spread like a holy fire as we all knelt round the altar in the midst of the nave. We nudged and jostled, so close that, when my neighbours opened their mouths to receive the Host, their bad breath got right up my nose. People say the rail was put up to protect the altar, but I can't help seeing that wooden barrier as just another version of the fence built round Peak Forest over threescore year ago to mark the boundary of the royal forest. A great man comes along and says, "This is mine," with no thought for what the people or the place itself might want.

Christ, I'm getting like Will. I smile wryly to myself. Nathaniel, who must suppose I'm giving him some sign of my attention, smiles back before turning to the front again.

"Did you see him looking?" I whisper to Mary.

Not taking her eyes off him, she replies, "What do you think he's after?"

"Might just be trying to vex us, make us—"

Will elbows me and shushes, as though he's been listening intently to the sermon all along.

After a long service, the church doors finally open. I breathe in the cold air as though it's a reviving tonic. Nathaniel has his sights set on us again. To hell with him—whatever he wants to say, it'll only test our patience, and I have precious little of that today.

"Come on," I say, rising. "Let's go before Nathaniel can catch us."

I weave through the gaggle of worshippers, Mary and Will following close behind me. Though there are only a handful of people standing in the way of our freedom, half seem to have been put to sleep by the rector. Behind us, Nathaniel is approaching in haste, bobbing up and being dragged back into the current of the crowd like a drowning man. I grab Mary's hand and push more insistently through the people in front of us.

"'Scuse me, sorry."

Elizabeth, a childhood companion of ours who was given in marriage to Robert Archdale this summer, veers to the side. "Go past, ducks," she says.

Others aren't so considerate. The smith, John Gleeson, refuses to move any faster, even though the tips of my shoes are bashing against his heels.

He doesn't seem to hear me asking him to step out of the

way, so Mary raps on his spine with three insistent taps. I swear to God I can see the hairs on his neck stand on end.

Soon after, we're out of the door and I'm pulling Mary towards the lychgate.

"Wait!" She breaks out of my grasp. "Where's Will?"

We look over the heads of the worshippers streaming past and spot him, caught in a conversation with the Archdales.

Mary tuts. "They've not spoken to us in ages. Fancy them suddenly wanting to talk now, this week of all weeks!"

Will must feel the same, for he's nodding along with whatever Robert is saying, but his eyes keep darting over to us.

"Come on," I say. "We'll see him back at the house."

There are too many folk around the gate to get through quickly now. We could jump the wall, but that would only give people more cause to stare at us.

"Da's grave," I say.

He's buried at the rear of the churchyard, near the wall. Like many graves here, his headstone is set at a slanting angle, threatening to topple over. Sometimes, I think all it would take is a heavy rainfall to wash the slurry of flesh and bone from this raised bit of ground into the heart of the village. I still can't believe that Da's is one of the bodies rotting away under there. Any moment, surely, he'll appear behind us with a pipe between his teeth and put his rough miner's hands on our shoulders.

"I tell you, childer, Death won't snatch me afore the age of ninety!"

His name's there, though, clear as day: *William Vernon.*

Harry Needham's quaking voice comes back to me: *Something's happened. An accident. Up at Highpit Rake.* Mam listened at the door, saying only *Aye* and *Right.* After Harry left, she went outside and scattered grain on the ground for the chickens, singing softly to herself. They brought his body down later that day, Nathaniel and Will and Harry. Da's head was bound by a cloth, soaked with patterns of blood that looked like islands on a map. Death by falling deads, the Barmaster ruled—in other words, Da's skull was smashed in by a pile of debris that should never have been stacked so high.

We left space on the headstone so that we could add Mam's name when the time came for her to rest beside her husband. We couldn't have expected death would sneak up on us again so soon, snatching first the baby and, with it, Mam's soul. In truth, she was dead even before she poisoned herself. She saved what was left of her strength for that cruel act of self-slaughter. We found her lying on her back in the marriage bed, clots of blood and vomit stuck to her mouth, a cup tipped over next to her blue hand. The fatal mash of foxglove and wolfsbane was scattered round the rim.

Grandam, that unnatural woman, outlived her own child. Not for very long, though.

Nathaniel Needham's voice drifts from round the corner. "The Vernon lasses! I need a talk with you."

Me and Mary exchange a glance. There's a hardness to the set of her mouth, like she's armed it ready for a battle of insults. Soon enough, Nathaniel comes striding up to us.

"Didn't you hear me calling back there?" he asks.

"Mustn't have," I say.

He crumples his face into a hobgoblinish scowl, then nods at my sister, almost taking her eye out with the jut of his chin. "Ey up, Mary. All going well at the White Hart?"

"Far as I know," she says, cold as a fish. "Unless you've heard summat from Mrs Bagshawe that I haven't."

"Only foul words."

"Oh, I've heard them plenty of times."

"Does she beat you?" he asks.

"If she tried, I'd turn the stick on her."

"I'll tell her that, I will, next time I see her."

"Go on, see how far it gets you. She'll probably give *you* a hiding. Not that you wouldn't deserve it."

They quarrel right well, Nathaniel Needham and our Mary. In a way, it's a pity they're not married. From the other side of the churchyard comes the delighted shrieking of children in play.

"Is this why you ran after us, Nathaniel? To be jeered at by my sister? You're a glutton for punishment."

"Not as much as you are," he says.

"What's that mean?"

"Oh, nowt." He smiles to himself. "Just making conversation."

"Enough of this shite," I spit. "If you've got summat to say, just say it."

Nathaniel draws a figure of eight in the ground with the tip of his shoe. "Would you rather we go somewhere quiet? I've heard the back room of the White Hart is good if you want a private word."

My stomach drops.

A girl child runs our way and hides behind a gravestone, poking her head round the side to check if her playmates are in pursuit. The three of us draw closer, me and Mary touching arms, Nathaniel leering at us. Up close, the freckles scattered across his nose look like a mud splash.

Mary whispers, "What of it? You know full well what goes on."

"I do. Find a stranger. Lure them into the hills. Give them a push." He mimes pushing someone, then switches roles to become the horrified victim, pulling his mouth open in a silent scream. The look of terror dissolves into laughter at his own clowning. "That's not all, though, is it? You sold his horse?"

"Aye, we did," says Mary. "And again I ask, what of it?"

"Fine animal, that. Very fine. Did he give you money for a new cow an' all?"

I start back, wondering how in God's name he knew that, before the memory of little Christopher running towards the water and pointing at Fie flashes into my mind. No doubt Margaret Needham told the whole family that the new cow nearly trampled the child to death while I stood by, laughing, or some such nonsense.

"I bought it with the money I got from the horse," I say.

Nathaniel nods, sticking out his fleshy lower lip. Then he replies, in a sing-song voice, "I don't believe you."

"Believe what you want, you daft bastard! It changes nothing."

"Jane!" A sharp pain needles the back of my wrist. Mary's nails are digging into me. "Quiet."

I look over my shoulder at the little girl, who's watching us from around the side of the grave. She's not from Peak Forest. She shouldn't be hearing any of this. Good thing Grandam's not here, or else that lass would have more to worry about than being found by her friends.

"What?" Nathaniel grins. "Are you worried someone'll hear how you robbed that rich man blind before you fed him to—"

"Shut up, shut up!"

I clasp my uninjured hand over his mouth and shove him up against the church just as a party of children run round the back, catch sight of their quarry and pursue her. Nathaniel is shaking, but not from fear. He's laughing, his breath puffing out between my fingers and making little fart noises. I push against him harder. He groans as the back of his head crushes into the rough stone of the wall. His hat lifts off his brow, as if he's giving me a sign of respect. He could use his strength against me, if he chose to. He probably doesn't think I'm worth the effort.

One or two of the children stop and stare at us, but fear of being left behind proves stronger than curiosity. They follow the fleeing steps of the little girl. When I'm sure they've all gone, I let go of Nathaniel. He wipes his sleeve across his mouth and takes a lungful of air.

"What do you want?" I ask.

"A p… portion," he says. "A share of whatever you got from him. If you don't… g… give…"

"You should catch your breath before threatening us."

He gives me a look of pure loathing and steadies his breathing. "If you don't give it, I'll talk. There's plenty of people outside the village who'd be interested in hearing what the Vernons get up to, starting with Reverend Daniels in there. It wouldn't take much to convince them. Touched by the Devil, you lot are."

It's too close to the truth. It reminds me of what Grandam said about the Spirit of Elden Hole: *She was an angel who fell from heaven. Wasn't Lucifer himself the brightest seraph, once?*

I take a deep breath. "Why would you try and stop us doing our duty, eh? When that's what keeps you safe from the curse?"

"Curse?" He titters. "The only cursed things round here are the Vernons. I reckon your family made up the story about what's down that hole, just so you could do away with folk and take their money."

"You're talking out of your arse!" I say, but I'm losing control over my voice and my limbs. "Besides, no one outside Peak Forest will believe you if you told them. They'd think it was a wild tale *you* made up when you'd drunk too much."

His eyes burn. "Then what if I told the rest of the village about what your brother did to my sister? About our Rebecca?"

I start, as if someone's shoved me, hard, in the middle of my back. "That was nowt to do with us, and you know it."

Mary's mouth opens and an absent expression clouds her face. She's thinking, but of what? The damage that Nathaniel could do if he spread this rumour round the village? Or of Rebecca Needham herself, God rest her soul?

"Say we give you a portion of what we've earnt," she says, "would you leave us in peace?"

"Mary!"

He'll strip us to the bare bones. It'll be a trifling amount first, then a bigger and bigger portion till we're left with nothing.

Nathaniel lifts his hands up to his chest, palms facing out. "I'd leave you in peace. For half of what you made from that man."

"We didn't get that much," I say, but Mary's talking over me, asking if we have his word.

He holds out his hand. "On Christ's rood, you have my word."

"Mary, no. Don't—"

"Then you have ours," she says. They shake. *You idiot, Mary.* He's got us where he wants us now. The way he looks at my sister—it's like she's a joint of meat he wants a good chew on.

He turns to me. "Swear it yourself, Jane."

I get a glimpse then of what Da had to put up with every day at the mine. This clod of a boy thinks he's better than us just because his name is Needham. Somehow, Da managed to put up with the mean-spirited taunts when he worked, because that's what he had to do. Then he came home and looked after all of us, his children and Mam. True, there were times when he drank so much he passed into a faint on the chair and didn't move for hours and hours. Once, he was in such a deep sleep that Mam thought he was at death's door. She had us kneeling about him, weeping and saying prayers, till his snores startled the life out of us. But Da wasn't a bad man, despite his vices. He took fools like Nathaniel in his stride.

Now Mam may have praised my kindness, but she never congratulated me on suffering fools.

"I'm not promising you anything," I say, and turn my back on them.

Mary walks slightly ahead of me all the way from Chapel-en-le-Frith to Peak Forest. Neither of us says a word to the other. I smoulder with anger at her, at Nathaniel bloody Needham, at the fact he managed to get the deal he wanted right beside Da's grave.

Will is singing, actually *singing* when we get in. He's making up the fire, a job he usually leaves for me, even if it means sitting in the cold until I'm ready.

"The Archdales were telling me about the bit of the royal forest they bought," he says.

Mary picks up a sampler—an intricate pattern of bell-like flowers and wild animals—and slumps on her bed, absorbing herself in needlework. I sit at the table, cradling my head in my hands.

"It doesn't cost as much as I thought," Will goes on. "We might not need much more, if we're careful with what we've got."

"Glad you had a good talk with them. Did you give them our news, tell him about the man we killed?" The words are out of my mouth before I have time to question the wisdom of deliberately ruining Will's good mood.

"Anyway, Robert said he can walk me around what they purchased," he says, as if he hasn't even heard. "He's invited me to his house for dinner beforehand. Fancy that! Dinner. You two can come as well."

His cheer snags on my temper. "Fat lot of good that'll do us," I say.

"What's wrong with you, eh?" He folds his arms, looking from Mary to me and back again. "Aren't you pleased? First time someone invites us to dinner in God knows how long and—"

"It's Nathaniel Needham," Mary says, sticking her needle into the side of a running stag. "He has to go."

There they are: the words I've been waiting for her to say all the way home. Of course Mary wouldn't just give our money away for nothing. She's more cunning than that. More dangerous.

"No." I hold onto the table to stop myself from falling off my chair. "We can't."

"If he talks—"

"Can one of you tell me what the bloody hell is going on?" says Will.

And Mary does, stabbing and pulling with her needle as if she's picturing sewing Nathaniel's mouth shut. Will lights a pipe as he listens. Once Mary's finished, quiet settles over us all. Will blows a cloud of smoke to the ceiling and says, "Mary's right. He needs to go before this gets out of hand."

"This isn't like doing away with an outsider," I say. "If Nathaniel goes missing, everyone in the village is going to know about it. They'll turn a blind eye to our family's doings as long as we target strangers, but you understand as well as I do that they'll cry murder if it's one of their own."

In the silence that follows, I'm almost able to convince myself I've won the argument. But Will's tongue is poking out at the corner of his mouth, which means he's concentrating, and if he's concentrating, it means he's not done.

"What if he doesn't go missing?" he says, his brow creased. "He has a mining accident, just like Da. The air trunks in the sump collapse; it becomes hard to breathe. He looks for a way out, but soil has fallen across the level, blocking his path. He's trapped."

A shudder runs down my neck. Da told me all about the steep, slippery wooden steps leading down the shaft and those pitchy warrens miles under the earth. Just thinking about it makes me aware of the smoke from the fire, clogging up my airways.

"That's horrible, Will."

He raises his eyebrows. "That's life, Jay Bird."

Will's always been quick. In the time it's taken to light a pipe, he's concocted an entire plan for how to murder the man down the road. But it may be that he's not as quick as I think. Lord knows how long this plan's been brewing in his head. As far back as Da's death? Further? Those snarky little remarks Nathaniel would make about Mam's peculiarities…

You ought to put a leash on her, Nathaniel said once to Da. *So that she doesn't go wandering off when the moon is full.*

Will threw a punch at him for that.

"Harry Needham would know," I say. "If anything foul happened to Nathaniel. He'd suspect us."

"He wouldn't know a thing," Will replies. "Like I said, it'd look like an accident."

"It's a good idea," Mary says. "Just a pity. If we make it look like an accident down the mine, then we can't feed Her."

The blood stills in my veins. "You said She was satisfied. That's why She rewarded us with the money and the jewellery, isn't it?"

Will twizzles the pipe in his fingers, but he doesn't answer. It's Mary who speaks.

"If She's satisfied, why do we have this problem on our hands? It's mighty bad fortune."

"It's not bad fortune. It's Nathaniel's nature."

"Bad happenings or bad nature, he's a problem," replies Mary.

"It's best to get rid of him this way," Will says. "There'll be plenty more opportunities to feed Her."

I stand. "You're getting us into terrible trouble."

"You're getting us into more trouble by pretending everything is all right," says Will.

"It'll make things worse!"

He and Mary give each other a look. If I didn't know them better, I'd say it were wordless mockery. *How simple our sister is.* But I do know them, and this look has another meaning, one that slips away from me as soon as I try to grasp it.

"Oh, Janey," sighs Mary. "Can't you see the way it's going?"

I see it: Nathaniel, drowning in a heap of soil, pushing aside waves of it with splintered arms, giving up as it blocks up the passage to his lungs and then fighting no more.

"I'm having nowt to do with it," I say.

I'm out of the door and halfway up the road before it occurs to me. The look that passed between them: it's the same one they used to exchange when Will, a young lad at the time, came back from his first trips up Elden Hill with Grandam.

In them days, I had a vague idea of what *duty* meant. It meant empty nests, the odd egg smashed on the ground outside our house as Will carried the unhatched brood back to Grandam's clutching hands. One day, I asked him what Grandam did with them. Did she cook them for tea? *She swallows them whole,* he said. It was only later I realised that *She* didn't mean Grandam.

When he reached fourteen summers, Will started going out for longer with Grandam. He'd come back with mud splashed up the back of his breeches, panting like he'd been running. He wouldn't say anything to Mam and Da, just go to bed or sit by the hearth and watch the flames like a stuffed thing. When Grandam came into the house, a good few paces behind him, he wouldn't greet her. He'd flinch if the door closed too loudly.

None of us asked what they were doing or why it took so long.

The only one he'd let near him was Mary, who'd sit by his feet or cuddle up next to him on the bed, neither of them saying a word. She was eight, too young to know what was really going on. But, somehow, she understood what Grandam was training him to do.

Chapter Seven

I stand a few feet away from the abyss. My fingertips tingle. I'm light, slippery, made of ice. Around Her edges, Elden Hole is scabbed with stunted trees, nettles, and ferns. But there's a place where the plant life can't and won't trespass—the void that is Her heart.

I breathe through the fear and tilt ever so slightly forwards. The walls of rock are covered in patterns that look like mottled flesh at the back of a throat. It's beautiful and dreadful.

"Are you really so unsatisfied?" I whisper.

A patch of nettles stirs. The wind? It's far more vicious up here than it was down in the village. But the wind doesn't make plants move like that, like something's unfurling under them.

"What do you want from us?"

I descend the grassy slope to a ledge of land that sticks out over the mouth of the Hole. Even so, I'm too high up to see all the way down. I lie on my front and crane my neck over the edge, gripping the ground. A wave of dizziness sends showers of white speckles, like snowflakes or ashes, pouring before my eyes. The inside of the pit is funnel-like—gaping at the top and narrowing to five yard or so a few feet below the surface. Great wedges of rock stick out from all sides, knobbly and hard, like swellings. How can a human body fall all the way to the bottom without getting stuck or smashing on one of those outcrops? Something must collect the remains and drag them down into the belly of the earth. A creature—the fallen angel, surely—with hooked wings and bristles that clack together like dry bones.

A swirl of air hits me in the face. It's warm as flesh, rank as rot. I snap my head up, gasping. She must have grown tired of holding Her breath.

"What does the angel look like?" Will once asked Grandam.

She sucked on her teeth—the few that hadn't gone brown and fallen out. "Nothing of this world, lad."

If I leaned over again now, what would I see? The angel clinging onto the rock face with splintered talons? A backwards skull or, worse, the other side of it?

Dread roiling inside me, I prepare to look.

"Be careful," someone behind me says, "I've heard it's bottomless."

A man is standing at the top of the slope. A man I recognise.

He must be made of air and wings. First, he turned up like an angel in the marketplace, watching over me when I was at my lowest. Now, he perches above me, a long tawny cloak folded round him, drawing me back from whatever is waiting down in the pit. Isaac—that was his name.

Shakily, I get to my feet. "I was trying to find out how far down I could see."

"And to what depth did your view extend?"

"Couldn't see much."

Wind whirls around us and spins off down the throat of the Hole. A rumble rises from deep below—the growl of a stomach. Isaac doesn't appear to have heard.

"What're you doing here?" I ask.

I should be worried, being alone with a man. A man of class to boot, who'd face no consequence if he were to ravish a woman like me and leave her for dead. Yet there's no twitching malice in his smile; his low, soft voice speaks of safety.

"I'm still looking for my cousin, Sarah Pulmer." He draws the cloak tighter.

"No joy in Tideswell, then?"

"Not a lot, although a couple of local busybodies did point me in this direction."

"I haven't seen her pass this way. I'd remember—we don't get fancy folk coming through here all that often."

"Hm, that surprises me. Did you know that Elden Hole is in Thomas Hobbes's *Wonders of the Peak*?"

The name *Thomas* jangles my nerves.

"What's that?"

"Oh, it's..." He gives a casual wave of his hand "...a poetical text. Hobbes is a scholar who wrote about the marvellous attractions of the Peak country. He describes Elden Hole as a sort of gateway to Hell, and he writes about throwing a stone into its jaws and hearing it echo throughout the entire Underworld. Sarah was planning on visiting Elden Hole. She was interested in sounding its depths. Isn't that what you were just about to do?"

"Eh?"

"You were lying on your front and looking down. Weren't you—?"

I suppose it did look like that to him. Thank you, kind Sir, for coming up with an explanation so I don't have to. "Aye. I was having a look."

"You won't be able to tell how deep it is just by staring," Isaac says, prodding the sloping ground beneath him with the tip of his buckled shoes. "Let me show you what to do."

"No, no." I hold my hands up, the hungry grumble from deep beneath the ground still echoing in my ears. "You stay put. It's not safe down here."

"Wait," he says, and goes off somewhere. What in God's name is he doing? I scramble to the upper ground. The wind skims moisture off the surface of my eyes and channels it to the corners.

Isaac's by the half-collapsed sheep pen, picking up a piece of limestone about the size of his own head. He tries to stifle a groan as he carries it across the hillside. I suppose weakness is the price you pay for a lavish life. Will must never set eyes on him, this man of gentleness and good manners. Not only is he a wealthy stranger; he wouldn't put up as much fight as Thomas. Will would be able to snap him in two. As long as I'm here, though, nothing can happen to him.

Isaac nears me, his arms trembling with the effort of lugging a hunk of wall.

"I can take that," I say, holding my arms out in a gesture that I realise, too late, looks like an invitation to embrace.

Isaac's got strength and sense enough to clutch the stone closer to his chest. "Please, there's no need—"

"Give it here." I want to add, *you daft thing*, but we're not familiar enough for that.

Reluctantly, Isaac passes it to me. I take it clumsily, my fingers fumbling against his. There's hardly a hair's breadth between us. He smells delicious, of lemon balm and lavender. The relief when I step back is followed quickly by regret that I didn't make more of that closeness. If I had no pride at all, I could've feigned a fit of weakness.

"What do I need to do with this, then?" I ask.

"We need to throw it down and count how long it takes to hit the bottom."

A stone's no worthy offering. She might suppose we're insulting Her, trying to choke off Her breath. Then She might taunt me as She did when I gave Her a sheep's skull, only, instead of bleating like the poor animal, She'll cry murder in Thomas's voice.

"It won't work," I say.

"You've tried this before?"

The stone suddenly feels too heavy. It touches too much of my skin. Could a speck of blood or shard of bone have flown from Thomas's head and landed on its surface? "Summat like it."

"It's quite simple," he says. "I'll show you what to do."

I almost laugh in his face. Even a rustic like me knows how to throw a stone down a hole. Still, his offer of guidance makes me feel at ease. It's like having Da back again. Not in terms of age—Isaac's far younger than Da was when he died—and not at all because he reminds me of my father in the way he looks. It's the reassurance he brings. The sense that he need but click his tongue and all the dark and wild things will obey his commands. He says testing the depth is a simple act, and it is—the way he's planning on doing it at least. There are no hidden monsters in Isaac's world.

"All right. Keep behind me," I say, bolder than I feel. "I don't want you falling."

"But I may still fall, and then I'd crash into you and *you* would topple down."

"Better that than the other way round." I pick my way through the nettle patches down the slope.

"Why?" he asks. "Does it not matter to you whether you live or die?"

It's a question I've asked myself too many times. What difference would it make to the world if I were gone? Will and Mary would be able to carry out their business without my objections. They'd get on well, I reckon. Outside our household, not a single person in Peak Forest would be sorry to see the back of me. All the more reason why I should make the most of this companionship while I can.

"It does matter," is all I say.

I place the piece of limestone by the edge, gather my petticoat and kneel. Not like Mam used to do, all loose hair and wailing and devotion to the Spirit of Elden Hole, the angel. No, however much Mam urged us to worship this thing, I never could send my prayers down there into the darkness.

Isaac kneels at a respectful distance from me.

"You'll mucky up them breeches," I say.

"They're already *mucky*."

He puts on my accent for the last word, and it sounds so much like me that we both laugh. Tremors, not at all unpleasant, thrill along my nerves.

You're being foolish, Janey. He'll do you mischief.

The last thing I want is to end up with a bastard child. It's bad enough ending up with a child who *isn't* the product of a tumble on the hillside with some gentleman. But again, an animal instinct tells me he's to be trusted.

"Would you like to be the thrower?" It comes out in a trembling whisper.

He looks at me sideways and wipes a hand across a forehead clammy with sweat. Then, he picks up the chunk of stone wall. "Yes."

"All right." I start counting. "Three, two…"

"One."

He lets go. The stone whistles out of sight. There's an echoing clack that sends a black flurry whirling out of the darkness. Harsh caws fill my ears. I wrap my arms over my head and shut my eyes, protecting them from the sharp beaks that peck at the faces of newborn lambs and corpses of men, till the squawks quiet down.

When I open them again, Isaac's no longer there.

I thrust my head down the Hole. Darkness echoing darkness. My insides swoop, as if I'm falling. He's gone, torn out of existence.

A cough. Isaac is standing at the top of the grassy slope, God be thanked.

"My apologies," he says. "They startled me."

I climb up after him and follow his gaze to the sky. Black wings cut through clouds.

"Pathetic, isn't it?" His cheeks turn ruddy as a maid's.

"Not at all."

A deep clatter comes from behind us, making me jump out of my skin.

"It's hit the bottom!" he says. "We weren't even counting."

"Oh! That's what it was."

"You thought you could hear the labours of Sisyphus in the Underworld, didn't you?"

I laugh nervously, wondering who Sisyphus might be, just as the clouds give up their load and rain spatters down. Isaac pulls his hat lower over his brows.

"I should go," he says, "or else it'll be dark before I get back to Eyam. The walk to Jumber House takes over two hours."

"You haven't got a horse?"

"I enjoy walking. Perhaps I can sit in the White Hart until the rain passes."

"Not there."

He scowls. "Why not?"

Because Mary'll be on the lookout for people like you—rich strangers who are ignorant of her tricks. Our tricks.

"It's not a friendly place," I say.

"I found it pleasant enough."

The breath catches in my throat. "You went in before?"

"Yes, before wending my way up this hill. I asked the hostess and a few customers whether they'd seen my cousin."

"And had they?"

"One man made some lewd comments. Other than that, they said nothing at all." His mouth turns down at the corners.

"As I say, we don't get many fancy visitors. Where're you going to look for your cousin next?"

He stands with hands on narrow hips, surveying the village. "I know she travelled in this direction. Since no one here has seen her, the next most likely destination is Castleton. There are two Wonders of the Peak in that area, and at least one of them was of interest to her. Are you familiar with Castleton?"

"'Course I am—it's the next big village along. But it makes no sense for you to walk all the way back to Eyam if you're going to Castleton, surely?"

"I have matters to attend to at the house," he replies, smoothing his already perfectly smooth beard.

I don't want to ask the next question, but I can't help myself. "A wife? Children?"

"No," he answers, looking down. "I'm staying with my aunt, Mrs Ruth Goodwin, at Jumber House for the time being."

"In Eyam, you say?"

"Just outside the village, near the moor. Oh, and you were

correct about the Ebbing and Flowing Well last week—it was an unimpressive spectacle."

I smile. "The folk round here know best. How long are you staying?"

The surface of Isaac's eyes shine like dark glass. "As long as it takes."

"And you've been looking for just over a week?"

"Yes, but she's been gone for a fortnight, since the end of August. I have ideas about what might have happened, but..." The earlier joviality has gone out of him. He looks lost.

I know what it's like to lose someone, to spend every day going over and over anything that could make sense of it. For him, it's not too late. He might still be able to bask in the warmth of a loved one returned. I should envy him for it, but I don't. I want, more than anything, to restore order to the world.

It'd be highly improper for me to spend time with him alone. Will would skin me alive if he found out. But he's not Da. I have no husband to keep me indoors, and with our role in the village, there's a good chance I'll die unwed anyway. Nathaniel's teased me about it enough times. Who'd want someone like me? I don't mourn for it. In all my imaginings of a life beyond Peak Forest, I've never seen a husband or children—only two great big dogs and as many cats as will fit in the house. What reputation have I to ruin by spending time with Isaac? I'll be all right. As long as I don't let myself get swept up in anything untoward. As long as I'm careful.

"I'll come with you, if you like, and help you find her."

Isaac shakes his head and smiles sadly. "A generous offer, but I've taken enough of your time."

"Not at all. Let me come with you. I know Castleton like the back of my hand—I used to go there a lot when I was young."

"You *are* young," he says. There are crow's feet around his eyes—not a lot of them and not deep, but enough to show he's lived a fuller life than me.

"I mean, when I was younger."

He digs the heel of one shoe into the mud, like he doesn't care how much they must've cost him. "You are *very* generous. Do tell me your name."

"Jane Vernon, Sir."

A smile curls under his moustache. "Isaac Latimer," he says, though of course I already know half of it.

We stand for a few moments, letting each other's names soak into our skin. Isaac—the sacrifice. No, not the sacrifice. The saved.

"All right," he says. "I'd be glad of your company tomorrow, Mistress Vernon. I spend far too much of my time wandering the countryside in solitude. A little companionship would do me good, I suspect."

For the first time in a very long while, I could float with joy.

Chapter Eight

ISAAC

A backwards, brutish county, where men scratch out a living belowground like moles. There are no ladies, only women who push out children by the dozen and drink themselves into an early grave. The cows, pigs, and sheep stink to high heaven. Even supposedly genteel Buxton is noisome, the town's hot baths spumy with sulphurous gases. A place of darkness, filth, and ignorance.

That was what you thought of Derbyshire at first, Sarah.

If you'd moved to the countryside under different circumstances, you may have relished the open skies, the opportunity to roll up your sleeves and get dirt beneath your fingernails. Yet any blossoming young woman would be resentful if they were plucked up from their home town and replanted in a lonely house atop a hill with a new stepmother and a father who seemed to have forgotten all about the woman who birthed you—a woman buried over forty miles away.

It never struck you that he might have been grieving, too.

When I visited you in your first year at Jumber House, far removed from your friends and relatives in Bolton, I could not even persuade you out of bed. The room had a sour odour. As you lay propped up by the bolsters, embroidering images of your deceased mother's face, I stared out of the window at the lashing rain and wondered if I'd lost you.

In truth, I dreaded my next visit.

Four years passed. As I watched my elder siblings marry and move away, my heart strained towards Derbyshire. By the time I returned at the age of twenty-two, you'd changed. Colour once again graced your cheeks. There was a new assurance in the straightness of your back and a sly smile on your lips, as if you were party to worldly secrets I could never know.

"You look so well, Coz," I said, as we took a turn around your garden. A fresh, savoury scent rose from the rain-dashed thyme and rosemary. "I'm so pleased you've found contentment in this life."

"I learned to make the most of it." You took a deep breath. "Ruth is not my mother, but she's a good woman, and none too observant."

I wondered how the two things complemented each other.

"And the Peak country is not as dreadful as I used to think. I see the beauty in it now."

"What caused this revelation?"

You stopped walking and took in the view of Eyam village, laid out at the foot of your garden like a model sculpted for your pleasure.

"Seeing what has been in front of me for so long."

It was a few days later that I saw the book poking out from under a cushion on your window seat. The leather binding shone. I slid it out, delighted by the earthy musk of its skin. With the speed of a mother protecting her infant, you snatched it away from me and clutched the volume to your chest.

"I am sorry, Isa. It's a very precious book."

"Your father's?"

"No. Mine. And you mustn't prattle to my father or… or Ruth about it."

Why such secrecy surrounding a book? My mind ran to Foxe's *Acts and Monuments*, then to the seditious work by Alexander Leighton which had angered the king and his Star Chamber so much that Leighton's back was whipped to ribbons, his nose slashed and his ears cut off.

"A tract against the Church?" I breathed.

You laughed. "Oh, good Lord, no. I'm glad to have left those god-fearing Puritans back in Bolton. No, it's *De Mirabilibus Pecci*, about the miraculous sights of the Peak District. There is a well that rises and falls with the tide, and the beautiful estate of Chatsworth, and…"

The spine cracked as you opened the volume. "The entrance to Hell itself."

As if it were made of newly formed flesh, you placed the book gently into my hands.

I scanned the page, bewildered. "When did you learn to read Latin?"

"A lot has changed since you were last here. Look." You

ran your finger over a line. "*Fovea… Eldenia*. Elden Hole."

The words Hobbes used to describe it—*terribilis*, *vastum*—must have been strange and thrilling to your mind. How terrible, that a gateway to the Underworld was lying wide open in Derbyshire! How marvellous, that you could stand inches away from annihilation. It was a luscious, round temptation just beyond your reach.

"It's very intriguing, Coz," I said. "But why must this stay a secret?"

Your jaw softened as you took the book away from me. "There is no good reason, other than it feels as though I've discovered these Wonders for myself and I wish them to be all my own."

"I hope you're not planning a midnight escapade to Elden Hole."

"It would be interesting, wouldn't it? To find out how deep it is?"

Well, now I have seen Elden Hole for myself, Sarah, and one part of me insists that it is a great nothing that captured your imagination. Thomas Hobbes gave a hole in the ground all of those blood-curdling names to make his poem on the Peak country more enthralling. He sees ordinary black birds in the air and calls them demons, much like those fellows who travel overseas and claim they have discovered headless monsters or men with a single foot, large as an elephant's ear, which they use to shade themselves from the sun.

The other part of me is inclined to seek out as many stories as possible and discover why these myths have such deep roots.

Certainly, they must have sprung from a seed of truth.

This rustic companion of mine stirs my spirit of inquiry. She is something of a wonder herself, not at all like the uncouth ruffians one hears about. She possesses a gentle soul. I have a strange conviction that we were destined to meet, that the book you showed me all those years ago put me on this path.

Chapter Nine

For once, Isaac's not here when I need him to be. The hills on either side of Winnats Pass, rising like fists into the soft-bellied clouds, don't so much provide shelter as channel the flaying air. My travelling cloak whips round my legs. I pull it tighter and try to allay my worries that he won't come and my worries that he will come. It makes so little sense that he'd see the value in someone of my standing. He's well-off, respectable—landed, no doubt. *He means mischief,* says that wary part of my mind. *He must do.*

A stronger voice tells me it's fate that brought us together. To meet on two occasions, when I've been at my most desperate… It must mean something, mustn't it?

Thought becomes flesh as a man in yellow and blue appears at the top of Winnats Pass. I've never seen him from this far away before. My eyes roam over every part. His legs are long and shapely, but thin compared to his broad chest. From this distance, he has the look of someone made up of spare odds and ends. Only when he draws closer do you see the curl of his smile under his moustache and that soft-looking beard, the sparkling eyes.

"Mistress Vernon! Forgive me for keeping you," he says, catching his breath.

"No matter." He needn't know that I rose while the sky was still murky with night to get all my morning chores done.

"My curiosity got the better of me. Look!"

From his pocket, he takes out a curled nub of stone, about the size of my thumb, covered in fine ridges. "What is it?"

"I chipped it out of the side of the hill. It's a sea shell, I think, preserved in the rock."

"A sea shell? Up here?"

"That's what it looks like. There may have been water covering this area very many years ago."

It's much more likely to be a snail shell that's turned hard and dirty over time. I know the land; he doesn't. But there's no point in contending with him. Besides, I like his idea better.

"It's pretty. Keep it safe," I say.

"Oh, I shall." He puts his treasure back in his pocket. "Thank you for accompanying me today."

My face could crack with smiling. "My pleasure."

Idiot girl, Janey.

We set off down the steep road to Castleton. I go slowly at first, as all it'd take to go flying head over heels is a jutting rock, but Isaac has the springing step of a hare. Sheep bustle across our path and take refuge in the craggy limestone hills that loom up on either side of us.

"Is there still a castle in Castleton?" asks Isaac.

"Hardly. There's Peveril Keep, and a wall running around

it, but no one looks after it anymore. Is it one of your Wonders?"

"No, Hobbes wasn't impressed either."

"Have you any idea where Sarah could've been round here?"

He gives a slight shake of his head. "I'll check in the inns and taverns. There are caves she might have visited as well. We were interested in seeing the Devil's…"

"Arse?"

A blush spreads across his face, and I conclude once and for all that he's a beautiful thing, thin legs or no.

"Why does it have such a vulgar name?" he asks.

"Well, it's a great big crevice in the hillside. Whoever came up with the name didn't need much in the way of fancy. The wind blows about in it, making it sound like… you know."

"Flatulence."

"Farting."

It cheers my heart to hear Isaac laugh and to know that I'm the cause of it, even though I'm being mighty unladylike.

"But why the Devil?"

"He's got the biggest arse, I suppose. It also stinks in there. It floods often, and all kinds of rotten things float about in the water."

"The name makes me wonder if it's believed to be another entranceway to Hell—an especially noisome and blustery one, perhaps, but rather like your wonder in Peak Forest. Tell me, do *you* really think Elden Hole leads to the Underworld?"

I almost trip over my own feet. "Not certain."

"You must have an idea one way or the other."

"Then no, I don't."

"Oh, but people must talk about it!" He brushes a lock of wind-blown hair out of his eyes. "If you live in the village, you'll have heard all sorts of stories, surely."

"I'm no good with old wives' tales. Can't remember them for the life of me. They're all nonsense, anyhow." It comes out louder, harsher, than I expected. Silence stands between us like an unwelcome third traveller.

"Hobbes was probably exaggerating," Isaac says after a while. "*He* might have been the one to invent the stories, as far as I know."

"Most likely."

Isaac clears his throat. "He even writes of a mountain overlooking the village here, which has earned the nickname 'the Shivering Mountain' on account of the fact that it sheds grains of rock hour by hour."

That phantom traveller who stood between us fades away.

"Mam Tor," I say.

"Yes, that's the one."

"It's just a great big ugly bulk, nothing like an hourglass if that's what you're imagining. You can't even see it move with your own eyes. But folk do say there's a great pile of dust at the bottom of it."

"That's the wondrous thing, according to Hobbes—it never seems to shrink."

How different my life might've been if my family had lived here, next to a hill that's never hungry, instead of near that guzzling maw. We wouldn't be luring travellers off route, baying for the blood of neighbours. We'd live simple, satisfying lives.

Then, I see why I'm here, and why Isaac's here, and why our paths have crossed: I've been given a second chance. If I can help this man find his cousin—if I can be the instrument of a union, and not a severing—I have a chance of being saved from damnation. He does resemble an angel, after all, and any time spent away from the corrupting influence of Will and Mary can only be good for my soul.

He won't harm me, surely. I've never met a kinder man.

"I don't know what you'll make of the Shivering Mountain," I say. "But Castleton's a good village, and good things happen here."

"I'm delighted to hear it," Isaac replies. "If prayers can move mountains, then by God, we're in the right place for it."

We head for a shop selling bread and meat pies. Isaac stands outside for a moment, arranging his hat and smoothing his beard. He's jittery all of a sudden, almost like I was before I walked into the White Hart on the night of Thomas's death; it's as if he's rehearsed a part, and he's keen to get it right.

In he goes, and I follow, welcoming the wholesome waft of baking bread and pastry. A tinkling bell sounds as Isaac closes the door behind us. The shopkeeper—a woman of about thirty with thick eyebrows and a double chin—hushes us. Isaac stills the bell, grimacing.

"Sorry, sorry, ducks," the woman whispers. "It's just… the bairn." She turns around to show us a sleeping infant the size of a piglet strapped to her back with swaddling. "The slightest noise… I feel awful, telling customers to be quiet but, you know, she's such a light sleeper."

Isaac's face smooths out. "No offence taken."

"Some people think I'm being rude on purpose, which is not what I'm like, not in the slightest. Anyhow, what can I get you?"

I'm eyeing the pork pies, but Isaac says, "Nothing to eat, thank you. We wondered if you could help us."

He reaches into his bag and brings out a small book bound in brown leather.

"We're looking for someone. Let me show you."

The woman leans forward and folds her arms on the counter. The slight movement causes the infant on her back to stir, though they do not wake. Isaac flips through some very fine pencil drawings until he reaches one of a woman who has the same heart-shaped face as him. Her cheeks are fuller, though, plumped with luxury. From his bag, he also takes out a pretty blue hood, embroidered with silver birds.

"She was wearing a headpiece like this when she left," he explains. "It was a favourite pattern of hers. She had several made."

"Lovely lass," says the shopkeeper, staring at the picture rather than the hood. "Jilted you, has she?"

Isaac laughs like someone mimicking jollity. "No, no. She's my cousin. Have you seen her?"

"How long ago do you think she was here?"

"I'm not certain, though it can't have been before the thirty-first of August."

The shopkeeper cocks her head. "Did she have anyone with her?"

"For her sake," says Isaac, "I hope not."

"For her sake, I hope she did," replies the shopkeeper. Her head bounces up and down as she firmly agrees with her own point. "Shouldn't be going round on her own, a good-looking lass like that."

Isaac grumbles. "It depends on the company you keep. Being alone is far better than being with a scoundrel."

"You think she was with a scoundrel?"

Isaac's silence is curious—very curious.

This casts a very different light on the missing cousin tale he's been telling. No longer is Sarah just a clever girl who's been taking herself off to see the not-so-wonderful Wonders of the Peak. She had *company*, possibly the company of a scoundrel.

Sarah, you little strumpet.

The shopkeeper seems not to take much note of his silence. "Wandering off round these parts without anyone with you… well, you're asking for trouble, aren't you?" she says. "The weather can turn foul in the blink of an eye. You go off and find yourself a cave to shelter in and, lo and behold, there's a huddle of robbers waiting for a lamb like you to happen across them. They strip you of everything, from your purse to your undergarments, then chuck you down a mine shaft."

It's an effort to keep my face from crumbling. She must mistake my expression for disbelief, for her head bounces up and down again.

"It's a true story, that. Happened last year to a lass from Buxton, that's what I've heard." She starts rearranging the pies on her table. "But you know, I don't think anything like that'll have happened to your cousin."

The bairn starts crying.

Isaac glances over at me in dismay. He looks as if he's aged years since the start of the conversation.

"So, you've not seen her?" I ask.

As she fumbles to undo the cloths binding the baby to her back, the woman repeats, "End of August, end of August… Ah!"

Isaac leans across the counter. "You remember something?"

A length of swaddling unravels in her hands. "Can one of you…?" She turns about so that the rosy-cheeked bairn on the verge of slipping out of its stays is bawling straight at us. "Grab hold of her, will you?"

I take the warm, squealing bundle from the woman, trailing the yellowish white bands all over the pies, and jiggle the baby up and down, hush, hush, hushing. She quiets in my arms, though she's still a wriggly little thing. I'm transported back to Christopher by the pond, to Mrs Needham's sharp words as she tore him away from me like I was diseased.

If Will and Mary get their way, she'll lose her eldest.

I'm relieved I hand the infant over to its mother. I shouldn't be in charge of such an innocent and breakable body.

I'm about to say we should leave when the shopkeeper comes out with, "I might've come across your cousin or someone who looked like her. My memory's been like a sieve since this one," she replies, looking down at the baby with an admixture of love and resentment, "but I think it must've been around the end of August. By herself, she was. Didn't look at all pleased."

Isaac raises his hand to his skull, as if trying to stop a thousand questions from bursting out. "Going from where? To where?"

"From town, up to Winnats Pass. I couldn't tell you whereabouts in town she'd been."

"What do you mean, she didn't look pleased?"

The woman drapes her baby over her shoulder and pats her back. "The lass had been crying, I reckon. Her hair was loose under… I think it *was* that hood. And the bottom of her petticoat was dirty. She looked like she needed a good wash and a meal down her. She looked like she needed to go home."

Under the shadow of Mam Tor, we flit in and out of the places Sarah might've been, from the Nag's Head Inn to the little shops along the river. But no one else remembers a well-to-do lass who looked like Isaac. The morning grows old and, still, fortune doesn't favour us. We take to stopping passers-by who trudge through the streets. Some don't even glance at the picture before telling us they've got to be off and pushing past us.

Isaac takes out a handkerchief and dabs his forehead. "It might be time for us to leave."

Leave? Despair attends that word. We leave, and both Sarah and my soul are lost.

"We can't," I insist. "That pie woman saw her, didn't she?"

"She *thought* she saw her."

"Aye, but how many ladies like your cousin pass through here? Besides, there's the rest of the village to see."

"How much more?"

"Another inn. A few more streets."

He sighs, looking like he did when he was carrying that piece of wall to Elden Hole. "I'm not certain that I have the strength for this today."

"It's all right, Sir, we can—"

"You don't need to call me *Sir*," he snaps. "I'm no gentleman."

My face glows hot, as though he's struck it.

"I've never met such a fine gentleman," I reply, quietly.

For a while, we stand in silence. He closes his eyes and rubs his fingertips over the lids. "I'm sorry. This business with Sarah—it's tiring."

"You don't need to say sorry to me."

"But I do. I do. I shouldn't have barked at you for paying me a compliment. I only meant to say that I'm from a family of merchants, not gentlefolk. It's rather a sore point for my father." The next moment, he claps me on the back. "Come. I owe you a meal and a drink. I hear the Cheshire Cheese is good."

Once he's gone through the ritual of smoothing his beard, he sweeps through the door of the inn with all the boldness in the world. He has quite an effect on people, Isaac does, and those few moments outside might help him achieve it. A table of miners drowning out the chatter with a song drop their voices and watch as this finely dressed visitor passes them. One man steps aside for him at the bar. When I come trailing along behind, panting like a mangy cur at his fine heels, looks of awe turn to bafflement.

The landlord has only a few strands of grey left on either side of his head and a wide nose. He must've been in the business long enough to learn where not to stick it, for he takes one look at the difference between me and Isaac and knows better than to ask questions.

"What can I do for the both of you?"

"A cheeseboard and two small beers, please. And…" As he's already done dozens of times today, Isaac shows the host the picture of his cousin's face and takes out her hood. "I was wondering if you'd seen this woman. She may have been wearing a head covering like this."

The landlord squints at the book. "Wait."

He places a pair of wiry spectacles on the end of his nose, and his eyes, now three times bigger, get three times wider. "Oh. Oh! You know, I think I may do."

"You *may* do?" Isaac asks.

"I do. I do remember her. That's right. She had that hood on, with birds on it."

Isaac throws back his head, like a man in ecstasy. "What

was she… What did she…?"

"Travelling with her husband, she was. Or someone who said he was her husband. About a week ago."

"I knew it! Was he an older man?"

"That's right." Our host pinches the bridge of his spectacles and puts them back in his pocket. "At each other's throats, they were. Some of my other guests made a fuss about the noise of them shouting in the early hours. I told them they couldn't stay another night here, seeing as they'd caused so much trouble, but the man said it was no matter, for they were on their way in any case."

"They left together? Are you certain of that?" asks Isaac.

"I am."

"Where were they going?"

"They didn't say much, apart from that they were off to see the sights. By that, I assume they meant the Devil's Arse. There's not much of note round here apart from that. Hm, caused quite some trouble, hasn't she, this lass?"

"She wasn't causing trouble," Isaac protests, "it was him. Tell me, was he physically violent towards her, this scoundrel?"

"What went on in the privacy of their own chamber is a mystery to me, but—"

"Ey! Am I going to get a drink today or not?" shouts someone behind us. The landlord fumbles with the barrels and pushes two quarts into our hands.

"I can't stand round here talking, Sir. That's all I know."

"His name?" I ask. "What was the man's name?"

The host shakes his head. "They gave their married name

as Jones, but most folk who come in here pretending to be wed do as well. Either that or Smith or Williams. Godspeed in your search for her. She was a pretty thing, deserving of better than him."

He nods at the people behind us, but Isaac side-steps and blocks his view. "If you see either of them again, would you send a message to Jumber House near Eyam? And to show you my gratitude…"

Coins pour out of Isaac's leather purse, spinning and clattering on the bar in front of us. He pushes the pile—at least twice as much as the beer and cheese costs—towards the host. If Will saw this, he'd pick Isaac clean as a bone and throw him down Elden Hole in an instant.

The man takes out his glasses again and holds them to his face. "I'll keep an eye out." He slides the money back to Isaac. "But I don't need paying for it, ta very much. Haven't I told you all I know without bribery?"

"Quite so. My apologies." Isaac hurriedly scrapes the coins into his purse. It must've embarrassed him out of his senses; as we're carrying our drinks over to one of the only free tables in the place, he glances over at the door and bumps into a pot-bellied man, slopping beer down the both of them. The man blurts, "Oy, oy, oy! Watch where you're stepping!" but Isaac hurries on, keeping his head down. He scurries to a different table, one that's further towards the back.

"What's the rush?" I ask.

Isaac pulls out a seat. "I've humiliated myself."

"We can go somewhere else if you'd like."

"It's too late now. I've ordered."

We sit in brooding silence till the food comes. Though my belly was rumbling not half an hour ago, Isaac's crabbiness makes my appetite dwindle. The thick slabs of cheese stick to the back of my throat when I try to swallow. Isaac breaks off a morsel of bread, brings it to his lips, lets it fall back onto the board, looks over his shoulder and picks at the skin around his thumb.

"So, this *husband*…" I begin, but Isaac waves away my words. His gaze isn't on my face, but somewhere over my shoulder.

"Not here," he says, "it's too public. We should go to the Devil's Arse. Come on." He pulls his hat low over his brow. "Let's leave."

"Now? We've only just started eating."

"Take your food with you."

Before I can finish wrapping the bread and cheese in the napkin, he's hurrying across the tavern, swerving between tables and drinkers. A man in the winter of his years, the tallest in the room by at least a foot, starts towards him from the middle of the queue. Isaac's too fast for him, though; the door of the Cheshire Cheese is already creaking shut by the time the stranger has crossed the room. His lean, fox-sharp face turns to me, sniffing me out as though I owe a debt. Whoever he is, Isaac must've thought he was trouble. Like my companion, I lower my head and weave in and out of customers to avoid him, but I'm not so quick.

"Excuse me, Mistress! May I trouble you for a moment?"

The grey eyes of the stranger meet mine. They're full of faded authority, cobwebbed memories of gentlemen and nobles.

"What is the name of that man you are with?" he asks in a voice dry as dust.

"Vernon," I say, without pausing to think about it. "Mr Isaac Vernon."

He nods. "Vernon. Right, right. Yes." The nodding stops. "Are you sure about that?"

"I am absolutely sure, Sir."

He might've been good at sniffing out falsehoods once, but not today. He shakes his head. "Yes, yes, of course you're sure. Forgive me."

It's as simple as that; he steps aside, and off I go. Outside, Isaac has already made it to the top of the road. It shows a strange lack of courtesy, leaving me behind. That man who talked to me might've been up to no good, and Isaac just left me in his clutches.

"Mr Latimer, wait!" I run to catch up with him. "Wait! Did you know that man?"

"Who?"

"The one in the Cheshire Cheese. He looked well-off."

"I cannot think who you mean," he replies. First, he hides what he knows about Sarah's lover. Now he tells me a lie.

"There was a man," I say. "Tall, about sixty-odd. He asked me who you were."

Isaac stops in his tracks. "And what did you tell him?"

"I told him… Oh, it sounds daft now, but I told him you

were Isaac Vernon."

He closes his eyes and sighs. "Look, I have not been entirely honest with you, but it is for a good reason," he says. "I will tell you about that man. But let us make sure we're somewhere private. Is the Devil's Arse always full of visitors?"

I force myself to move on from his confession of dishonesty and return to memories of childhood, when I went into the cave with Will and Da. The roof gets so low, the ground so waterlogged, that you have to lie flat on your back in a boat. There's chamber after chamber, reaching down into the hills. It reminds me of the mines: those endless depths; cold earth; traps made of stone.

"Depends on the weather and the time. It might not be busy today."

"Then you shall know more presently."

Chapter Ten

Peveril Castle looks down on the crack in the hillside like the tasteless joke it is. Think of the king, coming to visit his property and finding it's built on top of Castleton's most famous arsehole! The birds are cackling as they circle the blank sky and swoop to roost inside the puckered roof of the cave. In the entrance, a few people are gathered about a fire: men, women, and children in patched clothing. The young woman who greets us is comely enough for someone who spends all day leading rich folk down into the bowels of the Devil.

"Looking for a guide?" she asks in a thick accent. "I know all the ways. You'll be safe and have light."

Isaac reaches for his beard. "A guide?"

"It'll be a shilling, ta," the woman says, losing no time.

Isaac beckons me towards him. My heart thumps fleshily in my neck as he puts his lips to my ear. "Is it really necessary?"

"You've got to pass over a river—you'll definitely need a guide for that part. After that, you might not."

"Can *you* lead us, Mistress Vernon, once we've crossed the

river?" If it were any other man, I'd tell them to get lost. But Isaac's eyes plead for us to be alone. In darkness, we can talk of his cousin and the gentleman in the tavern. We can talk of other matters: things he wouldn't dare say to me in public. He's craning his slender neck to look at the cave roof. How soft and warm his throat looks, like an overripe piece of fruit. I'd like to kiss that pip of an Adam's apple.

"I'll lead." I drop a few pennies into the cave woman's palms. "Take us across the river, then give us a couple of candles and I'll lead from there."

"You know how dark it is down there? And wet? That gentleman wouldn't want a dousing under the waterfalls."

"I'm well aware," I say.

"Hm! As you wish."

She hands me the candles from her apron while Isaac goes through the rigmarole of asking about Sarah again. Given what the host in the Cheshire Cheese told us, I'm expecting the woman to say straight away that she remembers the lass, but she shakes her head.

"We see a lot of folk. There are a great many of us leading an' all. One might've seen the woman, but it weren't me."

"Can you leave this picture with the other guides while we're down in the cave?"

He hands the drawing to the woman, takes a pouch from his bag and puts three shillings into her palm. The more he flashes that purse about, the more chance he has of running into someone like Will. I'll have to tell him to be more guarded. The guide, thankfully, is not one to exploit him. She frowns at the glittering coins, as if she thinks they must be a trick and they'll disappear up Isaac's sleeve any instant.

"For your trouble," Isaac explains.

Her eyebrows knitted, the woman closes her fingers around the money.

"Ta very much." To me, she says, "Haply for you, it's not as rank-smelling today. Once I leave you, don't go wandering off down the side passages. There's some that think they know best, but they're the ones that don't come up again."

"I'll keep us safe," I say.

My breath coming in rags and tatters, I follow our guide along a crude path. Children with hollow cheeks and hungry eyes peek out from behind haycocks that stand like giants in coats of fur. Two men lift a boat down from a stack, and it looks like they're preparing a coffin for a rich man's funeral. The daylight is already a long way behind us.

"Careful," I say to Isaac. "Watch your head."

"Thank you for the warning."

"And mind where you're stepping. There are loose stones."

"Worry not. I trust you'll lead me on the safest route."

Trust. Safety. If only he knew what I did the other day.

Water dribbles from the stone and soaks through the linen coif wrapped round my hair, chilling me like a devilish baptism. Leaving behind the pale daylight and the chatter of the other guides, we descend a sandy slope to an archway formed of two merging rocks. There, a single boat awaits.

"I'll take you across one at a time," the guide says. "Who first?"

Isaac steps forward. "I'll go."

I laugh to see him clamber into the rocking boat in his fine shoes, holding onto the young guide for dear life. It's not quite so amusing when he crosses his arms over his chest, lies back, and disappears from view inside the coffin-shaped box.

"Wait for me on the other side," I call.

"Of course."

The guide ducks down at the front and, holding her candle aloft, she steers the boat through the dark waters with a small paddle. The light flits over the cave walls, getting smaller, fainter. Isaac drifts under the lowest archway and out of sight.

It takes entire days, entire winters, for the boat to come back for me.

"Is he all right?" I ask.

The guide grins. "He's waiting for you on the other side."

I fit my body into the dint Isaac's left in the straw. The guide pushes off from the sandy bank. On the low cave roof, a shadow boat sails above us.

"He's very dear to you, i'n't he?"

Is it so clear? Did Isaac mention anything to her on their way across? "We've not known each other long," I say.

"Doesn't make a difference, though, does it?"

My body feels heavy enough to sink this boat all of a sudden. "I suppose not."

"I told him to look after you. There used to be robbers hiding in here. Some say they still are. You hear about all sorts of goings-on deep in the cave."

Does every resident of Castleton want to scare visitors shitless? "I can do without the stories, ta very much."

"Suit yourself."

After another minute, the boat slides up the bank and lodges itself there. The guide helps me out as Isaac comes right up to the river's edge, asking me if I managed to stay warm and dry, pointing out the straw that's stuck to me. There's a nervous ruffle in his voice. It must've been a lot worse for him, waiting on the shores of the unknown, than it was for me over on the side of the people and the daylight.

"I'll be here," the guide says, "when you're ready."

"Many thanks, good lady." Isaac nods at me. "Lead the way."

"I'll stay by your side. It's safer that way."

"As you wish. You know best."

We walk together up a slope that leads into an immense darkness. It's broken only by the pale glow of a dozen or so candles resting on high rocks and our own small sticks of tallow.

"This reminds me of when we were on the top of the hill, staring down into the depths," Isaac says. "We'll have to drop another stone down Elden Hole and see if we can count properly next time."

The name *Elden Hole* has more power under the damp roof than it does on the surface. An echo stretches the *O*, deepening it, turning a word into a great circle of air.

"You won't find an answer," I say. "People've been down there before, and even they couldn't say how deep it was."

"So you *do* know some local tales."

My heart sinks. Of all the things we could be talking about.

"Have many people have been down Elden Hole?" he asks.

"Some."

"Miners?"

"Miners, yes, and people… urged to go down."

My chest feels as though it's being heated from the bottom. Fear and an age-old resentment begin to simmer. I walk on, hoping to get far enough ahead of him to make questioning harder, but he catches up with me soon enough.

"What could persuade someone to make that descent?"

"Money, for one thing."

"I don't think I could do it for all the money in the world."

"It's all right to think like that if you've got enough," I say, trying not to sound irked.

I thought we'd come here to talk about *his* private thoughts, not mine. Not these ones, in any case. A flinty drip of water trickles into my mouth. I shouldn't say another word, but somehow, I can't help myself.

"People have gone down there because they had to."

"You saw this happen?"

I hesitate. "People talk."

"I thought you said you didn't know any tales about the hole."

"They're not *tales*," I say. "They're real things that happened to real…"

A pattering. A hiss. My candle goes out, and pure blackness closes in. The panic I've been holding off since coming into the cave digs its claws into my heart. I curse under my breath.

"Here."

Isaac's candle touches mine, tallow dribbling from the pool at the top and down the stem. The flame grows bigger, splits in two. His face is close. It's soft with shadows, and so very lovely. What is he: an angel, or the greatest tempter of all?

"You were saying?" he whispers.

I could tell him to mind his own business and stop bothering me about Elden Hole. Or I could tell him about what happened to my grandfather. He's thirsty for stories—his parted lips would drink my vile history gratefully. He'd drain me of it. Then, doubtless, he'd turn with disgust and leave.

"The only tale I know is about a goose," I say, looking away from him.

"A goose?"

"A woman from Peak Forest threw a goose down Elden Hole to see if it was bottomless. They say the creature came waddling right out of the Devil's Arse."

"It travelled from Peak Forest to Castleton? Over three miles away?"

"Not only that. Its feathers were black and smoking. That's why people say the hole is an entrance to Hell. Think of it as the mouth. This is the other end. The goose walked through the whole slimy gut of the Underworld."

There's a moment of silence. Then, he laughs lightly. "Astonishing, what people believe around here!"

It's the second time today he's hurt me. "Is that why you want my company? To keep you amused?"

Shoving aside thoughts of being buried alive or lost down

some branching passage, I stride ahead. If I go deep enough, nothing'll come to find me. Not Isaac's mockery, nor the curse, nor my memories.

"I didn't mean to disrespect you," Isaac calls.

"A man like you doesn't owe respect to one like me."

"Nonsense! You deserve as much of my respect as anyone else. Good God, you're deserving of much more. How many others would have inconvenienced themselves as you have and offered me their help?"

"Glad I can be useful as well as amusing."

On I go, dodging the fallen rocks in my path, half hoping I'll lose Isaac, half listening out for his footfalls.

"Mistress Vernon, I've offended you. I'm sorry."

He catches up and grasps my elbow. The shock of his touch crackles along my skin and sparks like gunpowder in my belly.

"Pray, forgive me. I'm not originally from this part of the country. My home is in London. The ways of the people there are very… It's not that I'm suggesting your manners are rough and uncouth, or that your beliefs smack of superstition… Don't misunderstand me. It's only that—"

I shake him off. "I understand, Sir. We must come across as different to you. Ignorant. Childish, even. But everywhere has a past, and in the Peak country, the past never goes away. Aye, we feel it more than the here and now. Our stories are sinkholes."

The pattering of water is close and constant. We must be near the next chamber.

"You think I can't possibly understand, but I do," says Isaac.

"We're all in danger of losing ourselves in the past, letting our histories and the stories we've told determine our future course of action."

"Then we're all damned."

"No, Mistress Vernon." His eyes flash bronze in the candlelight. "We're all tempted towards despair."

"A grave sin."

"Indeed. But every day, the world is made anew. We are made anew. Every time we make a choice—"

"We have no choice."

"Therein lies the root of your despair—we always have a choice. See, at this very moment, I'm choosing to apologise for appearing to stamp all over your history and for treating your traditions lightly. I may sound like I'm being mocking and derisive, but I assure you, it comes from a place of genuine interest. I'm trying to understand, you see—understand Sarah by putting myself in her shoes. She was always so fascinated by places like this and the stories people told about them." He puts out his gloved hand. "Come, let us be friends. I can't bear to see your back turned on me as it was a moment ago."

I look down at the open palm. "You don't think I'm too ignorant for you?"

"Not at all. You don't think I'm too proud for you?"

I place my hand in his. The kid skin gloves on his slender fingers are soft as surrender. "No. But do me a favour and call me Jane, not Mistress Vernon."

"Only if you—Oh!"

A droplet of water from the cave roof makes a track down

his cheek. He takes away his hand and dabs at his face with his embroidered handkerchief, the same one he held out to me that day at the market. "None of this *Sir*-ing. Call me Isaac."

"Isaac and Jane it is, then."

"I am grateful for your company," he says, dropping his voice. "This trouble with my cousin is a terrible worry."

"The man the landlord mentioned—the one posing as Sarah's husband… Do you know him?"

Isaac takes a deep breath. "No. Sarah spoke of him occasionally, but never in particulars. All I know is that, as you might have already suspected, they were lovers. You see, Mistress Ver—Jane… my cousin was already married."

Of all the things he could've said, this shocks me the least. I'd assumed she was of marriageable age. It shocks me more that Isaac isn't married, but then again, neither am I. Perhaps we have more in common than it appears on the surface.

"Every part of the sordid business has been placed on my shoulders," he goes on. "Sarah confided in me about her miserable marriage to an older man in Foolow. Her husband complained to me of her temperament, quite shamelessly. He even seemed pleased when she disappeared, which is why he's made so little effort to look for her."

"Did he know she had a lover?"

"I strongly suspect so. As careful as she was not to disclose her lover's name, she made no secret of how much she longed to get away from Peter. She had known and admired this other man for a good many years—at least six, based on what she told me—but the scoundrel waited until Sarah's marriage to confess his love to her. He was married as well. Now, the two of them have disappeared off together. The stink of it all! It makes me glad her father is not alive to bear the shame."

His coldness takes me aback. "You should never be glad of that, no matter how bad things may be."

"I apologise, again." He stuffs his handkerchief up his sleeve. "I admit that I'm not expressing myself well today."

"Why do you think she went off to see these Wonders of the Peak?"

"She told me before that her lover had promised to take her on a tour of them. Where they were planning on going together after that, I'm not certain. From what the shopkeeper and the host in the Cheshire Cheese told us, it sounds like they may have already parted ways."

"'Appen they realised they were doing the wrong thing."

"Not everyone is as good as you are."

If he'd seen me on Elden Hill that night, he wouldn't say that. "I've done nothing to deserve your praise."

"Now, now. I could say the same to you. Yet you enjoy my company, do you not?"

I drop my gaze. "Of course."

"Then let's not waste our strengths debating whether we're worthy of each other's good opinion."

"I'm sorry. Only, I marvel that someone like you—"

"Shh, I said none of that."

He reaches out with one finger raised, as though he's about to lay it on my lips, and I step back, suddenly afraid. We're still—two rocks that've been standing across from each other in this cave since time began. Isaac drops his hand and looks away.

Disappointment curdles inside me. That was the moment. He could have pulled me towards him and kissed me right then. But oh, Janey, what'd be the good in that? Even if we had our fill of each other, what could I expect once he'd fastened his breeches and stepped out into the daylight? We'd have to come face to face under the glare of the sun, and Isaac wouldn't like what he saw. How could he? He'd be disgusted with himself, disgusted with me. He'd leave me, possibly with a bastard child planted in my womb that I'd have no interest in raising.

The truth is, whatever he might say about us being worthy of each other's good opinion, there's a vast gulf between us. I have to keep reminding myself of that—the distance that can't be bridged. Better to rankle him than get too close.

"That man in the Cheshire Cheese seemed to know you. Was he Sarah's husband?"

Isaac motions for us to walk on. "Yes, Peter. The fool despises me. He doesn't know I'm searching for Sarah. It's better that way."

"Why?"

"He is in no rush to find her. Peter is an unfeeling man, and her life with him was not a joyful one. Her absence probably affords him some relief. He must be waiting for Sarah's lover to tire of her, and then once she returns, he'll seek an informal separation. Sarah will go back to living with her stepmother—my aunt Ruth—and Peter Pulmer can return to his dreary little life. If he showed any concern in the inn, it was on account of his pride, not his love for my cousin."

None of this fully accounts for Isaac's nerves in the Cheshire Cheese and the way he so desperately tried to avoid Sarah's husband; his portrait of Peter Pulmer also doesn't quite match up with the man I met. While he wasn't at his wit's end, Mr Pulmer didn't seem uncaring either. Most surprising is that Mr Pulmer didn't recognise Isaac. Have they never met before, not even at Sarah's wedding? There must be more to this mutual dislike than Isaac's prepared to tell me.

We enter another chamber, where water showers down from the cave roof. Isaac walks round to the other side of the torrent, his mouth open.

"How beautiful!" The droplets glow silver in the light of his candle.

"It's like God's wringing out a cloud," I say.

"You have quite a way with words, don't you know?"

I can only see a smudge of Isaac through the water, but I get the sense that he's looking at me with admiration. A man like him—chucking lavish compliments at a rustic like me. I can't get my head round it.

"Come on," I say. "I can show you a bigger waterfall than this."

I lead Isaac to a slope that snakes down under a crushingly low ceiling of rock. Even the lanterns on either side stand no chance against the solid darkness at the bottom. In the distance—the deep, deep distance—water thunders.

"The source of the river's down there," I say.

"And all that lies on the other side is oblivion."

"If you keep going, you get to more chambers. There are some big ones, bigger than any we've seen up to now."

"We're not going to keep going, though, are we?"

I think of the roof pushing down from above, the cold waters below. The river would take us under another arch, then into the great cavern. I don't remember much about it, only the feeling of being somewhere you're not meant to be. "I'd rather not."

"Good. I was afraid you'd want to demonstrate how well you can navigate these maze-like underground passages."

I take one last look at the way the slope gives way to blackness, and to the hidden river where the beginning and end of all life stews and bubbles. In the air, there's a faint stench. Sulphur. Gone-off meat. How many have wandered down there and never found a way back out?

"I don't much feel like it," I say, and we turn back.

Chapter Eleven

On our way out of the cave, we find the picture of Sarah on the ground, muddy footprints stamped across it. Her parted lips, which looked so coquettish earlier, could well be open in a gasp of surprise at finding herself in the stocks, smeared with filth.

"Oh, look," Isaac sighs. "Look at what's happened to this."

He picks it up and smooths a waterdrop off its surface with his thumb. He's gentle, but the paper tears. With a flash of annoyance, he screws it up and puts it in his pocket.

"Well, it appears that this was a dead end. No one has given us any more information."

"At least we got to talk," I say. "It wasn't a complete waste of time."

A faint smile flickers across his face. "That is very true."

The two of us pass a group of men—fancier folk even than Isaac, with sleeves so big and wide that all it would take to send them floating off into the air is a fierce gust of wind.

One of the visitors looks down at the slick of mud on Isaac's stockings and his face drops.

"Not their kind of place, is it?" I say to Isaac once we're out of earshot.

"Laundry is none of their concern."

"Do *you* have servants?"

Isaac's brow creases. "Well… yes. My parents wouldn't have it any other way."

"You live with them?"

"We run a shop together. A drapery."

The path leads us towards squat cottages with ribbons of smoke unspooling from their chimneys. A river runs down from the Devil's Arse, a gentle thing that you wouldn't believe has its source in such infernal regions. On the grassy bank, a mother is holding her young child round the waist, the two of them watching ducks sail past.

"My parents are dead," I say. "Da passed a few months ago. Mam went soon after, when she lost a baby."

Isaac makes a soft moan of sympathy. "I'm sorry to hear that. The loss must still be very raw for you."

"Raw—that's just it. Feels like a wound that keeps bursting open with each little scrape."

I look down at my bandaged fingers. Mary's done a good job on them. I wish she could do the same for my spirit.

Away from the cave mouth and the riverside, there's hardly anyone on the back streets. I want to tell him all about what it was like growing up with Grandam, catching Da in tears, and, once they were all dead, having to take on the burden ourselves, but it's something only a Peak Forester would understand.

I ask, "Will it ever get better?"

"The grief?"

"The grief, yes. And the guilt."

Behind us, the child is laughing and clapping its hands.

"I've not yet lost a parent," says Isaac, "but I have, in a sense, lost my cousin. I feel plenty of grief and guilt about that. I should have taken actions to prevent her from getting involved with that scoundrel in the first place."

Will's sordid plans for Nathaniel fill my mind. "But how can you stop people from doing something terrible?"

"That, I don't know yet. All I know is that you are the captain of your own soul. One day, I hope to have an answer for you. I am thinking, thinking all the time of the past, of what I could have said or done that led to this. Sometimes, I want to turn back time itself. That's why… I know this sounds foolish, but I talk to Sarah in my mind as I traipse all over this county. I—"

He stops abruptly, his eyes drawn across the road. There's little of note on the other side, other than a brazen-looking woman carrying a basket of food, her dark hair loose and flowing down to her waist.

"Excuse me!" He runs over to her, waving.

She angles herself towards him, shoulders pushed back. There's a wine-red birthmark covering one eye and the top of her cheek, like a mask. I know her. I know *of* her.

"Excuse me! Where did you get that?"

Isaac gestures to a trinket round her neck. Her hand sweeps up to it protectively, but not before I see what it's made of:

glass, glistening like early morning dew. The last time I saw that necklace, I was scramble-headed through want of sleep, pain, and sickness of the soul. Now, those feelings hit me again.

"A young man gave it to me," says the woman.

"Who?"

"No one you'd know." She looks Isaac up and down, her eyes narrowed. "Strange one, aren't you?"

The woman makes to move past him, but Isaac stands in front of her. "Who gave it to you?"

"Get out of my way!" she says. "You can't have it!"

"I'm not asking for it. I'm asking—"

"It's mine!" Bess Jenkins, Will's former lover, throws me a look of appeal. "Are you going to stand there and do nowt about him? He's with you, i'n't he?"

"Leave her be, Isaac," I mutter.

Bess stares as if trying to work out where she knows me from. I turn my face away.

"Move now, will you?"

The next thing I know, she's given Isaac an almighty shove in the chest. Both of them look as shocked as each other. Bess's expression twists into a nasty smile. She gallivants off, shutting herself up in a house further down the road. Isaac seems to spend a moment thinking what to do next, before spinning on his heel and heading to her door.

"Open up! I haven't finished." From a house nearby, someone shouts out a bawdy cheer. Isaac ignores it and pummels the wood. "Tell me, God damn you! Who gave you that thing?"

"Leave it!" I shout. "You're showing us up."

Isaac hammers on the door again. "We're staying here until I can get some sense out of that woman who's wearing my cousin's jewellery."

To hear him come straight out with it frightens me. It means it must be real, this cold, heavy chain that links Sarah to Thomas and Thomas to Will. All Bess need say is that she got the necklace from my brother, and Isaac would be on his scent.

I gather my nerve. "You can stay. But I'm off."

"Off?" He's stricken. "I need you here to witness what's going on. If she knows who was with Sarah—"

"I have to go. I don't want to be involved in this anymore."

It pains me to say those words. But how can I stay here, now that I know Sarah's lover was Thomas Mace? Every step of this journey seems to be leading us back to Elden Hole.

"We're finally getting somewhere," Isaac says.

"We're not getting anywhere. All that's happening is that you're scaring the life out of that poor lass who has nowt to do with your cousin."

"It's *Sarah*'s!" His silken voice frays. "Can't you see? If I can find out who gave this foolish wench the necklace, I'll know—"

"Be careful where you're prying. If I were you, I'd give this up now. Your cousin's found her own way without her husband and without you. Let her get on with it, for your own sake."

I rush past him, up the back street and onto the main thoroughfare, where Mam Tor looks down on blameless little people living their blameless little lives and shivers out eternity. I keep my head low and push up Winnats Pass, my thoughts whirling. Thomas, that great bully of a man… what did he do to Isaac's cousin? They argued, that much is clear, and Thomas stripped the riches off his young lover like a hunter skinning a hind. In the best case, she's wandering through the Peak country now, too ashamed to go home. In the worst, she's lying dead somewhere between here and our village.

A villain, Mary called Thomas. *A violent rogue looking to wet his fists with blood*.

Didn't he say he'd spatter our guts all over the grass? It was no empty threat. Thomas Mace was dangerous. Christ knows what he did to Sarah.

Isaac might never find out what happened to her. He might never find peace, unless I reveal that I met Thomas, and he had Sarah's jewellery. If I did that, questions would follow. How did we get hold of that man's possessions? Why would he give them to us freely?

I could cover up what happened: say we found the bag under a tree or make up some other story. But chances are, he'd come to suspect that *we're* involved in Sarah's disappearance.

Even if I keep silent, there's trouble coming. He'll go on searching and searching, combing through every blade of grass, peeking into every cavern, asking in every inn, and, eventually, he'll hear Thomas's name. The trail will lead him to Peak Forest again and to us. What a betrayal it'll be, if he finds out I knew about Sarah's lover all along and was too much of a coward to confess it. Once he's lost all trust in me, I won't be able to protect him from Will and Mary.

I stop to wipe the sweat off my face and catch my breath halfway up the Pass. The thump of my heart makes me feel weaker than ever, so I dig into my bag and take out the bundle of cheese and stale loaf left over from earlier. My food's all mixed up with Isaac's. I linger on the first bite, wondering if it's touched his lips.

I should stay away from him, for the sake of my family. I should… but I know I won't. I'll think of something. There must be a way of leading him closer to the truth, of finding out what happened to Sarah, without putting Will and Mary at risk of accusations and Isaac at risk of much, much worse.

A gust of wind snatches the bundle of cloth out of my hand, and pieces of bread go trundling down the hill. Wonderful, that. A bit of good fortune to round off a fruitful day.

Cursing, I pick up a slab of cheese near my foot and brush specks of dirt off it, but black bits of muck are lodged deep in its grainy surface, and it loses any appeal it once had. One of the sheep is nosing around in the sackcloth. I throw the food to it instead, taking up the wrapping that would cause untold problems if it got stuck in the animal's guts.

As I lean over, my shadow spills across the grass—which is strange, as the sun's been hiding behind clouds all day.

Janey. The voice sounds as if it comes from something trying to speak for the first time. A scratchy, pained bleat.

I look over my shoulder. There's nothing behind me but limestone towering into the grey sky and sheep chomping on the cheese and bread, nudging each other out of the way for a bigger portion. We're all made for two things, and two things only: killing and eating.

When I look back down, the shadow's gone.

Chapter Twelve

ISAAC

You'd promised to sit for me so that I could draw your likeness, but you were restless that day, shifting about in your chair, calling one of your little dogs to your feet and declaring you absolutely had to eat an apple, though woe betide me if I drew your mouth stuffed with food.

"What *is* the matter with you, Coz?"

I feared the worst, that you were with child. It had been almost a year since your wedding—ample time to overcome any reluctance about sharing a marriage bed. There *was* reluctance. You were distracted as you took your vows, your eye wandering to the church door, the smile you gave Peter not modest, but disappointed. Your father boomed his good wishes to all the guests, delighted with such a lucrative match, oblivious to your doubts.

Yet people bend to their circumstances.

I tried to discern a bump beneath your bodice, but the lacing was tight. It hid anything that might have been growing—that might, one day, have killed you.

"What's making you ill at ease?" I asked. "Would you like another cushion?"

"I am quite well, Isa. Distracted, that is all."

"Distracted?" I laid down my charcoal. "About what?"

You scooped up the lapdog, the little bell attached to its collar tinkling, and strode over to the window. The view from the drawing room showed nothing but fields stretching up to the dark hills on the horizon. "It is lonely here in Foolow. Unbearably lonely."

"You have your husband," I muttered.

"Peter is no companion."

There, sang Hope in her golden voice. *She has not yet given herself to him.*

I rose from my seat, careful not to startle away the words on the tip of your tongue. "He is away often?"

"Not often enough," you replied. "It's bliss to have these hours to myself, but the more he is away, the more I crave his absence."

"Does he treat you badly?"

"He does not strike me, if that is what you mean."

"Does he treat you badly in *any* way?"

With your back to me, your expressions were directed only at the emptiness beyond the window, and yet the nervous movements of your hand, petting the same patch of dog fur again and again, told me of your agitation.

"Coz, please. You can be honest with me."

"Peter is guilty of nothing but being a bore," you said in a rush.

This afforded me some small measure of relief. If that was the only thing wrong with you, there was not much wrong at all. Still, I could not accept such a simple explanation.

"And?"

"He thinks my head is too full of fancies and wishes me to stay in this damned house whenever I'm not within his sight. And he is growing to resent me."

"Resent you? Why?"

"I refuse his advances. He has tried to insinuate himself into my favour, but I cannot do my marital duties with a man I do not love."

I stepped towards your silhouette. My hands, quaking, came to rest on shoulders that I half believed would dissolve as soon as I touched them. "Do you love another?"

You faced me. Tears glittered in your eyes. "You have always known me so very well, Isa."

I pulled you into an embrace. The dog, pressed between our ribs, wriggled free and scampered beneath the chair on which you'd been posing, and our hearts, finally touching, trembled together.

"It is such a relief—" you sighed.

I held you tighter, pressing my lips to the curls around your temples. "I know it is."

"—to be able to talk of him at long last."

My arms stiffened.

"Him?"

You broke away from me, eyes averted. "He does not wish

for me to tell anyone his name. Please don't think I mistrust you, Isa. I trust you more than anyone in the world, but… But we have our reasons for being discreet, as I'm sure you'll understand."

The table with my drawing on the surface, the box of charcoals, the chair with the lapdog cowering beneath it, your body next to mine—everything in that room tilted, as if a great wave had swept up the whole house.

"Who is he?"

"A man with a curious, open mind. He's so unlike Peter. He wishes to travel with me, not to tell me to wait at home until he gives me permission to leave."

I tried to put my thoughts in order, and make the most important question of all—*why does this man deserve your love?*—spring from my lips.

"You are no prisoner here," I said.

"At least if I were a prisoner, there would be an end in sight."

An end to all this wealth, all this comfort! Peter was not a good match for you; I knew that as soon as I met him. Yet it seemed obscenely foolish of you to risk so much for another man.

"Does he treat you with kindness, this… *paramour*?"

"With kindness and enormous generosity. Do you remember the book on the Peak's wonders? That was from him."

My breath stopped. "From five years ago? From before your marriage?"

"We were not *together* then. He saw I was melancholy and

he gave me a gift—that is all. Since then, we have grown ever closer, and last year, only a month after my wedding, he told me… he told me he could no longer keep it a secret anymore. It killed him to see me wed. He loves me, Isa. You should see the beautiful tokens he brings me from his travels abroad."

"Why do you care about such trifles?"

"They are *not* trifles. I will show you."

Taking me roughly by the arm, you led me upstairs to your chamber, and then to the small room attached to it, stuffed with your perfumed garments—a private space I had no right to enter. As you stepped inside, I hovered in the doorway, glancing over my shoulder to ensure no servant was lingering in the corridor. With heaviness, I remembered the times in our childhood we would slip away without your parents, the two of us together. A pair, in need of no one else.

Rather than rooting through your clothes for a concealed packet, you lifted up the upholstered seat of a chair and took out a leather-bound volume.

"*De Mirabilibus Pecci*?" I asked. "*The Wonders of the Peak?*"

"It used to be."

This time, when you opened it, there was no poetry. A large rectangle had been sliced out of the pages, so that the book functioned as a makeshift box.

"He brought me this from Venice."

From within, you drew out a necklace that looked as if it were strung with frozen water droplets.

I was less impressed with the jewellery than with your ingenious way of hiding it. Yet it could not be denied: the scoundrel had taste.

The trinket seemed to wake the eager young girl who still dwelt within you. Pushing aside the strands of golden hair that fell in loose ringlets over your ears, you strode into the bedroom and stood before a mirror. "Put it on me, Isa. I want you to see what it looks like when I'm wearing it."

If I objected, I would be revealing too much of myself. I had already revealed so much.

I fumbled with the clasp, my fingers clumsily brushing your slender neck.

"Be careful—it's delicate."

"I know," I said, resisting the urge to pull on the chain and send the beads flying through the air. "There."

I stood back and let you admire yourself in the blotched surface of the mirror. You turned this way and that, the glass catching the light. Another light shone from within.

"It's beautiful, is it not?"

I felt a chain tightening around my own throat. "It is."

"Look! It matches my other *trifles*."

From the hollowed-out copy of *De Mirabilibus Pecci*, you drew a pair of glass earrings. I hoped to God you wouldn't ask me to slip them through your lobes and untangle the twists of hair that caught on the backs.

I stood behind you in the mirror, an ungainly, unhandsome thing, while you slid in the earrings and admired your profile. Gleams of afternoon sunlight shot through the clearness of the ornaments and the crystal of your eyes. When you saw me watching, you became still.

"You must think me terribly vain."

I said nothing in reply.

"I like the jewellery he brings me, of course I do. But it is more than that. He is my world, Isa. If he had an empty purse, I would still want to be with him, simply to hear about the places he's been, the people he's met. He is my world, because the world is within him."

What had I to offer, compared to a man whose globe of a skull contained the continents and oceans, who transmuted the rain and dankness of Derbyshire into shining wonders and bought you jewels from abroad?

"If you cannot contain this passion," I said in a strangled voice, "you will bring disgrace upon your whole family, including me."

The earrings quivered as you shook your head. "No, Isa..."

"Take off those ridiculous baubles."

As my reflection marched off the edge of the mirror and disappeared, I swore to myself it would be the last time I spoke to you about *him*. I would tell Aunt Ruth. I would tell Peter if I had to.

Oh, the ways we deceive ourselves.

Chapter Thirteen

A mangled thing lies on our table, innards spilling from the knife wound. Its body is big—the clothes have been stuffed to bursting with straw—but the turnip head is nightmarishly shrunken. It lolls to one side, grinning up at me. Whoever's made it went to the effort of carving tiny, sharp teeth. The rest of the face is featureless, save the black slits of eyes.

I'm so distracted by the sight of it that I can't even respond to Will's cry of, "So! The prodigal returns. Good of you to join us, Jane. Where've you been all this time?"

Him and Mary are sat at the table like Mam and Da, back in the days when Mam ate at the table for a proper meal and didn't just nibble on crusts like a mouse.

"Did you make this thing?" I ask.

With a trill, Lordsmeer jumps up on the table to get a sniff of the effigy and a stroke from me.

"I found it on the doorstep," says Mary, reaching across to take out the dagger from the scarecrow's chest and slip it into her pocket. "It's a disgrace. They could've at least given him a hat. And hair. That bald head is unbecoming."

"Who's it meant to be?"

She pushes a handful of straw stuffing to one side and holds up a leather purse, empty but for a feather. "Guess."

Blood crashes in my ears. It's a wonder my heart can keep going day after day.

"It's got to be Nathaniel's doing," says Will.

Lordsmeer chews on a piece of straw. Idiot animal. I nudge him off the table. "We don't know that."

"They're Harry's old clothes."

"Surely it's meant to be Harry, then?"

Will doesn't even bother to answer this one.

"Waste of cloth, this is," says Mary, fingering the ripped shirt. "He wouldn't throw away all this on a stuffed thing without giving it some thought. He's serious. He's going to tell people about Thomas if we don't pay up."

So much for my earlier hope that Isaac would pull me out of this sinful mire. All he could advise was that I be captain of my own soul, but that's no good when your ship is storm-tossed.

"What's he going to tell people?" I retort. "He doesn't know anything. If he saw what'd really happened, he'd have mashed up the head like you did, Mary."

"It'll be worse than a scarecrow next time." She leans over the body and pins the arms down to the table, as if this really is Thomas and she has him laid out before her, ready to kill again. I can tell from her deep, quivering breaths that she would. She'd kill that man a thousand times over and relish it every time.

"What's your idea, then?" I ask. "Suffocate Nathaniel down the mine, like Will said?"

"Aye. Will can tell Nathaniel there's a problem with the sump on one of the deeper levels. The fool follows him down, and Will finds some way of blocking him in there."

"I thought I could make all the deads from the level above fall in his path," adds Will. "If I timed it right, the stuff might even fall on him and snap his neck. Hm! It'd be fitting, wouldn't it, if he died in the same way as Da? *Death by falling deads.* Anyway, I'd kick the sumps out of place so that even if he's not killed by the rocks, he'll suffocate."

He's taking pleasure in concocting this foul plan and making it *fitting*. Well, I know a way to dash that joy right out of him.

"You know that necklace we found, when we were going through Thomas's bag?" I say.

Will folds his arms. "What of it?"

"You told us you'd sold it."

"I did," he says. His voice betrays nothing.

"You took it down to Castleton, didn't you?"

"You know I did. Why are you aski—"

"To your mistress? Bess Jenkins?"

The back of my legs ache, I'm standing so stiffly.

"Is that where you were, then?" Will breathes. I can sense the stir of his temper under the stillness. "What do you want from her—wise words on how to please a man?"

"You sound like Thomas Mace."

Mary looks up from behind her veil of loose hair. "Is it true, Will? Did you give the necklace to her?"

"He did," I say. "I saw it on her today."

"How do you know it was the same necklace?" Will answers, all cocky. Then there's a bang under the table, and he winces. "Ow! Don't kick me!"

"I'll kick you all I want until you say whether it's true or not," Mary says.

"All right!" He holds up his hands. "I gave her the jewellery, for bloody hell's sake!"

Pride is the greatest of sins—that doesn't escape me. It's hammered into us enough at church, how Lucifer fell after he did battle with his creator. But Will's not God, and for once I want him to realise that I'm right. "Knew it! Not so daft, am I?"

"Shut your mouth."

"*Gave* it to her?" Mary says. "You gave it away for nowt? The ring an' all?"

"Not that, only the necklace. Christ, I don't want to be giving her ideas by handing over a wedding band! I had to get her off my back. She was following me around in Castleton, saying all kinds of bull."

"Such as?"

"Oh, that she loved me and shite like that. The woman wouldn't let me be when I went down to sell Thomas's goods!"

He pushes back his stool as he stands. It catches the edge of a flagstone and wobbles, and with a kick of his boot, he sends it clattering across the room. Despite my earlier courage, I flinch away from him. He stalks over to the hearth, spits in the fire and kicks the pile of wood too, for good measure.

"She started sniffing around the bag, trying to guess what was in it. I told her to take the necklace and sell it to get money for… for whatever she needed. But she had to leave me alone from then on."

"Why did she need the money?" demands Mary, searching him through and through.

"Do you need to know every detail?"

"Not every detail, no, but the bits that affect all of us. What are you so reluctant to tell us?"

He finally withers under her gaze. "She needed new cloth, for her and… and the… the… You know."

"The what?" Mary demands.

With a look of disgust, he sweeps an arm over his front, pausing at the top of his hips. "The baby."

The air is sucked out of the room.

Mary lifts one shoulder. "I had a feeling that summat like this would happen sooner or later. You can't go about sowing your wild oats and 'scape siring a bastard."

Will shoots her a poisonous glance.

"Are you sure?" I whisper. "She didn't look like she was with child today."

"That's because she's a damned liar!" he shouts. "I bet her belly's no fuller than mine."

"She might not be showing yet," says Mary quietly, "if it's not been that long."

We stand in silence as the fire burns lower. After a while,

Will lights a pipe and takes a long, deep drag. "The child—if there really is a child—might not even be mine. I reckon she just saw Thomas's bag and took the opportunity to trick me out of more money. Women are always lying to get their own way."

"Mam never lied," snaps Mary.

"Hm! She lied to herself. How else do you think she lived with all the things Grandam made Da and me do?"

All of us fall silent.

"Does she love you?" I ask. "Bess?"

Will blows a cloud of smoke through half-closed lips. "Bess loves everyone. She likes to dally around."

The way she stuck her chest out as she walked down the road shows well enough what manner of woman she is. That's all he can get, being a Vernon. Handsome as Will may be, he's in the same boat as me and Mary. No one in Peak Forest would want to wed him.

"Your mind's all scattered." Despite the dying fire, streaks of sweat drip down my face. "One minute, you need money for land. The next, you're giving it away to a woman with a reputation."

"What's reputation to you?" he snipes. "You've been out all day, God knows where! You should have been here, watching over—"

"Shut your gobs, the both of you!" Mary steps between us. "You're giving me a right pain in the head. And we're forgetting about the jewellery." She turns to Will. "Do you think she'd tell who she got it from?"

"Doubt it. I told her if she said anything about me fathering a child or giving her gifts, I'd make her sorry for it."

That awful silence tightens around us again. From the way he's talking, I know it was no casual threat. He meant it with every bone in his body.

He rests his dark eyes on me. "She didn't tell you where she got them, did she?"

"No."

He steps forward, pushing past Mary. "Did she?"

"No! Look, no one knows about this but us," I insist. "If Bess keeps quiet, we've nothing to fear."

"Nothing to fear." He laughs drily, dropping back into Da's chair. "That's a good jest, Jay Bird. A very good one."

When I'm full to the brim with melancholy, I go to the Shouting Cave. It's not too far from Elden Hole, near a barrow where Mary used to go digging for jewellery—the headdress of a queen and the like. She did find a few jet beads and bits of bone, though whether they belonged to a queen, I don't know. I'd always refuse when she asked me to help her dig. Grave robbing is grave robbing, whether the occupants have been dead for centuries or days. Besides, you never know what you'll disturb. Whenever Mary came back with one of her treasures, I'd lie awake the whole night. Every sigh of the wind was a curse hissing through the dagger-sharp teeth of an ancient tribeswoman who'd woken to find her grave goods gone and had come to get them back.

The cave mouth is a yard in width; I have to duck low to squeeze through. Once in, the cave opens out. It would frighten the spirit out of me if I hadn't been here so many times and from such a tender age.

I take twenty-four steps inside and stand in the middle of that vast, empty space where, as children, Mary and Will and me would shout our names, grievances, and dreams, till our voices blended together and we couldn't tell who was who.

It's a strange thing being in here all alone, though it's not the first time I've been back without either Will or Mary. I came up after Harry Needham told us that Da was dead, and after Mam wrapped our half-formed sister in a bloody nightgown, and after we found Mam lifeless. All those other times, I was so stricken with grief that I hardly noted the difference between me and the stone, between my own voice and the echoes. I didn't come here after Grandam passed. It felt like a burden had been lifted.

Wings flap high above, and it sounds like someone shaking muck out a large leather sheet. There must be all kinds of things nesting in here.

I wet my lips and whistle. The sound cuts cleanly through the cold air, and the bird above falls silent.

"I."

My voice is rough and croaky, but the slight echo gives it depth. I speak again, louder.

"I!"

This time, it splits into dozens of *I*s, none of them me.

"I—saac," I shout. The end of his name sounds too sharp in here, unsuited to his nature.

He touched me, when we were alone in the dark. It wouldn't have taken much for our companionship to tip into something more, something much less high-minded. I lean against a wall and think of what it'd be like if he'd lifted up my gown and shift. The only roughness would come from the scratch of his beard and moustache as he ran his tongue all the way down my belly. He'd part my thighs and slide his finger inside that dark, wet place, kissing me there. I pretend he's doing it to me right now, till my desires come bursting out and I shout again, shout in pleasure, tears spilling from my eyes.

Afterwards, there's no sound save my breath. A bird was here before, wasn't it? I strain my ears to catch the slightest movement elsewhere in the cave. Nothing. I'm alone, not lying with Isaac, caressing his head in my lap. I wipe my face on my sleeve, put my gown back in order and fade, fade slowly.

The dry swish of coarse material drifts in from outside. Someone's stalking across the hill. I know that purposeful stride. It belongs to the two members of our family still living, and the time between one footfall and another is too short for the legs to belong to Will.

A silhouette blacks out the twilight at the cave mouth. For a moment, it looms enormously large.

"Thought I'd find you here," Mary says, crouching down to enter. "You took off quick."

"I'd had enough."

She gathers her petticoat—a patched, sack-like thing she's had for years—and lowers herself down on the ground next to me. I hope she can't smell the filth of my longing.

"Will's worried about you," she says.

I'm too tired for another argument. Still, I snort. "He sent you here so that you could talk me round?"

"No, he didn't. It's as I said—we're worried. You seem… off."

"I wonder why that can be."

"Stop it, Janey. Come here." She puts her arms round me and squeezes. There's comfort in the warmth of her body. "I don't want to fight. I know all this has been hard on us. That's why I needed to check you were all right."

"I am all right. I just wanted some time to think."

"Can I sit with you, or do you still want to be on your own?"

Now that she's here, I don't want to send her away. The welcome solitude of the cave will soon turn to loneliness.

"You can stay."

We sit side by side on the cave floor. Silence rings in my ears. It must be ringing in Mary's as well, for she hums a few notes of a mournful tune. It ripples around us like dark water.

"Remember when we used to make up songs?" she says.

"*You* used to."

"*Little Magpie with the voice of a nightingale*, Mam said." She clears her throat. "I haven't sung in a while, so I'm not as good as I was. I miss it. *Dear Sir, the…*" Her voice cracks. "Wait."

She coughs, then starts singing again. Her voice is pure as

milk, but her songs have always had a bitterness to them. I once asked where she'd learnt them, and she gave me a smile and said, *Oh, they just come.* The one she's singing now is a favourite. It starts with a maiden under a tree, as most songs do, and goes on to her meeting a lad, as most songs do. Normally, this lad is a farmer or a shepherd, and his intentions are plain as day. In this one, though, the man is wrapped in a dark cloak and wears a hat so wide and low that the maiden can only see his eyes, and they glow like sparks struck from iron. She starts with the girl's part, a tune that travels down as if the lass has set her mind on bringing the matter to an end, before sweeping back up.

"Dear Sir, the night is drawing near.
I can no longer tarry here.
Homeward must I travel soon
Before the rising of the moon."

The man's part comes next. Mary doesn't drop her voice, but she makes it slower, more sure of itself:

"O, come fair maiden, come with me
The shady regions for to see.
Take leave of earthly riches bright
And step with me into the—"

"—Night," I finish.

The song creeps into the nooks and crannies, as though it came from there in the first place and isn't dying away so much as returning home. Mayhap, in years to come, two others will be sitting where me and Mary are now and it'll appear, words an' all, in their minds. We'll be long gone, but that melancholy little tune will carry something of us.

"I don't think you should do it," I say. "Nothing good can come of doing away with Nathaniel."

Mary starts fiddling with a stone, scraping it along the ground. "Jane, you saw what happened when She didn't eat for a little while. The chickens were walking around one minute, dead the next, without a mark on them. That wasn't anything natural. That was Her."

"I didn't say you should stop giving Her what's owed." I clench my fist so tight that the stitches throb. "All I ask is that you think carefully about Nathaniel. Very carefully."

"We'll try and get it under control without… you know. But if we have to… If there's no other choice…"

"If there's no other choice?"

She bashes the stone on the ground so hard that it sounds like musket fire. "Then that's it, I suppose. We do what we have to."

Before I can say anything else, she sends a loud *Ah!* up to the roof, and it bounds back. A mighty pair of bird wings flutter.

"Do you want to shout with me?" she asks.

Childish games, after that conversation.

"Not today, Magpie," I say, too quietly to make an echo.

That night, I dream I'm on Winnats Pass again. I stagger behind a line of people into the mouth of a cave. Inside, it's bigger than the church in Tideswell. About a mile above my head, near where the roof meets the walls, there's a ledge where a group of winged creatures are watching. Their beaks clack in applause as we gather round the guide. We have a guide, aye, for we've paid to get in here—a dear price, though I'm not sure how much. The guide leads us to an old man with a chisel and hammer.

The first traveller in line sits on a stool. I watch as the old man slides the metal chisel into the traveller's mouth and rests its rusty edge on the side of a tooth. Clutching the hammer, he lifts his arm, takes a swing…

The clang of metal on metal.

The traveller cries out in pain. Blood pours from his lips. In a stream of red spit, a tooth drops into his cupped hands. He gives it to the guide and gets up, following a path that leads deeper into the cave.

One by one, the others go through the same ritual. Some of them hardly shed a drop of blood, and the tooth comes cleanly away. Others are a mess of gore by the time the old man has finished. I stand back, putting it off as long as possible, but now it's my turn.

"This one," I say, pointing to a tooth far back in my lower jaw.

The old man grins, revealing empty, scarred gums.

He puts the chisel in my mouth. It's huge, so big it almost chokes me, and so cold that my cheek throbs where the metal touches the soft flesh.

He hooks his little finger around the corner of my mouth and raises his skinny arm.

The hammering blurs my sight. It goes on for longer, far longer than it did for the others. Still, I taste no blood. The old man lets go, and I head towards the back of the cave, thinking how fortunate I am to still have all my teeth.

There's a passage leading out and—oh!—the sunlight! It turns the grass pale yellow and throws light into a pit, a great open gash in the hill. It's a hundred times bigger than Elden Hole, though I know it must be Her. The world is wavering as I step towards the edge. Inside is the whole village. Houses are arranged in a higgledy-piggledy fashion on narrow ledges, which go all the way down to where the sun can't reach, and as the pit narrows, the houses look less like copies of ones in Peak Forest and more like twisted, trapped things that used to contain something alive.

Isaac! He's on the other side of the pit, a mile away, but clear, so clear. The back of his head shines with golden curls.

I call his name. "Isaac Latimer!"

He does not hear.

"I'll take what I'm owed." The guide, swathed in a long, black cloak with a hood over Her head, appears beside me like a shadow. Her voice is as sly as a fox's and as rasping as a rook's cry. It is a menagerie of a voice, made up of everything She's eaten. "My business is with you, Jane Vernon. I tire of scraps. It's time for you to give me what I most desire."

Isaac still has his back to me. "Not him," I plead, and I

know as I say it that he'd be perfect in all ways. A bite of Isaac, and She'd leave us be. It's tempting.

I prod my tooth with my tongue. A flap of flesh moves. I bite down onto bone, and other teeth work themselves loose. Half a dozen fall out into my palm, gleaming white as pearls. A sob works its way up my throat.

"I didn't know you'd take so much."

The guide opens wide Her jaws. Her gums are full of rows upon rows of teeth, reaching all the way down Her throat, packed together like pimples on pox-riddled skin. Yet, at the very back, are deep, red pits—the spaces left for mine.

I wake with a start, the taste of blood in my mouth.

Chapter Fourteen

Jumber House, pigeon-grey and solitary, roosts halfway up a hill outside Eyam. Its twin gables look ready to unfold and take flight in an afternoon sky that, for the first time in days, is free of rainclouds. The place has more glazed windows than there are houses in Peak Forest, though I can't see through most of them on account of the drawn curtains. Guarding the entrance, tall bushes stand like watchmen in need of a good razor.

Knocking on a door shouldn't be this hard. When I joined Isaac in Castleton yesterday, my motives were simple—to bring him and Sarah together and, in doing so, pull myself out of the stinking pit of sin. That's not changed, but the situation has. I've got to keep him away from Bess, or at least keep her quiet about her connection to Will if my brother's threats aren't enough. Today is not the day to trouble myself about that, though. We won't be going anywhere near Castleton. If Isaac accepts my proposal, we'll be venturing to a place where the creaking cogs of the world can, just for a little while, come to a halt. Yesterday, he said he wanted to turn back the clock.

If I knew how to do that, I'd take us straight to the cave in Castleton again, make the most of being alone with him and, this time, avoid running into Bess. Not knowing how to go backwards, I'll have to satisfy myself by taking him somewhere time can stand still—somewhere so beautiful that I won't even think about last night's dream.

I rap on the door. Inside, a dog barks. Isaac hasn't said much about his Aunt Ruth. I don't know whether to expect a haughty old woman or the kind-hearted sort, but the presence of a dog makes me inclined to believe she must be patient at the very least.

The door opens a crack, and a wet, black nose pokes out, followed by a floppy-eared head. A reddish brown spaniel squeezes through the narrow gap in the door and jumps up at me, resting its paws on the top of my legs, its tail wagging madly.

"Duchess! Get down, you naughty lass," says a woman.

"It's all right," I kneel to give the dog a stroke. She licks my face with a warm tongue until a finger hooks around her collar and drags her back.

"I am sorry, Mistress. She's not meant to do that." The speaker is wearing an apron; she looks about Mary's age, with the same drawn face that comes from days of hard work and nights of uneasy rest. I have to hold myself back from laughing from shock; for the first time in my life, a maidservant is answering a door to me.

"Don't worry about the dog," I say, all too aware of the dirt on my petticoat. "Is Mr Isaac Latimer in?"

"Who's asking?"

A woman in her fifth or sixth decade, stout, with a large mole on her chin, taps across chequered black and red tiles on a crutch. Her spaniel bounds up to her and stands to heel, a flash of colour against her sombre black gown.

"It's Jane. Jane Vernon. I met Isaac at the Wonders. He… he said it was all right for me to accompany him."

The woman—Mrs Ruth Goodwin, I presume—expels a long breath. "All right, Mistress Vernon, I'll speak to him. Wait a moment, please."

She motions to the servant to close the door. Left alone outside, I walk up and down the path that runs along the front of the house, doubt and worry snipping at my hopes of seeing Isaac. When the door opens again, I'm expecting to be told that I shouldn't have wasted my time walking here, but instead, the maidservant invites me into the entrance hall. It's warm, deliciously warm, and the smell of roasting meat sends hot juices shooting through my empty belly. I wonder if the servant knows how fortunate she is to work here instead of down the lead mines, like Will, or at the White Hart.

"Been here long?" I ask her.

She looks over her shoulder, checking I'm not addressing someone else. "Y… yes, Mistress."

Mrs Goodwin calls, and with a curtsey, she disappears off through one of the doors.

The sound of footfalls on the stairs towards the back of the house turns my pleasure at being in this grand place to panic. I run through what I want to say to Isaac and before I'm halfway through, there he is, all in yellow and blue, a vision of paradise.

"Hello, Jane." The smile Isaac flashes isn't his usual sort. It's less sure of itself. "What are you doing here?"

Sweat prickles on my scalp. "I wanted to come and say sorry for leaving you yesterday."

"Oh. Well, thank you. I… You shouldn't have come all the way here to apologise. You didn't need to, you know."

"No," I say, "I did, because it was wrong of me to leave you like that after you'd been so good to me all day. Anyway, that's not all I wanted to say. Have you heard of Wet Withens?"

In a daze, he nods. "The stone circle on the moor. I've heard of it, though I've never been before. Why, do you think Sarah might have visited?"

"That's not the reason I want to take you, I'll admit. It has more to do with something you said yesterday. I can tell you when we get there. That is, if you want to come along."

A reply catches in his throat. Have I done something wrong, turning up on his doorstep, standing in this fine hall and asking him to come out with me? I ready myself for a rebuff.

"I apologise for my appearance," he says, brushing down the front of his doublet. His appearance? He looks as fine as ever.

"I was about to take Duchess for a walk, you see. She always gets me covered in mud and Lord knows what else, and so I thought I'd wear the same clothes as yesterday, when I was scrabbling around in a cave." He pauses to catch a breath. "I'll take her to Wet Withens."

My heart leaps. "With me?"

"You proposed it, didn't you?" This time, I'm treated to his full smile.

"Is that woman all right with it?"

"Who, Aunt Ruth? Oh, yes. She very much appreciates someone else exercising her little girl. Duchess!"

The spaniel patters into the hall and up the stairs. Isaac bends to fondle her ears, calling her a scurvy rascal and all manner of mischievous names. Oh, to be that dog.

Under the afternoon sun, Isaac strides by my side, Duchess bounding in front of us. I haven't once seen him adjust his hat or smooth his beard today; the endless solitude of the moor seems to put him at ease.

I shield my eyes and gaze over the clouds of purple-brown heather. "I thought the stones were somewhere round here, but apparently not. They're not always in the same place they were before."

"To the untrained eye, the moor looks the same in every direction."

"If you kept coming back often enough, you'd soon learn to note the little landmarks. The dip over there, that rock, and—oh, look!" I point out a wizened tangle of branches. "That tree. We shouldn't be too far away now."

We head off again, treading a path only visible to me and the hares that run through the stubbly mazes. It feels like a return to normal—mine and Isaac's normal. Can you get used to such a thing after meeting someone only three times? A little further along, the moor opens its heart to us. It's wider, wilder, the edge of it blending in with the hills that circle the valley. We couldn't be anywhere more different to the Devil's Arse.

I point out a rock that looks a bit like a fox's head. "Look, there's one. Now follow my finger. Can you see the next one? And the next?"

They rise from heather, one like a chair, another coming up like an enormous fish breaking the surface of water.

"We're right in the middle of it," Isaac gasps.

His astonishment thrills me.

"This circle is where the ancients worshipped and danced. People say that, when the sun is in the right place, time stands still. You spoke yesterday about turning back the clock. Well, I can't do that, but I thought I could bring you here, to a place outside time."

I daren't look at his face, in case I've misunderstood him entirely.

"Thank you," he breathes. "It's a beautiful thought, and a beautiful place."

Sunlight fills the middle of the circle like melted gold. Stop now, time. Stay this way forever.

"Didn't the pagans make sacrifices at sites such as this?" Isaac asks.

Savage dances to a midsummer sun. Shadows flickering on rocks. A pit. A sharpened blade. Blood, soaking into the woody roots of the heather. I can't picture it. Not here, not now, with the sun draping the stones in sheets of light and Duchess rolling on her back, swiping her tail near our feet.

"Not here. It's too beautiful, as you say."

"There's a certain beauty in sacrifice. Look at Christ's redemption." Isaac crouches down and musses up the fur on Duchess's chest. "This place has an atmosphere, don't you think?"

"I think there's comfort here."

"So do I."

"Safety."

"Yes."

We're silent.

"I shouldn't have left you like that in Castleton," I say again.

"You don't need to apologise. You were under no obligation to accompany me."

He picks up a twig from the ground. Duchess immediately sits and fixes her eyes on it, her limbs quivering. Isaac throws, and off she dashes.

"I said I would, though, and I didn't keep my word. Did you manage to talk to her again? That woman?"

Isaac shakes his head. "You missed my finest moment. She appeared at the top window with a full chamber pot and tried to tip it over my head."

I can't help but laugh. "No! Did she really?"

"Oh, yes. Thankfully, I was quick on my feet." He rocks back and forth on his heels. "I do regret bothering her."

"Do you?"

"I suspect there was truth in what she told us. The villain who stole my cousin's heart was probably a lover of hers. I'm working on the assumption that he and Sarah argued, and so he gave the necklace to his mistress or a common prostitute, whoever she is."

"Someone with a reputation," I say, remembering Will's words about Bess.

"Quite."

Duchess bounds back with the stick in her mouth and drops it at Isaac's feet, sticking out her forepaws and dipping her back.

"Do you want to do it?" asks Isaac. He nods at the stick.

I pick it up and Duchess edges backwards, keeping her head low to the ground. I hurl the stick nearly as far as one of the rocks. She retrieves it from the tangle of heather without much of a search.

"Are you going to go back to that woman's place again? Ask more questions?"

"Not for now," Isaac says quickly. "She won't let me in. I may have to find information elsewhere. One thing is playing on my mind, though." Isaac plucks a sprig of heather from the ground. "A young man. The woman said that she got it from a *young* man."

A detail like that could lead Isaac to my brother eventually. And whose fault would that be?

Duchess brings back the stick, but dances away from me before I can take it out of her mouth. Isaac continues, "Sarah did not tell me much about the man she was seeing, but I do know that he was older than her, closer to the age of her husband."

"Do you know how old?"

"No."

"Well then." I find another stick behind us and throw. "*Young* gives us no clue at all, does it? She might mean *young* compared to the grey-haired fiends who normally bother her. It could mean your age or mine, or anything in between. I don't mean this as an insult, but you look young in some lights and older in others. Not old. But older. Like you're wiser than your years."

The laughter lines I've grown to love crease round Isaac's eyes.

"Jane," he says, threading a sprig of heather through the top buttonhole of his coat, "I am not wise in the slightest. If I were wise, I wouldn't…"

"What?" I wet my lips. Wouldn't be here with me? Wouldn't be messing around with a woman so poor and base?

"I wouldn't be searching for Sarah in this haphazard way at all. Look at what I'm doing today—playing with the dog instead of going back to speak to that woman. If I could find out his name… If I could only find out his name."

He rubs the sides of his face.

Thomas, I whisper in my head. *Thomas Mace.* All it would take is for me to press the tip of my tongue against the top of my mouth and say the first *T*.

Will's voice echoes in my ears. *What good would that do?*

Thomas is dead. We killed him. Anything he knew about

Sarah is gone, swallowed up forever.

"You can't be out looking for her all the time," I say. "You have a life to live as well."

Isaac nods, letting out a long breath. "I know. I think you may have been right in what you said yesterday."

"What's that?"

"She's found her own way without me." His voice is thick.

"I didn't mean that. I was—"

"You were right," he says. He plucks the heather out of his buttonhole and crushes it. "You are right. I have a life to live as well."

We head back to Jumber House when the shadows of the stone circle grow long. Isaac doesn't say another word about Sarah. He tells me about London: how there's a monstrous bridge where they stick the heads of people who've been executed; how boats from all over the world glide in along the river that stinks to high heaven on hot days; and how ale is much more expensive than up here, but not as good.

"It sounds marvellous, bad ale or no," I say. "Do you think it's better than here?"

He sucks on his bottom lip. "There's something about the Peak country that turns ordinary things into wonders. As you wisely observed before, the past is inescapable here. Of course, in London as well, there are traces of times gone by, such as ruins left by conquering Romans, primitive churches. But there are new goods flowing into the city all the time. Everything is novel. The old stories are there, somewhere, beneath the buying, selling, and rushing around, but they don't grow quite so wild."

"There's business aplenty round these parts as well, you know."

"I'm sure. But if you stroll along the Thames, you'll see boats laden with woollens destined for Spain, and cargoes of spices from the East. You'll hear sailors and shipbuilders speaking in tongues from all over the world, as far as India."

How must it be, to have the whole world a boat ride away? The very thought of it makes me feel like I'm standing on a precipice.

"You said you run a drapery?"

"My father does. He is also a cloth merchant, as was my uncle."

Cloth merchants. That was Thomas's line of business as well.

"Was?"

"Sarah's father passed last year, leaving my Aunt Ruth a widow."

"Last year? The same time Sarah cuckolded Peter?"

Isaac clears his throat. "The same time Sarah and her lover confessed their feelings to each other, yes."

Different words, same thing. Was Thomas an associate of Sarah's father, who offered her a big, broad shoulder to cry on when death ripped a hole in her family?

We reach the edge of the moor, and there's nothing else to see apart from the dusty road that leads us in different directions. The sky already has that pale, dull hue that'll soon give way to evening. In a few moments, Isaac will turn his back on me. If he's certain that Sarah's gone of her own free will, Lord knows if we'll ever meet again. This could be where our acquaintance ends.

"It's been good seeing you today," I say. "But I suppose I'd best be heading off. There's washing to do, and the animals need tending to."

Isaac doesn't answer for a moment. Then he says, too quickly, "Before you leave, you can come back to Jumber for dinner. It won't be a feast, but we have some roasted meat and other bits and pieces."

My heart lifts. "That's mighty generous of you."

I urge myself to refuse the offer. No matter what pleasures I may taste, they'd be short-lived. Mary's songs about men who lead young lasses astray with promises of riches and marriage taunt me. I never thought I'd be like other girls, falling into the arms of any fine-looking man who comes my way.

But Isaac isn't like a man from them songs. He's spent time alone with me in a cave and out on a moor without ravishing me. In all things, he's taken my wishes into account. The only danger, then, springs from my own desires. I must stick to the bounds of decency, however much I long to break them.

"I'd be honoured to have dinner with you," I say. "But I've got to leave before dark."

Isaac looks at me sideways on, holding my gaze so long that it feels like I've gobbled a bag of frogs. Softly, he replies, "I'd be glad to have your company, even for a short time."

Chapter Fifteen

Our whole house could be taken apart, stone by sorry stone, and rebuilt in Mrs Goodwin's hall. The thatched roof wouldn't even be within tickling distance of the beams; there'd be room between our walls and the tapestry that shows some battle of old. You could sneak round the outside and duck into the fireplace, which is like a whole room to itself, and delight in the warmth of the fire without getting a mouthful of smoke. Here, there are proper chimneys to suck the fumes away, not just a hole in the thatch that lets in the weather in winter and the flying, biting things in summer. The table in the middle of the hall at Jumber House could sit six or seven people. Isaac and Mrs Goodwin sit on one long bench, me on another, opposite them. Even before I've touched the cup of sack poured for me by the serving girl, I'm tipped off-kilter by the strangeness of it all.

"You've got a very fine house," I say to Mrs Goodwin.

She forces a tight smile. "It's not as grand as it once was, when my husband was living. We had a butler and a footman, then. I'm having to make do with just a few girls, Mrs Thorpe and Cook these days, but you get by."

Why two people, three with Sarah, would need more than a few servants, a cook and whoever this Mrs Thorpe is, I don't know. But Mrs Goodwin's standards are as different to mine as mine are to Lordsmeer's.

"Aunt Ruth knows she has plenty to be grateful for," Isaac says to me. "And she relishes playing the host."

The glance she gives him would suggest otherwise. He's taken some liberties by inviting me here for dinner, it seems. She must wonder what I'm doing with Isaac, what I can possibly hope to gain from the family.

"I'm so honoured to be here."

"Although I did tell Isaac not to invite guests back here without my say-so..."

"Aunt, p—"

She silences her nephew with a commanding hand. "Although I told him that, and I didn't expect another to be joining us at this table, I suppose it's well that I meet Isaac's friend."

Friend. What does she mean by that word? "He's spoken of me?"

"Once or twice." The old woman's smile betrays the pleasure she's taking in making Isaac blush.

I'd ask more, but in comes the maidservant again, and another, and one more, and they're all carrying dishes. Pies, cheese, bread, a whole roast chicken and bowls of soup are set before us. *Bits and pieces*, Isaac said. If this isn't a feast, my name's not Jane Vernon.

The surface of the soup glistens with globs of fat; beneath it swim slices of succulent-looking cabbage. I wait until a blessing's been said and both Isaac and Ruth have started before taking up my own spoon. It tastes as good as it looks, with a deep flavour that's as meaty as it is earthy. I finish it in a few mouthfuls and soak up the dregs with bread.

"You like it, then?" asks Mrs Goodwin, amused.

I'm too satisfied to be humiliated. "Isaac's very fortunate to have you."

"She reminds me of that every day," Isaac says.

Mrs Goodwin wields her spoon at him. "Now, don't you go making me out to be a tyrant, Mr Latimer. I've been very generous with you over the past fortnight, and I ask for nothing in return except your good opinion and manners. Is that not right?"

"That's right, Aunt. You'll have my good opinion forever and ever. Amen." He gives her a naughty look over the top of his bowl. "And my manners sometimes accompany it."

After dinner, there's more sack to go round. Mrs Goodwin, finally at ease, tells me about Eyam, the village down the hill. Isaac, who must've heard about it hundreds of times before, occasionally adds prompts and details to the stories about the ghost of the hooded monk that Ruth saw near the old carved cross down by St Lawrence's, or the time when one of the village lads put his head and hands in the pillory for a laugh and couldn't get out again.

"And Sarah said she'd help him, dear lass, and walked right up to it even as people were throwing eggs and animal waste.

She had a brave soul." Mrs Goodwin catches herself. "*Has* a brave soul. I meant *has*, of course I did, daft old thing that I am."

The crackle of the fire is too loud.

"I know what it's like to lose a loved one," I say. "Not in the same way, mind. I've at least had… some certainty. The not knowing must be terrible."

Mrs Goodwin closes her eyes. "It is. It is. But what can we do?"

"Keep looking," says Isaac. "Even if she doesn't want us to."

"I was worried you were on the verge of giving up earlier," I say.

"I had a moment of melancholy, that's all."

I could save them from this torment. They wouldn't have to keep wondering who stole Sarah away from them. The guilt would be lifted from my own soul. What else would I say, once the confession started? Would I also tell them they've been dining with a sinner, a robber, and a murderer?

"More sack, Jane?" Isaac asks with forced jollity.

I hesitate. "It's getting dark."

"Well, the maid can make you up a bed."

Mrs Goodwin's head whips around. "Can she, now?"

"No need to do that." I say. "I've got work to do early tomorrow morning. I… I've had a pleasant time this evening, but I never meant to stay the night, and I've got to see to—"

"It's no problem for us at all, is it? Abigail!" The maidservant who looks like Mary enters. "Abigail, make up a bed in the spare chamber, would you, please?"

"Aye, Sir." She fades back into the shadows of the hallway.

Mrs Goodwin stares hard at Isaac. "That room's not been opened for a long time. The air's stale."

"Mistress Vernon will have to make do with an open window, then."

It feels as if a storm's about to break over the table. The air is full of gathering thunder.

"Mr Latimer… Isaac," I start. "It's kind of you to think of me. As I said, though—"

"Do you *want* to stay?"

I desperately want to stay, my eyes tell him. I'd stay a thousand years if I could.

It's Mrs Goodwin who gives in. "All right then. All right," she says, barely holding back a temper. "I can't disobey the master of this house, can I? Even though he's only been here for a couple of weeks."

She rises from the table.

"Mrs Goodwin…"

"It's not you, Mistress Vernon." She gives me a pat on the arm and makes a slow, halting exit that I'm sure she draws out to make us ill at ease. At last, she goes back into the hallway, shutting the door on us, and the sound of her crutch fades to a distant tap. We're alone in that vast room.

"Will she be all right?" I ask.

"She'll bluster and grumble for a bit, but her ire dies down soon after it rises." He shakes his head in dismay. "I suppose she's worried about how it might look. She's making a fuss over nothing. I, for one, am glad you're staying."

"Do you think it is?"

"What?"

"A fuss over nothing?"

Isaac's cheeks are flushed from the heat of the fire and the drink. How he'd blush if someone pushed aside those waves of golden hair and kissed the fine skin of his neck. Has anyone ever done that to him before? Has he done it to any other lass? His cousin? With the thought comes a stab of jealousy and an urge to eat him up before anyone else can get their hands on him.

The door creaks open. Isaac's aunt, I'll be bound—deciding to stand her ground and not face banishment from her own table.

"Ah," says Isaac. "Duchess!"

Her little brown head noses into the room. Positioning herself by Isaac's feet, the dog nudges at his hand, asking for strokes or food.

"You stinking wastrel, you!"

He rubs her head with a tender roughness. She smiles up at him, saliva frothing on her black gums. Contented with his love, Duchess stretches herself out in front of the fire and yawns. He hasn't answered my question. It can't be a fuss over nothing, can it? Me sitting here in this grand hall with him after dining with his aunt, his eagerness to make me stay—they're not usual things. I'd ask again if he really thinks it's nothing, but the moment's passed.

"Your aunt takes good care of you. You said before that she was Sarah's stepmother?"

Isaac takes a swig of sack. "Yes. When Sarah was fourteen, her mother died of consumption. It was a terrible time for everyone. Sarah suffered the most, though. For two years, it was only her and her father. No one spoke of it, but I suspect Sarah's mother had miscarried many other children. Sarah was a miracle, really."

He looks into the flames as if they can show him where his lost cousin is now. She was more than his uncle's child, though, wasn't she? They were much closer than that. The heat from the fire is scorching my chest and neck. I shuffle a few inches along the bench, seeking the draught from under the hall door, but it does little to cool me.

"Then Ruth Goodwin came along," continues Isaac, so wrapped up in his story that he hasn't noted my discomfort, "and my uncle married her. There were no more children. Aunt Ruth's three boys had long since grown up and left, and she was at the age when any more pregnancies would have been both difficult and dangerous. Sarah was the daughter she never had. Aunt Ruth may seem hard at times, but she's as soft as Duchess underneath it all. She was patient, so patient, with Sarah. Obedience was not in my cousin's nature."

"It must be hard for your aunt," I say, "losing Sarah as well as her husband."

"It's hard for all of us." He stares into his cup. "What's your family like, Jane?"

Like no one you've ever met. Like no one you'd ever want *to meet.*

"Well, I've got a brother and a sister living. My brother's proud. He has ideas above his standing, but his impulses drag him down into baseness."

That devilish little smile I'm coming to know so well curls under Isaac's moustache. "He sounds intriguing."

"Believe me, he's not."

"And your sister?"

Good at sneaking up on folk with rocks. "Mary has a talent for the unexpected."

"An evasive answer! What is it? Is there a rivalry between you and your siblings?"

I shuffle on the bench. "Not a rivalry. I don't know how to explain it. It's just… everyone in my family—"

"Yes?" He leans forward.

"They're not… There's something…"

Isaac frowns. He leans back and knits his fingers together. They're so slight and delicate, each one milk-white with nails filed to perfect roundness. "What?"

"There's a sickness."

Now I've done it. If anything was going to cool the heat between us, it was this. I wait for him to laugh. But he merely sits, swirling his drink, musing.

"Were you going to tell me about this sickness when we were down in the cavern?" he asks.

I look away, into the fire that seems to hold all the answers. "If I told you about it, you'd think me insane."

"I know better than most that what looks like madness is nothing of the sort." He slides one of his perfect hands next to mine, not quite touching me, but not far off. "Tell me your story."

My lips pulse. "I've never told anyone before. I don't know where to start."

"Your family," he says, pouring me a drink. "Start with your family."

"My grandfather, George Bradley, would do anything to get his hands on money: gamble, rob, cheat. He was poor, aye, but only as poor as the other miners in the village. The difference was, he was cocky. His father told him that the Bradleys used to be well-off, and, far back, were related to a lord. Whether this was true or not didn't matter—George acted like he was denied his due, and anything that got him closer to a fortune was worthwhile.

"So it happened that one day, a star fell from the sky over the village. People said it landed in Elden Hole, because all around that area, the earth turned black. The rot spread to crops in the commons, animals in the farms. Then, it spread to the youngest people. Bairns, hale and hearty before, refused to suck. Children danced into fires and threw themselves in the great pond. They went wandering off and never came back. Such fear gripped the Peak Foresters that they gathered together a pot of money for anyone that'd go down there and face the fallen angel. Well, this piqued my grandfather's interest. He thought this act of bravery would earn him as much respect as money, and he was greedy for both. Grandam tried to put him off. 'Don't go down there,' she said. 'Remember the old woman's goose, how its feathers were all blackened and charred after it walked through the fires of Hell? You're ignorant of what's down there, George. No good being rich if you're dead.'

"That might've been the end of it, if one of the Needhams hadn't got a word in. Old Harry's da called George a coward, mocked him in front of the village, saying that he was afeared of elves and sprites. If my grandfather had any wits about him, he'd have told the man to go down there himself if he was so brave. As I said, though, George was not wise.

"The villagers went away to make preparations and came back with some marvellous engines that would allow my grandfather to be lowered down fourscore yard at a time. On the end of the rope was a bell, which he could ring if he could go no further or wanted to be raised up. Ropes were wound round my grandfather's middle and looped about the top of his thighs. He was laughing as they tied him up like a cut of meat. His laughter turned to howls of pain as he was lowered over the edge. He shouted out that the ropes were cutting into him, but the Needhams told the men to keep lowering.

"As George disappeared into the blackness, his protests turned to silence. Grandam panicked, but the men insisted that they could still feel George's weight pulling them forward. He was let down fourscore yard, and no bell was rung. He could, it seemed, go deeper. Those on the surface dropped him further down. Still, there was no ringing of the bell. So down he went again, almost another fourscore. Then all of a sudden, the tension slackened off. He'd either reached the bottom, or one of the knots had come undone. Grandam started to scream, certain she'd lost her husband.

"That's when the men holding onto the ropes were dragged forward, right to the edge. The crowd that had gathered around Elden Hole began to chatter and push past each other to get a look. Miles below the surface, a bell was ringing.

"It was only with the help of extra hands from the village that they managed to heave George back up. They heard his laughter long before they saw how his shirt and trousers were soaked in blood from where the rope had bitten into his flesh. There was something different about his eyes. They couldn't say what. And the ropes—along the whole length of them were curious knots made by nimble fingers. Surely no one could have untied the line of them, knotted them so thoroughly, and tied them back up again in the time that George was down there?

"When the villagers asked whether George had reached the bottom, my grandfather spoke gibberish. They untied him. He wasn't in control of his limbs. He'd been touched, they said. Something down there in the Hole had put its long fingers in his head and stirred his brain to mush.

"But Grandam, she knew the truth of it. She nursed him through his fevered gabbling, and the nightmares that would cause him to wake up screaming. But while George was an invalid for those first few weeks, he re-learned to walk, and more—within three months of George coming back up from the Hole, Grandam was with child. He also regained his power of speech, though his mind was never quite the same."

"Did he tell you what he saw down there?"

Isaac's voice brings me back into the room, to the death rattles of the fire and the candle, sloughing off its skin. Shadows from the dying lights lean in to listen. This was Grandam's favourite part of the story—the part where her husband tells of meeting the angel, the Spirit of Elden Hole, and making a deal with Her: his family would give Her a steady supply of offerings and in return, She would leave Peak Forest be. The words well up inside me. But I lock them in.

"He only said he was affrighted. He didn't say of what."

Us, the shadows, the whole house—we're bound in silence, a special, listening kind of silence as thick and pure as snow. Then, Isaac says, "Pah!"

He bangs his cup down on the table. "What a story to frighten children with! You do understand why they spun this yarn, don't you? It was to keep you away from the edge. A warning. A cautionary tale."

I frown. "But it happened."

"Who told you this?"

"The story was passed down. From Grandam to Mam, and from her to us."

"I don't doubt that your grandfather was lowered into Elden Hole," says Isaac. "The poor man was scared half to death and horribly maimed by the ropes. His wounds probably became infected, hence why he ranted and raved."

My throat is tight. "How do you explain the knots?"

"An elaboration," says Isaac.

Footsteps come creaking down the stairs, accompanied by

the knock of his aunt's crutch, and Duchess lifts her dozing head, her ears pricking.

"Stories, Jane, are living things," says Isaac with a new urgency. "They grow with each telling. Their hearts beat stronger. Look at those so-called Wonders in Derbyshire! Are any of them real wonders? Does the Shivering Mountain never shrink? Does the Devil truly lurk in caverns and fart out wind? Oh, I've tried and tried to see it through my cousin's enchanted eyes, but it's all too simple to see how beautiful things become fantastical. Your story has grown teeth and horns over the years. The darkness your relative saw has become populated with devils."

"It's not just a story," I insist. "I know. It happened."

"A *part* of it happened to an old man a long time ago. The other details were added to make it a more fearsome cautionary tale."

"It doesn't even work that way! If anything, it made us more eager to stand at the edge."

"Then ask yourself this: if a story, contrived to keep you safe, puts you in danger, is it a tale you should keep telling?"

We meet each other's eyes. Something leaps between us—an understanding that's more than words, like he's found the very thing in me that dwells deep in him, and it makes everything so light and clear.

He stretches his legs out under the table. They touch mine.

"Don't let other people's stories control you, Jane. You're too rare a jewel for that. What I said… about this being a fuss over nothing…" He reaches out for my hand. We lock fingers, and he leans towards me. "It's—"

The small flames in the fireplace waver as the door opens.

Isaac springs back, grabbing the bottle of sack near my elbow and mumbling apologies for having to lean over me. I gabber some nonsense in return, and then I force myself to look into the face of my hostess. It's hard and cold as flint.

"I was right," Mrs Goodwin says. "The air in the room is too stale. It's not fit for a guest."

My legs are shaking as I stand. "Not to worry. I'd changed my mind about staying anyway."

This time, Isaac doesn't object. He's got his hands wrapped round the cup of sack and is staring deep into it. Is he not going to say anything? Not a word?

I swallow drily. "I'll go now then, shall I?"

"I think that'd be wise," says Mrs Goodwin.

She stands aside, gesturing towards the corridor. I glance back at Isaac, whose head is still hanging low. "Thank you for coming out to see the stones with me, Mr Latimer."

At last, he lifts his face. His cheeks are ruddy, like a child's after a slapping. The lips that could have pressed to mine are turned down at the edges. "My pleasure, Mistress Vernon."

"Your cloak is by the door," the aunt reminds me.

"So it is." I want to curl into a ball. I've taken advantage of her hospitality. She's let me into her home, and I've brought dishonour to it.

"Ta for everything," I mutter.

I skulk past her. The maidservant hands me my cloak and coif. I avoid her eyes and slip out of the front door before my hopes of seeing Isaac for one last time this evening climb too high.

What a bloody mess I've made of this visit. Isaac's aunt will never let me near that house again. Isaac himself may well be too ashamed to speak to me. I won't be able to reunite him with Sarah. Everything is in ruins.

White rage scrubs out the rest of the world as I make my way home. What man of his standing invites a woman like me to stay, gives her drink, has a bed made up and seduces her into it right under his aunt's nose? What did he think would happen? Mrs Goodwin was hardly going to sit back with some sewing and let us do as we fancied.

Isaac wasn't thinking, and now that lack of foresight has cost us our companionship. He should have been more careful. *We* should have been more careful, for he's not the only one who let himself get swept up in passion. Telling him about the curse, *almost* letting slip about Elden Hole… What was I doing?

He didn't even understand what I was telling him. We belong to two different worlds. The rich man and the lazar, the draper's son from London and the rustic. An unbridgeable gulf exists between us.

The memory of Isaac's skin on mine taunts me. He was trying me out, daring himself, and I wasn't worth it. That's why he didn't protest when Mrs Goodwin asked me to leave. It's all right. It doesn't matter. His aunt was making a fuss over nothing after all.

I find a tree by the roadside and drive my foot into it again and again because I need something to suffer. When my toes are throbbing and I've exhausted my fury, I sink to the ground.

I weep out the bitterness that lies at the bottom of my anger. Isaac can't begin to understand me and my family. He dismissed what happened with my grandfather as a tale to frighten little children. He wasn't there. He doesn't know. Grandam, spiteful as she may have been at times, would never have asked Da, Mam, Will, Mary, and me to make the sacrifices we've made if there weren't any truth in her story. It'd be lunacy. It'd be evil.

I thought this day would end in joy, not regret. I thought it would be a pleasant distraction. I can tell myself that I brought Isaac to Wet Withens to make him feel better about his cousin. In truth, I went there for my benefit, to tug my mind away from that horrible business back home and indulge myself. There's no stopping the tide of time, though. Will and Mary and Nathaniel are still caught up in its current.

For all his misunderstandings, there was truth in what Isaac said. If the story of Elden Hole no longer serves us, why are we still telling it?

Thomas's sacrifice has brought us nothing but trouble. There must be another way to give Her what She needs. In the nightmare, She said Her business was with me. Me, not Will and Mary. Their plans for Nathaniel won't help the situation. It's time I showed them how I'd approach the whole matter.

Chapter Sixteen

ISAAC

Why must I find it so difficult to hold my tongue? Why can I not refrain from impetuous behaviour? I criticise others for mythmaking, yet I am far worse. I have come to believe in this version of myself—Isaac, who always knows best and is not afraid to speak his mind. I have made enemies of my parents, Aunt Ruth and now Jane Vernon.

I have also driven you away, Sarah.

Last Summer. Chatsworth gardens, by the fountains. Ingenious designs, bristling with pipes and spouts, water shooting into the mild summer air. The sea god in the middle of a stone basin, the waves at his command, dolphins lashed together under his feet.

And you, looking down at your troubled reflection and saying, "Do you know the story of Neptune's wife? She tried to hide from him at first. She was a maid and frightened of his majesty. He sent a dolphin to find her."

"Did it carry her back to him against her will?" I asked wearily, sensing your comment was a prelude to more talk of your lover. "Abduct her, like Hades did Persephone?"

"No, it persuaded her. She wanted to marry Neptune, despite her protests." You adjusted a pin in your hair. "Is that not how the gods curse us? That is how Eve was punished, after all. *'Thy desire shall be subject to thine husband, and he shall rule over thee.'*"

"If that were true," I said, "you'd be walking alongside Peter."

Several hundred yards behind us, your husband was reining in his long stride so as not to out-pace Aunt Ruth. Her shuffling gait had grown worse since your father died. When he saw me looking, he extended his neck and tried to attract your attention as well.

"He wishes to walk with you."

"He sees enough of me at home. This is one of the few times I need not look at him, and I intend to make the most of it."

You set off again in haste. Casting an apologetic glance at your husband and Aunt Ruth, I ran to keep up with you.

"The other week," you said, when I was within earshot, "Peter *pleaded* with me to perform my duties as a wife. It made me sick."

My own stomach turned. "Have you been ill since then?"

"I know what you're asking, Coz. And no, it was only the once, and I washed myself with a cloth and hot water afterwards, inside and out. But I cannot keep holding him back. He will ask more and more of me. This afternoon at Chatsworth, grand as it may be, is merely a way of winning my favour. And how he skulks around! How he drags his feet!"

"He is looking after your mother."

"She is *not* my mother!"

Pain flashed in my jaw. I'd been grinding my teeth without knowing it. I took a breath and gathered my patience. "Ruth treats you as well as her own children."

"I never asked to lose my own mother. I accepted Peter because my father said it would have made my mother so proud to see me—" Your voice broke. "To see me wed and settling down. But he is not the man I love."

"The man you love belongs to someone else."

"A damned Puritan who cries to the preacher because her husband goes shooting on a Sunday!"

We'd stopped by a statue of Orpheus charming the animals. Carved rabbits and deer sat at his feet. A fountain echoed his ancient song.

"She is the woman he chose," I said.

"He chose wrong. He says we'll go away together one day. He says we'll visit the Ebbing and Flowing Well, and Elden Hole, and the Shivering Mountain. He says he'll take me further still, and we can live together as man and wife where no one knows us."

"Then he's a lying rogue."

"You know *nothing* of him, Isa."

In that moment, I could have struck you. A spoilt child—that was how you appeared to me. A spoilt child indulging in a fairy story and taking it as truth because it suited you.

"You want freedom," I said. "Not a man who swipes married women from under their husband's noses."

Your eyes flashed. "How would you know what I want?"

"I've known you for most of your life. Longer than Old Neptune."

You laughed. It was not a pleasant sound.

"What amuses you so?"

"Your jealousy."

"Jealousy?"

"You are jealous of the attention I get from men. You always have been, Isa."

If I had been honest with you then, you might not have been compelled to run away and leave us all, to leave me. But you'd selected your sharpest dagger and thrust it straight into my heart without a thought, and I wanted to see you suffer in turn.

"I have no reason to be jealous of your small, inconsequential life," I replied.

The look you gave me then. You may as well have spat in my face.

On you walked, leaving me alone with Orpheus and the melody of the water until Peter and Ruth found me. I told them the grief of losing your father was taking its toll on your spirit, and you wanted to be left alone.

"I had days like that," Ruth said. "I understand."

Peter scowled. "I'm afraid I do not. She was distracted long before her father passed." He turned his cold eyes on me. "Did she say anything to you about it?"

"Nothing of substance," I said.

That was August. That was the last time I saw you.

Chapter Seventeen

Inside the White Hart, Alyson Bagshawe is showing off her talent for making customers feel at home. She's playing a game of piquet with the tubby little tailor, Dick Jones, the two of them red-faced with laughter and drink, while Walter the Weasel gives them jealous glances over the pie he's eating. Harry and Nathaniel aren't here, God be thanked, so I go straight over to Mary. With the hostess distracted, she's taken charge of pouring from the barrels. The customer before me doesn't seem too irked that it's her serving him instead of Mrs Bagshawe. I suppose it's what comes of working at the same place, year in, year out.

When she's done, she raises her eyebrows at me. "Evening, Janey. What urgent business brings *you* back from wherever you've been hiding?"

"I need to talk to you," I say.

"Come back later, when—"

"Move." Mrs Bagshawe nudges my sister out of the way and lodges herself between the table of tankards and the barrels. "Go and do something useful, Mary. You spend enough time standing round here, chatting."

"I was the one who started talking to her," I protest. "She told me to come back when she was less busy."

"She's not supposed to be serving in any case."

"I was only doing it while you were seeing to the regulars," says Mary with some cheek.

The hostess takes a laboured breath. "Well, I'm here now, and I'm sure there's more you can be getting on with."

"I'll go and sweep the floor in the back room," Mary says, more to me than to her employer.

"Mind there's no one in there. Don't go interrupting anyone's business."

"I won't."

Without ordering an ale, I follow Mary as she strides off. "You shouldn't let her talk to you like that, you know."

"I know how to deal with the likes of her," she mutters.

"By letting her trample all over you?"

"I can't bite her head off now, can I? People like that, you've got to show some patience to their faces—let them think they've got the upper hand. And then, when they trust you enough…"

Mary elbows open the door to the back room. She goes right in, but I linger on the threshold. I haven't been here since that night. How well has Mary scrubbed it? What if the dirt from Thomas's boots is still crammed down the cracks in the flagstone floor? What if the grease on his fingertips, a last imprint of him, worms its way into me?

"Come on." Mary takes a seat in the same chair he used

that night and sits back with her ankles crossed. “I thought you wanted to talk to me.”

Treading lightly, the way you would tiptoe through a graveyard, I go in and take a seat. I don’t know how long I can last in here; the smell of cooked meats on the shelves makes me want to heave.

“So, ta for leaving me to do all your duties at home today.” Mary gives me a sour pout.

“I’m sorry, Magpie.”

“Where were you?”

“Eyam.”

“Eyam? Why there?”

“Didn’t aim for it. I just walked, and that’s where I ended up.”

She regards me with narrowed eyes. “Castleton… Eyam… Where next, eh? Who did you meet?”

I drop my gaze to the flagstones where Thomas set his sack of wool and jewellery down. “No one.”

“I don’t believe you,” she says. “Not a bit.”

I imagine this is how a mouse feels when Lordsmeer’s pinned its tail under his paw. Mary’s always had this knack of knowing what’s going on. She’s Mam without the madness. Or perhaps it is a kind of madness. She’s got one foot in another world.

“I’m distracted,” I say. “That thing on our doorstep was upsetting. But it got me thinking… I want to end this with Nathaniel the right way, without any blood being spilt.”

“Jane—”

"Trust me. I know that if we get too deep into this, we'll regret it. Now, I need you to go back to the house. Get my share of the money from behind the butter churn. Give it to Nathaniel and tell him that's it, that's all he's getting, and in exchange for it, he's not to speak of Thomas again."

She shakes her head. "Only the other day, you were insisting that we shouldn't give him anything. And now, what? You're folding him in? Is he going to be part of our plans now as well?"

"We don't *need* plans, Mary. At least, not the same plans."

"Wait." She twists an apron ribbon around her finger. "What are you telling me?"

The words I want to say scatter as if blown by a strong wind. I catch one thought and hold onto it, tight. "I don't think we're going about any of this in the right way—the feeding, I mean. There must be another way."

"And that is?"

"I'm trying to put the pieces together. But I need more time. Mary, trust me. I think… I think I've seen *Her*. The Spirit of the Hole. The angel. In a dream."

She sits back with her hands in her lap, her forehead furrowed, puzzled. "You? She talked to *you*?"

"Why so surprised?"

"I'm not. It's… I mean, what did She say?"

If I repeat those first words—*I'll take what I'm owed*—Mary'll jump to the conclusion that we need to keep piling up the bodies, starting with Nathaniel's.

"She said Her business is with me and no one else," I tell

her. "She talked in riddles. For my ears only. I'll work it out in time."

Mary leans over the table. "And if you don't? All them people in the next room—if we don't do our duty, do you know what'll happen?"

"I know the—" I'm about to say *story*, but I bite my tongue. I won't dismiss it like Isaac did earlier.

My sister holds my gaze so long it makes my skin crawl. "It's not just summat that happened in the past. The families we know now will suffer. Elizabeth Archdale's bairn, when it's born, won't live to see a year. It'll starve to a tiny skeleton in its mother's arms. Do you want that? Do you want to be blamed for that?"

Elizabeth Archdale, withered to a husk, screaming over her dead child. "I don't want that," I say, almost choking on the words. "But if we give Nathaniel the money—"

"He'll drain us dry. That's what'll happen. And when we run out of money, and he spreads rumours of us far and wide because he's too pig-ignorant to know better, and we hang for it—people will die."

All that she's saying is true, and I fear it. More than the gallows, I fear people believing Nathaniel's branding of us as common criminals, and I fear the rot that'll spread from plant to plant, animal to animal, child to child, until Peak Forest is one mass of suffering souls. If Mary's right, my actions will only lead to destruction. Yet the Spirit spoke to me. What can *I tire of scraps* mean, if not Her dissatisfaction with how we're going about our duty?

"I'm certain," I say, "that killing Nathaniel won't solve anything. Please, Mary. Believe me."

Mary's determination flares for a moment longer, then vanishes into smoke. Her eyes slide off me.

"You'll have to hurry, then," she says, looking down at her hands. "Will's up at Highpit Rake now. He told Nathaniel to meet him there tonight."

Despite the cold, rivers of sweat are running under my bodice as I reach the rake on Gautries Hill. During working hours, the whole place shudders with the crank of the stow bringing the ore up the winding shaft and the crack of rock under the bucker hammer. Women, including Mrs Needham, chatter as they take baskets full of the smashed pieces of lead ore to a stream for dressing, while the men gather in the coe to fuel themselves with bread and ale. The only sound tonight is the *knock knock* of the coe door in the wind. I push it fully open and hold up my lantern. Picks and hammers on the wall wink in the dim light.

"Will? Are you in here?"

I edge my way around the entrance of the shaft in the middle of the cabin floor. It's a drop that goes fourscore feet straight down, with nothing to hold onto but wooden stemples wedged into the earthen wall.

A sharp rasp comes from the corner, and a spark flies out, yellow against black. A flame whoomphs into life as it catches a piece of wadding. The air fills with the stench of rancid fat as a hand brings a tallow candle towards the fire. Shadows pool in Will's eye sockets. He grins. For a moment, I'm afraid of him.

"So! You've decided to join us?" He spits on the wadding, crushing the heat out of it.

I mustn't show any weakness around him, no matter how much I feel like turning back. "I've decided to stop you."

He sniffs. "You can't. He'll be here soon. Mary's gone to fetch him."

"She's not fetching him. I've asked her to give him my share of the money." I hold my breath, waiting for Will's reaction. He says nothing. I've struck him dumb. For the first time in my life, I've stopped his tongue.

A bubble rises from my chest and bursts out of my mouth as a laugh. It's wonderful, this feeling of lightness, the same lightness I felt with Isaac before Mrs Goodwin burst in on us. I realise now what it is: the feeling of being the captain of my own soul.

"You'd better be joking, Janey," Will says, running a hand through his hair. "Because that would be a very, very bad thing to do, wouldn't it?"

"No joke," I say.

The thump of boots, a fist sweeping towards me, a crack of pain across my jaw. Warmth dribbles into my mouth, and it tastes of coins left to turn brown at the bottom of a purse.

"What do you think Nathaniel bloody Needham is going to do now, eh?" Will is shouting, his hand still raised. "He's going to squeeze us for every penny we have. People like that, they don't stop! They never stop!"

I wipe the blood off my stinging lips. "What's so important to you that you have to kill for it? The money? We can get that through honest work. You can marry Bess, and she can help me look after the animals and work the commons."

"And what about *Her*?"

"This is not about the sacrifices! You weren't even going to offer Nathaniel."

"But he'll stop us from offering others."

I try to spit the blood from my split lip on the ground, but miss, and it slops down my front. Faintness steals over me. I want to lay down and go to sleep right here. Only the memory of being fleetingly in control keeps me going.

"The one who'll stop you from offering others is me," I say. "If you mean to slaughter anyone who stands in your way, slit my throat. I know you've got Thomas's dagger." His eyes flick down to his belt, at the handle carved with the dead man's initials. "Do it, Will. Go on. Finish me. Feed me to Her."

I tip back my head, inviting him to draw the dagger across my windpipe. But he won't. In my heart of hearts, I know he couldn't really do it.

He grabs hold of a loose strand of my hair and pulls so that his furious face swims before me. "I want you gone, out of our house by tomorrow. Me and Mary can manage without you. And don't expect us to run to your aid when something nasty and wicked comes for you. Believe me, it will be coming."

He shoves me back and makes his way towards the door, no doubt to throw me out of it. But something stops him in his tracks: a glow from the shaft.

Da's tale of the knocker who lived in the bowels of the earth and led men to the deepest of seams comes back to me. Terrified, I stare at the hole as the light grows stronger, becoming like the halo surrounding a hearth fire; a lantern appears, and then a head.

"The Vernons," comes a wheezy voice. "I could've guessed it were you messing about with the levels." Old Harry Needham pulls himself out of the shaft with a groan, rising unsteadily to his feet.

Without even realising I'm moving, I find myself standing shoulder to shoulder with my brother. I try to speak.

"We weren't… it's not…"

Huffing like a pair of broken bellows, Harry waves away my excuses with a shaky hand.

"Don't take me for a fool. Nathaniel said that you two"—Harry's breath crackles and whistles—"are the worst kind of trouble. I didn't want to believe him, not even after what happened with our Rebecca. I wouldn't put summat like that down to you. But hearing you talk now, I *can* believe it. You know, your Da would be turning in his grave."

"At least we didn't put him there," snarls Will.

"Neither did I!" It's the first time I've ever heard Harry shout. "And if you think that killing my boy, my Nathaniel…" He beats a fist against his chest. His face crumples. "If you think devilry and sacrifice and an eye for an eye will bring your father back, you're wrong. All it'll do is get you a place on the gallows."

"You've got it wrong," I say, time slowing like it did on top of Elden Hill with Thomas. I dab my lip on my sleeve. It's still bleeding. "Mary's with him. She's giving him the money he demanded from us."

"Money we earnt doing our bit for the village," Will adds.

Harry's dry laugh rattles in his chest. "You think you can make Nathaniel the villain of the piece. It's no good making accusations when you're a Vernon. Oh, I know you've got to do your duty or we'll all starve to death or run mad. But the more I talk to Nathaniel about it, the more I think that maybe you're on the side of that fallen angel, working against us, not to benefit us. Aye, I can tell when the Devil's truly touched someone, and there's a darkness about you, William Vernon—summat wicked, summat wrong." He looks at me. "I always thought you and Mary were better, but happen you're just better at hiding it, as is the way of women."

Old Harry Needham has always been a man of few words. This is the longest I've heard him speak. It's the finest I've heard him speak. I'd buy him a drink and applaud him for it, if I wasn't so scared.

"It doesn't have to be like this," I say. The words are coming faster than I can think. "You can go your way, and we'll go ours. We can leave this place and let you and your family be. We'll move to Castleton. What do you make of that?"

"But how about this? We get to keep all the money," Will says. He's a quick one, is my brother, hopping on board with this new plan the minute it's out of my mouth. "None of it goes to Nathaniel."

The old man's veiny eyes search me for a sign that we're not going to mess him about. I nod, encouraging him, even though us leaving Peak Forest puts everyone in the most appalling danger. In truth, we can't leave. But for now, we need to put Old Harry's fears at bay and convince him that a life without the Vernons is a possibility. When he's of sober mind, then we can explain why we must go back on our word.

"You can keep every penny," he says. "As long as you leave us alone."

"If that's really what you're offering"—Will steps forward—"then I'm not going to say no."

He's changed his mind. He's really gone and changed it. I could cry with relief.

"All right," says Harry. He offers his hand.

Will takes it. I close my eyes and let out a long breath. It's over.

And then Will throws his whole weight against Harry Needham. He rams him in the stomach, sending him staggering backwards towards the mine shaft.

Harry's short, strong arms windmill through the air. He doesn't scream. There's no time.

In the blink of an eye, the man who worked with Da since they were my age, who used to bring us wild cherries and cobnuts from the market sometimes, who has a wife and six children and good, strong hands to make up for his weak lungs—

He's gone.

Neither Will nor I move for a long time. There are pins and

needles in my fingers. My feet are numb. Time freezes around us and cracks, shattering the coe into sharp fragments. When it thaws, many years later, I wipe the crusting blood away from my mouth and say, "Do you want to check?"

"Check what?" says Will. He sounds like the echo of a dream.

"If he's still alive."

"He's not, Jay Bird."

"How can you be certain?"

"It's…" Will bites his lip. "I just know."

Outside the coe, there's a shuffle of footsteps. Mary is saying, "Look, Jane's here. There's Will, an' all. They'll tell you what's going on."

Will catches my eye.

I shake my head. "No, Will, please…"

The door opens. Two figures are standing there, one of them small and slight and carrying a lantern. The other has all the bravado of a newly recruited soldier. He swaggers inside.

"Have you got the money, then?" asks Nathaniel Needham.

Will reaches for Thomas's blade.

Chapter Eighteen

The next day, I go about my duties, mucking out the new chickens, collecting eggs, kneading bread, making oatcakes, milking the cows. My bones march me up and down the hill; my heart commands: *Keep on, keep on, keep on.* Yet I'm in pieces. I dread the moments when some innocent action stirs up the memories of last night. When I pour myself an ale, I see blood spurting over Nathaniel's hands. I don't even try to skin a rabbit. One look at a knife conjures an image of Mary hacking at the side of the lad's face and holding up the mangled ear, bits of scalp and cheek still attached to it.

"Might as well make a little offering," she said.

My bladder needs emptying all the time. My guts are full of thorns.

Harry and Nathaniel are gone, and there's no way out, no way of taking it back now. It's a truth too horrible to bear, but I make myself go over and over it, testing and tasting and pulling apart all the things I've done, laying them out and forcing myself to look, damning myself to the deepest part of Hell.

By nightfall, news has travelled round the village: two of the Needhams have been found dead. The story goes that Will went to the mine in the morning as usual and saw Harry and Nathaniel at the bottom of the stemples. The younger man was horribly disfigured, face all torn up. Folk at the White Hart are saying that he did it to himself out of sheer grief after witnessing his father's fall. Margaret Needham, on hearing about her husband and son, screamed until she lost her voice, they say.

When my mind finally plays dead, it comes as a sweet relief I don't deserve.

In the early hours, Will comes home late, reeking of ale and smoke. His clobbering about wakes me up, but I keep silent; the last thing I want to do is talk to him, especially when he's in that drunken state. He lies in the bed next to me. Little moans and choking sounds come from his throat. With cold shock, I realise he's weeping. I open my mouth to say his name—and close it. He wouldn't take kindly to me poring over his sorrow. After a lot of sniffing, he falls asleep. The snores start. Each one gets louder and higher, till he startles himself out of his dreams with his own piggishness, rolls over, and starts snoring again. I get up. I'd rather go without sleep than listen to him all night.

At the other side of the house, Mary's up and busy with needlework. She sits on her bed, candles burning around her.

"Couldn't sleep?" she asks.

"No."

Thankful that wood is still smouldering in the hearth, I take Da's chair. Lordsmeer jumps on my lap and flops onto his back, curling his white paws. There must be some part of me that's still good, if he trusts me. Grateful for his simple love, I fuss him till his nettle-green eyes close and his purr becomes a steady sleeping breath.

Mary hums to herself as she pins cuts of taffeta onto a bodice. It's a tune I don't recognise—one of them songs that 'come to her,' in all likelihood—but it reminds me a little of the one she sang in the Shouting Cave the other day. *O, come fair maiden, come with me, the shady regions for to see…* Who teaches Mary these things? Does a presence glide through her dreams, too, telling her of ancient mysteries?

"Is there summat on my face?" she asks, without looking up.

I clear my throat. "No."

"Then gi'over staring."

After last night, I shouldn't take my eyes off her again. Not for one moment. "I'm looking at what you're making. Seems fancy."

She tilts the bodice forward so that pools of silk catch the candlelight and shine a rich blue. "A new robe for work. I've got to look proper, seeing that I'm taking over some of Alyson's duties as hostess."

"She's letting you?"

"I have to. She's not well."

"What's wrong with her?"

She smiles to herself. "My, your tongue is loose this morning, Janey. Want me to sew it back into place?"

I wince. "Did you buy that material with Thomas's money?"

"I did. Might as well make use of my share. It's time you did the same."

My stomach roils. "I asked you to make use of my share last night. Instead, you led him up the hill, straight to us."

"The plan was already in place. I couldn't have stopped it."

"Yes, you could've!" I get restless. Lordsmeer flips off my lap like a landed fish. "All you had to do was tell him what I told you to say."

"He insisted."

"Then you should've said no."

"A little thing like me, standing up against him?"

I laugh at that. "Come on. He wouldn't have hurt you."

She lays down her sewing. "Oh? And how do you know that? Do you know what it's like to work at the White Hart, always trying to judge whether a man's going to meddle with you or maul you? Do you think I liked being pushed about by that Thomas Mace?"

I tongue the split in my lip. "No."

"That's right, I didn't. You're not the only one who's been haunted by memories of that night. It's not the killing that bothered me. It was what came before—having his horrible hands shove me, not knowing what he was going to do next."

She's opened my eyes. It was us who put her in that position. What would have happened to Mary if Thomas had fought us off, and then found her all alone on that hillside? The very same thing that, I suspect, has happened to Sarah. And while I can't imagine Nathaniel hurting Mary, I wouldn't bet my life on it. He had his eye on my sister. God knows what might've happened if she'd challenged him.

"You still didn't have to lead him to us," I say.

"You didn't have to stay and watch."

I couldn't do anything else, though, could I? It all happened so quickly, and my feet were stone. I was helpless, useless, like I always am.

"Look, it's over and done, now," Mary says, her voice oddly light. "Best not to let it get in the way of anything else."

"Stop talking like that! We've got blood on our hands, Mary!"

"Don't you think I know?" she says through gritted teeth. "I'm trying, Jane. I'm trying to hold everything together here and at the inn. The way I'm doing that is by putting one foot in front of the other and taking each minute of each day as it comes. I'm not thinking about what could've been different." She picks up the top part of her new robe again and jabs a pin into the back. "It is what it is."

We barely speak to each other after that. She gets on with her work. My blood simmers, then cools as I drift into sleep. When I wake, the room is bright with unflinching day. The thought of the hours and hours ahead make me want to die.

"How does it look on me?" Mary asks.

She stands with the newly covered bodice loose around

her nightshirt, her arms held out at the sides. It lifts her into beauty, into womanhood. Mam would've been proud. I lower my face and weep.

The funeral takes place two days after Harry and Nathaniel are found. I say I'm too sick to go, but Mary insists it'd look odd if I didn't mourn with everybody else. When she says *everybody else*, she means it. The whole village has gathered outside the Needham farmhouse, as well as a host of people I don't recognise, who must be kith and kin from other parts.

"I don't want to stand near *her*," Mary says, cocking her head towards Mrs Bagshawe. The woman hardly looks capable of bothering Mary today. Pale and drained, she's leaning against Walter the Weasel, who has his meaty arm about her shoulders and his lip stuck out in an ill-fitting mask of woe. I didn't realise the hostess and him cared about the Needhams that much, but I suppose they've always been good customers.

I search for a better place to stand, hoping no one takes note of me. If they did, they'd surely be able to see the cut on my lip and the mark of evil on my forehead. My heart turns over when I see a small group of men who worked the rake with the Needhams and Will. Pipe smoke rises up through the middle of their circle.

"Let's not go near them," I say.

"Why not? We've nothing to be ashamed of," Will replies, too loud. One of them—a particular friend of Nathaniel's, arms tight with bundles of muscle—gives us a long, hard glare. He's about to break off from the others and come over, God help us, when a hearse draws up on the road, and the crowd falls silent.

The Needhams must be swimming in money. No back-breaking bier-carrying to Chapel-en-le-Frith for them. The only other hearse I've seen was passing through the village, probably on its way to one of the grand houses in Tideswell or Eyam, and this one's even more impressive. You could check your reflection in the polished coat of the horse. The inside of the carriage is hung with black. The sight of it strikes icy fear into me. It's like Death himself has ridden up to greet us.

Right by the house, the crowd parts to reveal four men bearing a coffin on their shoulders. They're big men, yet their bodies bend under the weight of their load as they pass by. I wrap my arms round myself, holding tight, afraid of screaming that we're the ones who did this. I almost do when the second coffin comes out, borne by two men, Mrs Needham herself and John, who at fourteen summers old is as tall as his mother. This coffin must be Nathaniel's.

Behind them, little Beatrice and Christopher toddle hand-in-hand under the watchful eye of Mrs Needham's spinster sister, and in her arms is the youngest of the Needhams, a bairn of under a year. Four children, all dressed in purest white. As well as Nathaniel, there used to be another: Rebecca. When she was laid to rest only six weeks ago, the body was carried on a bier for all to see. She looked like a little onion in her winding sheet, freshly plucked from the ground, making everyone round her weep.

The Needhams have almost lost as many family members as us now.

The graves of father and son are next to each other, in the same plot of ground where Rebecca and all the other Needhams of years past are buried. We're at the side of the crowd, pressed up against the wall that surrounds St Thomas's church, so I have to stand on tiptoes to see Mrs Needham bend and kiss the coffin of her husband and then her son. Her bairn, now in her arms, lets out a high-pitched mewl as she moves. Some of the other mourners babble and shush him.

"He's saying goodbye," says Elizabeth Archdale, loud enough for the whole crowd to hear. "He's telling us of his anguish."

"Jesus bloody Christ," Will utters dismissively under his breath. "The child's only fussing because it's being tilted upside-down."

"Same thing," I say.

Mrs Needham lifts her tear-blotched face up to the heavens. "In his will, Harry stated that he wanted his family to help bury him," she announces.

She gives the baby to her sister again and scoops up a handful of earth, holding it aloft like the Host, and lets some of it fall on each of the coffins with a wet thud. A part of me, the part I don't like, thinks that she must be relishing this spectacle. "Sleep peacefully, my dear ones," she says.

John Needham is next to sink his hand into the soil. He squeezes it between his fingers till dirty water runs down his arm and wets his white sleeve. For a long time, he looks at it, closing his fingers and opening them again. Reverend Daniels lays a hand on the lad's shoulder and gives him some gentle encouragement.

Little Beatrice Needham's next. She's the prettiest of the children, with a head full of dark curls and apple-red cheeks. She takes the soil in her pudgy, five-year-old fist and laughs as it patters down on the corpses of her father and brother. When it's young Christopher's turn, the boy buries his face in his mother's linen and sobs. Mrs Needham folds him into her, but her tender affections will be no substitute for the loss of a father. When Da died a few months back, we came unmoored. For days afterwards, we drifted in a grey mist. I'd go out to tend to the cow and forget what I was doing. I'd wander for hours before coming back to a house as big and empty as the open skies. Harry's children are too young to deal with that. It's not fair, what they'll have to go through because of us.

The sexton picks up a spade. It's almost done. I managed to get through the procession all the way here without speaking to a single soul, and I listened, without screaming, to the sermon about how Harry and Nathaniel ran the good race. I don't reckon we'll be staying for cakes at the Needham place; soon I'll be able to go back to the house and grieve in peace.

Margaret weaves round the mourners and presses bags of

coin into the hands of the needy. Hunchbacked Mrs Gumby, who was trampled under a horse as a young lass, looks up to her as if she were a queen.

"God bless your heart, Mrs Needham."

"It's not much," the widow replies. "Only a few shillings."

A few shillings for each of the poorest in this parish adds up to quite a lot. Foolish boy, Nathaniel. Why did you have to go and be greedy?

Mrs Needham freezes when she sees us. Her face is painted with the usual signs of grief. There are the red-tinged eyes, with blue bags beneath them, and her hair is matted under her cap. She's not old—Harry Needham was a full ten years her senior—but death has aged her in ways that motherhood could never manage.

"We're terribly sorry for your losses," Will says. Though he sounds sincere enough, his reminder that she's lost more than one loved one is a deliberate blow.

Mrs Needham's nostrils quiver. "I told him. I told him that working with you would only bring him trouble."

My heart stammers. Some members of the crowd turn to look at what's shaping up to be graveside entertainment. The very last thing we need now is all eyes on us and people baying for our blood.

I bend my head low. "We really are very saddened, Mrs Needham. Your husband was a good friend of our Da's."

"There's no love between our families," she replies quickly. "You're touched by evil. Come anywhere near me or mine again, and I'll burn your house to the ground."

"Did you hear that, everyone?" Will announces, spreading his arms wide. The people nearest us back away. "Margaret Needham, threatening us, and outside a church, too. Which of us is touched by evil, may I ask?"

He tries to catch the eye of Reverend Daniels, but the clergyman doesn't return his gaze. Robert Archdale, who invited Will to dinner only a short time ago, looks down at his feet. His wife is hiding her face behind a handkerchief. I think again of the image Mary put in my mind: of Elizabeth Archdale cradling a little skeleton child. Are we any further from that, now we've killed Nathaniel and Harry? How can I stand aside and let Mary and Will carry on with sacrifice after sacrifice? The next time, it could be someone like Isaac. It could be Isaac himself.

"Come on," Mary mutters, threading her arm through mine. "Mrs Needham's grieving. She doesn't know what she's saying."

"I do. I know more than you think. When did you get that, eh?" Mrs Needham reaches out to touch the cut on my lip. I flinch away. "When did you get that, I said? Same night my boys died?"

"Can't remember," I say, my face warm.

"But you must be able to remember *what* happened. Who hit you?"

It's so tempting to look at Will, and in that look to say, *Him! He's the one you want!*

I shake my head. "No one."

Mrs Needham's sister puts her arm round her shoulder,

saying, “Come along, now,” but Margaret pushes her away.

“You’ve got summat to do with this!” she shrieks. “I know you have. The Devil follows you out of that hole and whispers to you to do its bidding. You’re not protecting us. You are the curse upon this place!”

A scream ripping from her throat, she lunges at me. Her nails dig into my cheek and rake down, drawing tears from my eyes, and I lash out, but Will stands between us and shouts, “That’s enough!” and I feel myself being pulled away from the church, away from everyone else’s burning stares.

Mary asks me a thousand times if I’m all right. I say, *Yes, yes, don’t worry*, though my cheek is inflamed.

“She’s an old witch,” Will declares. “A scornful old witch, and everyone will see that now.”

“They won’t. They’ll see a woman mad with grief,” says Mary.

“We should go back and—”

“No point causing a big scene in front of the whole parish. We’ll sort her out later.”

I pull away from Mary. My eyes are stony with lack of sleep and crying, my cheek and lip are raw, but there’s strength in me yet. “Sort her out? What do you mean by that?”

“Oh, you know,” she replies, nodding back towards St Thomas’s. “Some families are ill-fated.”

“Would you make her youngest children orphans? They’ve been through enough.”

“At least they have graves they can visit,” she replies sourly. “Poor Mam, buried outside the church grounds just because she…"

Because she took her own life. Because her ghost, dark with despair, would stain holy soil.

"We have Da," I say.

"One grave doesn't make up for the lack of another."

"I know. But we *can* visit Mam, at the crossroads. We can visit her now."

Mary looks at Will, who's fallen quiet. Could it be that even he is having doubts about any more *accidents* after the scene that's just passed?

"We can visit the crossroads if you want," he says to me, looking over the scratch marks on my face. His eyes are filled with something I don't see too often: remorse.

"I want to see her," I say quietly. "I want to see Mam."

We head towards the crossroads at Sparrowpit. On the way, Mary collects witches' thimbles, fennel, and dandelions from the hillsides and ties them into a bunch with a piece of string from her hair, snapping off the longer stalks.

We weren't told precisely where they buried her, so Mary lays the flowers right in the middle of the meeting place of the roads to Castleton, Dove Holes, Chapel-en-le-Frith and home. She places a rock on top of the stems so they don't blow away.

We stand in silence, heads bowed. I want to reach into the earth and fold my arms about Mam's thin, broken body.

I want to go back in time and be by her side on the days she couldn't do much but drift in and out of sleep. If I'd tried hard enough, I could've cleared the fog in her mind. Too many times, I simply accepted it as the way things were. My God, if I could talk to her now, we could be each other's medicine.

"It's bloody cruel, putting her here," Mary says. "Her ghost'll never find its way back to us."

"Wait."

Will picks up some stones from the roadside. He makes an arrow with them on the ground, pointing down the road that leads to Peak Forest and Castleton.

"We'll leave a trail for her."

All of us gather enough stones to make two or three arrows, and every few hundred yards, we stop and make one. What we're doing, simple as it is, far surpasses the showy funeral with its coffins and horse and carriage. Burying Harry and Nathaniel with their own hands! I'll bet that was never in her husband's will. My earlier distaste for Margaret Needham's display of mourning comes back again, stronger than before. How much of what she was doing sprang from a need to be pitied?

We leave the last arrow a yard or so from our house. Putting it right outside our door would draw too much attention.

"There we are," says Mary, hands on hips. "Now she'll find us."

"What if someone kicks it about?" I say.

I sound like a child. Of course someone'll kick it about, whether they mean to or not. It wouldn't make a difference.

She's not coming back to us. Like Thomas, she's lost out there in the wild, wind-battered regions.

He didn't deserve to have a dignified resting place. If he got his rough hands on Sarah, the bastard probably left her ravaged and bleeding on the moorland. What's that he said about love? *An uphill struggle to a castle in the air, but up close, it's only a pile of rubble.*

A castle. Rubble.

He couldn't have meant… Could he?

At the time, I thought he was being poetical. But what if he was telling me, plainly, where he'd been with Sarah before he stripped her of the jewellery and left her? What if, all this time, me and Isaac have been overlooking the most obvious place? The host at the Cheshire Cheese said Sarah wanted to see the sights. Where better to see the sights than from Peveril Castle?

The revelation cuts through me like lightning.

Chapter Nineteen

I reckon it went like this.

Thomas rode from Bolton and stole into Sarah Pulmer's gardens after dark, as they'd arranged. She'd lit a candle in one window to signal she was waiting. At the sight of him, she flew past her chamber door, where her husband was sleeping off a generous serving of sack that deadened him to the world. She flung herself into the brawny arms of her lover. She was wearing the necklace he gave her in the heyday of their courtship, which glimmered through the folds of her black cloak.

In the saddle, she pressed against his back, wrapped her arms round his thick waist and let the waves of his breath lull her into dreams of a new life. Pride bloomed through Thomas, and, for each mile they travelled, another crease fell out of his lined face. Sarah would return him to the full vigour of his youth. They'd have many children, and he'd regain—

But wait.

If they were so content with each other, why would they tip into arguing so soon, as the man from the Cheshire Cheese said they did?

Let's say instead that they rode along in silence, unused to being so close, and by the time they got to Castleton, it was late. Sarah was weary. He wanted to carry on, until they were further from Hathersage. But she insisted that they stop at the Cheshire Cheese for the night. They bickered. She wept and said she wanted to go home. He told her it was too late for all that now.

They set off early the next day. Sarah reminded Thomas that he'd promised to take her to see the sights. She wanted to go to the Devil's Arse or climb Mam Tor. *There's no time for it*, Thomas said.

But he'd promised.

All right. They'd see Peveril Castle.

Sarah pouted. *It's not one of Thomas Hobbes's Wonders of the Peak.*

Isn't a castle good enough for the princess?

The hill to Peveril is so steep that I have to bend in the middle to give myself better balance. Several times I stop, panting, and scour the hillside for scuffed-up patches of grass, plants rolled flat, loose soil—any signs that someone might have fallen, or been pushed, from the top—and find nothing that causes the hairs on the back of my neck to stand on end. Above, the curtain wall rises high from the earth. From there, you'd see for miles. You'd feel like the queen of the world on a good day. On a bad one, the view might only serve to remind you of how small and forgettable you are.

Thighs burning, I force myself up to the summit of the hill and pass under a crumbling arch. Dust rains down on me. A rook takes flight, as surprised by me as I am by it. As I step into the bailey, the bird sails overhead and shoots through one of the windows of the castle keep.

I walk alongside the curtain wall, the sounds of horses' hooves and traders' shouts drifting up from street level, towards the foundations of what, judging by its size, might've once been a banqueting hall. The empty space in the middle becomes a stage, on which a scene is played out. Thomas, though quite some years his lover's senior, is more used to walking and riding, and he soon grows weary of traipsing around the ruins.

Let's go, he says. *Visiting places like this is too risky. People might see us, and then where would we be?*

I want to go home, Sarah replies. *My cousin will miss me. My husband will miss me.*

You didn't pay them much mind before.

I didn't know what I was doing.

Don't give me that. You knew exactly what you wanted, wench.

She lays a white hand on his. *Thomas.*

When he doesn't answer, she gets down on her knees. He likes her like that—begging, getting herself dirty for him. Out here, among the ruins of rich men, the blood comes rushing to his loins. He clasps the back of Sarah's neck and pulls her towards him. She pushes back against his calloused hand, but she's no match for his strength.

If he was going to do violence to her, he'd have done it somewhere no one could interrupt. The castle keep, looming ahead of me, seems like the most fitting place.

Care killed the cat, as they say. Still, that doesn't stop me climbing the groaning wooden stairs to the entrance. It's hard to believe that this place was still being used for prisoners and some official business when Mam and Da were small and Grandam was a young woman. Since then, people have stripped the lead off the roof and the open skies have worn away the walls, turning the stones a sickly shade of green. What remains of the floorboards looks too soft and weak in the middle to walk on. Some of the wood has been hacked apart.

Hacked, like Thomas's skull caving in with a wet crunch. I see the pulpy mess of his face under my hands; the way he rolled into the Hole; Mary, slicing off Nathaniel's ear along with half of his face. I squeeze my eyes shut till the green-black imprint of the stones fills my vision.

I search the old garderobe to see if I can find any objects that might've fallen out of Thomas's or Sarah's belongings. The only thing left behind, apart from the smell of shit, is a clay pipe that could've belonged to anyone. The other chambers contain nothing of interest either.

There must be something here that leads to Sarah. The idea of the castle came to me after so many dark days, came to me so blindingly, I can't see it as anything other than a revelation.

Oh, no, no, no, Janey. The voice of the Spirit claws inside my skull. *You're here because you're trying to convince yourself Margaret*

Needham is wrong about you, to persuade yourself that you're on the side of God. But the fallen angel does follow you, and She whispers in your ear.

"Leave me alone!" I shout.

Wings beat above me. When I look up, there's no bird, just an empty patch of sky.

I'm gripped by despair. When my life comes to an end and I'm waiting for my final judgement, God will unroll a scroll twice the length of my body, every bit of which will be covered with scribblings of the vile acts I've aided. I try to balance my family's evils with some good, but I'll never live a life of open-spirited generosity. No one will ever come to my door, asking for help, and then leave quietly so that I can have an evening to myself.

The closest I've ever got to such peace was in the stone circle with Isaac. For him, I'll do the best I can, whether it's a way out of my own life or not. It's all I have to give.

A staircase winds from the ground floor to the parapets, tight and slippery. The narrow steps look so damaged as to be unusable in places. I'm about to dismiss any thought of climbing them when something snags on the edge of my vision; there's a ball of paper on one of the steps. My stomach jumps. It's the most promising thing I've seen since I got here. The problem is, it's high up.

On my hands and knees, I begin to crawl. The stone is cold and slimy as a frog's back. Walls press in on either side. Thomas would have struggled to get up here, being the broad-shouldered man he was. Then again, if Sarah dashed away from him, up to the very top of the keep, he'd have followed. He'd have done anything, I suspect, to bend her to his will.

A few of the steps have ruptured into loose stones. I could get to my feet and climb over them, but that would mean balancing, and everything in my body trembles at the thought of toppling backwards down these twisting steps, of falling like Harry. Holding my breath, I clamber on all fours up the piles of stones that used to be steps, my petticoat soaking up dirt, rainwater, and the tiny scurrying things that now rule this place. The scrunched-up paper is just out of arm's reach. I stretch as much as my stays and bodice will allow. My fingertips brush it and knock the paper further away. Swearing, I stand, lunge forward and grab it.

The ink is rain-blotched, though not enough to be unreadable—if I could read whole sentences. The words dance in squiggly lines before me. Then, at the bottom, I see them, written in the same manner as the initials on Thomas's engraved knife: the letters, TM. I take a closer look. There's a date written above—the 28th—but the rest of the scribbles swim before my eyes.

Take it to Isaac. He's educated. He'll be able to read what it says. This is precisely what I wanted, isn't it? A sign of Sarah's presence. A token of my determination to help Isaac. No matter what Mrs Goodwin thinks of me, or what regret Isaac might have felt the other night, he'll have to see me now.

Unsteadily, I turn. There's more chance of me falling headlong if I crawl down the stairs on hands and knees, and so I tread slowly, carefully, avoiding the stones that could tumble.

And then I stop. At eye-level, there's a reddish-brown stain pasting a few golden hairs to the stonework. I peel away the hair. It's the same colour as Isaac's. Dry flakes fall onto my fingertips, smelling of the rags Mam used to clean herself after the dead girl-child was born.

Nausea rises in me as ghosts play out what happened here three weeks ago. Sarah, her gown torn, flees down the steps. Thomas's rough, prying hands grab her hair. With a sharp tug, he smashes her head against the stone. The side of her skull cracks, sense slipping out like an egg yolk. She staggers down two sets of stairs that bounce sickeningly before her eyes, missing her footing, falling to the cold stone floor below. The last thing she sees is Thomas striding towards her, fists clenched.

I fly towards the marketplace, feverish with the hope of seeing Isaac again, fretting over what I'll be able to reveal to him. I can admit that I've heard of Thomas Mace, even that I've met him once. All other details of that meeting, I need to keep to myself. I'll show him the letter and tell him of the bloodstain and hair. There were no other traces of Sarah. I checked the bottom of the keep and the hillsides, but there was no body. Thomas must've disposed of her in another way. He must've—

Dimly, I register that someone's calling my name. The market square settles back into place as I stop and take in the vagrant by my side, who wears only a tattered shawl over her head, despite the chill.

"I don't have any money on me," I mutter.

I'm about to cross the street when the vagrant pulls back the shawl, revealing a tangle of dark waves, her wine-red birthmark and a necklace hung with glass in the shape of teardrops.

"You're Will Vernon's sister, aren't you," Bess Jenkins says.

I should've known I'd run into her sooner or later. "Who told you that?"

She lifts a shoulder. "You look a bit like him. There's summat about the face. I thought I saw it the other day."

I can't help but feel some pride in being compared to Will, whom I've always thought handsome, even if it's not doing me any favours at present. "What do you want?"

"I need you to be on my side." She lays a hand on the slight bump of her belly. So it was true, what she told him. Will is a father. Something inside me melts.

"What do you want?" I ask, more gently.

"I want you to give him a message," Bess says. "Tell him to visit and bring the money he promised. I can't carry a bairn when I'm hungry."

"He won't see you again. He said so."

"Then can you take me to him?"

I imagine the fury on Will's face when he sees his mistress in the middle of Peak Forest, the necklace he stole from Thomas glinting on her raised collarbones. "No," I say. "You mustn't go there. You mustn't ever go there. It'd be better for you if you sold that necklace and got the money that way."

Her fingers flutter to her neck. "Still coveting it, are you?

Where's that strange creature who was with you last time? Money enough and still after my jewels. Hm! Both of you should leave off me."

She's a spirited wench. I can see both why Will was taken by her and why he wanted rid of her. "I'm being honest with you, Bess. It'll be better for you if you sell that jewellery and leave Will be. He won't be pleased to see you."

"Why? Is he ashamed?" She doesn't sound self-pitying, as I might expect.

"Not ashamed, no."

"What, then? He doesn't want to look after the life he put inside me? It'll be born in a few months. I'm not going to be left on my own when my time comes."

"Then you'll have to find another man to take care of you both. It might not even be his."

"Will's the only man I've lain with for the past year."

Somehow, I find it hard to believe. "Well, he says it can't be his. Let the matter end there."

I scurry across the square and down by the church. Bess's cries pursue me like wild dogs. "Don't you walk away from me, you bitch! I'll find him myself, if you won't show me. I'll knock on every single door and tell everyone in the village that the bairn is his. He'll pay for what he's done to me."

Bess doesn't follow. At least, not close enough for me to see as I hasten through Castleton, Hope, Bradwell. It's early afternoon by the time I reach Foolow. I'm faint, but still, I walk. I take the road that runs alongside Eyam Moor and allow myself to dream again. If I could go back to that day with Isaac, I'd do it all different. The stone circle—that's where I should have let him hold me, in the middle of that charmed embrace. What if I'd never gone home? I'd never have witnessed what happened to Harry and Nathaniel. They'd still be dead, but not burdening my conscience. I could have tasted the sweeter sin of lust.

A sin, that is, according to Reverend Daniels. Who's to say the ancients would have thought it so? The old gods might've lapped up our pleasure.

I stop in my tracks.

A figure with golden curls is walking about fifty feet away from me. It looks like Isaac, but it can't be him. She wears a bodice and petticoat the colour of dying heather and a cloak the colour of earth.

"Sarah?" I call.

As she glances over her broad shoulder, our eyes meet. The panic of a cornered quarry flashes across her face—a face that looks so familiar, yet so strange.

God be thanked, she must have survived whatever Thomas did to her back at Peveril Castle. She looks well, all aglow from her walk. Oh, how Isaac will jump for joy when he sees her again. Smiling, I open my arms.

"Sarah Pulmer. We've been looking all over for you."

She lifts the hem of her petticoat and runs.

"Mistress Pulmer! Wait!"

I spur myself on after her, but my legs are weak after the

long walk, and I watch, my heart sinking, as the billowing cloak glides across the moor. To get this close, and then lose her! As I run through the heather, my toes crash into something hard, and I stumble forwards, arms flailing, and fall. My thigh thumps against the ground, but the pain of that's nothing compared to the sharp scratch of my ankle smashing against a rock.

"Christ Almighty!" I stand and look at the damage under my petticoat. The skin is scraped off and beading blood. I'll have a bruise tomorrow, but nothing worse than that.

On the moor, there's no sign of Sarah. Still, the hairs on my skin prickle with the sense that she's nearby, watching me. My eyes dart over the skeletal trees.

"Listen! I know all about Thomas. I know how he must've done you wrong. I want to help. Isaac is waiting for you at home."

A rustle comes from a shrub on my right. A patch of shadow detaches from the green, hesitates for a moment and streaks away.

I run after her, stumbling over my own feet in the heat of the chase. The rainwater that soaked my petticoat drags me down. Sarah is swift, but her cloak is catching the wind and, rather than making it easier for her to glide, it seems to be keeping her from pelting at full speed. She tries to tear it off, which delays her more, and I leap forward to close the distance between us, wincing at the pain in my ankle as I land. Abandoning the efforts to rid herself of the cloak, she breaks into a sprint, but then a bump sends her flying, and she falls. Hardly has a curse escaped her lips before I've pinned her between my legs and crouched over her lower back. More curses come pouring out, this time, directed at me.

"It's all right. I won't hurt you."

I attempt to turn her over. She resists, thrashing and kicking.

"Stop it! I swear to God, I'm not going to—"

Then, entirely of her own free will, she flips onto her back and gives me a shove. I land, hard, on my arse, and there we are, looking straight at each other. I blink, my mind flickering in and out of reality. I can't be seeing what's right here before me—the kind, handsome face of Isaac, stripped of his beard.

Chapter Twenty

ISAAC

It was Aunt Ruth who first suggested it. You can buy yourself more freedom, she said. No woman of our family should be wandering the length and breadth of the Peak country alone, especially in a state of distress.

I would not be distressed, I told her.

"But what if Sarah is nowhere to be found?"

I could not answer that.

"Come along," said Aunt Ruth, heading upstairs.

A great chest stood in the chamber where she used to share a bed with my uncle. Aunt Ruth handed me the key. As the key clunked in the lock, I looked over my shoulder, seeking her permission to open the lid. Even with her blessing, I felt like an intruder as I opened it. The mustard-sharp smell of unwashed clothes wafted into the air. Aunt Ruth pressed a knuckle to her mouth, stifling a whimper.

"I don't have to touch them," I said.

She lifted one of my uncle's shirts from the chest, letting it fall out of its folds, and buried her face in the material. For a long time, she stayed like that, breathing him in. Eventually, she lifted her head.

"I should've given them away after he passed, but he always took such pride in how he dressed. I couldn't bear the thought of anyone else wearing them."

Then surely, I thought, I shouldn't be wearing them. I'd read what people think of the women who deck themselves in men's attire. The moralising pamphlets say that they become immodest, quick to anger, war-like; ruining the God-given image of Eve's form, they make themselves stranger than any beast that was ever aboard Noah's ark. I'd always thought such inflated rhetoric ridiculous, but now I was considering transforming myself, the words buzzed around my head like flies. It seemed irreverent to use my uncle's clothes for this purpose.

"I can find a shirt and breeches elsewhere."

"No, love." She gestured for me to stand. "These will look well. It'll be a pleasure to see them worn. Let me help you change."

She untied the bodice and stays that squeezed my ribs; the heavy folds of my petticoat fell to the floor; hen-flesh rose on my arms as I stood in only my undergarments. She slipped the shirt over my head. It was pleasantly loose and cool, though the sleeves were so long that they covered half my hands.

"We can always adjust," said Ruth as she rolled the material up around my wrists.

Next to go on were the blue breeches, which looked far too big until I pulled them up and fastened them around the middle. The bottom of the legs would need taking up, but other than that, they fit comfortably if a little loosely on my gangly body.

Piece by piece, I became a different version of myself. The last item to go on was a short yellow doublet, trimmed with blue. The garment buttoned securely about me—an embrace, but not a crushing one. For the first time, I was glad of my flat, unmotherly chest. Still, it would have to be bound so that not a trace of femininity lingered.

Aunt Ruth stood back, a soft smile reaching slowly to her eyes. "Go and look at yourself."

She led me to the mirror. My nerves tingled. I didn't know who would greet me. A cheap copy of my uncle? A monstrous hybrid of woman, living, and man, dead? The figure who stared back at me snatched away my breath.

"You make a handsome lad," said my aunt.

He was handsome indeed, this stranger who, I realised now, I had known all my life. He was there when my sisters invited me to play mothers and babies with dolls, and I would take on the part of the father. He was there in the afternoons I spent at my family's drapery, admiring the cut of a customer's garments, and how effortlessly I might be able to wear clothes like that instead of playing dress-up in my gowns. He was in my dreams of dancing and flying, and now, even though my feet touched the ground, I was filled with that same levity.

I loosened my hair and let it tumble past my elbows. Already my thoughts were running to how I might trim my locks and fashion a beard. My imagination was venturing over the hillsides, spinning me into dizzying joy, and now, now that my cousin had gone…

Forgive me, Sarah. Forgive me for finding myself, and not you.

Chapter Twenty-One

The eyes are the same—polished with flecks of gold, thick-lidded, scored around with laughter lines. Yet the straight, defiant set of the lips, the chin cleaving where it comes to a point: these aren't features of my Isaac.

"You're—"

"A woman?" Still breathless from the chase, the stranger huffs a humourless laugh. "I didn't think you'd have to grapple me to the ground to reach that conclusion."

Damn her for mocking me. As if crawling about in the dirt weren't enough.

"I knew something wasn't right."

"Did you?" She holds my gaze. There's a kind of pleading in it. I look away.

"Why?" I ask. "Was it all just sport, trying to bait me?"

"It wasn't about you." Red-faced, she gets to her feet. She grabs a handful of material at the back of her cloak and picks at the mud that's stuck to it. "I only dare walk alone in my own clothing near Aunt Ruth's house, and my search for Sarah takes me further afield, as you well know. It would've been neither safe nor seemly of me to stalk around the county like this."

"So Sarah exists, at least."

"Of course Sarah exists."

"Isaac doesn't though, does he?"

"Oh, Jane." She lets go of her cloak, and it flaps down by her legs. They don't look as thin as they did before. That'll be because she's only wearing a bodice and sleeves at the top, not layer upon layer of masculine garb. "I *am* Isaac. There is no difference between him and me apart from the clothes I wear."

There's a world of difference, I want to say. Isaac could have whisked me away to London, set me up in a home far from Elden Hole and Will and Mary. I'd have had to take on the role of mistress—I didn't deceive myself for a moment that he'd have married someone like me—but that would have been better than nothing. Now the promise of all that is gone.

The woman takes a step towards me, extending a hand, but then thinks better of it. I get up by myself.

"You tricked me," I say.

Her gaze drops. "I am sorry you feel that way. It wasn't my intention."

"You used me to try and find out more about Sarah."

"If that was my plan, it didn't work. The only time you told me the truth was when you mistook me for her. Who…?" She takes a trembling breath, as if a dozen birds are beating their wings in her throat. "Who is this Thomas? Is he the man who took my cousin?"

"I'm not acquainted with any Thomas," I reply. Why

should I trust this woman?

"Liar!" she roars.

I sink my teeth into my lower lip and wince with pain as it opens up the wound Will inflicted. As blood drips into my mouth, the affection I felt for Isaac flares into something hot and urgent. I want to wrestle this woman to the ground again, pin her under me.

"Funny, that," I say, "coming from someone who's been lying the whole time."

The lips that used to flatter me curl in contempt. "Tell me who he is, or—"

"Or what? You'll spread it around that I've been spending time alone with a man of much better birth? What if I tell people you're a lass? What'd they make of that, eh?"

That wipes the scornful look off her face.

"Who do you think they'd believe?" she says. "The merchant from London, who can pay handsomely, or the rustic with a head full of old wives' tales?"

There we have it: what she really thinks of me. Oh, the masks are flying off today.

"They'd believe one of their own," I shout, stung. "You're an imposter. You don't belong here."

She opens her mouth to answer, but nothing comes out. My words tumble into the silence. "You know nothing about me or this place. I wish you'd never come here. All you've done is cause trouble. If you know what's good for you, you'll go back where you came from."

She stifles a sob with a too-delicate hand. "Jane…"

"Don't use my name so freely. We're strangers."

I leave her weeping on the hillside. Isaac wouldn't weep like that. There's nothing of him left. She created him, then slew him without giving me a chance to say goodbye.

But what never existed can't be killed. I can't grieve for a person who never was. She had me blinkered like a horse and led me round the county by the nose. For what? To get a thrill from having power over me?

She called me a *rare jewel* after dinner at Mrs Goodwin's. It was cruelty, making me believe such things. I bet she had a laugh over it that night.

Shame hollows me out. What man like Isaac would take an interest in me? I'm too dull of mind to see when people like Thomas or her are using me for their own ends. No, not dull of mind. Wilfully blind. It suited me to think that Thomas was convinced by my show of interest in him, even though, if I'd have thought about it, I could've recognised that he was playing his own game. It suited me to think that the woman who tricked me was truly Isaac, a man who cared for me, despite where I came from and what I inherited.

Another sort of shame consumes me, then. I've reduced a lone woman, who walked by my side for days, to a state of distress and abandoned her. What I said to her was nasty. I never knew I was capable of such cruelty.

Don't fool yourself, Janey, the high voice of Elden whistles in my ear. *Only a few days ago, you stood by and watched two men being murdered.*

The house is silent. Not the kind of silent it normally is when Will and Mary are away. It's heavier than that, as solid as the carriage that bore away the bodies of the Needhams. Something that should be here—that's always here, like part of the house itself—is gone. There's another thing. It smells foul in here, as it does when an animal has emptied its bladder or bowels. It smells of terror.

I call Lordsmeer's name and get no trill or pad of feet in response.

At this time of day, he's usually sleeping on Mary's bed, a snoring circle of black and white. From time to time, he squeezes himself into the gap between the bed and the wall, and so, gripping onto that hope, I go to check. He's not there, but something else is: a wooden box, one that Da carved himself. The lid is engraved with what I've always taken to be a giant honeycomb. Tracing the pattern of chambers and passages, I see now it's Elden Hill. Da gouged out the top of it to make the Hole. Underneath is a hollow nest—chamber after sticky chamber of things that sting and bite.

Mary's box of keepsakes. My fingers twitch to lift the lid. Though Will disallowed her from keeping items from our sacrifices—*we feed and we sell*—I saw her cutting a lock of auburn hair from Nathaniel's scalp the other day. Her grim treasures make me sick. I put the box back where I found it.

With rising panic, I call for Lordsmeer again, looking in

Will's pile of tools and in the butter churner. Another place in the house, another sign of my guilt. The purse of Thomas's money is still hidden in that corner—my share, which could've gone to Nathaniel and ended this feud between our families.

"Lordsmeer!"

I go round the back, the cat's name on my lips. The sight that greets me robs my voice. Our new hens, all of them, are in a pile. Their heads have been twisted clean off.

Dear God, not again.

Knees smacking the ground, I clutch my stomach and retch. There's not enough air, and maybe that's it—I'm dead already and this, this is my eternal punishment: to bear, alone, the guilt of innocent lives lost.

The door to the storeroom is ajar. An odious smell comes from it, an odious mixture of urine and sulphur. Madness lies on the other side of that door. I picture our cow, Fie, lying on the ground, the globes of her eyes glassy and unblinking as flies land on them, her entrails snaking out of a steaming, bloody slit in her body. Yet it's worse, somehow, not knowing for certain what's there.

As in a nightmare, my arm reaches out of its own accord and touches hay, cold earth. And then, something soft. In that instant, I know why Lordsmeer wasn't coming when I called. I drag out a limp body. His green eyes are open, unseeing.

I press my face into his matted fur, curling my hand under his legs so that he's safe within my arms, and I howl.

That's how Mary finds me. She's saying something I don't

understand as she tries to get me to my feet. I can't move. She opens the door to the storeroom and slams it again immediately. Her chest rises and falls. She's got tears running down her face. It's one of the few times I've ever seen her cry. Even as a bairn, she never cried.

"Come on, let's get you inside," she says.

Mary brings me in and sits me down before the hearth, then sets to work making a fire. It takes her a few goes, she's in such a state. All the time, I'm nursing Lordsmeer, rocking him back and forth, telling him that everything will turn out well.

Once the fire's going, Mary kneels by the chair and strokes the damp fur. "Oh, little man. Little Lord." Tears dash from her eyes again. "Can I hold him, Janey?"

The flames are gorging on the wood in the hearth. A terrible fear possesses me that Mary will burn his body. I shake my head and clutch him closer to my heart.

"Please, Jane, please. I want to hold my cat."

She means him no harm, I see that now. I pass Lordsmeer into her arms as if he's a sleeping baby. She kisses his head, paying no mind to whatever poison has stopped up his veins, and strokes him.

"I'll wrap him up," she says, sobs choking her words. "We'll give him a proper burial tonight, all right?"

It's not all right. It can never be all right.

She lays his body on her bed and folds the sheet about him. "We'll give him a proper burial," she says again. "Our little man."

Mary presses her forehead into the bundle. She stands and

takes a deep breath. She goes to the cabinet, opens a flask of ale and pours us both a large measure.

"Here."

She presses the drink into my hand. I sip slowly, feeling guilty even for that, for being able to drink and go on breathing.

"You know the cows are gone, too?" she says.

I didn't think my heart could get any heavier, but it does. What a fool I was, to think I could save myself from damnation, to think that finding a piece of paper at Peveril could outweigh the punishment of a fallen angel. "Both of them?"

"Aye, both. Fie is in the storehouse. The older one died up on the hill. Elizabeth Archdale came into the inn and told me. What a terrible waste. It's not like we can eat them. It'd be like eating poison. I'll have to nick some food from the stores at the White Hart." Mary sinks down by my feet again. "Why, Jane? We gave Elden Hole a small offering the other day, not to mention the much bigger one recently."

"She doesn't want scraps."

Mary sits up on her haunches. "How do you know?"

I'm not supposed to be telling Mary what I heard in the dream, but the words are out now. "She spoke to me in my nightmare the other day. She's not asking for more people like Thomas. I don't actually know what it is She wants. That's why I thought we should leave off sacrifices for the time being."

"Jane, you know what happens—"

"That's what you'd think, isn't it? But look at what's happened today, Mary. We gave Her an offering of a whole man not long ago, and we've got nothing but death in return."

She lets out a pent-up breath. "Could it have been Margaret Needham that did in our animals, then? Margaret and John, together? They hate us. They'd gladly see us—"

"No, Mary. You don't understand."

I press the heels of my hands into my eye sockets until dark clouds burst. What if Mary's right? Mrs Needham could've taken revenge on us. God knows, we've done enough to her. I still remember the way Grandam looked at little Rebecca when she was first born. Mam and Da went soft at the sight of that plump angel with huge feet. Grandam, meanwhile, looked at her with cunning, like she was a ripe plum to pluck from under Harry's nose. Not that she'd do it herself. That was Will's job.

I heard them talking one night, after Mam and Da had passed. I heard how Grandam wheedled her way inside my brother. *An unsullied soul would be the greatest offering.*

Sickened, I haul myself back into the present time.

"It's not Margaret," I say. "No matter what we've done to her, she wouldn't do that. She couldn't, not without people seeing her."

"The village is on her side," says Mary.

"Elden Hole took our animals before. It's a message."

Mary presses my arm. "What if you speak to Her again?"

"I'm not certain I can. She comes to me. In dreams. In waking dreams. She speaks in my ear, but I don't call upon Her."

"Why don't you try?" asks Mary, her eyes desperate. "Go up to the Hole and… I don't know. Give Her something you think She might want."

"Like what?"

We've never had to do this before. Our grandfather spoke to Her once, but no one else ever has, as far as I know.

"Think about what She said to you," Mary urges, shaking my arm. "There must be summat you can give!"

My business is with you, Jane Vernon. I tire of scraps.

George Bradley gave himself: the blood from his rope-bound legs, the sweat of his brow, his sanity. If I give Her a taste of me, that might just be enough.

I use Thomas's dagger. There's a neatness to using the weapon belonging to a past sacrifice—the same weapon that Will used to stab Nathaniel, that Mary used to peel off part of his face.

The recent kill seems to have whetted its blade. It slices into my skin so cleanly that I don't even realise the cut's been made until blood starts to channel down my palm. Then the pain comes, like a high ringing in my ears. I grit my teeth and let the blood drip into the open mouth of the Hole, thinking all the time about the story of my grandfather's meeting with a fearsome being of wings and promises and blood, a thing that Grandam called an angel.

The offering gets caught in a trembling web of nettles and shrubs. I squeeze harder. A faintness steals over me. If I'm not careful, I'll feed the Hole more than I bargained for.

Wind cools the sweat-drenched hairs sticking to my forehead. "Come to me," I whisper. "I'm calling upon you."

The hillside sounds of cows lowing and sheep bleating grow distant. Rooks spiral off towards the heavens. I roll to follow them. Something's happening. It's as if I'm drifting into a dream without being asleep.

"I'm calling upon you."

The ground shifts beneath me, rocks grinding against rocks, delivering me into the Hole. And yet I still feel the press of the grass against my back. I close my eyes, and visions rush upon me.

A circle of light blazes in the sky: the sun, flattened like a coin. It shrinks away, getting smaller and smaller. Shadows swarm from all sides, amassing over the light and soon, all that's left is a pale slit of grey, and then that, too, knits together.

I'm enclosed in darkness. It's crowded, full of things that can only be felt, things that can watch you, even though you can't see them. The thrashing of blood in my ears becomes the beating of great, leathery wings above my head. Hot wind stings my eyes, carrying the stench of sulphur and the rot of carrion meat and the tang of blood. I hear the rustling of feathers and the clack of spines as the thing settles before me.

"You called."

From below comes a deep growl that makes the rocks shiver. A flash of red, like a fire raging in the depths, turns the blackness a muddy brown. For a moment, only a moment, I see a mass of bristles hunched before me.

My soul tries to scramble out of my body. I drag it back and take a quivering breath. "I did."

"What do you require?"

I'm here for answers, for justice. Questions spit from my mouth like burning sparks. "Was it the Hole that killed our livestock? Our cat?"

"She sends Her Spirit out over the face of the earth."

"Are you that Spirit?"

"I am."

Another flash of fire lightens the depths. It shows the bulky outline of the creature within touching distance of me. A rank stench grabs at the back of my throat. Dim light catches the gleam of a skull-like head that seems to be attached to the spiny body backwards. Darkness closes in again.

"Did you kill our livestock?"

"*You* killed your livestock," the voice of a hundred dead animals says.

"I did not, devil!"

"You didn't do as I asked. You gave Her inferior meat."

The foetid smell is so overpowering now that I daren't open my mouth too wide, lest the poison of the creature's presence seep into me.

"What in Christ's name are you?" I ask. Sweat trickles down the side of my face.

"Nothing, in Christ's name."

"Who do you answer to, then, if not God?"

"I answer to Her. I am Her—a Spirit, made manifest."

"What are you? A devil?"

A scream, shrill as a horse's whinny, bursts from the creature. I put my hand over my ears. The noise dies down to a low growl. "I am hunger," She says.

"What do you want?"

"Everything."

Hopelessness presses against the bars of my ribcage. "Then how can I give you what you want?"

"Elden Hole will never be satisfied. But if you give Her that which causes you the most exquisite pain, She may be pleased—for a few hundred years."

"So She'll… You'll… leave us alone?"

"I will do more than that."

A sharp claw or hook nicks my cheek. It stings, but only for a matter of seconds. The release that follows sends tingles rippling through my body. Something wet, warm, and firm darts out to lick the blood that trickles down my face. I like the feeling of it against my skin. The stench isn't there anymore—or rather, it is, but it's musty and mushroomy in a way that makes me want to eat or be eaten.

A breath of hot wind travels down my navel and between my legs. A warm and wet mouth presses against my loins. The rage that burns away inside me tips, oh so easily, into an itch of lust that throbs with the heat of a thousand infections.

"Will you do it?" The voice purrs from below.

I want to scream that yes, yes, I'll do anything to burst in an agonising and beautiful explosion. Let the bonds holding the elements within their limits come undone. Let disorder reign, direful and free.

Some unclouded part of my mind forces me to ask, "That which causes me pain? What do you mean?"

The heat in my loins fizzles out and twists into a sour cramp in my bowels. When the voice speaks again, it's far away, a whisper that might be made of the wind. "Think on it, Janey. Think on it."

The darkness peels back, and I'm staring up at a blank sky.

Blood oozes from the re-opened wound and pools in my palm. My eyelids are heavy, as if I've woken from a long sleep, and yet much of the panic from earlier has leached out of me along with my blood.

She sent Her Spirit out over the face of the land. She killed the livestock and Lordsmeer. I have my answer.

I have my answer to Her riddle as well.

That which causes the most exquisite pain: myself. My own unnatural desires that only She can satisfy.

We'll have peace for a while. Mary, Will, and his child will be safe. Never again will they have to make offerings or suffer the loss of their loved ones. All this, in exchange for my soul.

Chapter Twenty-Two

"Mrs Goodwin is not receiving visitors today."

The housemaid stands between me and a conversation I need to have. It's not her fault. She'll have been told to give the same excuse, no matter the hour or the day.

Duchess slides through a gap between the servant and the doorframe and jumps up. At least something is pleased to see me. I'll miss animals, the way they give their love so freely. I ruffle Duchess's soft ears, my eyes beginning to water, and step back.

"What about Mr Latimer? Can I see him?"

"I'm sorry, Mistress."

"Is he sick?"

"No, Mistress. He's not in."

"He's not in, or you've been told he can't see me?"

The maid's lips quiver. Poor thing looks like she's about to cry.

"Look, if he's here, you need to fetch him. This is important. I—"

A stern voice comes from the hall. "Thank you, Abigail. I'll take charge of this."

Tap tap goes the crutch across the tiles, and soon, the sleep-starved face of the servant is replaced by Mrs Goodwin's solidity. "Mr Latimer is not in."

Fate wouldn't be so cruel. Not when me and Isaac have crossed paths so often before. It wouldn't deny me one last meeting, a chance to say goodbye. "I can wait."

"He hasn't said when he'll be back."

"He?"

It's the only hand I have left to play, and it stumps Mrs Goodwin. She could be a thing carved of stone, so still is she then. "It's all right, Abigail," she says quietly, guiding the servant aside. "Let Mistress Vernon in."

The hall isn't half so welcoming as last time. Isaac's company lit up every corner. If the rafters had been falling down around us, I wouldn't have remarked on it. Without him, the hearth fire burns low. The long table, bereft of its fine pewterware, draws attention to how lonely this big house is with only Mrs Goodwin and her servants in it. My host takes the same place she occupied the other night and gestures for me to sit opposite. In the daylight, the armour worn by the soldiers on the tapestry gleams as though it's made of real metal. In that empty hall, I can hear the clash of swords as the armies meet in the middle of the bridge, and the scream of men as they fall into a deep blue river. One soldier has his foot planted on a fallen man's back while he drives a spear through his shoulder blades. Another is forcing the head of his enemy underwater.

"Did any of your ancestors die in that fight?" I ask.

Mrs Goodwin smiles. "No. The tapestry shows an ancient Roman conquest. Though it won't be long till the River Irwell is awash with bodies, with Lord Strange and his popish army about to lay siege to Manchester any time soon."

"So much cruelty and death," I say, "and for what?"

"For the right to be ruled as you choose."

"It means nothing. All of this will pass away."

"That's true. But is it not important for even the smallest of us to stand up against tyranny?"

Though they're not related by blood, Mrs Goodwin and Isaac share a quality more defining than hair or eye colour: they both refuse to meet the world as it is. My heart is flushed with tenderness for this family.

"Thank you for letting me in today," I say.

"My argument was never with you, Mistress Vernon. I was furious with Isabella for inviting you to stay like that."

"Isabella?"

"Isaac's birth name. You didn't know, did you?"

All at once, I could cry. What a thing to keep from me. "Why did she want me to stay?"

"I'm not certain," Mrs Goodwin replies. "I think she forgot herself."

Forgot herself? It hadn't seemed like that to me, but then again, what do I know about Isabella Latimer? I only learnt her name a few moments ago.

"She does as she wants these days. She's off now somewhere, or rather, Isaac is. She must've learnt this sort of daring from our Sarah. Now *she* was untameable. I put it down to not having a mother when she was a young woman. Her father spoilt her rotten. I kept telling him that he let Sarah get away with too much, but he said he didn't want to be one of those fathers who treats their daughters like horses, to be bridled and reined in. Well! I was worried at first, but then I saw what a clever little creature she turned out to be, and I—" She presses a fist to her mouth. Her eyes scrunch, and I pray she doesn't weep, because then I won't be able to hold back my own tears. "Wait a moment."

Gripping the table, she gets to her feet unsteadily. I come round to her side and put the crutch into her hand, which is bent and swollen at the finger joints. I've never seen a hand so old, apart from Grandam's.

"Thank you," she says. "I'll be back soon."

Once she's gone, I crush stale breadcrumbs on the table with my nail, as you'd burst head lice. It puts pressure on the skin round the gash in my hand. Mary dressed it again after my meeting with the Spirit yesterday, softening it with oil and applying honey to stop infection. The two of us were quiet as she worked: I, not daring to speak; she, more than a little envious of my talent for talking with things beyond our realm. I'd give her the ability, if I could. Afterwards, we burned the hens. There was no question of feeding them to Her. It'd anger Her to consume the livestock She'd killed as a warning; such things aren't good enough to be offerings. Besides, it'd stick in my own throat to nourish Her with what was stolen from us. When Will got home, he and Mary took apart the cows, limb by limb, and added them to the fire. Then we buried Lordsmeer in the shade of a yew tree near the old hunting lodge and chapel.

How long would it be, I wondered, until funeral rites were being conducted for one of us? If all goes to plan, it'll be me. Though there won't be a proper funeral for a woman who throws herself willingly into a pit. Will and Mary can make arrows out of stones to guide my soul out of Elden Hole and back home. Little will they know that I'll be bound in that Hell pit for eternity, the Spirit sucking me dry, bringing me to the peak of ecstasy, licking away all traces of redemption with a burning tongue. The good I'm trying to do now won't save me. But it may make other people's lives better.

Mrs Goodwin returns with a pile of papers, loosely stitched together.

"Isabella's drawings. I thought you'd want to see them."

It takes me a moment to remember who Isabella is. "I've seen the one of Sarah already. It was good."

"These are the ones she made when she was much younger, from when she came to stay with us. She often visited, though her parents despised this part of the country. They didn't get along, her mother and my husband. They fought like cat and dog. Isabella and Sarah, though, became close as twins."

Jealousy stabs me in the gut. "It was thoughtful of you to keep these pictures safe."

"Isa wanted me to."

Between the yellowed front and back pages are light, shaky drawings of this house, flowers, snails. Though they're not as good as the ones I saw in Castleton, they're still much better than anything I could ever make. There's one of a slender girl sitting by a stream. It's more detailed than the others; I can tell from the way the face is tilted up that it's a warm day in spring or summer, and there's hours of idling ahead. I ache to step into that picture.

"Is this Sarah?" I ask.

Mrs Goodwin strokes the corner of the page. "That's Isabella. Sarah drew that one. She has more skill than Isa—it's her who taught Isabella how to draw. Let me show you my stepdaughter."

She turns to a full-page drawing of a face with full lips and eyes round with wonder, but slightly shadowed underneath. It's similar to the sketch Isaac—Isabella—was showing people in Castleton, but in this drawing, coils of hair escape from a hood embroidered with birds.

"Did Isabella do this one recently?"

"No, no. This is Sarah when she was about… oh, fourteen, fifteen, I'd think. Not long after she lost her mother, in any case. That hood was her mother's last gift. Sarah wore it so much that we got copies made." Mrs Goodwin closes the book.

"She was very pretty," I say. I have no right to envy a woman who grieved the loss of a parent at such an age.

"Isabella used to be terribly protective of Sarah when they

were both younger. She was like a guard dog, snarling at men if ever they came too near Sarah. She must've taken her eye off her at some point."

"Yesterday..." The memory of it lies heavy in my heart. "I thought it was Sarah at first, on the moor. I was so pleased to have found her, but..."

"But you found Isabella."

"It astonished me."

"I'm sure it did."

I won't tell her about my anger and the cruel words I said. "I was trying to find Isaac—to tell him about this."

I press the crumpled paper into the widow's hand. Her eyes travel from top to bottom, two, three times. Her face turns ashen.

"Where did you find it?" she asks in a choked whisper.

"Up at Peveril Castle. We knew Sarah had been to Castleton—someone told us she stayed at an inn with a man." I press my nails into my palms. "A man by the name of Thomas Mace. Now, I can't write or read full words, but I do know my letters, and the initials TM are on that paper. I met him once. He's a scoundrel and a knave. If he's indeed the one with Sarah, then no good will come of their association. Can you understand what he's written?"

Mrs Goodwin nods. "My husband taught me to read, just like he taught Sarah her letters in English and Latin. He was a good man, my Samuel."

"What... what does it say?"

She wets her lips, and Thomas Mace's words pour out.

Bolton, August 28th, 1642

My dearest one,

I cannot match the authors you and I so admire, being a mere merchant and not a poet. But believe me, my lamb, my heart is flaming with longing for you. I count the days until we can live together as man and wife.

We will see some of the Wonders that so enchant you, including the cave whose name you blush to relate (false modesty!). From there, we will travel across the country by coach and horses and, at Dover, board a ship bound for Italy. In Venice, we will make a new life. I shall continue trading and you, my sweet, can glut yourself on sugared wine and the pleasure that has been denied us both in our dry, loveless marriages.

I have cloth to sell along the way. Do not overburden yourself with bags. You are leaving your old life behind, after all, and we can buy more as we travel. I have the wedding band I promised you. It will look fine on your pretty hand. If you must bring one thing with you, let it be the necklace I brought back from Venice. It was my first promise to you of a bright and shining future overseas.

You have had your doubts, I know. It is a dangerous and frightening thing to leave your home, but love shall lend you courage. Put aside those killers of joy—prudence and modesty. They are for old maids and foolish girls. You are neither, little lamb. You are my very own, just as I am your most true, most loving,

TM

Mrs Goodwin puts down the page with a trembling hand. "He can speak well when he wants to."

Shame he didn't speak so well at the White Hart. He must've been at his wits' end, having argued with Sarah and done away with her. His plans changed completely—gone was the prospect of sailing from Dover with the woman he claimed to love. Instead, he was untethered, heading for Liverpool port and causing trouble along the way to prove he was still a man. I'm rent apart in all directions. I'm disgusted by him. I'm angry with him. I pity him.

"You know him?" I ask Mrs Goodwin.

"Thomas did some business with my husband in Bolton, and they stayed in touch. They even talked of going into partnership for a while. My husband was impressed by him at first. Thomas was well-travelled, eloquent. But the better my Samuel got to know him, the more he saw another side to him. Mr Mace could be… scheming. His wife is very god-fearing. Likes to hear a preacher such as Richard Heyrick railing against the Catholics, won't allow any jollity on a Sunday, that sort of thing. They were an ill-matched couple if there ever was one. Doubtless, she tried to convert him to her ways. She's still living, as far as I know, and they have children together. How devastated she must be."

Marriage is a punishment, he said. A punishment harsh enough to drive him into the arms of his friend's married daughter. Harsh enough to send him out of his mind and into our path.

"And Thomas knew Sarah… well?"

Mrs Goodwin's face is swept clean of expression. "He spoke to her a bit whenever he came to visit us here. Pleasantries, nothing more. At least, that's what it looked like. He was married, God forgive him. I never thought… I didn't…"

She trails off into silence, staring straight ahead. Now is the time to tell her, while we're talking of Sarah and Thomas. Painful as it is, she's got to know.

"At Peveril Castle," I begin, "I saw that piece of paper screwed up on some spiral steps, and near it were signs that Sarah might've got into some trouble… as in, she might've slipped. There was a little blood—"

A sob breaks from Mrs Goodwin's throat.

"Not a lot, by any means. But she was hurt."

How badly did Thomas injure her? Enough to kill her? True, I found no fair young corpse on the mount, but there's no end of places to hide remains round there.

"The caves and hills in Castleton—you need to search them. Peveril Castle is right next to the Devil's Arse."

I take hold of the widow's papery wrist. Her pulse feels strong enough to tear through the skin. "Sarah might have… ended up in the cave after she was injured."

I wait for her to catch my meaning. Mrs Goodwin licks a tear from her top lip, distractedly. "This is our fault. We should never have let him near her."

"Did you hear what I said, Mrs Goodwin?"

She turns her face to me. "Bring them back to me, won't you? Both of them. My Sarah and my Isa."

My heart breaks for this woman who's lost so many of the half-wild things she's tried to tame. But she's not lost everyone. Not yet.

“I’d never let any harm come to Isabella, Mrs Goodwin. I swear it on my life.”

“You’d better honour that, Mistress Vernon.”

“I will. I will.” It’s as solemn as a marriage vow.

Mrs Goodwin, sighing, squeezes my hand with chapped fingers. She takes the letter, tears it to pieces and chucks the fragments into the hearth. I help her light the flame. Together, we watch Thomas’s words burn.

Chapter Twenty-Three

Lights from Peak Forest prick through the rain. At this hour, dinner will be over, children will have played the last of their games, and husbands, sore from a day's work, will be finding warmth in the bodies of their wives. When I think of other people's families, that's what I picture: something dull and predictable as the sunset and full of quiet shows of love. But no family's like that.

Once, there was a lad who lived in Wormhill. He loved the land and the secrets it held. *Wormhill*, he said, was named after a great, snakelike dragon or 'wyrm' that wrapped itself round the peaks in ancient times and swept birds from the air with a single flick of its tongue. Some appreciated his tales, but lasses found his manner odd, his tales frightening. Then, on the night of the Midsummer dance, he set eyes on a girl from outside the village. And so taken he was by her beauty, that he missed his step, recovered, missed his step again, and fell. When she laughed, the stars sang. She helped him up and followed him to the top of a hill. He showed her the lumps and bumps in the ground where the coiled skeleton of the dragon lay. She showed him how to make garlands for hobs and speak the language of blackbirds.

Six weeks later, they were married. He moved away from home and into the house the girl shared with her aged mother, Annie Bradley. The whisperings about her and her family didn't bother him, for he had a liking for anything out of the ordinary, and his new wife could mend clothes neatly and cook the best cakes he'd ever tasted. Several of their children died before they were born, but three lived, and they cherished each other, the five of them existing in a village within the village.

That's only one story. For every one of those memories I have of sitting by Da's feet and listening to his marvellous tales, there's another one of him coming back late at night, stinking of drink and his own piss and other men's blood. Mam was good at caring for us when we were young. When Mary was sucking at her breast, and me and Will played at her feet, she was content. I felt it as a slow pulse of happiness that spread from her to us. As we grew older, and Da stayed out longer; as Will learned from Grandam how to lure men away from the safe paths, she spent more and more time up at the Hole. I tell myself that things got bad after Mam and Da died, when in truth, the family duty has been hanging over us for a very, very long time.

Even so, nothing was as bad as that night six weeks ago, when my brother went up Elden Hill with Grandam and Rebecca Needham and only two of them came back.

A wave of faintness almost sends me falling to the ground.

There'll be little to eat at home, so I can only hope that Mary makes good on her promise to steal a few things from Alyson Bagshawe's kitchen.

As I approach the White Hart, I hear something that, for a long time, hasn't graced my ears—music. Through the misted glass of the window, I can see tables and benches have been pushed aside to clear some space in the middle of the room. To one side of this makeshift stage, the Weasel plays a lively tune on the fiddle, and drinkers—a fair few of them for a Tuesday night—stamp and clap along. For the first time since the Needham men died, folk seem to be passing time gleefully, even riotously. Edward, the kitchen boy, flits from table to table, serving up trenchers of food that make my mouth water. There's no sign of Mrs Bagshawe. It's Mary who's by the barrels. Arms folded across her midnight-blue dress, she's watching the room like a proper proprietor. Has she arranged for Walter to play music and told Edward to wait on people? Has she, one of the Vernons, compelled customers to forget what happened at the funeral the other day? She must've made that ale very strong indeed.

Walter's song finishes, the last note accompanied by raucous applause. He bows, revealing the table behind him, and the man sitting there.

The earth quakes. It's him.

Even knowing what I know, I can't see the smudged outline of the person inside the White Hart as anything other than Isaac. I wipe away some of the rainwater with my sleeve and press my nose to the window for a better view. The foul weather has turned the golden waves of his hair to yarn. Still, there's a dignity about him. A trio of men gathered about Walter the Weasel are looking across at this well-to-do outsider. Isaac angles himself away from them, and there, that's when I mark it—the fear of being exposed, set upon; a trace of the panicked woman I saw on Eyam Moor.

Mary is staring at him even as she passes a tankard to a thirsty Walter. The Weasel starts talking to her, but she mutters a reply that makes him leave quickly, drink in hand, tail between his legs. Then, she tilts her head back and gives a nod to someone over in the corner by the door.

Will nods back at her.

I duck away from the window and press my back against the inn wall, trying to push myself all the way through it so I can step out of the other side, grab those scheming bastards and wring their necks. They're not getting their hands on him. They are not.

Pain nicks my hand. I look down to see blood seeping through the bandage around my fingers. I've been picking at the wound again. Mary will tell me off for it, when she's done trying to lure Isaac to his death. Except, she won't have a chance to do that, because I'm here now.

The plans I've been weaving together over the past couple of days unravel. I was going to apologise to Isabella for the way I'd spoken to her and stay by her side as they dragged Sarah's body from the Devil's Arse or wherever the poor lass ended up. Before taking myself up to Elden Hill, I'd have given someone—John Needham, perhaps—a message to pass on to Mary and Will. *I'm sorry, but it has to be done. You need worry no longer.* And then I'd have thrown myself into Elden's jaws and ended the threat to the village for generations to come.

Now, my self-sacrifice would leave Isaac vulnerable to my family's schemes. Will and Mary might not even be convinced by the idea of my sacrifice sating the hunger of the Hole and, more likely than not, they'd carry out their plan to murder Isaac anyway.

I force my quivering body across the courtyard, through the back door and into the pantry. Having spent so long out of doors, the cold in the room doesn't hit me as it usually does. As soon as I catch the smell of food, I snatch one of the pork pies off the shelf. I'm too ravenous to pay much mind to the hard coffin of pastry that almost breaks my teeth. The inside is good, full of rich jelly, fat, and meat cooked with thyme and sage. I tear big chunks off it like a savage dog. Satisfying this most basic need puts me in a state close to rapture.

Licking my chops, I open the pantry door a crack and put my eye to it. The heat from the fire in the main room blasts the thin strip of skin running from my forehead to my chin. As chance would have it, the table closest to the hearth is also closest to me, and that's where Isaac has seated himself. If I took but a few steps forward, I'd be near enough to feel the steam rising from his damp clothes. Mary's over by Walter and his cronies, who're talking of Lord Strange's latest attempt to wrest control of Manchester from the Puritans.

"They're blocking up Salford Bridge, being shot at with musket fire," Walter's friend says. "Makes life bloody difficult for the merchants trying to get in and out of the city. Don't stop to think, do they, how all this fighting affects people just trying to get by? Won't be long before blood's spilt round here, you mark my words."

Fool. The affairs of king and parliament have little to do with us. The wild and desolate places of the Peak belong to nothing human. The autumn winds that rage around the hill-tops blow away laws like dust.

All the talk of war distracts people enough for Will to make his way across to Isaac unnoticed. My breath catches. I hold myself back from running out and breaking my brother's nose. After all, the more I know about what Will's planning, the better chance I have of stopping it.

"Mind if I join you by the fire?" he asks. He's rubbing his hands together and breathing into them with all the subtlety of a peddler belting out a ballad.

"Of course," says Isaac, gesturing towards a place next to him on the bench. He has a twitchiness in his movements that wasn't there before. Nerves, from being so close to a stranger? A stranger he's looking at with more than a casual interest.

My brother removes his hat, ruffling his crown of curls as he sits. "Cold weather, isn't it? Did you walk far to get here?"

"Not too far, thankfully."

"Tideswell, or…?"

"Eyam."

Will's already made himself quite comfortable in front of the fire with Isaac and found out where he's staying. Looks like my old friend opens his heart to anyone.

"And you heard so many good things about Peak Forest that you had to come and visit on a rainy night like this?"

"If we let the weather dictate what we did here in Derbyshire," says Isaac, "we'd rarely leave the house."

"That's true."

My brother wears a tight smile. Does he feel uneasy with Isaac? It wasn't like that with Thomas, who had money and wits but was so beastly that you couldn't envy him. Isaac is different. He looks and talks like a gentleman. Shame he's nothing of the sort.

As if he's picking up on my thoughts, Will says, "You don't speak like someone from around here."

Isaac takes a sip of ale. "I live in London most of the year."

"London? What brings you up to the Peak country?"

"I'm seeing the sights," says Isaac, every bit a man of leisure. "Thomas Hobbes wrote a volume on the Wonders of the Peak. I've seen most of them now. Only Elden Hole to go."

Every fibre of my body tenses.

Will's eyes flicker to Mary, but she doesn't see him. He bites his bottom lip. "What have you heard about it?"

"That it's the entrance to Hell," Isaac says steadily. "I don't believe it, though. Do you?"

A pause.

"There's more to this place than you might think," Will replies.

"Oh?"

"Back when my father was a boy, there were still plenty of deer, though they were kept inside the parish boundary by a high fence. Parts of it are still standing on the hills, rotting away now, and you might've seen the old hunting lodge opposite this inn. One by one, the animals were killed off—not by the king, but by us. There was no point in having them around, ruining the land for the sheep. When the commissioners came to divide up the royal forest into our part and the king's part earlier this year, they didn't find a single one. All the royal deer had been shot."

"All of them?" Isaac asks, turning to him, closing the gap between their bodies. His chest rises and falls under his doublet.

Will mirrors his movement. "Yes, all of them."

"Hm. I thought I saw an animal on the way here. It was too large to be a dog. Then again, it disappeared into the copse of trees before I could get a good look."

"There are other wild animals here," Will says. "My own father killed a wolf with his bare hands."

A disbelieving smile spreads over Isaac's face. "Did he?"

Will glances over at Walter's group of companions, wary, it seems, in case they want to join in the telling of this famous local tale, but they're so absorbed in their conversation with Mary that they don't seem to be listening to what's being said. Will's gaze slides across the wall, and I crouch down before it falls on me.

"Come into the back room," he says, "and I'll tell you some tales that'll freeze your blood."

My heart knocks inside my chest like a cannonball. *Don't snatch the bait, Isaac. Don't fall into the trap.*

"Tomorrow, perhaps," he says. "I'm heading to bed now. But thank you for the offer, Mr…?"

"Hollis," Will says, too softly for anyone else in that room to hear. "John."

"Mr Latimer. Isaac."

I imagine Isaac's bare, delicate hand sliding into my brother's. It makes me want to scream. It makes me want to smash this place to splinters.

I grind the fear and anger under my heels, stomping about the village until my head has cooled—if not completely, at least enough for me to face going home. Yet my blood still boils away as I'm trying to sleep. What does Isaac think he's doing? This is no flying visit. He's bedding down for at least one night. His trail has led back to us, as I always feared it would, but it won't end as he expects.

I once followed Mam all the way up to Elden Hole to see what she did there. At a distance from the sacrifices, her devotion to the angel was of a different character to Da's and Grandam's duties. I watched from over the top of the tumbled-down sheep pen as she cut nettles and thorns from the grassy slope that ran down to the edge of the pit. She crushed the stinging plants into her eyelids, pricked at her arms until they bled. I wanted to scream for her to stop, but Mam had told me before not to interfere with her worship. *It's very important, Jay Bird, that She witnesses our dedication. We are so small and insignificant and filthy compared to Her, the great angel who fell from heaven, who is everything and nothing.*

And so I watched in awful silence as Mam, her body inflamed and bloodied, felt around in her belt for a pouch of herbs and stuffed them into her mouth. She lay on her front, her neck dangling over the Hole, and screamed and wailed like a thing possessed. And as I watched, the darkness moved, like water flowing upwards, and it covered her head, her shoulders, working its way down her body. She made even more terrible noises then, her body jerking and spasming. They were the sounds of pleasure.

The door opens. Startled, I turn towards the wall.

"I keep expecting to find him here," Mary says. "Poor little lad. We'll have to get another one from Mrs Barnes. She's got cats coming out of her ears."

"You know what I could do with now?" Will says, as if she's not mentioned the Spirit's latest kill at all. "A hot pork pie. Crust an inch thick and dripping with lard."

"One went missing from the pantry. Edward the kitchen boy must've nabbed it."

Will starts singing. *"So passing my degree, not so contented still—"*

"But a king thyself to be!"

"How does the rest of that verse go? You're the one with the good memory for songs. *Wringing every wright, wringing every wright*… Oh, oh! That's it! *All the realm doth rue. That all the realm doth rue.*"

"Anyway, as I was saying…" Mary coughs. "The other day,

I caught Walter fondling the hem of my dress."

"Fondling?"

"Aye, and he was sniffing it an' all, like some pup around another dog's arse. I says, 'What're you doing, Walter?' and he goes all red and says, 'I thought I saw a stain on it.' So I go, 'Do you usually go about wiping stains off women's dresses?' To which the Weasel replies, 'Only if the dress is as pretty as its wearer.' The cheek on him!"

"Careful," says Will, stifling another laugh. "He might touch more than your clothes next time."

"I'd like to see him have a go. He'll wake up in the morning smooth as a… well, as a very smooth thing."

"A pebble?"

"Aye, but not as hard. Smooth and soft. An eel without length."

"An oyster, then," Will shouts in glee.

"Yes! He'd wake smooth as an oyster. You can do that, you know."

"Cut off his cock? I'm sure you could."

"No, I wouldn't even have to go that far. I'd only have to charm his eye so that he thinks he's lost his manhood. And the poor sod would be so bereft that he'd never bother me again."

"You'd miss the attention."

"I bloody wouldn't."

They talk for a while longer about the Weasel's father, who apparently caught the falling sickness and who got so used to staying in the house and having his wife and children tend to him that he's now round as a boulder, and how they wished they could grow fat and have folk wait on them, and whether Robert and Elizabeth Archdale's children are going to be pretty like their mam or have squinting eyes and a pug nose like their Da.

I listen for Isaac's name, but they don't mention it. Whatever plans they've made regarding the solitary traveller, they made them while out of the house. I've got to find out what they are and get to Isaac before they act on them. As if my legs are trying to carry me to him already, they kick out of their own accord, rustling the sheets.

"Look! Janey's back," says Mary.

Footsteps cross the room. The darkness behind my eyes turns from black to a deep, fleshy red as someone leans over me with a candle. Its heat licks my face. I suck breath in slowly, release it in a trickle.

"Sleeping the sleep of the innocent," Will says softly. "Either that, or she's tired out from fucking whoever she's off fucking these days."

They muffle their laughter. The chaff beneath me rustles with each thump of my heart. *Go. For Christ's sake. Leave me be, before you realise I'm awake.*

"It's a shame," Mary says with a new solemnity. "I love Janey."

A heavy silence presses down on the sheet.

"It is a shame," agrees Will.

He blows out the candle, and I'm swallowed by darkness.

Chapter Twenty-Four

ISAAC

I wonder what you'd have thought of him, Sarah—the man I met tonight. He had striking features. The dark curls of his hair around the angular face gave him a sharp kind of beauty. His eyebrows were identical lines, accentuating eyes that glinted like coal. He smiled charmingly, and yet there was rot between his teeth.

His looks may not have made an impression on me, if it weren't for the wide nostrils and his lips, pulled into a bow above a round chin. Those gentler features reminded me of someone. My curiosity was further awakened by all his talk of stories that would make my hair stand on end—an echo of what Jane told me that night after dinner. By the time I bid him goodnight, I suspected that I had finally met the brother she seemed to hold in such low esteem.

Certainly, they are different. While he talks in a measured manner, weighing every word and adding lead pellets to give his speech more gravity, there is no art in what Jane says. Yet it is true that she has hidden the name of Thomas from me, and more besides. Was her concealment *art*? Or did I simply choose to be blind and deaf to the hints she gave that all was not as it seemed? There is still so little I understand about Jane. Her heart is both pure and in shadow.

Upon leaving the so-called *John Hollis*, I happened across a woman sitting halfway down the back staircase, clutching her middle. She refused my help at first, insisting that, as I was a guest, it wouldn't be seemly. The poor creature seemed to imagine she was running the place. Finally, with a grunt of resignation, she leaned against my shoulder. I angled my body to the side, afraid that she'd feel the press of my breasts against her own, even though they were tightly bound.

"Shall I send for a physician?" I asked, once we'd ascended the final few steps.

"No need." She paused at her door, her chest heaving. "Was it William Vernon you were talking to just now?"

"He gave his name as John Hollis." My pulse quickened as I remembered the curved hook of that man's smile.

She gave me a dark look. "There is no John Hollis. That man talking to you downstairs is a Vernon."

I forced the next question from my throat. I had to. It was why I came back to this wind-blasted part of the county. "What do you know about the Vernon family?"

"A fair bit," she said, unease shaking her voice. "That girl, Mary—I don't know how she's doing it, but it's wicked, it's…" Her face twisted, as though she were experiencing an attack of colic and, holding onto her middle again, she drew a breath in through her teeth.

"Look, if you want to hear the history of that family, talk to Mrs Margaret Needham, who lives in the big house near the pond. Her husband and son worked with William."

"They no longer work together?" I asked, suspecting a feud of some sort.

She looked at me over her shoulder. "They were both put in the ground recently."

With a final grimace, she retreated into her room.

The shadow of dread that follows me grows ever more solid. It reaches into my chest and crushes my heart.

Did not the woman in Castleton's cook shop say she'd seen you walking towards Winnats Pass, in the direction of Peak Forest? I fear that Jane's presence at the Wonders, her secrecy, and now, her brother, all point towards one terrible truth.

Sarah, if William Vernon has wronged you, believe me—he will rue the day he was born.

And Jane? I cannot think what I'll do if I discover Jane has wronged me.

Chapter Twenty-Five

I can't sleep all night, not with those conspirators under the same roof. I stay as still as I can, sweat prickling my flesh, while Will snores in the bed next to me. Every time I change position, I hear movement from Mary on the other side of the room, as if she's keeping track of my tossing and turning. Her words echo in my ears. *It's a shame.*

Will's reply was swift as the thrust of a knife between the ribs. It's what he didn't say that bothers me most. They must've already spoken about how to get rid of me before I cause any more trouble.

I must be on my guard against them, more than ever before.

I wait till I can hear the steady breathing of both Will and Mary before heading into the early morning. It's fresh and cold out. Yesterday's rain has cleansed the land. Birdsong purifies the sky. It'd be a beautiful start to the day, if threats weren't stalking my every step.

No one gets in my way as I walk through the yard of the White Hart and up the stairs to the lodgings—no one, that is, apart from Walter the Weasel, who steps out of Mrs Bagshawe's quarters and almost sends me flying. Christ Almighty, Mrs Bagshawe must be desperate. This close up, the man stinks of onions, pipe smoke and dried sweat. He mutters a *'Scuse me*, before stopping to look at me properly.

"Jane Vernon! What are you doing sneaking round here at this hour? Paying a quick visit to someone, are you?"

Refusing to take the bait, I muster all the dignity I can. "I'm looking for the man who arrived last night. Isaac. Isaac Latimer. Do you know which room he's in?"

"The one dressed in fancy clothes?" Walter nods down the corridor. "Last door on the right. Why do you need to speak to him at this hour of the morning? Do you know each other?"

"We've met before."

"Hm! Well, I reckon he won't appreciate being roused so early."

With a throat full of rattling laughter, the Weasel salutes me and wafts past, no doubt on his way back to his long-suffering Jennet and their litter of squealing bairns.

"Wait!"

He stops.

"Mrs Bagshawe. Alyson. Is she all right?"

"She's been better," he says. "Why? Do you know what's afflicting her?"

"No. But I thought you might."

"It's not *that*, if that's what you're thinking," he whispers, looking over his shoulder towards the corridor. "No disrespect to the woman, but she's past the age when she can bear fruit. I don't know what's wrong. To tell the truth, I'm worried about it."

"Have you tried taking her to see anyone?"

He crinkles up his veiny nose. "It's woman's business. She's got to sort herself out. Trouble is, she's as stubborn as they come."

"She might need your help, then," I say. "Whether it's woman's business or not."

"Aye. Aye, I could ask. No harm in that." He nods as if he's never considered the thought before, and slides an oily smile across to me. "Ta, Janey. You're all right, you know. You're all right."

The quality of my character, praised by the biggest lecher in the village. Lord help me. I wait till he's gone, then walk down the low-beamed corridor towards the end room. I knock quietly, so as not to rouse anyone who's managed to sleep through my chance meeting with the man who gives weasels a bad name.

On the other side of the door, a bed frame creaks. I knock again, louder, mimicking the pounding of my heart.

As footsteps approach, I stand back, smoothing down my gown.

The door opens a little, not enough for me to see a face. "Who is it?" says Isaac. A version of Isaac, anyhow. One who speaks more slowly, more hesitantly, as if the mask is not fully fitted yet.

"It's Jane. Look, I'm sorry for turning up like this so early, but—"

The door shuts on me. I'd rather take a hundred of Will's slaps to the face than a single one of those decisive thuds.

"How did you know where I was staying?"

Though muffled, the voice is spiked with anger. It's risen, and I'm in no doubt it's Isabella I'm speaking to, rather than her more welcoming self. She *is* talking to me, though. That gives me some hope.

"My sister told me," I say. "She works here."

"And how did your sister know who I am?"

"She… she didn't. Just talked about someone who looked like you, and I put two and two together, given you've been here before." I catch my breath. "Did you come to see me?"

"Why would I come to see you?"

"We didn't leave things well."

"Indeed."

Another pause. I put my ear to the door. No sound comes from the other side. I wouldn't put it past her to be lowering herself out of the window with knotted bedsheets at this very moment.

"Let me in. I need to talk to you."

"I'll have no truck with people who hide the truth."

I slam my palm against the door. "*You* hid the truth from *me*! Why did you ask me into your home and invite me to stay the night? Were you mocking me?"

"Of course I wasn't mocking you." She sounds more hurt than angry.

"Then why?"

When she doesn't reply, I rest my forehead against the door

and wait for my heart to stop its mad galloping. "Look," I breathe. "I've come to tell you something."

"Do you know where Sarah is?"

I clench my fist. "Let me in and I'll explain. I think I know what happened to her, but there's something even more important you need to know. You're putting yourself in terrible danger. If you're not careful, you're going to end up dead. Do you understand?"

Behind me, a door clicks open. Footsteps come charging up the corridor, and Mrs Bagshawe grips my shoulder.

"Jane Vernon, what do you think you're doing, disturbing my guest?"

"I'm not disturbing anyone."

"Are you going to leave my premises without any more fuss, or do I have to chuck you out on your sorry backside?"

"You don't have to touch me." I shake her off, pulling down the sleeve that's rucked up. "I'm going."

She prods the small of my back, goading me away from the door. "Go on, then. Off with you."

I'm halfway down the corridor when I turn back. The woman who was Isaac hangs out of the door, golden hair tumbling over her white shift. In this light, she could almost be him. Longing splits my heart.

She dives back into her room before the hostess has the chance to see who's really staying in her chambers.

"Wouldn't have had you down as a drunkard, Jane Vernon," Mrs Bagshawe says.

"I haven't been drinking. But…" Will's flabby-throated

snoring comes back into my mind. "Was my brother in here till late last night?"

"None of your business."

"Was he?"

"How should I know?" she grumbles. "I was early in bed."

The hostess drives me out into the yard and stands blocking the door, a big hoop of keys swinging from her waist. I'm seized by the nightmare thought of never seeing Isaac alive again.

"Mrs Bagshawe, keep an eye on Mr Latimer, will you? Don't let him leave here."

"Don't tell me what to do with my own guests, you bloody Ver—"

She doubles over, grimacing and clutching her belly. The attack lasts for a good few seconds. I lay my arm across her shoulders till it passes. When she straightens, her usually ruddy face is drained of colour. With a scowl, she shrugs me off.

"If I… if I see you in here again… then I'll cut your s—sister's wages."

The back door of the inn slams. A key clunks in the lock.

Poor Alyson. If she thinks she has any power over Mary now, she's even more ignorant than I am; and if Isabella thinks I'm going to give up my guardianship over her, then we truly are strangers.

There's almost nothing left of the royal hunting lodge now. Long before Grandam was born, it was a small court, where those who dared to poach or trespass on royal land were tried. Some say that kings drank wine and played chess there, then took communion in the chapel next to it before setting out across the hills with dogs and horses. The chapel is far too small to fit the congregation of villagers, hence why we have to traipse miles to Chapel-en-le-Frith for our services, and the roof shingles have been plundered by villagers short of coin.

The lodge's altar, once draped with white cloth and set with chalices, is spattered with bird shit. Ruined as it is, I think twice before standing on it; the chapel is still God's house. Yet if the Almighty objects to me using a piece of furniture in this way to save a soul in peril, He's got His priorities all wrong.

I push aside the branches that prick through the roof rafters. From here, the view to the White Hart is clear. Soon after I begin my watch, Mary arrives at the inn in her deep blue dress, lifting it off the ground so as not to sully the hem. She looks occupied with thoughts, though I can't tell if they relate to the running of the inn or affairs at home. I watch the miners come in for the first drink of the day, and set off to work a short time later, louder and more cheery. Will is not among them. Edward the kitchen boy runs in late, buttoning up his shirt as he goes.

The sun rises higher in the sky, and still there's no sign of Isaac. What if Mary is doing the deed alone? She could sneak into his bed chamber and hold a pillow over Isaac's face. Then again, she'd have to get the body out if she's intending to use Isaac as a sacrifice, and she'd need Will's help for that. I'm beginning to worry that Will's managed to get into the building without me seeing, when Isaac steps out of the front door. Relief floods my veins. Under the inn sign, he smooths his beard and adjusts his hat in the customary way that melts me a little inside, and sets off towards the pond.

Standing and waiting for him to appear was simple, if tedious. This next bit is much harder, given I've never been blessed with grace of movement.

I picture the shadow in the story of the Tideswell Butcher, how it flows like quicksilver alongside Robin Moody. I become that shadow, dropping soundlessly from the altar and drifting over the cracked stones of the aisle. When I emerge from the chapel porch, Isaac is already a fair way down the road.

He passes our house and heads straight to the big pond, where three ducks enter a gabbling argument and one mallard sends his weaker rival skidding over the surface. In the calmer waters, a reflection of Isaac treads the sky and stops at the gate-post of the Needhams' house. What can he want with them? I run through the conversation he was having with Will last night, and I'm sure that the Needhams weren't mentioned. He must've heard news about the funeral swilling round the White Hart. There can be only one reason why he'd involve himself in it, and that's to find out more about me and Will.

I almost run towards him then and tell him not to believe whatever Mrs Needham says, but John comes out into the yard. Isaac introduces himself to the lad graciously and asks to speak to his mother. John, older and sadder by years since last week, walks Isaac into his home.

I sit on a rock by the pond and wait. The sun's heat sups up all traces of last night's rain, though it's too weak to send down much warmth. Weariness creeps up on me and covers my eyes. A few times, my chin drops to my chest and my mouth falls open, and in my half-awake state, I'm certain that something is slinking round me, circling. I rouse myself, and the presence dissolves to nothing. I'm shivering. I should have coated my skin with a thick layer of grease and wrapped myself in woollen blankets. I'll freeze to death before I find out what Isaac's doing.

Finally, he emerges. On the doorstep, he clasps both of Mrs Needham's hands in his. She embraces him, a thing I've never dared to do. I envy her, then, even in her mourning.

Isaac's face is a blank as he leaves. It's an expression he must've picked up from his aunt. I know from my meeting with her that it means the very opposite of blankness. Inside, he's getting as churned up as the waters under the webbed feet of waterfowl. I should've eavesdropped by the casement and born witness to the bile Mrs Needham spurted against me. At least then I'd know what I was dealing with. Oh Christ, if Will had an inkling of what Isaac was doing, he wouldn't let him live another day.

He walks in the direction of Elden Hill. His broad-brimmed hat tilts back as he stops and looks towards the summit, regarding something up there. The Spirit of Elden Hole, rising to greet him? The hairs pricking up on my neck tell me She's not that far away. She's at my back, twig arms within slitting distance of my throat. I whip my head around and see an empty road.

Rather than turning up Elden Lane and walking the path that leads to the Hole, Isaac continues onwards, along the road that runs through the valley, all the way to the Chathams' house. Gilly Chatham is famous round these parts for coupling with her husband's brother, Stephen, a few days after her marriage. Her husband promptly took Stephen's lady love, and the four of them now live together in relative quiet, breeding horses and selling them, among other things. I can understand him visiting Margaret Needham if he'd heard rumours about how my family acted during the funeral, even about Will's work up at Highpit Rake, but why he wants to pay a visit to the Chatham household is beyond me.

As Isaac wends up to the farmhouse, I squelch through the waterlogged field opposite, trying not to make too much of a splash. I dip behind a barn and watch as Isaac knocks. Gilly answers the door. They exchange a few words, too quiet and distant for me to hear, and, once again, the outsider is invited in with a warmth I've never experienced.

This time, I fear the wait. I turn slow circles on the spot to get a full view of my surroundings: the hills rising behind, the road that winds out towards Castleton, the Chathams' house in front, the road back to Peak Forest. Hills rolling, the road to Castleton, house, Peak Forest; hills hemming me in, the bustle of Castleton far removed, the house a blur, Peak Forest—Peak Forest stretching on and on into the hills hollow as honeycomb, a writhing mass beneath the ground, blind things striving against each other with open jaws, lunging towards soft flesh to kill and suck.

I stop, disorientated, and catch my breath. The house is still there. The sun in my eyes made it seem to disappear.

Isaac comes out of the house with something in his hands. It's nothing pertaining to horse-riding, as I suspected it might be, but two lengths of thick rope—the type you might use in mining or to make a noose. He pulls it, testing the strength, and smiles to himself.

The sun sinks like an impurity to the bottom of the sky. Somewhere in the distance, a fox shrieks. From the chapel, I've watched miners return to the White Hart, wash the dust down their throats, and go home to their farms. I've watched Walter the Weasel sneak round the back a few times. His wife must be blind, an idiot, or simply relieved that she isn't getting the share of his attention. Since this morning's trip to the Needham and the Chatham households, Isaac hasn't been out again.

The cold has crusted my joints, thickened my bones. I'm as stiff as a tree that's grown up through the centre of the altar. Stiffer, even. There's life in the branches behind me that causes the leaves to rustle. Whenever I squint through the darkness to see what's moving, inky shapes of dark blue cloud my eyes.

The mystery of that rope tightens and tightens. My mind twists itself away from the most obvious possibility—that Isaac's found out something about our family that, wrongly, ties us to Sarah, and he seeks revenge. His slender hands could never knot a cord about our necks, could they? Not without a malign influence guiding them. But if Elden Hole can send Her Spirit out over the land to kill, what's to say She can't worm into people's heads and make them do Her bidding? After all, Her hunger is great, and I haven't yet given myself to Her as a sacrifice. She may be devising other means to get me down Her throat: having my own siblings turn on me; forcing Isaac to commit an act of murder.

A quick, strong shudder of the branches behind me awakens the instinct I share with the birds, rabbits, and mice. Though my vision is weak and the darkness thick, I stare through the glassless window of the ruined chapel, deep into the trees that surround it. There are shining dots in the distance, but they're too far apart to be eyes. They're wavering as candlelight wavers in the breeze.

I hold my breath. I'm both a hundred miles from myself and reined to my galloping heart as I stare harder into the night, trying to discern what's out there.

Something the size of a cat brushes against my leg.

It *brrs*, just like Lordsmeer used to do. But it can't be him, because he's dead and gone. The Spirit of Elden Hole can take on the voices of other things. Slowly, I look down. A clot of darkness slips off the altar and hides beneath.

"Get out," I breathe.

A limb, dark and paw-like, reaches over the edge of the altar, lengthening and bending in a way that no living creature could. It pats softly, trying to feel whereabouts I am. I stagger backwards, pressing up against the wall. Then another limb, this one made of a bundle of twigs yet agile as a spider's leg, plants itself by my feet. From below the altar, a heaving bulk of darkness rises up with an agonised groan.

I half leap, half tumble to the ground and land face-down in the weeds that push their way through the cracked flagstones of the old aisle. Behind me, the sounds of mewling, bleating, and pained breath grow louder as the Spirit of Elden Hole advances towards me. Her footsteps are uneven, the gait a strange mixture of bird hops and the dragging of heavier body parts. I close my eyes, frozen. What will I see when She finally turns that skull head round?

A sharp nick on the skin of my ankle sends a bolt of panic shooting through me. I try to push myself upwards, but the Spirit grasps my foot with Her bramble-like fingers and pulls me back, so I fall again, hands and knees scraping against stone. A hot, warm mouth closes on the cut in my palm and suckles, and it's good. Teeth scrape against flesh, barely sinking, teasing. I twitch with desire. Then I'm dragged backwards, the lights of the White Hart fading, shrinking, and I'm at peace. The Spirit can have me, if that's what She wants. That which causes the most exquisite pain. Aye, myself, myself. I'll give all I am to Her.

And what about Isaac? I am not protecting him. I must get him away from Peak Forest, from Will and Mary.

I look back over my shoulder. The only part of the Spirit I can see is the twigs wrapped round my foot. The rest of Her has disappeared into the shadows under the altar, where She is taking me. A den of foulness, set up in the very house of God.

I kick out. The Spirit strengthens Her grip.

"One more day," I cry. "Let me have one more day, and then I'll give you what you want."

I have waited long enough, Janey, She says.

"One more day, or else you won't get me. Will and Mary'll give you Isaac instead."

Does he not cause you the most exquisite pain?

Is that what She meant—not myself, but Isaac? Isaac, who treated me as someone worthy of his respect, who followed me through the dark and into the stone circle where, for an afternoon, the sun stood still in the sky? It is a pain sweet as childhood's end, to think how he was never mine. Even so, there is hope. When Isabella hung out of her door to watch me go this morning, I saw a glint of Isaac in her eyes.

"No," I say, "not he."

I kick again. This time, the Spirit lets go.

One more day, She says.

A single day to convince Isaac to get out of the village before Will and Mary pounce on him and divide the spoils between themselves and Elden Hole. My brother stands between us. He would not hesitate to do what must be done if I get in the way. A single day. It does not seem possible. And yet, many things in this dark and wild part of the country are.

"One day. Then I'll come to you," I vow.

I clamber to my feet and scurry out of the chapel, just in time to see Will walk through the front door of the White Hart.

Chapter Twenty-Six

The back door of the inn is locked. Mrs Bagshawe must be making good on her earlier threats to keep me out of this place, despite her feebleness. Going through the front is out of the bounds of possibility, if I want to 'scape Mary and Will spying on me. The only way in is through a window. As chance would have it, one of the ground floor windows is unlatched. It's on the wrong side of the building to the pantry, where my brother will no doubt try to lure Isaac for the promised conversation that will make his blood run cold. At least I'll be out of earshot as I scramble through the open window. I can only hope that no one else is in here.

To check, I give the pane a nudge. It scrapes along the wood, and I listen for any gasps of surprise or complaints about the wind. When none come, I push it all the way open. The room beyond is darker than the night outside, as even the endless sky is lit by stars. The impression of dim shapes, humped together, is created not by sight, but by the thickness of the air.

I'm reminded of a time, many years past, when I woke

at an ungodly hour to find the house full of grunting figures. With sleep-bleared eyes and a head full of Da's tales, I thought they must've been hobs come down from the hills. I curled closer to Mary, for we shared a bed back then, and pulled the sheet over my head. If I was still enough, I told myself, they wouldn't know I was there. As I pricked up my ears, their grunts transformed into familiar words, spoken by voices I knew. Peeking out from a gap in the covers, I saw by the firelight Mam, Da, Grandam, and others whom I soon recognised as Mr and Mrs Needham. There might've been more people, though I know not whether they're the figments of my mind or miners whose faces I've long since forgotten. Intrigue triumphing over fear, I wormed out of bed.

Old Harry Needham smiled down at me. "Janey!" he wheezed. "Did we wake you, love?"

Shy, I curled up in Mam's lap and wrapped my arms about her neck. Her thick, matted hair smelt of wood fires and the safety of her body.

"Why's everyone here?" I asked.

Mam kissed me wetly on the ear and whispered, "It's Christmas Eve, Janey—the most magical of nights. And here you are. The magic has brought you to my arms."

A magical time of year it must have been, to draw other people around our hearth in the middle of the night without fear of who we were and what we did.

I pull myself headfirst through the window, struggling and striving like a bairn coming into the world. Halfway through, I get stuck, the wooden frame pressing into the nubs of my ribs, my stomach being pushed back towards my spine. I thrash my legs and tip far enough forward that my head feels leaden and my eyes feel ready to pop with all the blood rushing to them. Then I grab hold of what must be a wooden table leg and *thunk* to the floor. What a sight I'll be when I see Isaac tonight. I'd worry about it, if it weren't for the bigger troubles like not getting him or myself killed.

The room, as I thought, is almost full. My hands slide over the dusty surfaces of chairs, tables, and dressers Mrs Bagshawe must've decided to store away when she made the downstairs of her home into a place for guests to drink and make merry. She's got a lot, apart from her health. I wonder if her son, sired on her by a husband ten years dead, will come back here and claim it all after she's gone. The world's full of widows like her and Mrs Goodwin, and there are more to come if the fighting between the King's men and the dissenters continues.

I creep out of the room. A puddle of light spills from under the pantry door. There's talking. There's the grey perfume of pipe smoke. I've made it to them, nearly.

As I turn to close the door of Mrs Bagshawe's storeroom, I'm caught off guard by a face staring back at me through the gloom. Her lips part in a gasp of surprise. As I raise my hand to take off my skewed coif, she does the same. We loosen the riot of dark hair tied at the back of our necks, and it tumbles between our shoulder blades. I've never thought of my wide, flat face and square jaw as pretty, but tonight, I look at myself in the dust-veiled mirror on top of the pile of furniture, and I'm struck that Mam's unearthly beauty and Da's strong features weren't all given in unfair proportion to my brother and sister.

Isaac saw something in me, after all. But now he's talking to my brother, alone. What if he sees the Vernon features that charmed him when he looks at Will? Would that make him forget whatever impulse drove his purchase of the rope? What a mixed blessing that'd be. I stalk along the corridor on tiptoe until I'm outside the door of the pantry. I crouch down and listen, breathing as lightly as possible.

A silken voice says, "You've never made the descent?"

Joy leaps in my breast. I'm so glad to hear him within arm's reach that the only words I catch of Will's response are, "… good enough price as yet."

They can only be talking of one thing. Isaac asked before whether anyone has been lowered into Elden Hole. What is his aim—to use our family history against us?

"And what if I were to offer you a considerable sum?" he asks. "Would you do it?"

I hear the rustle of Will's clothes. "Depends how much."

"Nine pounds," says Isaac.

Will's laughter echoes round the room. "You don't mean that."

"I do, Mr Hollis. I have the money with me."

That's the very worst thing he could have said. It will do nothing more than whet Will's appetite and make him all the more eager to push ahead with the offering.

A chair creaks.

"Why?" Will asks, and it's suspicion I hear in his voice.

"Why do you want me to go down there?"

"I've heard that Elden Hole is bottomless. I would like to see if it's true."

I could fall into the silence that follows and be falling forever.

Finally, Will says, "I'll do it for nine pounds, if you hold to your promise."

"I will," replies Isaac. I hear no traces of fear and uncertainty. He is firm in his resolution. As much as I admire Isaac's resolve, he is not strong. He wears a mask that could slip at any moment. By agreeing to his plan, Will knows that he'll be able to get the upper hand, I am sure of it.

"When do you want to meet?"

"Tomorrow, at dawn."

"Will you have everything we need?"

"I have a length of good, strong rope, and—"

A knock makes me jump out of my skin. I spring back, then curse myself for making too much noise. I doubt either Isaac or Will hears me, though, for it sounds like another person is in their midst.

"Mr Hollis, you're wanted out front." It's Mary.

"I'm talking to Mr Latimer," Will snaps.

"Please," says Isaac, "if you have other business to attend to—"

"I don't."

"Mr Hollis," Mary replies with some urgency, "I'm sorry, but you're needed."

A pause. "All right. I'll be back soon, Mr Latimer," Will

says, and the sound of fiddle playing flows into the back room before the door blocks it out again.

This is my chance.

I go inside. Isaac is slouching in the chair Thomas sat in weeks ago, the top button of his shirt undone. His mouth falls open when he sees me, and he leaps up, using the chair as a barricade.

"Get away." So my friend is, once again, revealing his true self. The clothes and beard are Isaac's, but the manner is entirely different. In short, he is not my friend.

"Shh, don't—"

"The hostess banned you from coming here."

"Listen to me." I put up my hands in a gesture of surrender. "I'm not going to hurt you, understand? I'd *never* hurt you. But you have to stop whatever it is you're doing."

His gold-brown eyes narrow in suspicion. "How long were you listening at that door?"

"You don't know who or what you're playing with."

"You mean your brother?"

How could he know? Is that what Mrs Needham was telling him—that the man he'd been talking to last night is a Vernon and a murderer? I'm still reeling from his words when a guttural scream cuts through the air. In the main room, a woman is drunkenly hurling insults.

"I'll go and see what's happening," I say.

Isaac is at my side in a moment. "I'll come as well."

It gives me such comfort to have him standing beside me that I have to remind myself who I'm really dealing with.

"Don't involve yourself in any of it, Isabella."

My companion turns to me, lips parted. They're close enough for me to suck into my own mouth. "You know my name?"

"You're not the only one who works things out," I say, quelling the desire that's rising unbidden in me. "How did you know he was my brother?"

"He told some of the same stories as you. Besides"—colour rises to those ripe cheeks—"you share some similarities."

"I'm nothing like him. Whatever you've heard from the people of this place, believe me, Will and I are as different as they come. I don't involve myself in what he does. Not directly. Not if I can help it."

Isaac—for he always will be Isaac to me, however much I try to tell myself otherwise—searches my face. "I want to trust you, but..." His eyes come to rest on my mouth. "You've injured yourself again. What happened?"

"Oh." I squeeze my lip between my teeth and taste the pain of that night at Highpit Rake. "Nothing."

"You're always coming to harm, aren't you?"

His finger touches the tender, swollen spot. It's a blessing. I put my hand over his and press it to my lips, kissing it hard enough to make the split bigger and deeper, to spill blood for his sake. His finger dips into my mouth. I stroke it with my tongue.

The woman in the room next door screeches, "Coward!"

Isaac draws back his hand. I want to grab it again and have him touch me all over, but the voice of Bess Jenkins has gone and ruined it all.

"You're a coward and a scoundrel!"

She has Sarah's necklace. She can testify that Will gave it to her. The answers to Isaac's questions are scattered all around him. All he has to do is gather them up to get a complete picture—a false picture—of what happened. Without knowing about our sacrifice of Thomas Mace, he'll think Will is guilty of doing something ungodly to Sarah.

"You need to leave," I repeat. "Forget whatever it is you're trying to pursue with my brother. Go home tomorrow and don't come back, or else your life is in danger."

His face hardens.

"You see, *that* sort of talk is why I can't allow myself to trust you. You are keeping things from me, still."

Isaac flings open the door to the main room. Weakened by staying up all night and standing guard all day, I'm frail enough for him to give me a push out. He follows smoothly behind me. A dozen heads turn in our direction. Will, seeing me with his quarry, takes a trembling breath.

"Jane? What are you doing with Mr Latimer?"

Bess starts towards us.

"You!" she snarls at Isaac. "You're the funny thing I saw in Castleton."

"Lady, I have travelled much of the Peak country," Isaac replies with a lift of the chin. I hate how fully in control of himself he seems. How can he be, after what's just happened? "I doubt not that we have crossed paths, though there is no need to turn your wrath towards me. I bear you no ill will."

"You wanted my jewels!"

She turns, teeth bared, to Will. "How do you two know each other? Did you rob him and give me the spoils?"

Will grips his former lover's arm, his knuckles turning white. "Quiet, wench, or else—"

"Or else what? You've taken everything from me already."

"I've taken nothing."

"My honour!"

"You had no honour when I met you."

The Weasel, warming himself by the fire, chuckles. Bess points a finger at Will. "This is the man you should be laughing at. A thief who doesn't even have the decency to admit he planted the baby in my womb. A poor little boy who used to weep after he fucked me."

A tide of laughter surges up to the ceiling. It stops abruptly when Will raises a hand and, pulling his arm right back, strikes Bess across the face. It sounds less like skin on skin than the snap of bone.

She moves slowly. She touches her birthmark, wipes away the tears knocked out of her with the force of the blow. Her silent shock is more powerful than a barrage of screams.

"Now you see," she whispers. "Now you see what sort of man he is."

In the middle of it all, Will writhes under everyone's gazes.

"What?" He lifts his arms, thrusting his neck forward. "Did none of you hear the way she was talking to me? The harlot deserved it."

"That's enough," says Mary. No longer a young lass, she

stands before the barrels in her robe of midnight blue, queen of her domain. "I think you'd better leave."

Will looks from person to person, trying to garner support. But he meets a wall of hostility. He turns to me then, mouthing *Janey*. I shake my head. His hands crunch into fists.

"Fuck the whole lot of you."

He turns his back and goes off, alone, into the night.

Chapter Twenty-Seven

Mary approaches Bess with all the confidence of an aged matriarch and loops her arm about the woman's waist. "Come to the kitchen with me. We'll get a warm cloth on that injury and some spiced milk down you. How does that sound?"

Bess, keeping her head low, nods.

"Walter, carry on playing," my sister commands, and the Weasel reluctantly takes his fiddle up from a bench. She addresses the crowd. "A free round for everyone! Edward, you're serving."

The poor boy looks as if she's offered a reward for the first person who can catch him and strip the pelt off his back. Customers, full of agitated talk about Will and Bess, surge towards the barrels while Edward entreats, "One at a time! One at a time!"

Isaac, ever the cunning cat, tries to slink away amidst the hubbub. I catch up with him as he enters the parlour. "Wait! That necklace—"

"How many more things have you kept from me?" Blazing

with anger, he scrapes the table across the floor to form a barrier between us. "Thomas Mace, the necklace, your brother… I fail to understand how you expect me to believe a word you say."

At times, attack is the best form of defence. "You were the one buying ropes this morning. I saw you!"

"Spying on me! You've spied on me, you've eavesdropped at the door… My God, Mistress Vernon, if you're innocent in all this, you're not doing a good job of showing it."

"I am innocent! Not of… not of everything. But I've got nothing to do with Sarah's disappearance, if that's where your mind's taking you. Is it? Is that what you think?"

Isaac lets out a pent-up breath. "I don't know what to think anymore."

"You went to see Mrs Needham, didn't you? Has she filled your mind with poison against me and mine?"

"You are the ones who've filled my mind with poison. Everything I've seen of you and your brother makes me realise how foolish I was to put myself in vulnerable positions with you."

"Vulnerable? I'd never harm you or your cousin. All I've ever wanted to do is help you. Believe it or not, I'm trying to help you now by telling you to stop whatever you're planning on doing to my brother."

"Convenient, isn't it? That you'd protect your own."

"He's…"

Still, I can't bring myself to betray him. It surprises me—this stubborn loyalty. Even though I'm content to stand in the way of my brother's scheming, I couldn't bear to see him carted off to the gallows.

"I'm nothing like him," I say.

"That is not what I've seen, Mistress Vernon. And if you bother me tonight by knocking on my door or listening in on me, I'll make sure none of your family can step foot in here again."

He makes for the door at the back of the room with a self-assurance that gets right under my skin.

"You think you can treat this inn like your own?" I shout. "My sister's in charge. She won't pay any mind to you! You're a stranger here. You're no better than us. No better!"

He stops. "There. You have proved the very point I was making: you band together against outsiders. You loathe anyone who's not from your own stock. Worse." He stabs me with the sharpest of looks. "You hurt them."

Then, he leaves.

I stand in the cool night air outside the White Hart. Despite my regrettable outburst, it's still not too late to put things to rights. If I rise early enough, I can stop Isaac reaching Will tomorrow, even if it means grappling him to the ground and tying him up with that rope he's so fond of. The question is, what to do till then? I'm not welcome here. Will is, in all likelihood, at home. To say he wouldn't be pleased to see me is an understatement. He'd be ready with a pillow to snuff the life out of me. *It is a shame.*

A door creaks, and light from inside spills across the ground. Bess Jenkins walks out front, a leather flask in her hand. When she sees me, her arm curls round her womb.

"Oh. It's you." The air drains out of her in a sigh, though it's not all relief. There's some disappointment in it as well.

"How's your face?" I ask.

"I'll live. What were you doing with that hybrid?"

I baulk. "What do you mean, hybrid?"

"The one who coveted my necklace. The mannish woman."

She knows? Is that why Isaac gave up on pestering Bess so soon? She's wrong, in any case. Isaac is no more a mannish woman than Bess is a princess. Isaac is simply his own person, and a beautiful one at that.

"He didn't covet it," I say with bitterness. "You were right. Will stole the jewels from Isaac's cousin."

Bess's shoulders slacken. Her neck bends with the weight of this new knowledge in her head.

"I told you to keep away, Bess. Why did you have to come here and stoke the fire?"

"Keeping away i'n't easy, even though Will's a nasty piece of work."

"Think what it must've been like growing up with him."

Taking pity on me, Bess passes me the flask. I must be in a sorry state if an abandoned lover carrying a bastard child thinks I'm more in need of a tipple than her. Despite the fusty smell that arises from it, I drink. The stuff sets fire to my throat. I cough, my eyes watering. Bess takes it off me and gulps as though it were small beer.

"Will isn't going to help you," I say. "You must see that."

"Mary told me he was coming into more money very soon."

I raise my eyebrows. "Did she now?"

"She said that sometime in the next few days, someone's going to pay him a debt. I'm going to stay here till that happens. She's a good woman, is Mary. I wouldn't have thought two decent ones like you and her would share *his* blood."

"It's not about blood," I say, taking another drink and keeping the cough locked away in my chest this time. Flames spread through my veins. "It's about what you do. We all have choices. Besides, I wouldn't lay all your hopes on Will getting this money. He might not."

"But I can't carry on like this." She draws a circle on the ground with the flapping pieces of leather that constitute her shoe. "I'm famished."

"Mary runs the White Hart, near enough. Why don't you ask her if she'll give you some work?"

Bess looks up. "Do you think she'd do that?"

"She might."

The possibility is enough to make Bess stand a bit taller. "I wouldn't mind that. It's honest work. I've considered doing other things."

"Like what?"

Her eyes glaze over. I offer her the flask, but she shakes her head.

"You know," she says, "when Will first started seeing me, he didn't even try anything. He just sat on my bed and cried."

"So you said."

She smiles, pride shining from the face that felt the sting of Will's hand. "He wasn't what I thought he'd be like. He seemed gentle. Sweet, even."

He was, very long ago. Before Grandam got to him and Bess made his acquaintance. "People aren't always what they seem."

"Never a truer word spoken." Her smile droops. "He changed. Bit by bit. But he was at his worst before he cut ties with me. Turned up drunk one night. Threw things about. I chucked him out of the house."

"It sounds like he deserved it."

"Folk get drunk. Bet you do."

I lower the flask. "Not like Will."

"No." Bess's eyes flicker over my face. "Deep down, you're not like him at all."

"You really don't think so?" Those words I said to Isaac tonight could've come straight from my brother's resentful mouth.

She wraps her thin arms round my neck, her belly pressing into mine, and kisses me sloppily on the ear. "You take care, Jane Vernon. You're a good 'un."

Without looking back, she goes inside. *A good 'un.* She was closer to the truth when she said I was the lesser of two evils. Her flask is still in my hand. It takes more effort now to bring it to my lips—my body's turned numb—but when I manage,

I drain every last drop.

"A bit presumptuous of you, to say she could have work without asking me first."

I whirl around, and Mary spins into view. How long has she been leaning against the side of the inn, listening? Waiting? A tingle of ice works its way down my back.

"Bess is in a bad way. She needs work, food, a roof over her head."

"What makes you think I'll agree to it?"

I speak quietly. "Because she's carrying Will's child, and neither mother nor baby will be long for this world if she doesn't get help. The more people who die, the more attention will be on us, and you can't run things round here if you get sent to the gallows."

Mary crosses her arms. "You'll leave me to run things round here, will you?"

"So long as you leave them be."

"Them?"

"Bess." I take a deep, quavering breath. "And Isaac Latimer."

"Mr Latimer? Why him?"

Why him, indeed? He shared his candlelight with me. He listened to my story. He could have had me all for himself if it weren't for Bess's untimely screeching.

"Isaac's a good person," I say.

"All right, then, Janey. A deal. You leave me to my own affairs here, and I'll look after those two."

A pale hand writhes out of the darkness and grips mine, cold as stone.

"Deal," I say.

The hand pulls me forwards, and I'm no longer by the side of the White Hart under a new moon, but under a canopy of trees tipped with silver. The stars crackle, exploding in white bursts and shrinking. They blind me. A shriek of something not quite animal and not quite human echoes as if I'm in the cave, and then I am, and the stars are insects on the cave roof, squirming towards a tunnel stretching on and on, into the hill as deep as an ancient forest tipped with silver, where stars crackle, exploding in white bursts and—

"Jane!" My sister is standing over me, her eyes bulging. "Jane, thank God! You fell into a faint." She fumbles to untie the bandage around my hand. "It's loose. You've not been keeping that cut clean, have you? I told you. Now it might be getting infected. Have you eaten today?"

I shake my head, still not sure when and where I am. "Not much."

"Go home. Make some oatcakes. You can borrow some milk from the stocks here."

Home. Home makes me imagine Will's coarse hands pressing over my nose and mouth, blocking off the air until my body jigs like a hanging man's and goes limp.

I'm trembling. "Not home. I want to stay here."

"I don't know about that. I've given Bess a room free of charge, as she's too upset to go all the way back to Castleton tonight. I can hardly do the same for you."

"Mary, please."

She must hear how scared I am. "Just for tonight, then."

I'm carried on a hazy cloud up the stairs, down the long corridor where we pass Isaac's room. I call goodnight to him as we pass and almost knock at his door, but Mary says, "Come along, daft girl," and puts me in another room.

She cleans the cut made by Thomas's knife twice over with soothing, fragrant water and dabs it with the sweetest honey. She feeds me broth made with stringy bits of meat and buttered hunks of bread. I eat like I can never be filled. Later, she lays sheets and woollen coverlets over me, tucking me in like a mother.

"I'm too hot."

"You'll get colder as the night goes on."

As sleep creeps up my body, lulling every limb to stillness, I'm dimly aware of asking, "Did we make a deal earlier?"

"A deal?" She brushes a sweat-soaked strand of hair out of my eyes. "You were mumbling summat about giving Bess a job, and I said yes. Is that what you mean?"

I know there was something strange about it, though I can't remember what. It doesn't seem to matter now that Mary's humming a low tune, sad but beautiful.

"Aye," I say. Weariness pulls me down into a bottomless pool of healing waters. "That's it."

Chapter Twenty-Eight

ISAAC

The search for you has led me to fountains that ebb and flow with the tides, through the guts of the Devil, past an ever-running hourglass of a mountain, and now to the edge of this hell pit. I rose while it was yet dark and, with my hat on my head and rope slung over my shoulder, trod softly down the corridor. Somewhere nearby, Jane was sleeping. I heard her call to me last night and spent the hours that followed wishing I had answered.

I still had time to find her, to change my mind. Once in her chamber, all I had to do was kneel by her bed and brush the messy locks of hair from her cheek, and then she would open her eyes to me. There would be no early morning trek out into the wilds; there would be no justice, only forgiveness.

It is a pity that I am not quite ready to forgive. Not when the Vernons are still keeping the truth from me. Hardening my heart, I let Jane sleep on.

Milky daylight spilt across the sky, imbuing the mists on

the hills with a white glow. I walked with small steps for fear that, having misremembered the way to Elden Hole, I would find myself teetering on its edge. Yet even through the mists, I recognised the path that led up the side of Elden Hill and curved around its summit. Eventually, I came to the ruins of a sheep pen from which I'd taken a stone so many days ago, when I saw Jane for the second time. Knowing what I know now, that memory does not seem so golden. I'd thought it peculiar at the time, the way she was staring into the void, but I had not entertained the idea that she may have been checking for traces of a deed she desperately needed to cover up.

This morning, Elden Hole looks deeper and more forbidding. The darkness at its centre seems to flow upwards, like water rising up the sides of a pail by its own accord.

What happened up here, Sarah? I'd like to believe that, finally freed from obligations of husband and lover, you lowered yourself down with a rope firmly fastened around your slender waist and explored those caves in the flickering light of a candle. I'd like to believe that you emerged into the daylight, newborn. But I cannot fool myself any longer. In all likelihood, you're lying in a broken heap at the bottom of this hellish pit.

Did William Vernon, seeing you heartbroken and bedraggled from a solitary journey over from Castleton, try to rob what little remained of your honour? And when you resisted, did he throw you down here? Perhaps fearful of what would rise from the earth, he called upon his sister to check that nothing wicked was emerging. I found her staring into the open grave that day and she, knowing well that I was too close to the truth in Peak Forest, leapt at the chance to accompany me to Castleton. What a fool I was, to trust so readily. I deserve to have this pain in my heart after a lifetime of chasing after the wrong things, the wrong people.

At least now, I have a plan to get to the truth of the matter. When William Vernon sees a rope slithering into the darkness, he will assume that I have descended and lie on his front, as Jane did, craning his neck to see if I am dangling in the midst of the void. That should give me ample time to emerge from my hiding place and loop a second piece of rope around his neck, my knee pressing down on his back and pushing the air from his body. He may have strength, but I can tighten a knot as well as any man. Soon, he will go purple in the face. In that breathless and disturbed state, he will be primed to make his confession, especially when he hears me lift my voice and speak as if you have risen from the grave.

As I make my way down the grassy slope towards the brink of Elden Hole, I can only hope that the theatrics will achieve my purpose, and William Vernon will not throw me off him like a wild horse. If he does, and I plummet into the circles of torment beneath the ground, know that I did it for you. Though I may have failed in my vow to protect you always, I have tried to make amends.

I tie one end of the rope around a rock that juts from the ground and throw the other into the waiting darkness. The wind drops, Nature itself barely daring to breathe. Despite the stillness, the earth trembles just a little. *Terribilis. Vastum.*

If Will were to rear up while I was on top of him, if I were to go over the edge, how far would I plummet? Would anything reach out from the crevices of stone and tear at my flesh? Jane told of a star falling from the skies. Even now, something with huge wings wrapped around its ribcage may be nestling on a ledge deep in that pit. Something, she said, had stirred its long fingers in her grandfather's brain. Fear itself could not drive a man to madness, could it? What did George Bradley see down there?

"It's me, Sarah," I call. The sound of my own voice gives me some courage. "It's me. I'm here. You are not alone. I am coming for you."

The abyss absorbs the sound. Then, from deep in the earth, a voice too old and gnarled to be mine echoes, *I am coming for you.*

Chapter Twenty-Nine

Outside the window, mist swathes the earth, white and still. White and still, as it were a few winters ago when the air was chock-full of snow and we walked to Chapel-en-le-Frith—me, Will, Mary, Mam, Da and Grandam—to receive the Lord's meal. The mist is the colour of angels' gowns and fills me up with the memories of thick cuts of beef and plum broth and apples drowning in bowls of spiced ale, of card games and carols on crisp evenings.

I close my eyes again, smiling. Brightness shines through my lids, diamond patterns in the leaded windows flashing.

Brightness. Daybreak. I've slept too long. Isaac and Will might already be at Elden Hole.

I slam my bare feet to the floor, and the room tilts as if I'm aboard a listing ship. Still in yesterday's clothes, I go out to knock on Isaac's door, but it's open, and the room is empty.

Whatever Isaac's planning on doing with that rope, Will can twist it to his advantage. Convinced of his own ingenious plan, Isaac'll play directly into my brother's hands.

The sound of a clattering from the kitchen brings my mind

to Mary. Did she put a herb in my food or drink last night to send me off into a deep slumber, well aware that I'd sleep fast until daybreak? We made a deal; I asked her to keep Isaac from harm. Isaac… but not Isabella. Could she know about Isaac's double life, and be using that knowledge to trick me? The shiver that creeps over my scalp says it's well within the bounds of possibility.

I have to leave without her seeing.

Alyson Bagshawe's room oozes Weasel musk. It's in the sheets wrapped round Walter's legs and pot belly. His hairy arse is hanging off the side, and the temptation to give it a kick is almost too great. Mrs Bagshawe is sleeping on her back, snores erupting from her open mouth. The skin around her lips is dry and crusted.

I give Walter a brief but firm pinch on the arm and whisper into his waxy ear.

He moans, but doesn't wake. I try again. "Walter! Get up."

This time, the lout's beady eyes flicker open. Before he can exhale his morning breath into my face, I lay what I hope is a soothing hand on his arm.

"Mary's asking for you in the kitchen," I whisper.

"Eh?" My God, his breath is worse than Lordsmeer's used to be.

"Mary. She needs your help with the cooking. Edward's sick today." Any other time, I would not have put my sister in this position. But if she put me to sleep last night, it's an eye for an eye.

The drawstrings of his mouth slacken, and he gawps at his sleeping lover. "What time is it?"

"Shh. Don't wake Alyson. She needs rest. Woman's troubles, remember?"

He nods. "Aye. Aye, that's right."

Walter pulls back the cover to reveal his full glory. I allow myself a quick glance (it's got a bulbous, beetroot-like head) and make a show of turning away while he scratches and pulls on some clothes.

"How do you know Mary needs help?" he asks once he's decent. "Did she come up to tell you?"

"I went down early, very early, for a drink. She was at her wits' end, what with Mrs Bagshawe not feeling herself and Edward stuck at home with fever."

"How did she know Edward was sickening?"

The man's not as empty-headed as I thought. "His brother sent a message first thing."

Mrs Bagshawe turns in bed as we leave the room. Her eyes open, take me in without understanding, and close again.

"Now, be sure to give her lots of instructions," I say to Walter as we go downstairs. "She'll appreciate it."

"Aye? She doesn't seem like the sort."

"Oh, that's just a front. She's used to Will telling her what to do."

As he lumbers towards the kitchen, I turn off towards the back door and make a hasty exit. It'll be a while before they get out of the argument that's coming, time enough for me to make it to Elden Hill. You may have won one round by putting me into a deep slumber last night, Mary, but I'll win this one.

I run past the ruins of the hunting lodge and chapel, turning onto the road that leads to Elden Hill. None of the Needhams are out yet. I hurry by their house anyway, fearful that Margaret is watching me from inside, her mind bent on revenge. A splash from the pond stops me in my tracks. There are no ducks on the water at this time; Mrs Needham always takes care to lock them away from foxes overnight. I watch the ripples spread outwards from a half-submerged bulk on the far side. It's like the stump of a tree where no tree should be, and it's watching.

"One more day," I whisper. "You promised me one more day."

I keep my eyes forward and set on the hill, even when the splashes get nearer, and from right behind me comes the sound of something large and heavy slumping onto dry land and drawing a laboured breath. I break into a run again, stopping only when I've reached the foot of Elden Hill and the only breathing I can hear is my own.

The path leading up to Elden Hole looks longer than ever, the slope so much steeper, disappearing into the snow-thick mist.

Come on, Janey. You've walked this way a thousand times before.

I push on, though my head is floating off like a sycamore seed and my legs are stone. Halfway up, a tall shape trembles into view.

"Isaac! Will!"

I dash unsteadily towards it—but it flees, only a sheep. I could have sworn it was walking upright. I look behind me. Nothing is pursuing, unless it's managed to conceal itself.

If I sit down to rest, it'll be impossible to get back up; if I close my eyes, it'll be like coins are stuck to my lids, weighing them down. But the tiredness is too great. It forces me to lie and rest my head on the dewy grass. It's as soft as last night's bed. I could wrap myself in my coat and sleep and sleep till the trumpets of the Last Judgement blow.

As I start to drift, I know it's too late. By the time I get to the Hole, the meeting between Will and Isaac'll be over. There's nothing I can do to stop it. Everything has conspired against me. I become a dandelion, drifting away bit by bit into the wind, senseless, directionless—

Spineless.

I pull myself up. The world wobbles, then falls into place. What I said to Bess last night is true. Hard as it may be to believe now, I do have a choice. I can lament my fate and my cursed bloodline, chide the weather and lie down here to sleep out the last few hours before the Spirit of Elden Hole drags me away, or else I can take possession of myself and stand up to Her tyranny. Be the captain of my own soul.

I heave myself up to the top of the hill, along the path where, buried somewhere deep under layers of mud, traces of Thomas's last footsteps are stamped into the earth. At last, the ruins of a sheep pen jut out of the mist. My steps slow, grass hissing under my feet as I approach Elden Hole.

The mist eddies around Her like frozen breath.

"Will?" I call, though I keep my voice soft, afraid of disturbing something that's not human. "Isaac?"

Sweat courses down my back. The air feels thinner here. You could take a few steps forward and find yourself in the land of the dead.

Trembling, I peer over the edge of the grassy slope that leads down to the open mouth of Elden Hole. At first, what I see baffles me. When I finally work out what it means, my nerves crackle.

A few feet from the brink of the Hole, someone's tied a rope around a rock. The end of the rope dangles into Her gullet.

Isaac, what have you done?

I scramble down the slope, my feet skidding where the ground has been churned up. To steady myself, I grab onto a clump of grass. Something wet and sticky slicks across my skin. I pull away with a shriek. Sarah's bloody hair, smeared across the wall of Peveril Castle, looms large in my memory. But there's nothing like that here; nothing but a slug trail and morning dew.

At the bottom of the slope, I lay flat on my front as I've done so many times before, thrust my head over the edge of Elden Hole and trace the shape of the rope that hangs in the darkness. It's visible for a good three yard before it drops out of view, hidden by a ledge of rock.

"Will! Isaac!"

Echoes bounce off the sheer walls and are lost.

Inching away from the edge, I gather the part of the rope that's above the surface and give it a gentle tug. It moves a little, but something's weighing it down. I pull again, harder this time. The weight attached to the other end is heavy. Heavy enough to be a person?

Panic mounting, I tug it more sharply. A pull the other way almost drags the rope out of my hands.

"Will? If it's you, pull twice."

Nothing.

"Isaac?"

Two distinct tugs.

I let out a sob as I imagine him on a rocky outcrop below, a jagged bone sticking through his flesh. But he's alive, he's alive.

"Are… Are you hurt?"

Two tugs. Hope and despair contend in my breast, one whispering that Isaac is well enough to respond and so must be in one piece, the other stating in cold, flat tones that there's nothing I can do unless I run to the village and beg a group of strong men to come with me and lift him out. But why would they? Isaac is an outsider here. Everyone in Peak Forest knows that outsiders belong down the Hole.

"You're going to have to climb, if you can," I shout. "Hold on to the rock face as I pull. Can you do that?"

Two tugs, weaker this time.

"Try. Please, try."

I gather loops of rope on the surface and wind them about my middle. The cord presses into my hips, but I can bear the pressure if I grit my teeth and tell myself that this is the only way to pull Isaac to safety. I walk backwards, past the rock where the end of the rope has been firmly tied, and up the grassy slope. The loops of twine tighten around my guts with each step, squeezing the breath out of me. Walking becomes too painful. I get on all fours and crawl up the slope, pushing my fingers deep into the soil to stop myself rolling backwards. Once or twice, there's a sharp pull, and I'm afraid Isaac's banging against the sides of the Hole and doing even more damage to his body than he must've already done, but then the burden becomes lighter as he seems to right himself.

The top of the slope is within reach. I channel all my remaining strength into my arms and heave, tears streaming, viscera about to burst. My scraped elbows have just made it onto the flat ground above the slope when a sudden, sickening pull draws me back an inch.

There's a moment of stillness in which I see, clear as day, what's about to happen.

A second later, I'm dragged backwards again.

Screaming, I grab at the sliding earth, holding onto clusters of stinging nettles, but they're ripped from my hands and there's nothing I can do as, feet-first, I'm sucked into the mouth of the Hole, hands flailing, grabbing at the rock—

My feet kick out into empty air.

I'm not falling. By some miracle, I'm not falling. I can no longer feel the weight at the other end of the rope. Isaac must've let go.

The vast, hollow depth under my feet fills me with cold

terror. I imagine a hooked finger rising out of the darkness, ensnaring my ankle and pulling me down. It feels like there's ice all over my hands and the surface of the rock. One ill-judged movement, and I'll slip.

Slowly, very slowly, I heave myself up, arms shaking, muscles round my ribs and belly bruising with the effort.

The edge presses against my legs and, with a blinding rush of relief, I drag myself onto solid ground, dripping with tears and slobber. I fumble to untie the rope from my waist, but it's too tight to undo now that my hands are all scraped and, apart from clumsily hacking at it with a stone, the only thing I can do to stop myself being pulled into Elden Hole again is to gather up the rope that now hangs loose, without the weight of Isaac on the other end.

In spite of the weakness in my arms, I'm able to gather it up out of the Hole with ease this time. The rope itself feels strangely weightless, glowing in the mist.

My eyes must be playing tricks on me, for it seems to be feeding itself up to the surface of its own accord.

I let go.

The rope continues to snake upwards, a living thing, coiling at my feet. I step away, afraid that, if I touch it, it'll writhe up my body and crush my insides. The last bit of rope slides upwards over the edge. The end has been unravelled. Each bit of twine is tied in hundreds of fine knots, too small and delicate for human fingers to make.

Chapter Thirty

It's my grandfather's blood that pulses in my throat as I make my way over to Highpit Rake. George Bradley had the guts and the idiocy to stir this curse into life. The Spirit speaks to me as if I'm his natural successor, the next in line to wear a crown of briars. If I'm to confront what's down that cursed pit, I need the right tools.

The Needhams' mine is a haunted place, abandoned after the bodies of Nathaniel and Harry were found last week. The veins had been drying up anyway. Better to move on to a site with richer seams and fewer memories. Will told me that no one's been back to empty the coe house of supplies yet. No one could face it, especially not Mrs Needham. The door blows open and shut in the wind. *Knock, knock.*

I step inside. On the table, I see what I'm looking for: hard leather hats and strings of tallow candles. There's also a pile of leathers in the corner, shed like the blackened skins of salamanders. Tools are lined up against the walls, off-duty. A pile of waste material, broken up by the washers, lies in a wooden tub. In the middle of the floor, the mouth of the shaft is sealed with sheets of metal and weighed down by rocks. That's all there is left of this place.

With a trespasser's shame, I cross over to the leathers. If only Isaac were around to see this: Jane Vernon, donning man's attire. The hairs on my legs stand on end as I strip myself of my ripped petticoat and tug on a pair of breeches that only fit over my hips with some difficulty. The leather is cold and has a musty whiff of sweat and earth about it. I doubt these clothes have ever been washed. I pick a jerkin big enough to fasten over my chest. It flaps about like the wing of a giant bat, and I'm filled with a newfound respect for Isaac who can make men's clothes look decent.

Once I've swapped my shoes for boots, I get myself a light source. It'll be darker down in Elden Hole than anywhere I've been before, which means I need a good supply of candles and wadding. I strike the flint against the wall and, after a few goes, produce a good enough spark to set the wadding alight. The flame hides in the folds of the material. I coax it onto the candle wick. The stench of rancid fat clings to the back of my throat as I stick the candle onto the rim of a hat with a blob of clay. The hat goes on my head and a string of spare candles goes round my neck. I put the flint and wadding in a pocket. The simple part is over. Now for the part that makes every fibre of my body burn with protest.

To journey into the Hole, I've got to tie one end of the rope to the rock and the other end round my waist, lean backwards over the void, and take one step, then another, unable to see what's behind and below. I won't know whether the rock is in the ground firmly enough, or whether the rope is capable of holding my weight till I'm doing it. Even here, in the shelter of the coe, it seems like a leap into the arms of death. Already, I can feel the sudden, sickening drop as the rope loosens and I go slipping out of existence, spikes of rock rising towards my spine and skull. Yet I've vowed to give myself to Elden Hole by the end of today. If I'm to die in Her jaws, I may as well die trying to find Isaac.

Janey.

The door of the coe swings open. I flatten against the wall, choking on my breath. My pulse jumps in the top of my legs, where the leather breeches are tightest. Strange, that. I've never felt my heart in my legs before. Perhaps that's why they say men think with their cocks. I laugh and it comes out an empty, hollow sound.

There is another way in, says the voice of Elden Hole. Do I dream it, or has Isaac's tongue joined the thousands that used to belong to beasts and men and now speak together for the void?

I swallow down my fear. "Where?"

Follow.

At first, I see nothing. Then I'm aware of a shimmer in the air, such as is made by heat on a summer's day or the smoke from a fire. It twists through the open door and eddies off in the direction of the Shouting Cave.

"Isaac?"

Instinct screams at me not to go into that darkness. No one should trust the word of a fallen angel. Demons speak the language of lies. But what choice do I have? It's either this, or an ill-fated backwards descent down Elden Hole.

Steeling myself, I stride headlong into the middle of the cave, counting my steps as I go. When I get to twenty-four, I stop.

"Isaac? Isaac Latimer?"

His name is immediately lost. The usual echo is gone, as if the once empty space is thronging with unseen yet substantial forms.

"Will?"

I edge forward, my quaking arm outstretched only as far as the light from my candle reaches. I dare not stretch it out any more for fear of touching something I can't or don't want to see. Something bristling with spines, with a backwards skull for a head.

I thought I knew every inch of this cave. It's always been forty-eight steps from one end to the other. Yet I've already gone fifty and I haven't touched the back wall yet. I'm playing games with a creature that can twist and bend the world out of shape. Breathy with fear, I sing one of Mary's songs.

"Dear Sir, the night is drawing near.
I can no longer tarry here.
Homeward must I travel soon
Before the—"

Janey.

The sound is guttural and close, so close that I feel the sting of hot breath on my ear. My head snaps over my shoulder and, at the same moment, light streaks through the black, blinding me, and I'm still blinking and dazed when something cracks by my feet. I cry out and wait for the leathery sound of wings to clap around me, but nothing comes. Nothing comes. I let go of my breath. The crowd of ghostly spectators fades. The chill of emptiness crawls over my skin.

I gather my senses. The light, the clacking noise—it was only my candle, falling out of my helmet.

Astonishingly, it's still burning. I pick it up, and, as my shadow travels over the wall, I see a feature I've never marked before: a narrow tunnel. Has it always been there? How could I have missed it all these years?

Janey.

I stumble back, almost dropping my candle again. The voice is coming from inside the tunnel.

In here.

No. I'll get stuck. No one will ever find me.

They're in here.

They can't be. How could Will and Isaac have crawled into that suffocating gap themselves? Unless they didn't go by themselves. Unless they were dragged, claws digging into their ankles, piercing the skin, blood running in rivulets down their legs.

"No," I say aloud. It's tighter in there than down the shaft where Da's head was crushed.

There's no other way, Janey.

My heartbeat crashes in my ears. Hot piss trickles down my legs. I'm going to die. No one can be this afraid and yet live. No wonder George Bradley went mad. The things he must've seen. The things I'll see.

The inside of the tunnel is rough with yellow incrustation, similar to what covers the walls of the cave. It smells of stagnant water and soil.

The body that used to be mine crawls inside. There's about two feet of room between the head and the ceiling of rock, and even less on either side.

This body worms along on forearms and elbows, the skin on the palms peeling away, raw grazes gathering dust. Knees and elbows knock against hard rock, and bright, clear pain shoots up through them. I hear it breathing, this soft shell, breathing hard and heavy, and I wonder, dimly, if it'll run out of air. I wonder also whether anything is creeping along behind it, waiting for the last movement, waiting to rip open the steaming guts and slurp them until only a husk of slack skin is left. Maybe something is ahead, and it'll spring out like a spider from the corner of its web.

The body that used to be mine stops moving. The way ahead is blurred with tears and sweat. In here, the stench of that tallow candle is overwhelming. Panicked breathing and sobs fill the space that's tight as a coffin, rebounding on themselves. It sounds like drowning.

The air is thick. An immense tiredness weighs down my limbs like a woollen blanket. Dying would not be so terrible. It would be rest.

My back arches in a fresh wave of panic, spine cracking against the low ceiling.

No. I can't let this happen. I can't lose control or drift away from myself. I must keep going.

Go slowly. Go carefully. Keep your breathing steady.

Repeating these words, I inch along on my knees and elbows. My shoulders and neck are sore. A headache hammers behind my eyes. The flayed skin of my palms rings with pain. *Go, go.* I keep dragging myself along till my breathing gets louder, as if it's echoing back at me, bouncing off—

A dead end. It was a trick. The Spirit of Elden Hole has bottled me up.

I use the last of my strength to scream.

I'll starve. After I've eaten those foetid lumps of fat that serve as candles and torn off parts of the leather waistcoat, I'll have nothing left but the dead flesh on my hand to strip away. I'll become a skeleton in the dark. With divine mercy, I'll run out of air and sleep will blend into death before I'm aware of my insides turning to water.

A whisper of breath tickles my ankle, and I convulse with fear. Then comes acceptance. The Spirit is here to eat me up. I squeeze my eyes closed and wait to be sucked down the pulsing throat, to feel sick pleasure ripple through my loins as She wraps Her tongue round me. She makes no movement. The breath keeps blowing on my raw skin. It's not breath, I realise then, but air. Air. Could I have missed another opening?

I push myself backwards, ignoring the sharp pains in my elbows and the deafening scraping sound of the hard leather hat against the low roof because, at last, I might have a way out. I run my fingers along the wall. My hand dips into cold emptiness. Without thinking about where it might lead, I delve into it headfirst.

I don't have to crawl for long before I see a half circle of dark grey light before me. Tears of relief stream from my eyes as I drag myself towards escape. When I finally break out of that crushing tunnel and into the great space beyond, I'm possessed by a dizzying joy. I am in paradise.

Giant, lumpen shapes loom up around me. The grey light and burnt-down candle aren't strong enough for me to see them in detail. I fumble for the flint and wadding and, striking out sparks on the rocky floor, light a new candle. It's blinding after the dimness of the tunnel. I close my eyes, and the ghost of the flame explodes in white behind my eyelids. When I open them again, I look up and away from the flame.

Paradise is a cave.

In small glimpses, the candle reveals its wonders. Rocks that look like icicles hang from a sloping roof, huge and ancient as dragon's teeth, but even these are dwarfed by the columns that rise behind me, towers made up of hundreds of rocks in the shape of open roses. The one that stretches high up into the shadowy roof of the cave is the same deep yellow as the icicle-shaped rocks; the smaller tower, about my height, is a deeper, richer shade. The walls glimmer like wet honey. Beautiful as this place is, the air isn't wholesome. A dank, rotten smell mars its beauty.

It takes me a moment to remember why I'm here.

"Isaac?" I call. The echo is flung back at me.

From the far side of the chamber comes the distant thrum of running water and a breeze that bends my candle flame. If I follow the river, will it lead me to the surface?

I cross the cavern floor, stopping one last time to marvel at the rocks biting down from the ceiling. There's no sign of the river, though it gets louder as I travel to the side of the cavern opposite the larger column of encrusted stone, and the smell gets so strong that I hold my sleeve over my nose. I lift the candle, trying not to breathe too deeply, and then my breath stops altogether.

To one side of me is a deep gash in the ground. Judging by the gurgling noises that issue from it, the river flows at the bottom. That in itself would take all my attention, if it weren't for what lies straight ahead.

I may well be looking at the entrance to the great hall of the Underworld itself. Arching ribcages and spines like rows of sprouting white mushrooms are strewn along a slope of loose rocks and stones. Pale light washes in from above. A way out! All I have to do to see day again is walk this bone road and go through an arch of rock, and then I can shout and shout until someone comes to my aid.

I begin to climb the slope. Countless animals have met their ends here. A whole sheep's skeleton lies on a bed of stained, rotten wool. The horns of a cow's skull prong out from the mass grave like a demon's trident. Still keeping my breath shallow, I crunch over the muddle of remains, heading towards the light, trying not to turn my head as I go. But how can I not look? How can I draw my eyes away from the tree branch that looks oddly like a fleshless hand reaching through the dirt and decay? For they're here, mingled with the animal bones: Grandam's offerings, Da's offerings, Thomas. I'm at the bottom of Elden Hole. I've wormed my way straight into the stinking belly of the monster.

Rolling and skittering under my feet are the hundreds of rocks people have thrown into Her mouth over the centuries. Somewhere along this path, there'll be the stone Isaac took from the sheep pen at the top, the stone which he dropped into the abyss with me at his side. I wish I could find it again. It'd bring me so much comfort to touch what he's touched.

Through the arch, the source of that ungodly odour gets stronger. It doesn't take me long to see what's causing it.

Cold air sweeps in from above, blowing into my face the sickly sweetness of rotting meat and cabbage left to go putrid in the sun. My stomach heaves. I face the wall and count slowly, willing it to settle. When I turn back, I force myself to take a closer look at the body that lies, broken, on a wide stone ledge a few inches above the ground. Its arm is hanging down. The sleeve, once fine, is spattered with droppings and blooms of greenish mould. To approach the body goes against God's laws. But I have to see it.

As if caught in a terrible dream, I find myself beside the corpse.

The time I spend looking at that abomination isn't long enough for me to take in every detail. But it's long enough to see what's left of the head. The jaw is skewed, snapped out of place by the fall. There are no eyes, just empty sockets. Thomas still has his long, grey hair, clotted with dried blood and filth. There's a hole where Mary brought the rock crashing down on his skull. Things teem inside it.

My candle falls. I press my hand to my mouth as my insides come rushing up, and I run blindly down the slope towards the other cavern, skidding on the loose stones and bones. I'm still seeing that head, an infested mess stripped of muscle, fat and humanity, when I slide and fall not onto the cave floor, but down the hole that leads to the rushing underground river.

In my nightmare, there's nothing to catch me as I plummet.

My shoulder crashes against one side of the tunnel and I'm shoved in the other direction and back again, bumping all the way down, my helmet flying off, ragged edges tearing the skin not covered by leathers.

In my nightmare, I scream just as icy water closes over my body. I sink into a deeper blackness than before. My heart must stop. It must do, because I feel nothing and I see nothing. I know then that this is not a nightmare and there's no waking from this.

I drift, letting the river take me to a world beyond this one, where there's no hope, but also no worry because life is worry and there's none of that. At last. At last, I can be at peace. The low voices of the water chatter in ancient tongues. I cannot understand them. Not yet. But I will. Soon.

Chapter Thirty-One

Something's trying to scratch its way out, or in. It's raining, but warmth enfolds me like a blanket here, before the hearth. Da's in his chair, and the smoke from his pipe curls round his head, covering his face in thick, grey bandages. I don't need to see his expression to tell that he's not best pleased to see me; his leg jiggles, as it does when he's agitated.

"Let the cat in," I say. "He's at the door."

"I'll do it." Mam gets up from Mary's bed. She looks down at me on the floor and smiles. Her eyes are white as cooked egg. There are flecks of vomit all over her chin.

She opens the door. Lordsmeer dashes in, grumbling, discontented mews trembling from his throat. His green eyes flash towards me. I pat my belly. He comes padding over and puts his wet paws on my chest, then rubs his face against my chin. A purr rumbles from deep inside him.

Da bends over me, his head still swathed in smoke. "Get up, lass."

"I can't," I say.

"Come on, now."

He yanks me up with cold hands and my eyelids flicker open. I'm not at home. Where I am is dark, all dark apart from a small fire and the glowing outline of the figure that crouches by it. He turns something over in his hands, making the scratching noise. The figure lays down his tools.

"Thought you weren't coming back," says Will.

I sit up. A thick cloak lays heavy on my shoulders, and beneath that, my body's a knot of agony. "Where are we?"

"You won't believe me when I tell you." He nods up at the cave roof. "We're in the very rump of the Devil."

I cough, and the muscles between what used to be my ribs spasm with pain. "How? How did I get here?"

"You tell me. I fished you out of that river."

That's where the sound of rain is coming from—the churning, black waters to the side of what I now see is a narrow bank. The cave grows around me. We're in a small chamber, with a sloping roof that's at its lowest just behind where Will is sitting. Beyond that, there's only darkness.

"I was inside Elden Hole."

The firelight captures the lift of Will's brow. "Well, you know what they say about Elden Hole and the Devil's Arse being connected. I suppose you found out for yourself."

He picks up the knife and starts chipping at the wood again. It comes away in flakes, like peeling skin.

The stench of Thomas's rotting body lingers in my nostrils. "Am I dead? I think I drowned."

"No, Jane, you didn't drown," Will says slowly, as though

talking to a dim child. "I've just said that I pulled you from the river."

"Why're you here? Were you following me? I thought I was following you, but—"

"I came in the regular way, through the Devil's Arse."

"How did you know I'd be here?"

"I didn't." Will pats the ground beside him. "Come and sit by me, Jay Bird. You're hurt."

Everything's hurt: my body, my spirit. But Will has the answers, doesn't he? He always has the answers. I rise, then limp stiffly across the cavern to the fireside. Will helps me to the ground, shushing me as I whine. The fire lurks behind charred lumps of wood, a mean-spirited, dirty flame that makes me cough again, but I'll take any warmth I can get.

"You're weak as a pup, and you're shivering. Here."

He passes his pipe to me. I groan and push it away.

"Suit yourself." He takes a long drag, closing his eyes.

The next question is too big to ask. It sticks in my chest. It drives against my heart like knuckles. "You've not… you've not done anything, have you? To Isaac, I mean."

His voice is flat and colourless. "No, Jane, I haven't."

"Swear to me. Swear on all our lives that you've not laid a finger on him."

"Christ, Janey." He prods at the fire with a stick. Blackened clumps tumble and send up a shower of sparks.

"You swear it?"

He sighs. "I swear on Mam and Da's memory, all right?"

If he was feeling uneasy about the words he just said, he'd

gnaw his bottom lip. His mouth stays firmly shut.

"All right," I say. "All right."

"Good. I'm glad we got that out of the way. How do you know him? Isaac?"

My insides flip at the mention of his name. "I'm not sure I *do* know him."

"Come on, now. You were speaking to him last night. I saw you both come out of the back room."

I consider lying, but we've passed that point. "He was visiting the so-called Wonders of the Peak, looking for his cousin. I ended up accompanying him."

"Why?"

The memory of him handing me the embroidered handkerchief in Tideswell market floods me with the sweetest pain. "I suppose he was there when I needed comfort."

"Comfort?"

"I met Isaac the morning after… what happened with Thomas. I was tired and hurt and Isaac was so kind when he didn't need to be and… I'm going to sound like a right clod, but…"

"Go on."

I shake my head. "When I was with him, it was like I could see the good in the world. In me. Like it wasn't all horrible. He took me to see these Wonders, and they weren't wonderful, not really, but he made me think… he made me think…"

"I suppose it's like being a child again," Will says. "Seeing things through a stranger's eyes is like seeing them for the very first time, before the rot sets in."

All at once, I feel heavy. The churn of the river is a hush after a lullaby. I rest against Will, sinking into him. "I knew you wouldn't touch him. You're all right deep down."

"Now don't go all soft on me just because I pulled you from a river."

"That's what I mean. You always look out for me."

He lets out a dry little laugh.

"Your heart is thumping away," I say, my face slack against his chest.

He's silent. I hear blood thrumming through the channels of his body.

"You do know, don't you, that we can't leave things as they are?"

"Hm?"

"Isaac will find out about Thomas, especially with Bess poking around in all this."

He can't be saying what I think he's saying. I try to uncurl from him, lifting my head off his chest. But he holds fast, pressing into a sore patch on my arm. "We won't mess it up this time."

"Will…"

"It'll be clean. Not like it was with Thomas and Nathaniel and Harry. And—" His breath hitches.

There's a high-pitched ringing in my ears. "And?"

"There was another. About a week before Thomas."

A week before Thomas. Last month, then. August. The last time anyone saw Isaac's cousin.

"I always tell Mary not to have keepsakes, but I couldn't

bring myself to burn it. It's a reminder to do things better next time."

He pulls something out of his pocket. In my mind's eye, I see Isaac's drawing of Sarah, the one that showed her heart-shaped face, her full lips and coils of hair escaping from the hood decorated with little birds. The bloodied scrap of cloth Will is holding has the very same pattern.

"I didn't know her name. She was wandering round on her own, just outside Castleton. She had a head injury, blood all down the side of her face. Couldn't remember how she'd got it. Said she was trying to go home, but didn't know where it was. I said I'd take her there. She was half dead anyway. Thought I might as well not waste her. It was soon after what happened with Rebecca Needham and Grandam. I wasn't in my right mind."

I shake. My teeth clack.

"Things got… well, she panicked and ran back towards Castleton, down Winnats Pass. I was rough with her, and that only made her panic more. She started screaming and yelling. I tried to shut her up. Put my hand over her mouth. She turned quiet." He draws a sleeve across his lips. It comes away bloody. "I hadn't meant to do it there. I'd meant for her death to be painless—just a knock on the head and a push into Elden Hole, nothing more. I'd made a mess of it all, Janey, such a mess."

He struggles for breath. Is this why he's never said anything about it before? Is he ashamed, not of killing an innocent woman—Isaac's cousin—but of his failure to do it right? Is that what he cares about?

"I went back to Bess's, tipped the place upside down in a temper, then went to find something to… You don't want to know what I did. Suffice to say I carried her down here in bags."

I push him away. The flames of the fire cast a dance of red and black on the stone, making the space around me shrink and grow, shrink and grow. Mary's song flutes over the crash of blood in my ears. *Dear Sir, the night is drawing near; I can no longer tarry here…*

"Then Bess started talking about a stench coming from the Devil's Arse. I thought this was her attempt at humour, but others were talking about it as well. It was the remains of the woman. I hadn't hidden them well enough. I should have carried them all the way up to Elden Hole and thrown them down, but I acted too quickly, impetuously, when I hid them in here. I needed to burn what was left. She never fully goes away, though. There's always a part of her here, no matter how hard I try to get rid."

The black hunks in the fire; the shrunken, blunt clubs. Surely, they'd have burnt to nothing by now if they were made of wood. One of them is round at the end. You don't get firewood shaped like that.

That day, when I came in here with Isaac, the guides said there were villains hiding out in the depths of the cave. Villains like Thomas, I'd thought, but it hadn't been him. Villains, like my brother.

Will's fingers dig into my shoulder.

"The funny thing is, Jane… somehow Isaac seems to know. And I've got this feeling you might have something to do with it."

A nonsensical sound spills off my tongue.

"What's that?" asks Will.

My face contorts. "Have mercy."

"No, Jane. Not this time."

"But… before. Rebecca. Rebecca Needham." I force myself to look at him, at his swollen eyes and the blood dribbling from his gnawed bottom lip. "You showed mercy then."

Will holds the next breath for a long time, then releases it with a pained groan. "I thought I was doing the world a favour, saving Rebecca and getting rid of Grandam. That she-wolf needed to be sent straight to Hell. But the Needhams never forgave me for wandering off with Rebecca, even though I gave her back to them. When she did die a few days later, I wondered…" He clears his throat. "I wondered if that wet night out on Elden Hill had weakened her heart. And Grandam—I thought Elden Hole would appreciate the offering. But it made things worse. I don't know why. It made everything so much worse."

My mind refuses to understand that mere weeks have passed since the night Will came in from the rain, dazed as though someone had bewitched him. *I've got to wash*, he said, and he stripped to his waist and ran a damp cloth over and over his body while me and Mary asked, *Where's Grandam, Will? Where's Grandam?* When he finally told us what had happened, how he'd offered her in place of Rebecca, we were too shocked to speak. And we didn't speak of it again.

All at once, I understand. "It was you, Will. Your sacrifice of Grandam. It gave Elden Hole a taste of our blood, and that's what She's wanted ever since our grandfather went down there. That's why She won't leave us be. Why strangers are mere scraps to Her."

A mumbled objection dies in his throat.

"Killing Isaac won't do any good," I say, a desperate hope rising in me. "It's us. It's our blood She's after."

His face that I once thought so handsome creases into an ugly frown. "Even if what you're saying is right, and I'm not sure it is, we need to get rid of anyone who knows too much."

The flames waver as smoke stings my eyes. "But I *love* him, Will."

My brother rubs my arm. "I know you do." He sounds like he means it.

"I can't let you do it. I won't."

His hand hovers above my head, as if he's pondering whether to stroke or strike. It comes down, cold, on the back of my neck. He takes a deep breath.

"I thought you'd say that."

My head is yanked backwards. Thomas's knife gleams above my throat. I let out a strangled cry and search for pity in Will's face, but all I see is a terrible resolve. He boils in the red glow of the fire, his stern jaw trembling, sweat gushing from his temples.

"Will, no, n—"

He covers my mouth and lifts the knife.

I bite his hand. With a howl, he lets go. Scrambling away from him across the cavern floor, every muscle in my body cramping, I grope around for any weapon I can find. Will crawls towards me, Thomas's dagger still in his hand. I kick out at him, and the toe of my boot glances off his chin. He falls sideways, putting out his hands to catch himself, landing straight in the fire, and I watch, too afraid to move, as his sleeve catches the flame. Screaming, he darts over to the river, flailing like a mad man. For a moment, I think he's going to throw himself in, but he falls to his knees and dips his arms in the water, whimpering. The smell of cooking flesh fills the dank air of the cavern.

Now is the time, while his back is to me. All it would take is a push.

That which causes you the most exquisite pain.

Of course. It's him. It's always been him: my brother, whose love and attention I craved, but never got; who only involved me in his schemes when he needed someone else to blame. William Vernon. My defender and my tormentor.

From across the bank comes the flap of heavy wings. A black shape crouches there. Something is sprouting from its head and growing, puffing up like a column of smoke, until the beast has reached the height of a man. Then one leg, made of a bundle of twigs and briars, snaps out to the side, hinged in the middle like a spider's leg. Another stretches behind, covered in the black and white fur of a cat. There are a dozen legs, I see now, some hooved, some ending in bloated human feet. A great pair of wings opens up wide to reveal the front of Her body. Every bit of Her skin is covered in hedgehog spines the size of knitting needles, every bit except for Her breasts, which are naked, with nipping claws writhing out of them. Where the genitals should be, there's a pair of fat, wet lips, and behind that, a glistening snake of a tail that whips back and forth.

Her skull head, facing backwards, turns slowly around. The face is a patchwork of human flesh. The weather-beaten cheeks and grizzled beard belong to Thomas and the bloodied ear, auburn hair still clinging to it, is Nathaniel's. But the eyes that stare out at me from across the water are Grandam's.

She opens Her mouth, packed with teeth both sharp and grinding, both human and animal. *Do it.*

I step towards Will.

It'd be no good simply pushing him in. I'd have to hold him down under the water till the air bubbled out of him. Then I'd leave him here, to be digested in the gut of the Devil.

By the remains of the fire, my foot knocks against something. It's Thomas's knife. Will doesn't move from the bank as I bend to get it.

"I know what you're doing," he says. He sits up, cradling his blistered hands in his lap. "I know you want rid of me."

I shake my head. The knife in my hand says otherwise.

"It'd be good for us all, wouldn't it?" he says. "It'd feel right. The one who gives the offerings becomes an offering himself. Sounds like a story they'd tell on a winter's night." He looks down, dropping his voice. His shoulders slacken. "It's easier than you think, you know. You don't really have to think at all. Your soul goes somewhere else when you're doing it. You'll dwell on it afterwards, over and over again, until you're sure you're going mad. You might go mad, if you're not there already. But in time, even the memories of killing someone fade."

He looks up at me. He's crying.

"You'll have a good life, Janey. Believe it or not, it's all I've ever wanted for us."

"Quiet!" I storm towards him, thrusting the knife within an inch of his neck. Will and the angel that waits on the other side of the stream are but smudges seen through my tears. "Why do you have to be like this? Even when I'm the one with the knife in my hand, you're telling me what to do!"

"Do what you have to."

"Stop it! You're no martyr. A minute ago, you were ready to slit my throat."

"I wouldn't have done it."

"It didn't seem like that to me. And now you're all, *You'll have a good life, it's all I ever wanted.* Well, bollocks to that! You're a sly, heartless bastard, William Vernon, and you'd have left me down here to rot if I hadn't fought back."

The Spirit flicks a wing, losing patience. She must've led me down here for no other purpose but this. The trick at the mouth of Elden Hole and the voices in the Shouting Cave were Her doing. This is the final temptation. If I give in, there'll be peace in this life, and sweet damnation in the next. If I don't, I'll suffer in the here and now—but there's a chance, however small, that I might be saved.

"If you're going to do it," Will says, "get it over with."

"Why should it be up to me?"

He laughs without humour. "I thought you wanted to make your own decisions."

"How can I? If it's not you controlling me, it's the Spirit."

He narrows his eyes. "The Spirit?'

The hellish thing stretches forth a wing across the water, nudging the back of Will's collar. He doesn't flinch.

"And if I don't do what it tells me, I have to answer to God. All our lives, we've been doing what some greater power or other wants us to do. Even you, come to think of it—even you… Christ Almighty!"

The coins poured from Grandam's hands into his for each thing he killed. Will trusted her. Everything she said took root in his young and corruptible heart. He was made a slave to her, a slave to Elden Hole, before he knew how to protect himself.

"What choice did *you* have?" I sob. "You were a child."

There's silence in the cave. Even the river seems to have stopped flowing.

Will clasps his burnt hands to his mouth. A low, deep cry comes from his throat. He doubles over, his back heaving. I look down at the dagger, thinking I must've stabbed him without moving at all, but the blade is clean. I throw the god-forsaken thing into the river. The Spirit bares Her teeth and folds into a crack in the wall with a low growl.

I hold my brother.

He clasps me round the middle, buries his face into my stomach and weeps. I weep with him for all the lives we've taken and for the lives we were denied. I run my fingers through his dark hair and hush him like Mam used to do when we were small enough to curl against her chest and feel her heartbeat against our ears. Slowly, the sound in the cave comes back. The water flows, as it's always done.

"What'll we do now?" Will asks.

"We head back to the village," I say. I take the piece of Sarah's hood from his pocket and place it in my own. "And we confess."

Chapter Thirty-Two

The Shivering Mountain watches us push through pain and tiredness all the way out of the village, past the ruins of Peveril Castle, arriving at the foot of Winnats Pass, breathless. There's no talk. All our strength goes into keeping our legs moving up the steep path and keeping thoughts of what Will did to Sarah at bay. We're making good headway, till, halfway up, Will chokes on the thinning air. Coughs turn to sobs—the same heaving, wrenching cries he loosed in the Devil's Arse—and he doubles over. I want to help him along, but I'm drained. The wind has no sympathy, lashing our broken bodies.

"Come on, Will. We need to get home. It's not too far now."

He holds his hands up before him as if he realises for the first time that his skin is blistered.

"We'll get you help for those burns when we get back. Mary can make a poultice for you. She'll…"

What am I telling him? Both of us know full well that life can't carry on as it was. The road that leads through these mountains will take us to the hangman. The best we can do is distract ourselves while making the final journey, without making false promises.

"Someone found a rock imprinted with a seashell up here," I say. "He reckoned there used to be water covering this bit of land."

Will looks up, seemingly as surprised by the words that come out of my mouth as I am. "Can't be true."

"That's what I said. But think about it. The great flood was supposed to have drowned everything, barring what was on the ark. Some fish and shells could've got washed up to higher ground."

Will wipes away a trail of snot. "Do you really believe that?"

On a morning like this, I'd almost believe it. The mist lying over the higher land ahead of us might be the waters of a deep sea. "I believe all kinds of shite. Come on, let's keep going."

We talk. Not of what's going to happen next, nor what led us there, but of summer dances, when the whole village would gather in Old Tom Archdale's field and the Weasel would play the fiddle, turning from a drunken lout into a nimble-fingered musician, and Alice Walsh would follow Will around like a spaniel, hoping for a dance.

"Did you even like her?"

Will lifts his shoulders. "She was all right. Not as ugly as people used to make out, anyhow. It's a shame. If she'd survived her fever…"

I try to steer us back towards more joyful times, reminding

him of when we found an abandoned house all the way out near Wormhill and used it as our hiding place till we were chased off by a hermit—we thought it was a hermit, anyhow, since he was covered in lice and had a big beard—but Will's too mournful to laugh about it.

Enough mist has shifted to show the turning for Peak Forest up ahead. We slow to a stop.

"Let's go by the top road," Will says.

I look at him out of the corner of my eye. "You sure?"

He veers off. "We'll see better from there."

"See what better? I can see all right."

As soon as we get to the top, I understand what he's talking about. Behind us, the sun is rising, sailing above the white swirls of the ghost sea. Last night's blue-black sky has turned the colour of ripe wheat, ribboned with bands of silver and purple. In the distance, the very tip of Mam Tor nudges a cloud. In all my years on this earth, I've never looked hard enough and long enough to really marvel at a sunrise. It's a shame that I'm doing it now, of all mornings.

"I'm cold," I say, tears welling up in my eyes. "Let's keep walking."

Will doesn't move. "A little while longer."

We stay there until the sun hangs high enough in the sky to start burning off the mist. Bit by bit, crests of hills dotted with cows and sheep come into view. Birdsong fills the air.

"I want to get back before too many people are around," I say.

Will nods. I wonder if, like me, he thinks of running in

that moment: taking off to Hull or Liverpool, boarding a ship and starting a new life overseas, just as Thomas wanted to do. Who'd come looking for us? Isaac wants the truth, but he wouldn't follow us wherever we went, would he? That, I remind myself, is the very reason why we can't just run; we'd be leaving behind too many people who deserve to know what really happened.

Will turns his back on freedom. "I'm ready."

Dread starts to stew in me. I know where we're heading. Home, and then Derby gaol, and then the gallows. It was a premonition, that rope. Isaac has put it round our necks, in a way. Which of us will die first, I wonder? I hope it's me, so I don't have to watch Will suffer.

My brother pushes on. Sooner than I'm ready for, we reach Elden Hill. The scar in the land comes into view. It stops us in our tracks, that great and terrible nothing.

Will bites the corner of his bottom lip. "People who aren't from here won't understand why we did what we did."

"They don't need to understand. They only need to know that it was us who killed them. Sarah Pulmer. Thomas Mace. Nathaniel Needham. Harry Needham." Each name is a stone in my mouth.

Sarah was an innocent. A wandering soul who'd taken one too many wrong paths.

Thomas Mace, nasty piece of work that he was, has left behind a wife and children.

Nathaniel and Harry—well, they were in the way. They were always in the way. But that doesn't make it forgivable.

"You've forgotten Grandam," Will says.

"Oh, yes. Annie Bradley."

"Five people. Five." Will walks to the side of the Hole that doesn't have any ledges to break a fall. It's where we stood when we rolled the body of Thomas Mace into the abyss. Sweat gathers on my palms.

"Get away from there."

"You didn't kill any of them, Janey. It was all me."

I shake my head. "No. No, Will. It was Mary who killed Thomas."

"It was me who killed Grandam. It was me who gave Elden Hole a taste of our blood."

It's the truth. But that doesn't mean… that can't mean… "Get away from that edge, Will. Stop being daft, now."

Keeping far away from the drop, I take a few staggering steps towards him, but he puts out his arms and moves away from me, closer to the mouth of the Hole. "Don't come any closer, or I swear—"

"Listen to me, Will, you need to step back."

"It'll go on and on!" he shouts. "She'll take Mary. She'll take my child."

My child. The tenderness and sadness of it shakes me to the core. "I thought you didn't care for Bess."

His eyes are flaming wild now. "I didn't say anything about Bess! Why did you have to bring her up?"

"I'm sorry, I—"

"I was talking about the baby. You listen to me! Why should an innocent have to suffer because of what I've done?"

Will's jaw trembles, as it did when he held a knife above my throat. "You said I didn't have any real choice, because I was a child. What choice would I be giving my own offspring, if I let this curse go on and on? It's our blood She wants, you said that yourself. You're wise, Janey. Wiser than I've ever given you credit for."

"You're not a child anymore," I say, my voice faint. "You can choose to do good."

The wind drops. Will looks at me from across the void.

"That's what I'm doing."

He takes a step forward. My legs turn to liquid. This is wrong. This isn't how it's meant to be.

"Will!" I cry. "Come back. Come home with me."

Something of Mam's spirit softens the plains and edges of his face. Then his mouth curls, impossibly, into a smile. He coughs up a laugh, shakes his head. "You know, I never did buy that piece of the royal forest."

It takes him an eternity to step over the edge, an eternity in which I could run across to him and grab him. He's in no hurry. He walks into the air as if setting off for an evening at the inn.

He screams, once, a cry that sounds more like defiance than fear.

And then there's only the screech of the rooks.

I stare at the empty patch of ground where he was standing, but my mind can't take it in. It makes no sense. He was there, and now he's gone.

I wait for him to shout for help or come climbing up to

the surface, smeared with dirt and blood, but grinning in triumph. I wait for him to tell me it was all in jest, all of it. I wait. I wait.

There's a cloud in the sky that looks just like a crown. The wind smudges it out of shape. I never picked up that carving Will made from the cave floor. It'll still be there, no doubt. I can ask one of the guides to collect it for me.

The sun climbs higher and sears the back of my neck. Hunger gnaws at my belly, then slinks away. When I'm too weak to stand any longer, and a bludgeoning tiredness hits me over the back of the head, I allow myself to sink to the ground, but I won't sleep. He can't find me sleeping when he comes back.

Someone—I don't know who—asks if I need help. When I say I'm on my way to Mary, they leave me be, though I can tell they're still staring.

She's at the White Hart, cleaning the long table. Bess is there as well, making herself useful by washing tankards. Good girl, Mary. I knew you'd look after her.

When my sister catches sight of me, she drops the cloth and hurries over.

"Janey, where…?" Her eyes widen at the sight of my dirtied mining gear. "What's happened?"

"Is Isaac in?"

She looks over at the barrels, towards Bess. The bruise on

top of her birthmark is a ripe ring of mauve. It's among the last remaining traces of Will in the world. I want, fiercely, to kiss it.

"I need Isaac," I say. "Get me Isaac."

My knees tremble, about to give way. Mary manoeuvres my shaking body onto a bench. "We'll get him for you, worry not. You're all right. You'll be all right." She nods at Bess. "Wake Mr Latimer."

"Yes, Mary."

Bess gathers her petticoat and goes upstairs, while Mary pours a large measure of sack. I drink it in one. "Will's dead," I say.

Do I say it? They can't be my words.

Mary's mouth is agape. "You what?"

"He's dead."

Taking infinite care, she sinks down next to me. "How?"

"He jumped."

Her eyes wander back to the cloth on the table. She picks it up, wrings it out. The water drips off her chapped fingers. Absently, she wipes them down the front of her apron.

"Oh," she says. "Oh."

From upstairs come muffled voices. I strain my ears to hear if one of them belongs to Isaac, but I can't tell from this far off.

"He told me he killed a woman," I say.

Mary twists the apron tie round her hand, making a fist so tight that her fingers mottle with purple. "I know."

Of course Mary knows. He shares everything with her.

"We were coming back to confess."

The White Hart, so peaceful at this time of day, so normal-looking, wavers. I hold my breath to stop the tears from coming.

"Supposing… supposing we didn't say anything? About…" Mary drops her voice. "About the murders. Dead men don't talk, do they?"

I blink. Tears streak down my cheeks. "You mean we let him take all the blame? He always said, if one of us swings, we all do."

"You can't hang a dead man." She grabs my leg and shakes it. "We could be all right, you and me. Look at what I've done here, at the White Hart. I'm in charge now. It's my place."

"Aye, by foul means."

She lets go of me. "What do you mean?"

My tongue darts out to lick the salt tears off my top lip. "I looked through your collection of keepsakes."

Our eyes lock.

I opened it before coming here—the deep, lined box, filled with an inky bed of magpie and rook feathers. Beneath were pins of bone, jet beads, shards of flint, a button ripped from the shirt of Harry Needham and a lock of Nathaniel's hair, tied with string: treasures pillaged from the world of the lost. There was another object in the box, off-cream in colour and made of wax. A little doll, with iron nails driven into the stomach and womb.

No wonder Alyson Bagshawe's been complaining of pain lately.

"What were you thinking?" I whisper. "If anyone found

that doll, it'd be the end of you. Remember them witches from Bakewell that were hanged back in Mam and Da's time?"

"I'm not like that," she mutters, twisting her apron strings about her hands again. "Besides, this isn't bloody Lancashire. No one's been carted off to the gallows for witchcraft in ages."

"You realise once all this about Will comes to light, you won't be able to get away with pulling the wool over people's eyes? You've got to leave."

She turns on me like a feral dog. "We made a deal! You said you'd let me run this place."

"I didn't know you were doing *that*. You were double-dealing with me as well, making me sleep in and miss meeting Will and Isaac at Elden Hole. Besides, you've got no reason to stay here anymore. It's over." I close my eyes and see Will falling again, in that obscene way that took forever and no time at all. "She's got what She wants."

"Why… why are you talking like this, when Wi… when my brother…" She rips the ties loose, tears off her apron and screams into it, again and again, as if she's bringing a life into the world rather than grieving a loss. I drape my arm around her quaking shoulders and cradle her head.

"Look, it's not safe here for you anymore," I say. "Go to Castleton, or further away still. Take Bess. Elden Hole is satisfied for now, for a long time. She—"

Footsteps are coming down the stairs. Two sets of them. Fear and a kind of sick excitement tumble about inside me.

I part from Mary. "Will won't bear the guilt of this alone."

As my sister lifts a bewildered, tear-stained face, Bess

walks in. She's clutching the arm of another woman, boasting, "Look who I've found in Isaac's room! Here's your Mr Latimer."

Half-dressed in breeches and an untucked shirt, her long pale hair plaited over her shoulder, Isabella is angry and tired and beautiful—as beautiful as Isaac ever was.

"Where were you?" I cry, staggering to my feet. "Where were you yesterday morning? I went looking everywhere. I thought something awful had happened."

"Jane! I was… Get off me." She shakes herself free of Bess. "Leave us in peace."

Bess looks to Mary for approval and sees my sister wiping her face on the apron.

"Everything all right?" she asks.

Me and Mary exchange a glance.

"Come into the kitchen," says Mary. "We need to have a little talk."

Bess's face drops. "About what?"

Mary doesn't answer.

"Is it Will?" Already, her voice is breaking. "Has summat happened?"

"Come on," says my sister. "Not here."

As she steers Bess towards the kitchen, Mary looks over her shoulder. While my brother, fearing discovery, would frighten me out of confessing at this moment, Mary does something far worse. She regards me with pity, as if my fate has already been sealed.

Then they're gone, and I'm alone with the person I cherish

most in the world.

"Isaac—"

"Isabella," she corrects. "I'm Isabella now."

Her hands stray up to her face to check for a beard and, finding nothing there, come to rest by her sides.

"What happened to you?" she asks quietly, almost shy. "You look like death."

"Tell me what happened to you first."

She closes her eyes. "I went to meet your brother at dawn, but… I wanted to frighten him—make him think I'd descended into the pit on a rope and then catch him off-guard, get some confession of guilt out of him… It was an ill-conceived plan, and then I became afraid. I thought I heard… It was nothing. I was afraid, that was all. I left the rope dangling there and instead of waiting for your brother, I went back to my chamber. I had a lot to think about. Margaret Needham has told me some curious things about you and your family."

"That I'm a murderer?" I ask. "A thief? That I bear the stamp of Satan?"

Isabella steps towards me. "Did you really rob Thomas Mace? Is that how your brother came into possession of Sarah's necklace?"

For so long I've been keeping the truth from her. I can hide it no longer, no matter what she might think of me. If this is the last time I see her, speak to her—if I die knowing that she bears me all the ill feeling in the world, so be it.

"Yes."

Gently, she twines her arms around me, her cheek resting

on my neck. "I knew you hadn't hurt Sarah. I thought, when I met your brother, and Bess said he was the one who gave her the jewels… I thought the two of you had… But no, thank God, no."

She kisses up my neck to the corner of my mouth. We find each other's lips. I press into her slender body, covered only by a thin linen, and feel the warmth in my breast flow through my skin as it touches hers. I want her to know how dear she is to me, how dear Isaac is to me, how it doesn't matter which of them I meet, the feeling is the same.

Despising myself for what I'm about to do, I push her gently away. I reach into my pocket and draw out Sarah's blood-stained hood. It's like a charm that freezes Isabella to the spot.

"W… what's this?"

"It's hers."

Her eyes meet mine. "Where did you find it?" she asks, each word slow and laboured. "Did Thomas Mace have it as well? Why is there blood upon the fabric? Jane?"

"My brother took it," I say. "He took it off Sarah after he… after he did away with her."

Isabella reels back, hand clasped to her mouth. With each step she takes away from me, another gash opens up in my heart.

"Believe me, I had nothing to do with that. I didn't even know until last night what he'd done." I take a deep breath. "But I did know all about Thomas, because me and my brother killed him together. We robbed him, and then we pushed his body down the Hole. Will took the jewellery and gave it to Bess."

Her mouth twists into a silent question.

"Mary knew nothing about what was happening. It was us: me and Will. We killed Thomas Mace. Then I let him kill Nathaniel and Harry Needham. If Margaret told you that, it's true."

She nods, her face a mask of horror. "Why? Why did you do it?"

Will was right. No one outside our family can possibly understand.

"It was in our blood," I say, as if that's really it. As if that explains it all.

Chapter Thirty-Three

The lad who's in for forgery is carving his symbols again. During the five months we've shared this cell, he's covered the wall in daisy wheels and pictures of men hanging by their necks, and now he's hacking at the door itself.

"What is it this time?" I ask from the pile of filthy straw that serves as a bed.

Without taking his eyes off the task, he replies, "It's us."

I know from experience that if I go to look at his work before it's finished, he'll get into a temper. So I lie on the hard floor and wait till he chucks away his stone and says, "You can see it now."

My back protests as I rise. It's never fully recovered from the fall into the river down in Elden Hole, and months without a proper bed hasn't helped it either. The one thing I can be glad of is that the Spirit of Elden Hole doesn't come into my dreams anymore. I can only hope it's because Will's sacrifice was worth it.

That's what I dream about now: my brother, falling. Sometimes, I'm the one who pushes him, and I wake thinking that the rumours must be true—I must've gone mad after that night in the caves and shoved him into the abyss with my own hands. Sometimes, I dream he's alive, and I wake with a wonderful feeling, like light spreading through my veins. Then, the choking stench of the cell and the pressing walls remind me of what really happened. Those dreams can put me in a state of living death for days, or what seems like days anyhow.

Pain still cramping my lower back, I drag myself as far as the chain will allow. The picture on the door is of a box with two stick people inside. They take up most of the room in the box. Their mouths are straight lines. In the corner is a bucket surrounded by dots, which I take to be the flies. In the background, a tiny gallows pole waits for them.

"A good one," I say. "Life-like."

The lad sticks out his lower lip. "Ta."

He reminds me a little of Will, a little of Nathaniel Needham. He's not long for this world. If the hangman doesn't get him, he's bound to end up dead after a brawl sooner or later. He's good company, as good as you can get in Derby gaol. I can be thankful I'm left in here with him and not with the man who beat his love rival to a bloody pulp. He called me a monster for what I'd done to *my own flesh and blood*. How they got wind of Will's death, I don't know. I can only assume that these walls, damp and scurvy as they are, absorb the stories people whisper about us, and all you have to do is put your ear to them and listen to hear the most blood-curdling tales.

We both start back when a knock comes at the door and

a guard shouts, "There's someone here to see you, Vernon."

It must be a trick. I've not had word from anyone in Peak Forest since I got here, months ago. Yet the guard who opens the door is one of the better sort. He's doled out extra food and water to us before and given me sheets when my monthly blood comes.

I lift my head. "Who?"

"A woman."

"Mary? Mary Vernon?" My heart scrambles out of place. "Or Isabella Latimer?"

"She didn't give her name," replies the guard. "I'll go and fetch her."

At the start of my time in gaol, this announcement might've prompted lewd remarks from the men in the cell. The coin-clipper's wife visited on a couple of occasions, but anyone hoping for an intimate reunion was disappointed; the woman was too upset to even finish the conversation about who'd get the man's possessions after he'd passed on. Soon, the heat went out of the men. Their eyes became glazed and glassy, like the eyes of rabbits caught between the metal teeth of traps. One after another, they succumbed to the bad air in this place and died of gaol fever. I don't know what happened to the bodies, or why, injured and weak as I am, I didn't follow them into death.

Now the forgery lad says, "I'll leave you in peace," and he slouches against the wall near the rancid bucket.

There's the sound of footsteps, and then the woman who's come to see me steps in, hood raised against the cold. It takes me a moment to recognise her as Mary. Her thin cheeks are plump and rouged. Where her scarlet robe once hung off her frame, it now fits snugly. She's grown up.

"Hello, Janey."

She puts down her hood. Her fingers are decked with rings. I wonder if I should kiss the hand that looks so much more regal than mine.

"Hello, Mary."

Of course it wouldn't be Isabella. She wouldn't want to see me ever again, not after what I confessed. I despise myself for being disappointed. Isn't my own sister, devilish as she is, enough?

"My, this place is something of a shithole, isn't it?" she says.

I laugh, and it sounds like someone coughing up ash.

"How's Peak Forest?"

"I'm not there anymore. You were right. I needed to get out. I went Castleton way and married an old widower."

"You're married?" How could so much have changed in the time I've been in this mouldering cell?

"Aye," she says. "We run an inn—the Black Feathers."

The name's familiar, but I can't think from where.

"Not for long, though. He's very sick. Lord have mercy on his dear soul."

"What's wrong with him?"

"Old age." She admires the glinting wedding band on her finger. "A weak heart."

A succession of images spring into my mind: Mary, jumping out at him from the top of the stairs; the old man whirling in panic when Mary tells him there's a band of robbers outside the inn door and collapsing, a hand clutched to his chest; the husband staring down in horror on his wedding night when he sees he's smooth as an oyster between his legs.

"You ought to be careful," I say. "You don't want to end up in here with me."

"I am careful," she replies, low and serious. Then she adds, her voice rising to the ceiling, "Ooh, and our Bess has had a baby. A healthy little boy. She's named him William."

The smile and the tears come at the same time. I lean against the coolness of her shadow across the cell wall. "That's wonderful," I say.

"Walter's left his wife and is living with Alyson now. They run the White Hart together. I thought you'd be pleased to hear she's made a miraculous recovery."

I nod, tears dripping into my mouth. The salt in them is more palatable than anything we've been given to eat all these months. "I am."

We're silent for a while. I sense the forger, who's been listening to us, drift back into his own broken mind.

"Do people talk?" I ask eventually. "About me and Will?"

Mary wobbles her head. "From time to time."

"What do they say?"

"Oh, all sorts."

The air here is too stale and thick to breathe. "They believe the worst of me?"

"They believe what you wanted them to believe."

"What I wanted," I echo dimly. "Aye."

She frowns, as if I might point the finger at her here and now, in front of the guards. It'd be satisfying, in a way, if they chucked her in here beside me. If one of us hangs, we all hang.

"You don't hate me, do you?" she asks.

She touches my shoulder. Her fingers have worked dark magic. They've stuck pins into the belly of a doll and pinched dead men's possessions. But they've also healed my wounds. I fall into her arms, warmth surging through me despite the freezing air.

"I could never hate you, Magpie."

"Good. I miss you, Jay Bird," Mary whispers. "You know, there's still time."

I pull back. "For what?"

A pause. "Say it was all Will. Say you had nowt to do with it."

"Margaret Needham will speak against me, whatever I say."

She'd gathered a crowd on the street outside the White Hart, set up a court of her own where she condemned me as the murderer of her husband and son. "And so steeped in wickedness is she," Margaret spat, jabbing her finger at my face, "that she killed her own flesh and blood. Her brother."

Gasps. A single cry. Murmurs of *Will? Will Vernon, dead?* A protest rose in my throat and got stuck. Why defend myself? Isabella had left me. Will had left me. I had nothing to fight for. So I stayed silent while Margaret flayed me alive before my neighbours and then carted me off to Constable Cresswell.

"What did you tell the Justice of the Peace?" Mary speaks in a hush. "Surely not everything?"

"Not much. But he wrote enough." He scribbled page after page of notes while tears drowned my words. My story has become his and Margaret's. "I can't change anything now, Mary."

Will would have patted me on the back for taking on his burden, but he'd be turning in his grave to know Mary was talking about me walking away, a free woman. The trust he put in her: what did it bring him, in the end? If things had turned out differently on that morning, and it was him standing here, would she be just as eager to lay all the blame on me?

"You get on with your life, Mary. Take care of Bess and the child. That's the best I could wish for. It's what Will wanted."

There—is that it? A flash of sadness in her eyes, regret for how she's been talking about him?

"I wish there was summat I could do for you, in return for all you've done for me," she says.

"You can do one thing." I wrap my arms round her again and whisper in her ear, "Have you still got mine and Will's share of Thomas's money?"

I'm afraid she'll say no, she's spent it all on the new inn or on wedding finery. But she replies, "Aye. What do you want me to do with it?"

I give her a firm squeeze. "Send it to Mrs Goodwin of Jumber House, Eyam. She's the stepmother of the woman Will… the one he killed. Isaac's cousin." I stand back to search her face for loyalty—if not to Will, then to me. I can't tell. My own sister, and I can't tell if she'll do what I'm asking of her. "Please. And tell Isaac I miss him and—"

"Don't fret, Janey, I'll do as you ask." Her voice drops to a whisper. "You've given me this chance to live. I'm not going to let you down. I have to go now."

"All right." I already feel the terrible loss of her. It tears my heart out. "All right, Mary. Keep well."

"And you, Jay Bird."

She kisses me on the cheek. It may be a trick of the light, but I could swear that, as she turns to go, her shadow doesn't move after her, but stays where it is, looming high and thin on the gaol wall. Then, as if remembering to catch up with her, it moves sinuously towards her heels and blends into the darkness cast by her cloak.

There was some small part of me that wondered if Mary would save my skin at the last moment, but there's no sign of that now. When the sun rises tomorrow, I'll be judged at the Lent Assizes. Doubtless they'll find me guilty of robbery and murder, and I'll be carted off to the gallows. I'm willing to bet that Mrs Needham will be in the crowd on the day of my execution, watching with a smug smile while they loop the rope round my neck. She'll probably bring the children for a family day out.

And my sister? Will she be there to watch me die, a horrified face among a sea of gleeful townsfolk baying for my blood? Or will she be too afraid to make an appearance, worried that I'll send up a hue and cry of, "It was Mary who smashed in Thomas's skull!"

Lord, may it be quick. May Will be waiting for me on the other side, and may he know I'm doing this for him, so that he doesn't have to bear the burden of guilt alone. In time, people will talk only of Jane Vernon wandering the hills on a moonlit night, lurking behind half-collapsed walls and trees to push unwary travellers down Elden Hole. Already, I can feel myself turning into a ghost, a cautionary tale designed to scare children into behaving.

It's what I chose, and it's the right thing, even if it doesn't feel like it now.

The tiredness in my limbs is a great mercy. More than tomorrow's judgement, I feared lying awake all night, each moment bloated with worry. But now, as I lay on the mat of straw, my breathing becomes steady and a heaviness settles over me, and I sink.

The world turns upside down.

I'm on top of a hill overlooking Peak Forest. A long, high note rings out from the moon, warbling over the valley, causing each blade of grass to prick up like the ears of a hare. In the village below, Walter has his arms round Mrs Bagshawe, who breathes out the last wisps of pain. The Needham children are packed into beds, close as newly whelped pups, as their mother looks for traces of Harry in their sleeping faces. The land around the old hunting lodge is silent but for the gentle pawing of hooves. The last of the deer disappears into the memory of the royal forest. All is at peace.

I pull on my horse's reins. She tosses her head, fire flicking up from her mane and dissolving into sparks in the hot night.

Away we turn from Peak Forest, from Elden Hole, heading across Tideswell Moor towards the place where the circle of stones has waited for us since the sunrise of the very first day. I look down at the shadow, my shadow, that ripples along beside me; and, for once, I am not afraid of it.

"You know, Janey," says Will, for he's here as well, standing in my path. "It's all right. You don't have to go."

"But I don't want you to be lonely," I say.

He looks over at Elden Hole. "I'm not alone. I'm part of Her."

The hills call, *Vernon! William Vernon!*

He smiles, then, showing the gaps where his teeth have been ripped out by the root. "And She wishes to repay you."

I keel over. A boulder has smashed against my side, knocking the air from my body.

"Vernon! Get up."

Another blow to my ribs brings me, gasping, spiralling, back to the hard floor of the cell. A guard stands over me, his face wrinkled with disdain. It was his boot that kicked me awake. This is the man who likes to dole out beatings and drag people to their fate in the Assizes. So, it's time to face my judgement. I mustn't resist. I must meet what's coming to me with as much dignity as I can muster. The lad is still asleep. Why wake me and not him?

"Someone's come for you," the guard rasps, as though I've spoken aloud. I might've done.

A gnat buzz of hope whines in my heart. It's quiet, painful.

"My sister?"

"No." He gestures to the thousand feet of darkness beyond the cell. "This one."

A man appears in the doorway, a bright vision of yellow and blue. The visitor has an impossibly soft-looking golden beard. His eyes shine with what, despite everything, looks like love.

My tongue is too dry and swollen to ask if all this is real. They say people dying of thirst see visions of water.

Isaac hands the guard a purse. "For your troubles."

The bastard opens it up, counts the money inside and slouches away, closing the door of the cell without locking it.

I stand, but my legs are straw and collapse under me. The visitor rushes over and kneels, brushing my matted hair from my face. Somehow, I find the words to say to him. "I thought you'd never want to see me again."

"Mary told me," Isaac replies, his lips barely moving, his hand still resting on the back of my head. "She told me that you never lifted a hand against a single one of those victims. You are innocent, Jane."

I try to make sense of his words. Was I not there, by Will's side, when Thomas, Nathaniel, and Harry were killed?

"I said… I told Margaret Needham…"

"She has dropped her charges against you and won't be appearing as a witness tomorrow. Mary saw to it."

Stomach cramps for her as well, I wonder, or did Mary simply tell her that Will was to blame and beg for my life?

"And the Justice of the Peace? He has my deposition."

A frown darkens Isaac's brow, but only for a moment. "He's been well compensated for accurately recording what you told him—which, I hear, is a very small amount indeed."

It sits ill with me. I did so little to help the Needham men. My fight was always for Isaac. Will wanted to do away with him, and yet here he is. Here he is in the living flesh. I reach out and stroke his cheek. He turns aside.

"You know I never would have let anything happen to you," I say. "I wasn't trying to—"

"Jane, you were trying to do the best for your brother, just as, in my own way, I was trying to do the best for Sarah. Our efforts were woefully inadequate and misguided, and they ended disastrously—yet I believe that we were acting out of goodness."

Tears glimmer in shining seams down Isaac's face. How can I tell him? That before we met, I acted out of nothing but fear, but after, after…

"There's no one in the world dearer to me than you," I say. "It hurts me to the marrow of my bones that I caused you misery or harm of any sort. I wish I could have been what you deserve."

"People are not rewards for a life well lived, Jane," he says, looking at me again. "We do not win better or worse hearts according to our merits. We love who we love."

I close my eyes. "This is a dream, isn't it?"

"No, Jane."

"Then you must be a thing of darkness. Isaac would not say these things. He could not love me after all that's happened."

"Could he not?" His hands enfold mine. "Do you love me, after all that's happened?"

Isaac has an ease that could charm the world. Isabella strains against her shackles till they break. Now, when I open my eyes, I see both of them—the man who does what he wants to and the woman who does what she has to—and around us, the gaol house falls away to dust.

"I love everything about you," I say.

"Then that settles it, Mistress Vernon." The soft pad of a thumb rubs against the scars on my fingers, made by Thomas's blade. "I suppose we're stuck with each other."

"I suppose so, Mr Latimer."

In the corner, the boy stirs. Upon seeing me and Isaac, he sits bolt upright and slurs, panic-stricken, "'S't morning?"

"Not yet," Isaac says. "I'm a visitor."

He stares about him at the grimy walls, as though he's never seen them before. Poor lad. I wish Mary could have helped him as well as me.

"What'll happen now?" I whisper.

Isaac takes a hitching breath. "My hope is that the Grand Jury will write *Ignoramus* on your bill of indictment—that is, without Margaret as a witness, they'll decide there's a lack of evidence to put you on trial, and the case will be thrown out."

"You hope?"

He nods once. "I hope."

If anyone else from the village comes forth and contradicts Margaret… Lord knows the Vernons are despised enough. Mrs Bagshawe might crawl out of the woodwork and speak against me and Mary. The jury might decide they've got enough evidence to go forward with the trial anyway. So many things could happen between sun-up and sun-down.

"Will you stay with me until the morning?" I ask Isaac, knowing this could be the first and last night we have together.

"Of course."

We lay down on the filthy floor, him in all his finery, me in the clothes I've been wearing for months. Even the few inches between us create too much distance. I wrap my legs around his, and he slides his arm under my head like a bolster. It's no marriage bed, but it's as good as it can be.

"I hear there are wonders outside Derbyshire," I say. "Could you take me to see them?"

"Be warned," Isaac replies. "The beer is not as good."

And he tells me stories, new stories, of a life beyond Peak Forest, where no one will take any note of us because we're but two natural lovers travelling through a world of the wonderful and strange, and I pray that I will live to see that day.

September, 1662

Chapter Thirty-Four

ISAAC

I carve your name upon a stone, along with the year you were born and the year you died. It is the best I can do, given that nothing remains of you, and there is no headstone to mark where you rest. William Vernon has no grave marker either—a small consolation. His reputation, however, is still very much alive in these parts, especially at the inn which now bears a sign of an oak tree by its door. When I stopped in for a drink, an elderly man regaled me with the tale of one rainy night twenty years ago, when a scoundrel robbed a stranger, ravished his wife and threw their bodies down Elden Hole.

"She was not his wife," I said. "And they did not die on the same night."

"That's how the story goes. Ask anyone. Ask Edward over there."

He nodded at a portly fellow behind the bar. His name was vaguely familiar, though I did not recognise his face.

Much of Peak Forest has changed since I was last here. I cannot recall what used to be on the site where a church now stands. The Duchess of Devonshire herself established it in memory of the monarch and the royalists who died fighting in his name, including her own son. His body, one local told me, was pickled in brine and kept in a barrel until the time came when she could give him a burial fit for nobility. It comes as no surprise that the owners of Chatsworth House would behave in such an eccentric manner; what astonishes me is that so many ordinary people around here were prepared to lose their lives for a king who had wrung so much wealth out of their land.

But the ones left behind have taken back what belongs to them. During the war that watered our fields with blood, the monarchy had greater concerns than the former royal hunting grounds. The new king does not seem to take much interest in the affairs of Peak Forest either, and everywhere I go, villagers are carving out their own piece of land. The wooden fence that once ran around the outskirts of Peak Forest no longer exists. If any deer survived the mass slaughter, they are free to roam anywhere but Elden Hole.

A dry-stone wall prevents them from venturing too close to the edge. In years to come, curious travellers will disassemble the barrier, dropping rock after rock into the depths, whispering a lurid tale of murder to one another. For that is the way: some events are so painful that they must be retold as a story with frills and bells attached. How else could we cope with a tragedy?

It is one of these rocks that bears your name. I clamber over the wall, descend the slope, and lie on the grass where, many years ago, a girl with broad shoulders and a big heart lay by my side and counted with me before we tested the hole's depth.

The memory is fresh despite its age—a piece of ancient pottery without a trace of damage dug from the earth. It is, I think, because I do not dwell on pleasant memories of Peak Forest. The ones that plague me are more disturbing. Too often, I find myself back at Elden Hole on that misty morning, the day before Jane made her confession to me, and then I remember the words she said, how they numbed me. I remember that night in the stinking gaol where I found the ragged, starved creature who'd once guided me around the county with such assurance, and I wish I had no capacity for thought at all.

"One, two, three."

The stone falls from my hands as my prayer flies up to the heavens. For you are there, Sarah, with God, though your body may have washed up on the shores of the Styx. It pleases me to think that the underground river which connects Elden Hole and the Devil's Arse will, in time, carry the marker to you and lay it at your final resting place.

I wait until a clatter echoes off the walls of the hole before I stand and brush down my breeches. They are getting tattered now. I do not have to don this male disguise; more and more women are walking abroad these days, travelling without a male escort to places like the Peak country. Yet there is a comfort in becoming Isaac. When I am him, I can breathe more freely—safer from harm, more at ease in my body and less preoccupied with other people's expectations of how to behave. And although Jane has taught me how to love Isabella and Isaac in equal measure, she relishes seeing me as I was when we first met.

As much as she appreciates the Isaac of yesteryear, her memories of this place are more harrowing than mine, and she will not be tempted back. She is not the same person as she was then. The edges have worn off her accent; a pity, though she can be more readily understood by my family. She is less prone to flights of fancy, preferring to draw and label types of bird than listen to stories or visit the theatre. My siblings know her as my very good friend, the woman who helped me search for my cousin. The customers and apprentices of my linen shop in the Exchange know that Mistress Vernon, the milliner, is my compeer, not my competitor. If anyone could understand the true nature of our relationship, it would be Aunt Ruth, but she died shortly after that hypocrite, Cromwell, became Lord Protector.

Would you understand, Sarah? You, once the sole object of my affection? I spent so much of my youth wishing you would acknowledge the feelings that thrilled through me whenever we met. I waited, and you never came. You left, and I followed. It took a journey across this dark and turbulent region to find the woman who would descend into Hell for my sake.

It was right that she should stay in Castleton today; the place is bustling with visitors, eager to explore the Wonders, and she is surrounded by the family she has not seen in so many years. Her nephew, William, now a grown man, wishes to sing and play the fiddle for us over dinner. Mary and Bess have instructed him in many of their own songs.

I sing to myself now, a melancholy little tune that Jane taught me.

"Dear Sir, the night is drawing near.
I can no longer tarry here."

The wind snatches up the tune and carries it towards the hole, where it snags on the branches of a stunted tree and is lost. I wait, holding my breath, for a reply: an echo that is too old, too animal, to be a true copy of my voice. Sheep bleat on the hill. In the distance, men shout to one another in gruff tones. Always, the wind buffets my ears. For a moment, I imagine a great, unknown Something flickering on the edge of wakefulness. Then the rooks cry, and that Something becomes nothing once again. Even the birds who love lonely places have found another home in the copse of trees fringing the village, and it is towards their cries I turn. I cross the land that belongs neither to kings nor fallen angels, heading for Winnats Pass and the shelter of the Shivering Mountain, because life is waiting for me there.

THE END

ACKNOWLEDGEMENTS

When my parents announced they'd moved from the house where I grew up to a roofless fixer-upper in the middle of nowhere, I was not impressed.

"There's a big hole near it," they said, in an attempt to win me round. "It's famous."

Though Eldon Hole is the largest visible pothole in Derbyshire, the opening is obscured by tree branches and ferns. A flimsy fence stands between a curious visitor and a drop of over 200 feet. It took me all of five minutes to walk around it. Yes, Eldon Hole was big, but I couldn't understand why it justified my parents sleeping under a wind-buffeted tarpaulin roof.

I later discovered the area had a rich folkloric and literary history. The likes of Thomas Hobbes, Celia Fiennes, and Daniel Defoe had visited Eldon Hole and written of its terror. Due to its immense depth, it was hailed as one of the Seven Wonders of the Peak. Even Defoe, who was underwhelmed by five of the seven, was grimly fascinated: "What Nature meant in leaving this window open into the infernal world, if the place lies that way, we cannot tell: But it must be said, there is something of horror upon the very imagination, when one does but look into it" *(A Tour Through the Whole Island of Great Britain)*.

I hope *The Brink* captures something of that horror.

My first thank you must go to my parents, then, for moving near a literal hell hole and inspiring this tale.

The talented and dedicated team at Ruadán Books has my eternal gratitude: R. B. Wood, Anna Koon, Deborah Brannon, Steven Pamplin, and Leah Donell, you are amazing. Richard and Anna had faith in this book from the start, and Anna's insightful editorial guidance made the story sparkle. Kip Ayers made a beautiful cover.

Enormous thanks also go to the writing professionals who read and commented on my drafts, including Colleen Anderson and Kathleen Foxx. Matt Telfer, thank you in particular for suggesting *The Brink* as a title. Donna Freitas, your mentoring was transformative.

Emma Albrighton, Mark Ruskin, Selena Slater, and James Stafford, I can't thank you enough for supporting my writing journey. 'Best Writers Ever' lives up to its name. It's a privilege to be part of a group where I can write freely and be myself without judgement.

T.J. Price, I won't forget your encouragement—it made me feel like a 'real' writer. Heather Clark-Hope, thank you for co-founding Artemis Writers with me.

Sam Hirst and Elizabeth Sulis Kim have given me platforms to promote an understanding of Eldon Hole and its history. Long may Romancing the Gothic and *Cunning Folk* continue.

Robert Murray Gilchrist may have died in 1917, but I want to thank him for showing me that Derbyshire can be weird and queer.

Thank you Bobbie Harvey and Andy Bentham for welcoming me into your home in Eyam, indulging my interest in the aforementioned Gilchrist, and taking me to Wet Withens on a glorious summer afternoon.

George Walkden and Robert Skidmore helped me understand the dialect features of Tideswell and Peak Forest more thoroughly. Tony from the Peak District Mining Museum was a fount (or should I say, pit?) of knowledge.

The final thank you goes to Tim, my teammate for life.

About Sophia Adamowicz

Sophia Adamowicz is a writer and tutor based in the UK. As the co-founder of Artemis Writers, Sophia runs workshops on all aspects of the craft. Sophia is an alumna of the Faber Academy, through which she completed two long courses on novel writing. Her short stories, flash fiction, and nonfiction articles have appeared in several publications, including *Cunning Folk*, *Crow & Cross Keys*, *Haven Speculative*, and *Trash Cat Lit*. Her flash fiction "Wixton Fen" was nominated for the Genrepunk Awards (2025). She lives in Cambridge with her partner, two cats, and a Bernese Mountain Dog.

Delicious. Dark. Fiction.
WINTER IN THE CITY
A COLLECTION OF DARK SPECULATIVE FICTION
EDITED BY
R.B. WOOD & ANNA KOON
THE BLACK FIRE CONCERTO
MIKE ALLEN
120 MURDERS
DARK FICTION INSPIRED BY THE ALTERNATIVE ERA
MEG GARDINER
JOSH MALERMAN
SILVIA MORENO-GARCIA
PAUL TREMBLAY
AND MORE
EDITED BY NICK MAMATAS
PORTRAITS OF DECAY
A NOVEL BY
J.B. BLANES
A COLLECTION OF DARK SPECULATIVE FICTION
SPRING IN THE CITY
SINISTER SOCIETIES
Six Novellas of Secrets and Horrors
Michael Burke • Tom Deady
Errick Nunnally • Cindy O'Quinn
Sarah Read • Mercedes M. Yardley
"It's an eerie gem."
FIVE FUNERALS
by Jeff Somers
Nick Mamatas
"Darling is an unflinching horror novel—an unsettling story about what constitutes true evil."
DARLING
Mercedes M. Yardley
RUADÁN BOOKS